AGE OF GODPUNK

AGE OF GODPUNK

AGE OF ANANSI // AGE OF SATAN // AGE OF GAIA

JAMES LOVEGROVE

SOLARIS

First published 2013 by Solaris
an imprint of Rebellion Publishing Ltd,
Riverside House, Osney Mead,
Oxford, OX2 0ES, UK

www.solarisbooks.com

ISBN: 978 1 78108 129 7

10 9 8 7 6 5 4 3 2 1

A CIP catalogue record for this book is available from the
British Library.

Designed & typeset by Rebellion Publishing

REBELLION

Printed in the US

FOREWORD

THE THREE NOVELLAS which make up *Age of Godpunk* were published originally as three separate ebooks. This is the first time they have appeared in physical form. They weren't designed to be read as an ensemble, but now that they've been united between two covers, I think they sit together pretty well, each counterpointing and complementing the others in interesting ways.

Those who have read any of my Pantheon series of novels may feel they know what to expect of a story by me with a title beginning *Age of...* The novels are military-SF action-adventure thrillers which take time out to muse on the nature of the relationship between humankind and its various gods. Each standalone book offers its own particular slant on the material. They're as alike, and at the same time as different, as I can make them.

These *Godpunk* novellas take another tack. They're lighter in tone, with the science fictional elements stripped out. They're still about us and our deities and our myths and belief systems, but they allow room for greater ambiguity and a buttload of irony. They demonstrate, I think, the potential breadth and scope of this subgenre I've invented (or, if not invented, defined). They are, I hope, above all else *fun*.

A novella is a strange chimera, a hybrid I'm very fond of. It gives an author the chance to be experimental, as a short story does, but also to let the narrative breathe, as a novel does. You can have a slightly unsympathetic protagonist whom the reader is prepared to stick with for a hundred-odd pages but would lose all patience with over any greater length. You can pack a great deal of plot into a novella and make it feel momentous even when it's only modestly proportioned. It's a format that's both epic and intimate.

Age of Anansi is itself about storytelling, about the fabrications that sustain us and the tricks we're prepared to play to keep ahead of our peers and rivals. Is it coincidence that the words "liar" and "lawyer" sound so similar? Yes, of course it is. But still...

Age of Satan pays tribute to Dennis Wheatley's fiction and the Satanic-horror cinema of the 1970s, but is also an enquiry into ethics and – oxymoron alert – political morality. Plus: blood sacrifice.

Age of Gaia takes a sidelong look at eco-activism and rampant capitalism, at the same time riffing on a certain recent publishing phenomenon (I won't say which one – no spoilers here). I have never been mistaken for James Lovelock, the scientist who formulated the Gaia Hypothesis, despite the closeness of our names.[1]

I must once again give credit to my publishers, Solaris, for coming along with me on this Pantheon lark and being as encouraging and supportive as they have been. Particular tribute is due to editor-in-chief Jon Oliver, who was very accepting of *Age of Satan*'s rather jaundiced irreligiosity in spite of his own faith. Jon is that rare thing, a broadminded Christian with a sense of humour and a refreshing lack of piety. He even fucking swears. Thanks must also go to publishing manager Ben Smith, who suggested the basic concept of *Age of Gaia*. It's a good one and I hope I've done it justice. Finally, desk editor David Moore should take credit for being the coiner of the term "godpunk," although Pornokitsch's Jared Shurin came up with the word at roughly the same time and so can lay equal claim to that honour. They have yet to settle the matter between them decisively, and a bout in Thunderdome surely beckons. Two men enter. One man leaves.

Off with you now. Go and read the stories. You're about to meet the African spider-god, the Devil

---

[1] No, actually I tell a lie. A dentist once asked me, somewhat grumpily, if I was the man who publicly advocated building more nuclear power stations as a way of solving the energy crisis, as Lovelock does. This was as she was on the point of injecting anaesthetic into my gum. I assured her she'd got the wrong writer. She said, "Just as well. Otherwise this might have been a very unpleasant experience for you." True story.

AGE OF ANANSI

JAMES LOVEGROVE

NEW YORK TIMES
BEST-SELLING
AUTHOR

Everything would have been fine, if it wasn't for the spider.

The spider came along, took a perfect life, a life that was well planned and blameless – *my* life – and wrecked it.

Maybe I should begin this the way my grandmother taught me to, by reciting the traditional incantation: "We do not really mean, we do not really mean that what we are about to say is true. A story, a story. Let it come, let it go."

Nanabaa Oboshie smelled of spices and fat-lady sweat. I'd cuddle up on her capacious lap and she would tell me the old Ashanti myths. Her English wasn't good, thickly accented, but I loved the cadences of her speech, the singsong rhythms, the occasional incomprehensible lapses into Kwa phraseology.

Most of the stories, the best ones, were about Anansi.

Anansi is lord of stories. He won ownership of them off his father Nyame, the Sky God. He bought them by trapping Onini the Python, Osebo the Leopard, the Mmoboro Hornets and Mmoatia the Dwarf, and handing these prizes to Nyame. Through stealth and subterfuge he captured the creatures, and so all the world's stories became Anansesem – Anansi stories.

Which is, of course, a story in itself.

"We do not mean that what we are about to say is true."

Only it *is* true.

It happened to me.

MY NAME IS Dion Yeboah, and up until not so long ago I was a respectable and respected barrister, specialising in criminal law. I had a sterling reputation as a defence QC, the man you want on your side when you're in a jam, the man whose silver tongue and sharp legal brain could scoop you out of hot water and land you safely on the right side of the bars of a prison cell.

I charged the going rate for my services, which is to say 'a lot,' and I can't confess to ever feeling guilty about that. And yes, there may have been a time or two when I acted as counsel for a client whose innocence I wasn't entirely convinced of. But everyone is entitled to a fair trial, and that means a robust defence. Besides, I did my share of *pro bono* work as well, mostly on behalf of kids from rough council estates who'd got unlucky, been busted for first-time possession – drugs, concealed weapons, whatever a random police stop-and-search turned up – or else were facing charges of assault or GBH when they were only trying to protect themselves or their family.

Those kids, they'd look at me in frank wonder sometimes. Never seen someone with the same skin colour as them who wore a suit and spoke the way I did. "What, you posh or summink, bruv? You Prince Charles or summink? How come you don't talk right?"

No, not posh, I would tell them. I come from the same place you do. I grew up on the London streets. My parents had no money, same as yours. But I studied hard at school. I went to university on a scholarship and got a Graduate Diploma in Law. I was called to the Bar at Lincoln's Inn. I worked my backside off to make a success of myself.

And you can too.

I WAS A success, I don't mind admitting it. Nice flat in St John's Wood. Tenancy in a well regarded set of chambers based near the Barbican. Steady and enviable income. I kept myself in trim – weight training twice a week, a jog round Regent's Park every other morning. I kept my home in trim, too. Very house-proud, me. Had that instilled into me by my mum. "A clean home is a good home," she'd say as she hurricaned from room to room with vacuum cleaner and feather duster, hands gauntleted in Marigolds. We had a tiny council flat, and it was always immaculate, not a speck of dust anywhere. My pad in St John's Wood was the same – spotless. Windows gleaming bright. Floors swept to within an inch of their lives. Bathroom dazzling. Did it all myself, what's more. I could easily afford a cleaner, but nobody else could keep things to my exacting standards. My mother, God rest her soul, would have approved. She cleaned other people's houses for a living and felt no shame in that, but she did believe a person should be responsible for their own domestic hygiene.

"It's your mess. Don't do you no good paying someone else to make it go away."

I CAN'T REMEMBER when exactly I noticed the first web. Sometime in midsummer, late July, but I can't be any more precise than that. It wasn't big, covering one windowpane. Flick of a dustcloth and it was gone.

The second appeared a couple of days later, stretched between a bookcase and the ceiling cornice. Bigger than the first, but just as easily got rid of.

The flat had never been troubled by spiders before. Insufficient prey. Flies and their ilk didn't flourish at my place. Not enough of the dirt and debris they thrived on.

A week passed, and one day I came home and there were a good half-dozen webs. They hadn't been there when I'd left that morning. One was draped around the light fixture in the living room. One linked the kitchen sink taps to the drying rack. One neatly filled the ring-seat on the toilet.

They were beautiful webs, I have to give them that. Pristine. Exactly how you imagine a spider web should look. The radial strands neatly equidistant, the concentric rings laddering out at steadily larger intervals, as though according to some fundamental mathematical principle. A certain silveriness to the silk, a gossamer iridescence. If they'd been anywhere else, anywhere but my home, I'd have admired them, marvelled at them.

As it was, I eradicated them. Angrily. Then I called in a pest control company.

THE MAN IN the Bug Blasterz overalls searched and searched, but couldn't find any trace of spider infestation.

"No eggs," he said. "No cocoons. No husks. Nothing. You're sure they were webs?"

"Yes, I'm damn well sure they were webs," I replied sharply. "What else would they have been?"

"Only asking."

He squirted insect repellent everywhere and advised me to stay outdoors for at least three hours. When I returned, the flat reeked of chemicals but felt somehow purified, as though I'd had ghosts and a priest had come and exorcised them.

My orderly life resumed. For a fortnight, my routine was as it had ever been. Work, fitness, cleaning, sleep. I found time to go on a date – a blind date set up by a well-meaning colleague, who thought I was working too hard and not "playing" enough. She was a nice enough girl, a solicitor, petite but curvy where it counts. West Indian, though, and sorry, I can't help it, but my parents' prejudices are my own. I remember my dad saying, "The stupid ones got caught. The clever ones knew how to run and hide. Those slave traders did Africa a favour, leaving the best and taking the rest." It's not true; what many of the clever Africans did was sell their countrymen to the slave traders. That's how they survived. But we all tell lies to ourselves about our ancestors, to make us feel better, and those lies are persuasive.

So the date ended with a polite peck on the cheek and me about a hundred and fifty quid out of pocket for dinner at a Michelin-starred restaurant.

And I got in that night to find my flat *swathed* in spider webs. Literally hundreds of them. Spider webs everywhere.

It was like some sort of practical joke. As though a prankster had broken in and gone mad with those spray cans they use to make cobwebs on movie sets. I couldn't move without sticky silk wrapping itself round my hands, my legs, my head. I scarcely dared breathe for fear of getting some of the stuff in my mouth or up my nose.

This is insane, I thought. *This can't be happening.*

I took myself in hand, told myself to get a grip. It was just spider webs. Just dirt that shouldn't be there. I fought my way through the webs to the cleaning cupboard and fetched out dustcloths, broom, brush, dustpan, Dyson upright and Mr Sheen, then tied a bandanna over the lower half of my face and set to work. It took the best part of two hours, but by midnight I'd got the job done. Not a scrap of web remained. It was all inside a pair of large black bin bags, which were stuffed full but weighed next to nothing and which I dumped in the wheelie bin outside with equal parts satisfaction and irritation. Bug Blasterz would be getting a very stern phone call in the morning. You do not bill Dion Yeboah £175 plus VAT for "services rendered" if said services have patently not been rendered.

In the middle of the night I woke to find a huge spider squatting on my chest.

It was black against the pale bedcovers, lit by the streetlight glow coming through the curtains. Its carapace glinted dully. Eight long legs straddled my torso, their outermost tips reaching from my collarbone to my navel and from one side of my ribcage to the other.

I lay there in a paroxysm of horror. It was the biggest, blackest, ugliest spider I'd ever laid eyes on. I didn't dare move. I had an urge to hurl the thing off me, but at the same time I didn't want to alarm it, provoke it. What if it was venomous? A spider that size – if it bit me it would surely kill me.

A dozen shiny eyes regarded me carefully. The mandibles beneath them rustled and clicked, mouth parts folding in and out of one another with machinelike precision.

Dion.

A voice. A whisper inside my mind.

Dion Yeboah. I am here for you. I have come for you.

I WOKE AGAIN. I was still in bed, still on my back, bathed in fear sweat. But there was no spider. No giant black arachnid perched on top of me, gazing at me with myriad jet-coloured eyes.

I'd dreamed it, of course. Spiders had overrun my flat with their webs earlier in the evening, so naturally I'd had a spider-themed nightmare.

Made perfect sense.

I didn't sleep again that night, however. Not a wink.

MR BUG BLASTERZ came back and did the same as before, namely doubt the veracity of my claims and souse the flat with poison. At least he had the good grace not to invoice me for the cost of the repeat visit.

THE FOLLOWING NIGHT, the spider returned.

Dion, it said.

I had no doubt that the whisper I was hearing inside my head – a mental tickling that was as much sensation as sound – was the spider's voice.

Dion, I have come far. I have travelled thousands of miles to find you. I have chosen you, you out of the many I could have chosen, to be mine.

"Who are you?" I challenged that black monstrosity. Its face, if you could call it a face, was just inches from mine.

Who am I? Its mandibles flared. I heard a raspy chuckle. *Oh, you know who I am, Dion. You know full well. I am he whom your grandmother told you about all those years ago. I am Kwaku Ananse. I am Ananse-Tori. I am Nansi. I am Kuent'i Nanzi. I am Ayiyi. I am the god of countless names and countless stories. Everything your Nanabaa Oboshie told you, that is who I am.*

"What do you want?" I demanded. "Why are you here? Why me?"

I want to be with you, said Anansi. *I want your story to become mine and mine yours. I want our tales to intertwine. I want us to be together. We have work to do.*

"Work? What work?"

Let me in, Dion. Let me inside you. See what we can do together, the two of us. See what we can achieve.

"No!" I cried. "No! Leave me alone! I don't believe in you. You're just a myth. An African old wives' tale. A story for children. I have nothing to do with you. You don't belong in my world."

Let's see about that, said Anansi. *Let's just see.*

* * *

Things started to go wrong.

Nothing major, on the face of it. I missed the bus to work a couple of mornings in a row, or rather, the bus failed to turn up as scheduled. The second time, I walked to Edgware Road and took the Tube instead, only for the train to get held up in the tunnel for an hour – a suicide further down the line, apparently. So I was late into chambers both those mornings, and late to court. Everything was a rush, but I compensated. None of my clients was short-changed and the verdicts went the right way.

Then a case I'd been nurturing for weeks and feeling confident about suddenly veered off-course and seemed headed for disaster. We were ready to go to trial, but a key witness changed his testimony, deciding almost on a whim that he *had* seen the accused commit violence at the pub that night after all, removing a vital plank in our defence. I scrambled to find someone who could shore things up for us again. Eventually I convinced a lesser witness to be, shall we say, more certain about her facts than she had been previously. I managed to gloss over the discrepancies between her statement to the police on the night itself and her statement in court in such a way that the jurors hardly seemed to notice any difference. Busy, crowded pub. Alcohol imbibed. Under those circumstances, recollections are often clearer some weeks later than they are in the immediate aftermath of the event. Skin of my teeth, but I pulled it off, and our man walked free.

Then I got word from various mutual acquaintances

that the girl I'd gone on that blind date with had begun making disparaging remarks about me. She was saying I'd behaved badly, been rude, snobby, insulting, even racist. It was absurd, of course. I might have been somewhat distracted that evening, maybe not paying her as much attention as she thought she merited, and possibly I'd alluded to the West Indies once or twice in less than complimentary terms, but snobby? Racist? Preposterous. I phoned her to straighten the matter out. She maintained that she'd been misquoted. I suggested that if she was unhappy with the way the evening had panned out, there were better ways of dealing with her disappointment than bandying slanderous accusations about. The conversation didn't end on a positive note, but I felt that I got my point across.

Little things. Minor annoyances. In and of themselves, nothing much.

But this sort of stuff simply did not happen to Dion Yeboah. I organised my life precisely so that there would be a minimum of grief and disruption. I worked hard to maintain my routine and keep everything on an even keel.

I did not like my shipshape little boat being rocked.

"ANANSI," I SAID to my empty flat. "I know you don't exist. I know you're not listening. But – if you *are* there..."

Silence. Only the murmur of traffic outside and the purr of the refrigerator.

"If you *are* there, please go away. Please stop interfering. I've done nothing to deserve this. All I wish is to be allowed to carry on as before. I've done nothing wrong, nothing to offend you. Find somebody else to bother. Leave me be."

I felt foolish, talking to thin air, addressing a spider deity who had appeared to me in dreams alone. I wished Nanabaa Oboshie was with me, so that she could confirm that I had only imagined Anansi. "A story, a story." That was all he was. Nanabaa Oboshie knew that. Much though my grandmother had loved to tell me of Anansi's escapades – his silly stunts that almost always backfired, the tricks he played and the trouble they got him into with his fellow gods and the other animals – she was perfectly well aware that he was a fiction. She herself had learned the tales from her own grandmother back in Ghana, sitting in the wattle-walled hut, by the fire. Anansi existed solely as oral tradition handed down from generation to generation, a way to entertain the tribe on a dark hot night while the lions roared in the hills.

Anansi certainly did not have a place in twenty-first-century London, in the flat of a sophisticated and highly intelligent lawyer.

I kept insisting on this to myself even after the improbably large black spider descended in front of me from the ceiling, suspended from a delicate thread of silk.

* * *

So you believe now, do you? Anansi said.

"I don't know what to believe," I said, hesitantly. The truth.

Good. An open mind. That's progress. But you mustn't be afraid, Dion. Above all else, not that. I shouldn't frighten you. I'm here to help.

"Help? How?"

If you'll just accept me – fully, wholeheartedly – then you'll see.

"Accept?"

Am I real?

"You – you *look* real."

Think how you could know for sure.

I thought. I studied the spider's fat round abdomen, the wormy spinnerets that extruded the thread, the tiny hairs fringing the legs.

"I could touch you," I said.

Touch me, then, said Anansi. *Feel my solidity. There will be your proof.*

I was repulsed by the idea. Who would want to touch a spider that size? Who in their right mind would want to go anywhere near it? Even Sir David Attenborough would think twice.

My hand went out, shrank back, several times. Anansi hung there, patient, waiting.

Finally, in a mad dash of bravado, I brushed my fingers against the creature's back.

For the briefest of moments, barely a millisecond, I felt *something*. The coolness of chitin. The hardness of a living shell.

That was all it took.

The spider vanished.

But it wasn't gone.

Anansi was within me. I felt him there as surely as I could feel my heartbeat, the air passing in and out of my nostrils, the gurgling of my digestive system. I had allowed Anansi in, and now he was a part of me.

Yes, Anansi said. *Yes, that's better. That's so much better, isn't it, Dion?*

I nodded. I could hardly speak.

So let's go and have some fun, said Anansi. *You and me. I'm looking forward to this.*

FUN? I HAD no idea what he meant.

Then, the very next day, I was summoned to HMP Wandsworth. There I met a man who was up on a charge of possession of a class-A controlled substance with intent to distribute and sell. One look at him – gold teeth, a ring on every finger, razored haircut, a plethora of tattoos – told me "drug lord." No doubt this wasn't his first time on remand. Nor would it be his last.

"I've just ditched my brief," the fellow said to me. "Useless cunt was wanting me to plead guilty. I've heard you're the dog's pods when it comes to getting a bloke off the hook. I'm hiring you."

"I'm very expensive."

"Money's no object. Fix this shit for me, and I'll pay whatever you ask. I ain't doing another stretch. Too much business going on. Too many irons in the fire."

The case against this charming specimen of humanity hinged on a single, crucial piece of evidence – an exchange of text messages between him and an accomplice.

Reading the transcript, it looked pretty watertight to me. The conversation was clearly a deal, some sort of transaction, and the weakly-coded references to the drug, cocaine, were unmistakable.

There is a way, though, Anansi whispered in my mind.

Was there? Well, maybe. But it would take an audacious person to pull it off.

And aren't you that person, Dion?

IN COURT, I tore into the case the police had built up.

"Ladies and gentlemen of the jury, you will note the recurrence of the word 'Colombian' in these texts, used in connection with weight – pounds and ounces – and monetary value. From that, the prosecution wishes you to infer that the accused and his associate, a trading partner, were negotiating the sale of a quantity of cocaine. This is perfectly possible. But is it not equally possible, if not more so, that the goods in question were of an entirely innocent nature? I put it to you that 'Colombian' could easily be taken to mean 'coffee.'"

There was an audible gasp from the viewing gallery. My learned friend, the counsel for the prosecution, could barely stifle an incredulous groan. The judge remained impassive, as he should, but I detected a glint of wry amusement in His Honour's wrinkled old eyes.

I soldiered on. Nobody was going to buy this line of argument.

But what if they do? said Anansi.

"My client is no fool. As we all know, no text-message conversation these days can ever truly be considered private. Who in their right mind would openly, overtly conduct a drugs deal via this medium? I put it to you, members of the jury, that the transcript before you centres on nothing more illegal or sinister than a purchase of ground coffee in bulk, coffee being of course one of the exports for which the country of Colombia is famous. Indeed, I myself drink a cup of Colombian blend every morning."

One or two of the jurors began nodding. By God, it seemed to be working. I was winning them over.

"If there is any doubt in your minds that this principal piece of evidence is in any way suspect," I went on, "if it is at all conceivable to you that the prosecution's case rests almost wholly on the misinterpretation of a string of innocuous text messages between two law-abiding individuals going about their legitimate business, then you have no alternative but to acquit the man in the dock and let him walk free from this courtroom without a stain on his reputation."

And what do you know, they did.

The champagne corks popped in chambers that afternoon, I can tell you. One of the senior barristers, who was also my former pupil master, professed himself amazed that I'd bamboozled the jury with such an obvious ruse.

"It wasn't what I did," I told him. "It was how I did it. It's all in the delivery."

"Still and all, dear boy," he said, "a fine example of legal sleight of hand. I'm proud of you."

"I had a good teacher," I said.

Yes, said Anansi. *Yes, you did*.

FLUSH FROM THAT success, I decided to exact revenge on my one-time blind date, who was still spouting uncomplimentary things about me behind my back. I phoned the Law Society and gave them an anonymous tipoff that the young lady was conducting an improper relationship with a senior partner in her firm of solicitors. I'd done my homework. I named the man, who was married, a father of two, a churchgoer, a charity fundraiser, a pillar of his local community. Whiter than white, in so many ways. Never in a million years would he be likely to dally at the office with an employee, especially one of colour – which somehow made it all the more plausible that he might, not to mention all the more outrageous.

The bigger the lie, said Anansi, *the more credence people will give it*.

And he should know. Had he not wooed and won his wife Aso by convincing her he was greatly in demand among the female animals and hence a worthy "catch"? He did this by tying a rope to each of his eight legs and having hidden animal friends tug on the different ropes. He told Aso the ropes were attached to other prospective wives, who were tugging to get his attention. If Aso wished to marry him, she should agree to it quickly, before one of her rivals hauled the oh-so-eligible bachelor off and claimed him for herself.

Unfortunately – and there's almost always an 'unfortunately,' in any Anansi story – Anansi's eight animal friends happened to pull on the ropes at the same time, and with all their might. The result was that Anansi was suddenly and violently yanked in eight directions at once, and his legs, which had been short and stubby, were stretched out like toffee. And that is why all spiders have thin, spindly legs.

But the good news as far as Anansi was concerned was that Aso laughed at the sight of him being hauled in different directions and stretched like a piece of chewing gum. She laughed so hard that she found herself falling in love with him, and next thing she knew, she was consenting to be his bride.

It was a decision she would come to regret, for Anansi was famously unfaithful, and all his cunning schemes seemed to come to nothing, and he often made himself and his family a laughing-stock. In legend, Aso has become synonymous with the exasperated, long-suffering wife.

My lie, at any rate, gained traction and ran. The Law Society made discreet enquiries, as it was duty-bound to do. It found no evidence of impropriety, but the very fact that it was investigating the firm at

You may have read in the newspapers about the BBC higher-up accused of taking bribes in return for insisting that a certain mobile phone company's latest product feature prominently in several drama serials he commissioned, in direct contravention of the terms of the Corporation's charter. I was able to get the charges dismissed on the grounds that the items in question were so desirable, so up-to-the-minute, so lusted after by those who love technology and progress, that the BBC would have been remiss in its duties as the Voice of the Nation if it *hadn't* shown them regularly on our TV screens.

You may also be familiar with the plight of a Member of Parliament who chose to claim the cost of a visit to a massage parlour in Pimlico on expenses. Remember the tabloid headlines? "We Pay So He Can Get His End Away"? It wasn't difficult for me to rescue him from ignominy by drawing attention to the stresses and the long working hours that his job entailed. I implied that the use of parliamentary allowances to reimburse him for this particular form of relaxation was in fact a wise investment of public funds. A rested, revitalised politician was apt to make calm and clear-headed decisions, was he not? Certainly more so than a tense, frustrated one.

And what of the footballer with a couple of dozen England caps to his name? Snapped by paparazzi leaving a Mayfair hotel in the company of a girl reputedly several months shy of the age of consent? I obtained a High Court injunction on all reporting of the case and ensured that it never came to trial. Beyond the paparazzi photos, there was no proof of any sexual liaison between the two. Demonstrably my client had adopted an avuncular role towards the child, as evidenced by the arm he placed fondly round her shoulders in several of the pictures and the chaste kiss he gave her on the forehead. I maintained that he and she had enjoyed an innocent breakfast together at the hotel, where the topics of conversation had been his career and her education. Furthermore, the meeting might be regarded as being in the nature of an interview, for the girl had her eye on a media career and could well have been intending to contribute an article about the footballer to her school magazine as a first step on the road to becoming a journalist. Far from being her lover, he was merely her scoop.

The judge swallowed it. The press were more sceptical but, gagged by the injunction, could do little but mutter obliquely and darkly.

Anansi, inside me, simply squirmed with glee. Pulling the wool over other people's eyes – there was nothing that delighted him more.

PLEASE DON'T GET me wrong, I didn't represent only unscrupulous rogues. There were plenty of cases during this time in which the innocent were exonerated and justice was done. None, however, demanded much in the way of ingenuity or subterfuge; nor was any of them especially dramatic or memorable. It's a sad truth about being a barrister that one gains greater satisfaction from reversing the course of the law than from merely seeing its natural status quo preserved. It is when one is the law's master, not its servant, that one feels one has genuinely achieved something. It is like being in a daily battle of wits with the ponderous, imposing bulk of jurisprudence, and sometimes, if one is clever, one wrestles it to the mat.

Anansi is a trickster god, a creature of intrigue and stratagems, weaving artful ploys like he weaves webs.

Perhaps we lawyers are the same, in our way. If we brethren of the law were to worship a god, by rights it would be Anansi.

IT WAS A terrific joyride, those months of one spectacular victory after another.

But like all joyrides, it couldn't last. It had to come to a screeching, crashing halt.

I was out jogging when Anansi announced that our partnership would be entering a new phase. It was not long after sunrise on an autumn morning, and there was a misty haze in the air that you could taste as well as see. While I huffed and puffed along the Regent's Canal towpath, Anansi and I chatted, as we often did, about an upcoming trial, the various tacks the prosecution might take and how best to deal with them.

Then Anansi dropped the bombshell.

You realise, of course, Dion, that there's a price for all this, don't you?

"What? What do you mean?"

You don't get the services of a god for free. No one does.

"What are you talking about?"

I'd fallen into the habit of speaking aloud during my conversations with Anansi, even in public. It was easier than keeping them confined to my head. At first I'd received some strange looks when doing this, but I'd got around the problem by the simple expedient of wearing a Bluetooth headset whenever I was out and about. It wasn't switched on or even connected to a mobile, but people didn't know that. All they saw was a man taking a phone call on the hoof. I didn't appear to be different from any number of businesspeople you see on the street, working as they walk. The only distinction was that whereas they were talking to a colleague or a stranger, I was talking to a god.

"Explain yourself," I said. "Is this some sort of joke?"

No joke, Dion. We've been working well together, haven't we? Quite a streak of wins we've had. We make a good team. But who's benefited from it more, do you think? You or me?

"Me," I admitted.

Absolutely. Your stock has never been higher. Dion Yeboah is in demand like never before. You've been billing enough in fees to make your peers and rivals gnash their teeth. Your name has cropped up in the papers – not just the Law Society Gazette, *but the national dailies. You're a star in the legal firmament.*

But Anansi... Well, what has poor old Anansi got out of this?

"Entertainment," I offered, lamely.

Oh, yes, entertainment indeed. But is that enough? I'm a god, after all. Gods cannot be expected to get by on entertainment alone.

I was passing London Zoo. My pace had slowed. The animals were grumbling and hooting to themselves, a soft, wild dawn chorus.

No, Anansi continued. *Our association is a two-way street, Dion. I scratch your back, you scratch mine. You've had your go. I've done you a favour. Now it's my turn.*

"You want something from me."

Naturally I do. But don't panic. It's nothing terrible. You might even enjoy the challenge.

"I won't do anything illegal," I said firmly. "I just won't."

Nor would I expect you to. What if I said I'd like to give you the opportunity to exercise your skills at coercion and skulduggery in another theatre of combat, outside the courtroom?

"Go on."

You'd be pitting yourself against some of the greatest swindlers, backstabbers and double-dealers the world has ever known.

"I'd say my career so far has been ample preparation for such a thing."

A pair of pretty women ran past me, bouncing beautifully in Lycra. I followed them with my gaze, and Anansi, with his many eyes inside me, looking out through mine, followed them too. Neither of us could help himself.

Yes – ahem – now, where was I? said Anansi. *Oh, yes. You see, Dion, once in every generation an event occurs – an event like no other. You could call it a convocation of likeminded individuals. A competition. A kind of divine Olympics.*

"Divine...?"

I am not the only trickster god in existence. You must realise that. There are, oh, dozens of us. Perhaps even hundreds – no one's done a census. Just about every pantheon that's ever been counts a trickster amongst its number. We're kind of fitted as standard. You don't get the full set of gods if it doesn't have one of us, just as you don't get a full pack of cards if it doesn't have a joker in.

"But they don't... I mean, they're not..."

Not real? Anansi chuckled. *But I am, aren't I? And if I am, then all gods must be too, surely. Stands to reason.*

By this point I had slowed until I was plodding along like a donkey, almost at a standstill. What Anansi was telling me was hard to process. Somehow, without meaning to, I'd become embroiled in something far bigger than I'd thought, far bigger than I could readily imagine. Until now, Anansi and I had just been fooling around, toying with the legal system, enjoying ourselves, getting one over on judges and juries. But this – all at once, this seemed serious. Deadly serious.

"Other trickster gods," I said. "And what do you

do when you get together once in a generation? Drink? Party? Dance 'til the early hours?"

There's a certain amount of that, sometimes, said Anansi. *Depends on the venue and the circumstances. Mostly we play tricks one another.*

"Play tricks? That's it?"

We are, are we not, trickster gods? Clue's in the name. It's a free-for-all contest of chicanery. Each of us attempts to outwit the others. Last one standing is the winner.

"Why do you need me for this?" I asked. I was searching desperately for a way to excuse myself from participating in this contest. Anansi was doing his best to make it sound like it was all just one jolly jape, but I wasn't convinced. I sensed there was more to this contest than he was letting on. "Does it have to involve me at all? Isn't there some sort of divine meeting place where all you gods can go, up in heaven or another dimension or wherever?"

That's not how it works, said Anansi. *All of the pantheons dwell in separate, discrete planes that don't intersect with one another. The only place they do all meet up is here, the mortal realm, where our followers and worshippers are, where our stories are told and retold and spread.*

"Earth."

Exactly. Earth. And the only way we can manifest on Earth is by assuming a living form. For some that's simply a matter of transubstantiating their incorporeal selves into flesh. For most of us, however, the vast majority, it's a case of temporarily 'borrowing' a host body, usually a human one, and using that as an avatar.

"Rather like getting into a car."

Rather like, only in my case it's taking with *owner's consent, not* without. *I'd never dream of entering a body unbidden. It's more of a... a* cohabitation *than an act of possession. Think how it's been lately, with me inside you. I'm not riding roughshod over you, am I? I'm not making you behave in any way against your own wishes. We've just been rubbing along, mutually cooperating, haven't we? And it hasn't been so bad. I think you've been finding it quite bracing, as a matter of fact. Quite liberating.*

I couldn't deny this. "But," I said, "perhaps I'm not keen on going any further. In fact, perhaps the time's come for you and I to discuss dissolving this partnership of ours."

Oh, I wouldn't advise that, Dion. Not at all.

"Why not?"

Well, remember how it went for you after we first met? When you refused to acknowledge my existence? Remember how bad things got for you?

I did – the coincidences that had left my secure little world wobbling perilously on its axis.

My doing, of course, said Anansi. *And I was hardly even trying. If I wished, I could make your life a living hell. What I did then would seem like paradise compared with what I* could *do. The torments I could put you through... You'd be begging me to stop, and do you know what I would say? I would say "No," and just carry on.*

His voice had become brittle and awful, like ice cracking underfoot, like tinder sticks breaking, like dry bones snapping. I felt a surge of nauseating dread, unlike anything I'd ever known. I stopped in my tracks and bent double, bracing my hands on my knees. To a passerby it would have looked as though I had paused to catch my breath and maybe work out a stitch in my side, not as though I was fighting to keep myself from throwing up, which I was.

Could Anansi truly do as he threatened and throw my life into utter chaos?

I had no doubt that he could.

But let's not make this a matter of browbeating and intimidation, he wheedled. *That's really not how I prefer to operate. I'd much rather you just agreed to do as I ask of your own free will. Everything would be much more agreeable that way.*

I straightened up. At that moment, the canal looked very tempting. To hurl oneself beneath that greasy brown surface, to expel the air from one's lungs and let the cold brackish water come flooding in...

"No," I said, determinedly.

No?

"I mean yes. Yes, I'll do it. Not because you're forcing me to. Because, never let it be said that Dion Yeboah does not repay his debts."

Excellent. I knew I could count on you.

"But Anansi?"

Yes?

"If we do this, we do it to win. Get me? No half measures. I do not take on a challenge unless I'm

40

going to go flat out, all guns blazing, to come out on top. That is my way."

Of course, of course.

"You have brought me further along in just a few months than I could ever have managed alone. I owe you for that, and I will honour my side of the bargain, but in return I must have your full and unstinting collaboration. I must be able to rely on you."

You will, believe me, said Anansi.

"Good. I'll hold you to that."

Oh, I have chosen well. I could feel him inside me, happily rubbing his forelegs together. *It was worth leaving Africa to find you. Aso told me I should stay home, content myself with someone local again, but she was wrong. I've tried that so many times and it hasn't worked. You may not be* African-African, *Dion, but your bloodline is still strong in you. You're only one step removed from your true homeland, and you carry its traditions within you, with all the sophistication of the industrialised West. You're the best of both worlds, and with you, I'm sure, this time I will take the crown.*

"*We*," I corrected him. "We will take the crown."

THERE WERE PRACTICAL preparations to be made. The contest was taking place at the end of the month, in America. I needed to book tickets and block out a week of holiday in my hectic work schedule. There was also research to be done. I hate to go into anything half-cocked, uninformed. Just ask any of my juniors. We know our brief inside-out before we enter the courtroom. We've looked up the precedents and nailed down the references and made provision for every contingency we can think of. Nothing should catch us by surprise, if we've done our homework properly beforehand.

And so it was in this instance. With Anansi's help I drew up a list of our potential opponents and studied them and their histories and habits. Not every trickster god makes it to every contest. Some balk, some fail to recruit a suitable avatar in time, and some are so neglected and forgotten about that they lack the will or the strength to put in an appearance. A god is only as mighty as the obeisance he or she can command. The less revered, the less remembered, the less empowered.

Not all the contest entrants are gods, either. At least, not in the sense that we understand the term "god." Figures from folk tales also attend – the wily fictional characters whose exploits have been celebrated down through the centuries and become the stuff of legend. Adored, if not necessarily worshipped, by many, they have carved out a place for themselves among the trickster fraternity. Lesser cousins, perhaps, but entitled to show up and compete nonetheless.

I researched them all, focusing especially on a core of regular attendees. In my spare hours I trawled the internet, finding out what I could about them. I haunted the Mythology sections of bookshops, buying armfuls of material. I immersed myself in lore, rather than law, for a change. Within a fortnight, I was as well informed as any comparative religion student on the subject. I was armed with knowledge, and ready.

I FLEW FROM Heathrow to Las Vegas on a grey Thursday morning. As I approached the departure gate, Anansi proposed we try a little stunt. *It might work, it might not*, he said. *Let's see.*

I had bought a Club Class ticket – though I have money, I'm not reckless – but at Anansi's prompted I elected to give myself an unofficial upgrade. When the plane was fully boarded but not yet moving, I sauntered through to the First Class cabin and plumped myself down in the nearest empty seat. I acted as though I belonged there and nobody had the right to tell me otherwise. I waited to be questioned, challenged, checked, but none of the team of flight attendants batted an eyelid. One of them poured me my complimentary glass of champagne. Another took my meal order.

Sometimes it's all about balls and bravado, said Anansi as the plane taxied towards the runway. *A confidence trick doesn't involve just gaining a victim's confidence. It's your own confidence that matters too. Have plenty of it, and results are more or less guaranteed.*

We took off, and England and its sheath of cloud fell behind. I sat back in my seat, lacing my hands behind my head and stretching out into the acres of legroom available. Eleven luxurious hours later, we were descending over the dry sunburnt plains of the American south-west.

AT MCCARRAN INTERNATIONAL, I witnessed what turned out to be the contest's first elimination.

In baggage reclaim, as I waited for my suitcase to appear on the carousel, I caught sight of a Middle Eastern man haring across the hall. He was being pursued by half a dozen plainclothes and uniformed security officials in full cry, all demanding that he stop. The man darted a glance over his shoulder, then collided headlong with a luggage trolley. He sprawled to the floor and the security men pounced. The man struggled, and someone produced a Taser. There was a high-voltage sizzle, and the man shrieked, writhed and lay still. The security men carted him off unceremoniously. A passenger asked them what was going on. The curt reply: "Terrorist suspect."

It was enough. It was all anyone needed. Almost everyone present started cheering and applauding, and a couple of suggestions were offered as to what should be done with the Middle Easterner: essentially, imprisonment, interrogation and execution.

That's no terrorist, Anansi scoffed. *If he's an Islamic extremist, I'm a tarantula. That's Juha, that is.*

I didn't have my Bluetooth on just then, so I gave a kind of mental shrug, as if to say *Really?*

Oh yes. Undoubtedly. Juha's avatar. And if I don't miss my guess, one of our opponents "dropped a dime on him," as they say.

It made sense. In the paranoid post-9/11 United States, anyone looking remotely Arabic was automatically under suspicion. A phone call to the authorities, or a tap on the shoulder and a few words whispered in the right ear, and people would see bomb vests and phials of anthrax where there were none, and overreact accordingly.

Juha, who, annoyed by his local muezzin's calls to prayer, cut off the man's head and threw it down a well, then threw a ram's head down there too in order to allay suspicion...

Juha, who sold his house but drove a nail into the wall before he left, then kept coming back on the pretext of inspecting the nail, meanwhile preying on the new owner's hospitality until eventually the new owner fled the property in high dudgeon without asking for his money back...

Juha, who borrowed a large sum of money off his rich-but-stingy neighbour and refused to return it, then asked the neighbour to lend him his horse, robe and shoes as they made their way to see the judge, who he hoodwinked into believing that Juha himself must be the rich one and the neighbour a liar...

Now out of contention.

One entrant down already, and the contest hadn't even officially begun.

THOUGH IT PERHAPS ought to have been, Las Vegas was not the location of the contest. Our ultimate destination lay some one hundred and fifty miles outside the world capital of tourist fleecing: a tiny town that went by the name of Sweetwater, stuck out in the Mojave Desert.

So, after a night in a decent enough hotel some distance from the lights and hurly-burly of the Strip, I caught a westbound Greyhound. The bus rolled away from the city into a landscape so arid and barren it almost hurt to look at it. Everything that was not rocks was scrubby, barely-there plant life.

Anansi was enthralled. *Reminds me of the savannahs of home*, he said wistfully. *The Serengeti. The Rift Valley. Olduvai Gorge.*

"I'm a city boy," I told him. "All I see is wasteland, without a Starbucks or a Marks and Spencer in sight."

"Is like Mars," said a voice from across the bus aisle.

"Excuse me?"

He was big and thickly bearded, with a lumberjack shirt and a snake tattoo on his forearm. His accent put him somewhere east of the Caucasus. "I said is like Mars. All this red desert. No wonder peoples is always seeing flying spaceships out here. If Martians are coming to this planet, here is where they are likely to be landing. Somewhere like their own home."

"Oh. Yes. Fair point."

"Do I know you?" The man squinted at me, his bushy eyebrows knotting together like a pair of caterpillars mating. "I am thinking we have met before."

"No, I'm sure I –"

Veles, whispered Anansi.

"I'm sure we –"

He is Veles. Trickster god of the Slavic folk.

I consulted my trove of research data. Veles. Storm god. Able to transform himself into various kinds of animals and even people. Protector of sheep and cows. Famous for...

Anansi chipped in. *Famous for fighting Perun, god of war, after stealing Perun's wife, or his son, or some of his cattle – depends which version of the story you read. Their battle raged in the heavens as a lightning storm. Veles lost, and his blood fell like rain. He looks after peasants, bringing them wealth, and is also the god of sorcerers. Those who weave spells as well as those who weave wool look to him for patronage and inspiration.* He concluded, *Slippery customer. These shapeshifter types always are. Keep your wits about you, Dion.*

"Yes," said the man. "I am recognising you. We are both here for the same reason, no?"

Without being invited, he heaved himself across the aisle and squeezed his bulk into the seat next to mine.

"Ivan Rodchenko."

I shook a hot, powerful paw.

"Dion Yeboah."

"Someone is riding with you, yes? As with me." He tapped his skull. "A secret traveller."

I glanced around at our fellow passengers. The bus was a quarter full. Nobody seemed to be interested in us. People were dozing, reading, messing around on their phones and tablets, or listening to music through earbuds. Nobody was eavesdropping.

I nodded to Rodchenko.

"Yes," he said. "I thought so. I know for sure when I am hearing you talk to yourself. Is hard sometimes to remember to not speak aloud when you are having conversation with guest in head. Maybe, to others, you are looking like mad person, or too much this..." He mimed glugging down alcohol.

"Normally I'm careful," I said. "I must be feeling a touch of jet lag."

"We have come long way to compete," said Rodchenko. "Others are coming from even further. China, Japan, Australia, all over. Is big world. Many gods. Only a few from America itself. Including last time's winner."

"Coyote."

"Yes, yes. The oh-so-wily Coyote. He wins, meaning he is getting to choose site for next contest. He chooses home turf. Well, of course. Why not? And you are being from... England, is correct?"

"Is correct."

"You are with Robin Goodfellow, then? Also known as Puck?"

I shook my head. "Anansi."

"Ah, Anansi! You speak like Englishman, but your ancestry is African. Interesting. I suppose, wherever we live, wherever we go, we are always carrying our true roots with us. If I am not having my home in Mother Russia, maybe Veles is still finding me and asking will I help anyway."

"Comfort stop coming up," the bus driver announced over the intercom. "Fifteen minutes and not a second more. You ain't back in your seat by the time I fire up the engine, 'fraid I've got to leave without you. Rules are rules. Can't mess with the timetable."

WE ALL DECAMPED into a roadside pit stop that boasted a gas station, a car wash, a fast-food outlet, a minimart and a tolerable set of toilets. I relieved myself, washed my hands with my usual fastidiousness, then went to see what snacks and refreshments were on offer at the minimart. Candy, carbonated drinks and vast bags of corn and potato products were the main fare available, all of which, as a man conscious of his health and appearance, particularly his waistline, I shun. I opted for a packet of peanuts and raisins, some beef jerky, and a large bottle of mineral water.

I joined the queue for the till – as luck would have it, directly behind the considerable girth of Rodchenko. He glanced round at me and winked. In his arms were great quantities of the very things I'd avoided, including what appeared to be a gallon bottle of Coca-Cola. He looked as content as only a Russian could on finding himself a voyager in the Land of Excess.

"Must stock up on energy," he said. "For when fun and games begin tomorrow."

Yes, tomorrow, said Anansi. *The official start of the contest. But why wait? Someone took Juha out of the running early. Let's do the same with Veles.*

On the counter, just by my right elbow, stood a

spinner rack filled with Zippo lighters. They had a map of the state engraved on them – the outline reminiscent of a guillotine blade – along with the quip *I GOT BURNED IN NEVADA*. I checked out the minimart's security cameras. The one trained on the counter was tightly aimed at the till clerk, no doubt to ensure the honesty of employees as well as of customers. There was another camera in the far corner of the premises, but I was well out of its range. Best of all, a Highway Patrol officer had just ambled in through the main entrance and was busy denuding the Krispy Kreme doughnut stand of most of its stock.

Quick, Anansi hissed. *Now*.

I palmed a Zippo off the rack and slipped it into Rodchenko's back pocket.

Two minutes later, Rodchenko was heading out across the forecourt to the Greyhound and I was informing the patrolman that an act of thievery had just taken place.

"Him," I said, pointing at the burly form of Rodchenko. "I saw him. He took a cigarette lighter without paying for it. It's in his back pocket."

"Big fella with the plaid shirt?" said the patrolman. "You sure?"

"Saw it with my own eyes."

I sounded plausible. My clean-cut English diction helped. I set my face, as any good lawyer can, in the expression that said, *Would I lie to you?*

The patrolman set down his box of doughnuts and hurried outside. "Hey! Sir. Excuse me, sir? Hey! I want a word with you."

I sauntered by as the patrolman grilled Rodchenko. The Russian fixed me with a curious frown. I feigned obliviousness.

Out of the blast-furnace heat, back in the air-conditioned bliss of the bus, I watched as Rodchenko obeyed the patrolman's instruction to empty out his pockets. He evinced surprise at finding the Zippo on his person. The patrolman demanded to be shown the receipt for Rodchenko's purchases. It didn't take him long to establish that the Zippo was not on it. He led Rodchenko indoors by the elbow, the Russian protesting and remonstrating volubly.

Just before he was taken back inside the minimart, Rodchenko turned and aimed an angry look towards the bus. His gaze met mine. He spat out some curse in his native language. I smiled serenely at him and waved.

"Guess he won't be rejoining us, then," said the bus driver. "Doors closing. Everybody, please take your seats. Next stops: Roach, Primm, Sweetwater."

Excellent work, said Anansi, congratulating both me and himself.

I wondered whether what I'd just done might be considered cheating.

Cheating? Cheating!? Anansi dismissed my concerns with a scornful laugh. *In a contest of tricksters, what's fair and what's not? I'll tell you. Everything and nothing. Just because hostilities haven't been declared yet, doesn't mean we can't get in a pre-emptive strike or two. Veles would have done the same to us, given half a chance. Initiative and ruthlessness. That's how we're going to survive to the end, Dion. Initiative and ruthlessness.*

SWEETWATER, JUST ACROSS the state line into California, had once had something going for it, namely a large lake. In the 'fifties and 'sixties, the town had been a handy stopover point for people travelling from Los Angeles to Vegas, and a resort besides, even if it had lacked the lure of the slot machines and gaming tables that lay in wait just a few miles further east. Boating, swimming, fishing, water sports in general: these had been its attractions, on a lake filled with cold limpid snowmelt straight from the slopes of the Sierra Nevada.

Then, however, the main river that fed the lake basin had been diverted and dammed some way upstream to create a reservoir and a hydroelectric plant, providing hungry, ever-expanding LA with power and leaving Sweetwater with nothing but a swampy pond fed by a trickle of a stream, and sad memories of its boom days. The town was mostly forgotten now, in spite of the billboards lining the freeway at five-mile intervals announcing to drivers that they were getting closer to The Best Little Burg You'll Ever Pass By. Most people seemed content to do just that, pass by, and Sweetwater had sunk slowly into sand and obsolescence.

That was certainly the impression I got as the bus turned off Interstate 15 and followed the narrow road into town. Everything about Sweetwater appeared to belong to a bygone era. A gas station with clockface-dial pumps. Diners that looked like railroad cars. Everywhere, that low-slung American architecture that spoke of space-age optimism and the capacity to spread outwards into infinite acres of wilderness. Sprawling aingle-storey structures. Polygonal blocks of concrete and plate glass and steel.

The bus halted opposite the town's one remaining hostelry, the Friendly Inn And Conference Center. Only I alighted. For a moment, as I felt the weight of the midday sun on my head, I wavered. It wasn't too late to climb back aboard and go elsewhere.

No, warned Anansi.

And then it *was* too late. The Greyhound pulled away with a diesel growl, executing a hundred-and-eighty-degree turn and sending a fine cloud of dust over me that stung my eyes as it trundled back to the interstate.

I crossed the street, tugging my roll-along suitcase behind me.

THE FRIENDLY INN And Conference Center had one of those cheap display signs outside it, the kind you see almost everywhere in the USA, with simple cutout letters that clip onto thin rods. It read:

THE FRIENDLY WELCOMES
18TH ANNUAL JOKE SHOP
PROPRIETORS JAMBOREE!!!

I couldn't help but smile to myself. I'd read a feature about this little trade fair a couple of years ago in the *Sunday Times Magazine*. The article described how retailers and wholesalers in the American novelty retail industry got together once a year to compare notes, buy and sell the latest items, and discuss the ins and outs of their rarefied business. I recalled photographs of rather odd-looking men, and a few women, poring over trestle tables laden with stink bombs, hand buzzers, sachets of itching powder and suchlike. The tone adopted by the journalist had been a mix of wistful and snide. Joke shops were dying out, he averred, kids in our computer age no longer as attracted to pocket-money prank wares as kids used to be. How brave and foolhardy these people were who strove to uphold the tradition.

In that respect, Sweetwater was the ideal spot for such a convention to be held. For all concerned, their heyday had passed.

A joke shop trade fair was, of course, perfect cover for a gathering of trickster gods to come and conduct their tournament of one-upmanship. Amid all the plastic hilarity of squirting buttonhole flowers and fake dog turds, who would notice us divine avatars fooling and foiling one another? Who would care? We would blend right in, camouflaged like tigers in the jungle. No one would look twice at us.

I CHECKED IN at the reception desk, which was staffed by an elderly lady with a beehive hairdo and those pointy-tipped schoolmistress spectacles that I didn't think anyone made any more, let alone wore. Gladys, as identified by her name tag, wished me a pleasant stay in a voice like gargled gravel.

"Friendly by name, friendly by nature, that's us," she drawled, a motto that had been leached of all warmth and meaning through decades of repetition.

The hotel was a ramble of long corridors and branching annexes, arranged in a complex geometrical pattern around a sun deck and a drained swimming pool. My room, which overlooked Sweetwater's main drag, proved to be small but serviceable. There was a TV set from the era when no technological device was complete without fake-wood panelling; a window-mounted air-con unit that crackled and wheezed like a catarrh sufferer's windpipe; and a bed which crunched when sat on. The mattress had a deep hollow in the middle, and I imagined countless coupled bodies thrusting up and down, hammering out this concavity over the years – then tried not to imagine it.

Just jealous, said Anansi.

"Am not."

You need a woman. Why don't you have a woman in your life?

"You sound like my mother."

You're thirty-two. Why aren't you married yet?

"You're married. Has it made you happy? Complete?"

Of course.

"And yet you're a serial philanderer."

A man has needs, Anansi said defensively. *Besides, my marriage has brought me children, and they definitely make me happy.* He reeled off his offspring's names. *Akaki. Toto Abuo. Twa Akwan. Hwe Nuso. Adwafo. Da Yi Ya. And my precious little Intikuma. I love them all more than life itself. I fought Death for them, did I not?*

"I know."

If you had children of your own, you'd realise how important it is, being a father, said Anansi. *How it fixes your priorities and grounds you in the nitty-gritty of life. Then you would understand, too, why I dared trick Brother Death to protect them.*

"You were so brave."

I was. I was. I know you're being sarcastic, but I was. Death had us cornered in our house...

"After you antagonised him by eating his food and drinking his water and not thanking him."

True, but let's ignore that, shall we? I and my family were clinging to the rafters while Death prowled below us with a burlap sack, catching each of us one after another as we lost our grip and fell, until only I was left, grimly clinging on.

"But you persuaded him to use the flour barrel to catch you instead, saying it meant you'd be nicely crumb-coated for him, all ready to be fried and eaten."

And I landed on his head and his face went in the flour and he was blinded for a moment, and we all escaped. Hee, hee, hee! Anansi wriggled inside me, overcome with his own cleverness. *But, Dion,* he continued, serious again, *I mean it. You need a family of your own. Nanabaa Oboshie, wherever she is, must be beginning to think there's something wrong with her grandson. A proper Ghanaian, by your age, should have a brood of rug rats scuttling around him and a nice plump wife in the kitchen.*

"Busy," I said. "High standards. And I'm British, not Ghanaian."

Too uptight, Anansi opined. *Too self-obsessed.*

"Are we here to criticise Dion Yeboah or are we here to win a competition?" I said testily.

A pause. Then: *A competition.*

"Very well. So let me rest. I'm worn out."

I lay down on the much-used bed and closed my eyes, trying to blot out all distractions.

But it was hard when one of those distractions was a rustling voice inside my head that wouldn't ever be fully silent but perpetually whispered and nagged, nagged and whispered...

THAT EVENING, WE gathered in one of the hotel's small conference rooms, the Sagebrush Suite, for a preliminary meeting. Several of the joke shop people wandered in with a view to joining us, then wandered out again. Instinctively, they sensed this sidebar event had nothing to do with them. They didn't belong. One man, dressed in full mime makeup and costume, pretended he kept bumping up against an invisible wall just inside the doorway which wouldn't allow him into the room. The wall could almost have been real. If you weren't a living vehicle for a trickster god, something inside told you you were barred from entry.

We took our seats on plastic chairs, eyeing one another up. It was weird, seeing the faces of all these strangers, random individuals culled from across the planet, and somehow recognising them. It was like meeting one's own extended family. We looked utterly unalike and yet there were similarities, something in the set of everyone's features, a shared look behind the eyes, unifying us.

Susanoo-no-Mikoto, said Anansi, indicating a young Japanese man with an imperious, brooding air. *And over there, that's Crow*. A thickset Australian Aborigine with impossibly black eyes, as though he had no irises, only great dark pupils.

Between us we put names to several other faces. A Chinese man with a certain simian cast to his appearance was Sun Wukong, the Monkey King. A swarthy little chap with quick green eyes had to be Gwydion from Wales. A young Greek with long ringleted hair who kept relentlessly checking his texts on his mobile phone was clearly Hermes, while next to him squatted a middle-aged Latino whose expression was as sinisterly sly as anyone's I've seen.

Eshu, from the Santería tradition, Anansi confirmed. *And as for that Scandinavian blonde...*

Well, who could fail to identify Loki? The famous Norse gender-switcher had come in the guise of a woman. A beautiful one at that. Slender, angular and icily lovely.

He's pulled this stunt before, Anansi pointed out. *And he'll use it to his advantage, you mark my words. Someone or other will think with their penis, not their brains, and get caught out by him. It's as inevitable as sunrise. Just make sure it's not us, heh?*

I took the advice on board: think with brains, not penis. Ironic, coming from him.

Then a figure went bounding up onto the small podium. He was a Native American with weathered ochre skin and iron-grey plaits. He wore jeans and a denim waistcoat, and his bootlace tie was secured by a silver clasp in the shape of a coyote's head.

Coyote – who else could it be? – raised a hand in order to command silence, although truth be told, the room wasn't that noisy to begin with. We fellow avatars turned towards him, waiting for him to address us.

Yawn, yawn, said Anansi.

I told him to pipe down.

"Greetings, all," said the Native American. "My name is William Gad. I have another name, which I'm sure you know. For the time being, we all do. But you can call me Bill. I'd like to welcome you to my homeland. These are the desert plains from which I sprang. Here are the canyons and arroyos I haunt, the salt flats and mesas where story-craft and ritual continues to keep me vibrant and alive. It's a harsh, unforgiving landscape, but it teems with secret life and its beauties are plain for all to see."

He smiled whitely – good, sturdy American dentistry.

"So, we reunite again," he said. "The wheel of seasons has turned, the years have flown by, a new generation has been born and grown to adulthood, and once more we are ready to compete. I see there are..."

He performed a quick head count.

"...forty-five of us. Not as many as last time. In fact, maybe the lowest turnout we've ever had. Sad to say, our numbers are in decline. Some of us cannot even muster the power to manifest on Earth now. Those guys' stories are so poorly preserved, their reputations so sidelined and diminished, they may as well no longer exist. We mourn their absence. But..."

He brightened.

"But we should celebrate our presence, too. Our continued puissance, if you'll forgive the fancy French word. We're still here, still hanging on, still known and noted, even in a world as godless as this. That's got to be worth a round of applause. Can I hear one?"

Most of us did clap. I was one of the few that didn't. Not my style.

"All right," said Bill Gad. "Down to business. At this stage in the proceedings, it's customary to restate the rules of the contest, such as they are. So here goes. As of dawn tomorrow, each of us is entitled to bring mayhem, chaos and disarray into the lives of any or all of the others. The means can be fair or foul, pleasant or offensive, so long as the victim is left significantly and materially disadvantaged in some way. Anything that achieves this result is allowable. And those are the rules."

We thought he'd finished, but it seemed he had more to add.

"Mischief. You know as well as I do that *mischief* is a broad term, a whole lot broader than most folk nowadays think. It isn't just naughtiness, it's the active upsetting of the order of things. Derangement, rearrangement. That's what we do. That's what we've always done, since creation. We live to undermine orthodoxy, mock the establishment, say and do what most wish to, but are too cowed and downtrodden to try. We're the anarchy that lies in the heart of every man, woman and child, the urge to tear down what others build, the seething rebellion that lurks beneath the surface of every civilisation.

"Our exploits tell people that it's okay to bend the law, okay to be different, okay not to toe the line. Sometimes you've just got to stick a finger up, or two fingers, or whatever your culture's preferred gesture demands. It frees you. It reminds you that individuals make a society, not the other way round. We're the gods of that. We're the worm in the apple barrel of every pantheon. We're the ones who make deities fallible and human. The rest may look down on us, but they need us. They couldn't do without us screwing up and dicking around. We're the balloon prickers, the ego deflaters, the court jesters, the circus clowns. That's us. Remember that.

"So, to sum up. Have a ball. Let your hair down. Go wild. Do your thing. We keep the contest going until the last deceit has been played. That is all. Any questions?"

A hand went up. It belonged to a Peruvian, short and flat-nosed, with a deadpan stare. He wore a zigzag-striped poncho and was carrying a brightly coloured cloth bag. Huehuecoyotl of the Aztecs.

"Is it true that two of us have already been taken out of the running?" he asked.

"Yes, I've heard that," Gad confirmed. "I guess you could call it a violation of the rules, but what the hell. Those fellas should have been more cautious. Probably will be, next time. Any other questions?"

None.

"Then we're done. Best of luck, all of you. May the tricksiest trickster win."

LATER, I WAS nursing a soda water with a lime twist at the hotel bar when Gad sidled up to me. He took the stool next to mine and ordered a double shot of Jim Beam, straight, no ice.

"Bill," he said.

"I know. Dion."

He clinked his glass against mine. "Good to meet you. Again. For the first time."

We both smiled at his little witticism, him more than me. Around us, attendees of the joke shop trade fair milled and chatted. For people whose livelihoods centred around laughter, they were a morose bunch.

Gad noted this. "Reckon running a joke shop must be a serious business."

"In the current economic climate, more than ever. Suicidally serious."

"Ha! Yeah. So tell me. Veles. That was you, right? That's the rumour doing the rounds."

Say nothing, Anansi advised.

Saying nothing is anathema to lawyers, so I said, "I can't comment," which amounts to the same thing.

"Don't worry, I'm not going to judge you for it," Gad said. "And I'm certainly not going to demand you withdraw. If nothing else, it would be damn hypocritical of me."

I put two and two together. "Juha. That was you?"

"I can't comment," he replied, his mouth creasing slightly at the corners. "What I will tell you is, I know you, spider man. I know you're a down-and-dirty, stop-at-nothing kind of guy. We've done this dance so many times before, I've lost count, and the two of us, we're among the best. The elite. I admire you and have respect for you. And I'm going to be watching out for you, or rather watching my back for as long as you're around. That's the highest compliment I can pay anyone in these circumstances."

"Thanks," I said. "I think."

"I have a feeling this is going to be one of those occasions where it comes down to you versus me at the end. And I just want you to know: it's going to be me."

He gave a wolfish grin.

"We clear on that?"

"Crystal."

"Good." Gad drained his whisky and melted into the crowd.

Arrogant son of a bitch.

Quite literally, assuming female coyotes are called bitches.

I assured Anansi that Bill Gad didn't bother me.

But he's beaten me before.

"And you've beaten him too," I said to my reflection in the mirror behind the bar. "And you can do it again."

"Excuse me?" said the bartender.

"Nothing. Just talking to myself."

"Can I freshen that drink for you?"

"No thanks. Long day ahead. Time I turned in."

"Sure, buddy. Sleep well."

I didn't. But I slept enough.

Dawn broke, and somebody screamed.

THE COMMOTION CAME from the room three doors along from mine. A man was letting out hoarse yelps of horror and disgust. Several of us avatars gathered in the corridor outside.

"Whose room is this?" someone asked.

"That Frenchie's," said a redheaded Irishman so tiny he was almost a midget. "What's the feller in him called? Ronald, something like that."

"Reynard," I said.

"That's him, so it is. But what's he setting up all that racket about? Yelling like he's got a snake up his arse." He pronounced it *erse*.

"Maybe he has. Maybe someone put a poisonous snake in his bed, a rattler or some such."

"Jaysus, do you think so?" exclaimed the Irishman.

Looking at him, the only word that sprang to mind was *leprechaun*. "Well then, who's going to go in? Not me, that's for sure. I'm from a land of no snakes and I'm happy with it that way."

"I will," said an Egyptian with fine, almost feminine features. Anansi told me he was the host body of none other than Set, as if I couldn't guess. "Snakes don't bother me – if it *is* a snake."

"Could be a trick, of course," I said.

The Egyptian's hand, raised to knock on the door, hesitated. "And you could be bluffing me by saying that," he decided.

"And you," the Irishman said to him, "could be who's behind this, and it's all an elaborate ruse to sucker one of us in."

Oh, this is a hall of mirrors, said Anansi with approval. *I'd forgotten how tangled these situations could become, and how quickly. Kidders kidding kidders, ad infinitum.*

"Just do it," I said to the Egyptian. The Frenchman's screaming had subsided to a loud, fretful gasping, but still the noise was getting on my nerves. So unseemly.

"All right, I will," the Egyptian replied. He knocked. "You in there. What's going on? You've woken up half the hotel. What's the matter?"

The door was opened, not by the Frenchman, but by the Scandinavian woman, Loki's chosen avatar. She was dressed only in a lace-trimmed black silk bra and matching panties. I have to say the sight of her left us all agog, some of us trying hard not to stare, others frankly staring.

"Good morning, gentlemen," she said. Glacier-blue eyes sparkled. She knew full well the effect her body, in that underwear, was having on us. "Apologies for disturbing you. Not my fault, however."

I managed to tear my gaze from her and peer into the room. The Frenchman was sitting cross-legged, stark naked, in an armchair in the corner of the room. His lean, foxlike face was distraught. He was biting one knuckle and gibbering.

"Excuse me?" I said. "Reynard? I know that's not your given name, but we haven't been formally introduced. Are you all right? What's the matter?"

"*Elle...*" the Frenchman stammered. "*Elle va pisser... et elle...*"

"I don't speak French. In English?"

"Her." He pointed a trembling finger at the Scandinavian. "She use the toilet."

"So?"

"I see her. Through open door. She – she use it standing up."

I looked back at her.

"What?" she said, innocently.

"You're..."

As one, our gazes migrated down to her crotch. Now that we knew what we were looking for, it wasn't hard to make out a telltale bulge in the front of her panties.

"I'm Solveig, by the way," she said. "Though that wasn't the name I was christened with."

She held out a hand to me that was just a little larger and bonier than a woman's hand ought to be.

I couldn't bring myself to shake it.

Well, this is a new twist on an old theme, said Anansi.

"A monster!" the Frenchman blurted out. "A crime against humanity!"

"Oh, *now* you're picky," Solveig said to him. "You weren't so bothered last night. You couldn't have been more eager."

"Last night I did not know," the Frenchman protested. "I was drunk."

"That's what they all say. If you ask me, you knew damn well."

"But I'm French. A French man." He let out a heartfelt groan of injured Gallic male pride.

"I know, my love. That makes it even more delicious." Solveig began gathering up her clothes from the floor. She slipped her feet into a pair of high-heeled slingbacks and walked out with her outerwear bunched to her chest. "One up to Loki, I'd say. Wouldn't you? And Reynard is out of the contest."

"Noooo!" the Frenchman cried, but there was no getting round it. His humiliation had been public and total.

Solveig sashayed down the corridor to her own room. We watched her go, and the Irishman spoke for all of us when he said, "Now that is one fine figure of a lady. If I didn't know what I know now..."

A FURTHER ELIMINATION occurred during breakfast. Someone left their table to fetch more pancakes from the restaurant's self-service counter. When they returned, they discovered that someone else had put urine in their coffee.

The culprit was a Filipino who was riding tandem with his people's trickster, Tikbalang. The victim was an Inuit, avatar of Amaguq, the wolfish god of deception. The Inuit took his defeat stoically, clapping the Filipino on the shoulder and ruffling his horselike mane of hair.

"You had it on you all along?" he asked.

The Filipino produced an empty hospital sample jar. "Just waiting for my chance."

"You know, American coffee is so awful, you actually made it taste better."

The Filipino laughed.

The Inuit clapped him on the shoulder again. "Kind of makes me feel bad about the piece of rotten walrus liver I slipped into your air con unit from the outside."

"Huh? When?"

"Just this morning. Your room should be stinking up real bad by now."

The Filipino looked dubious.

"Don't believe me? Go check."

The Filipino left the restaurant and returned five minutes later looking green-gilled and rueful.

"Bastard. That was awful. The smell...!"

Bill Gad stood up and congratulated them. "Superb work, both of you. A textbook two-way strike. But now, I'm afraid, you both need to pack your bags and go. You are done here."

The trade fair people in the restaurant were pretty bemused by all this. They grasped the gist of what was going on, but not the purpose. To them we seemed to be prank specialists, a kind of elite force of jokers. I overheard one remarking to another that he thought we must be a form of entertainment laid on by the convention organisers.

"Living theatre," he said. "That's what this is. These guys are showing us how it should be done."

"Yeah," said his companion. "I see that. We peddle the stuff, but these guys are, like, improv geniuses. Experts. They're the marines, and we're just grunts. Never seen anything like it at the Joke Shop Jamboree before, but, I tell you, whatever they're being paid, they're worth every cent."

"Agreed. We should watch and learn, my friend. Watch and learn."

TAME, SO FAR, Anansi commented. *But it's only just getting under way.*

"Should we go for Coyote?" I wondered. I was back in my room, so speaking aloud was an option. "Take him out early?"

Dear me, no. Start low, work our way up. Weed out the weaklings first. Show them who's boss. That's how it's done.

"Who do you have in mind?"

That obese German. The one with Till Eulenspiegel in him. Him or the Tibetan, Uncle Tompa. Or maybe your fellow countryman, Puck.

"Why not all three in one fell swoop?"

I admire your ambition, Dion. Tell me more.

*   *   *

TILL EULENSPIEGEL, UNCLE Tompa and Puck. Quite a trio. Till Eulenspiegel, whose surname means 'owl mirror' in High German and 'arse wipe' in Low German, would do anything to fill his belly, once even taking the job of watchman and pretending the town was under attack so he could steal the food off the table of the count and his knights as they rode to defend the walls. Uncle Tompa was a real rascal, who among other things hoodwinked a naïve young virgin into having sex with him by asking her to go to the toilet for him and filling her with his semen, convincing her that it was urine. Puck, as any aficionado of Shakespearean comedy knows, waylaid travellers, whether for his own amusement or at his master King Oberon's behest, and was also fond of stealing food at parties and blowing out candles with his farts, not to mention sexually teasing stallions.

Did they have anything in common?

Answer: not much.

But they were all of them creatures of carnal appetite, and if I've learned anything from my years spent wearing an itchy horsehair wig and being obliged to come into regular contact with drunkards, thieves and rapists, it's that such creatures are easily led. And indeed misled.

Anansi himself, after all, wasn't immune to the wiles of others. In one Anansesem he cheated a farm-owning chameleon out of his smallholding, but the chameleon turned the tables by stitching together a cloak from vines and decorating it with buzzing flies and offering it to Anansi, at a price. The price was enough food to fill a hole in the floor of his barn. Anansi, overcome with desire for the cloak, sent two of his children to the chameleon's house with sacks of grain. What he didn't know was how deep the chameleon had dug the hole. Day after day the children trekked to the barn and poured grain into the hole, and it never filled up. Eventually the chameleon got back in grain the value of the land which Anansi had stolen from him, and Anansi didn't even have the cloak to show for it. By the time he got to wear it, months after agreeing to buy it, the vines had withered to bare twigs and the flies were all dead.

I reminded him of this sorry episode, and his response was a sheepish, foot-shuffling, *Yes, but...*

"I'm just saying, there's none so gullible as a beguiler."

Lovely little slogan, that. You should have it made into a cross-stitch sampler and hung on your wall.

"You know what? I think I might."

FIRST ORDER OF business was hiring a car. Sweetwater's one and only vehicle rental place – Mojave Motors, "We Getcha Rollin'" – was run by a bickering elderly couple in matching dungarees, Jed and Gertie. A ten-year-old Ford Taurus was the best they had to offer. Jed said not to mind the patches of rust on the wheel arches, the car was still as reliable as anything that ever rolled off a Detroit assembly line. Gertie, meanwhile, alerted me to the fact that the gas tank was near-as-dammit empty and I should fill up at the Amoco on the way out of town, otherwise I'd be going no further than ten or fifteen miles.

Ten or fifteen miles sounded okay to me.

The next stage was to round up my three intended victims. I cruised the hotel, quizzing other avatars as to the whereabouts of Till Eulenspiegel, Uncle Tompa and Puck. Soon enough, all three got wind that I was after a meeting with them, and we congregated in the lobby.

They looked cagey, understandably enough, and I went to great lengths to put their minds at ease.

"I'm proposing a little road trip," I said. "Just the four of us."

"Where to?" demanded the German. His name was Gunther, and with his pig-bristle ginger hair and red blubbery lips he was almost a caricature of the *bierkeller* Bavarian, a living archetype.

"There's a pueblo Indian village not far from here."

"So?" said the Tibetan, a wizened individual by the name of Rinzen.

"I don't know if you've heard about it, but there's a place there that serves amazing food. It's quite famous in the area. Little family-run restaurant, half a dozen tables, Mexican cuisine, generous portions, very exclusive."

"And you're inviting us there?" said the Englishman. He was a children's party entertainer called Robin. The sprite inside him liked to keep things straightforward. "Why?"

"Why not? No fun going on my own. You're all appreciators of fine dining, and you seem convivial sorts. I thought you might like to come along and check it out with me."

"Forgive me," said Robin, "but this smells very like a trap."

The other two nodded and grunted in agreement.

"I'd be astonished if you *didn't* think that," I said. "But look at it this way. How can I possibly be hoping to trap you? There's three of you and only one of me. Each of you is my equal in intellect and cunning." In my head I heard Anansi snort. "To try and take on all three of you at once would be rash indeed. More than likely it would backfire on me and I'd wind up the loser. All this is is a comradely, peaceable gesture. We get to go out of town, have a look-around, see some of the sights, and enjoy a feast into the bargain. The chimichangas, I'm reliably informed, are delicious, and the burritos are stuffed so full you can barely get your mouth round them."

Their eyes, to varying degrees, lit up.

"Plus," I added, "there's beer."

Gunther moistened his lips with a glistening pink eel of a tongue.

"So what do we say, gentlemen? Are we interested?"

They remained wary, but I knew I had them.

"We do outnumber you," said Rinzen.

"And the hotel food's nothing to write home about," said Robin.

"But if there is any funny business..." Gunther growled.

I smiled serenely. "Transport awaits. This way, my friends."

WE GLIDED OUT of Sweetwater in the Taurus, straight past the Amoco without stopping. For a time the road followed the erstwhile shoreline of the lake. Disused, decrepit jetties reached out aimlessly over a deepening depression in the ground. The lakebed – dry, cracked – shelved into the distance, dotted here and there with the sun-parched hulks of motorboats and kayaks. Perhaps a mile away, a thin ribbon of water glimmered, writhing in the heat haze like a trickle of mercury.

I followed the interstate for approximately twenty minutes until a turnoff appeared. I remembered it from the bus journey in. The road was pitted and potholed, its asphalt cracked at the edges. I slowed to around 20mph, dodging drifts of dust and the occasional, honest-to-goodness rolling tumbleweed.

There was indeed a village at the end of this unimpressive highway. What my passengers didn't know was that its residents had abandoned it thirty years ago. I'd looked it up on Google. A handful of adobe dwellings, some of them dating back to the late nineteenth century and once occupied by a Zuni tribe, now lay uninhabited, home only to scorpions and lizards. The village was protected by some sort of heritage status, but to be honest, it was unlikely that a property developer was going to happen along, deem the spot a prime site for commercial exploitation and try to raze the buildings to the ground. It was more a case of the American government wishing to be seen to be actively preserving indigenous culture, compensation for the many long years when it had tried to do the exact opposite.

Anyway, we didn't make it to the village. Some six or seven miles after we left the interstate, the Taurus's engine began to plink and splutter. Moments later, I was coasting to a halt, the driver of a car that was most assuredly going nowhere.

"What's this?" snapped Gunther. "We cannot be stopping. I see no restaurant."

"Or any village," said Rinzen.

"Is there something wrong with the car?" Robin asked.

"Not as such," I replied. None of them had noticed the fuel warning light that had been glaring on the dashboard all along. Nor had any of them cottoned to the significance of the fact that I was wearing running shorts and trainers. "Nothing a tank of petrol couldn't fix."

"What!" Gunther roared. "You mean to say the car has run out? You let it?"

"Looks that way," I said, opening my door and getting out.

"Where are you going?" Rinzen asked.

"Back to town."

"How?"

"On foot."

"That's insane," said Robin. "It must be a hundred degrees out there."

"Hundred and eleven, according to the thermometer on the dash," I said. "But I'll be fine. At a steady jog I can make it to Sweetwater in under an hour, I reckon. I'm pretty fit. How about you lot? You fit too?"

Judging by their looks of dismay, Gunther's especially, the answer was: not very.

"Phone," said Robin, fishing a Nokia out of his pocket. "I can call for help."

"Really? And how many bars have you got there?"

Robin frowned at the screen, then hissed in annoyance. "None. No signal."

"That's funny, there weren't any on my iPhone either, last time I checked." Which I did, surreptitiously, while driving just a few minutes earlier. "This is the back of beyond. Network coverage's pretty much nonexistent. Tell you what, when I get to the hotel I'll arrange for someone to come out with a can of unleaded. Can't say fairer than that. Until then, you three sit tight, don't exert yourselves, stay in the shade, try to keep cool."

"And the restaurant?" Gunther said plaintively. Even now he couldn't quite give up on the dream of those plump, grease-dripping burritos. "The meal?"

"Oh, Till Eulenspiegel," I said with a sorrowful shake of the head.

I set off, leaving them to their own devices. A last look back showed me Robin clambering onto the roof of the car, vainly angling his phone to the heavens; Rinzen watching me go, hand shading his eyes, his posture phlegmatic; and Gunther stamping around in impotent fury, filling the air with guttural Teutonic oaths.

IT WAS A hard run, the hardest I'd ever done. The heat was atrocious. Every mile seemed to sap a bit more of the life out of me. The sweat on my face dried to a salty crust. My throat burned with dust and dehydration.

But Anansi lent me the stamina to keep at it. He drove me onwards, telling me I had the body of an African, designed to cope with lack of water and withstand the blaze of the sun. It was in my blood, in my very DNA, to endure these sorts of conditions. I was as much a creature of harsh, arid lands as Nanabaa Oboshie had been, as all my ancestors had been, as Anansi himself was. We'd both agreed beforehand that I could do this. We were both counting on it.

Reaching Interstate 15, I got lucky. Some Good Samaritan in an RV saw me trudging along by the roadside and pulled over.

"Need a lift, pal?"

I got round the "What the hell are you doing out here on foot?" questions by simply saying my car had broken down.

Minutes later I was back in Sweetwater, where I gulped water from the drinking fountain in the hotel lobby until my stomach could hold no more. I was planning on phoning Mojave Motors from my room to tell them where their Taurus was and ask them to send help, but first I needed to lie down and recover from my ordeal.

Let those three stew for a while, Anansi said. *Rub their noses in their shame.*

In the event, I sank into a exhausted doze, and it wasn't until mid-afternoon that I managed to make the call. A couple of hours later, Gunther, Rinzen and Robin were brought back to Sweetwater in the cab of a tow truck, with the Taurus hooked up and trundling along behind. Gunther was moaning about the awful headache he had from his hunger and thirst, while Rinzen and Robin simply professed themselves glad to be alive.

All three, it goes without saying, were out of the contest.

THAT SAME DAY, more fell by the wayside.

Mullah Nasruddin, the Islamic scholar cleric renowned for his pithy aphorisms, was tripped up by his own vanity when he responded to an invitation to give a lecture in one of the conference rooms, only to find there was no audience when he arrived.

Bulgaria's Hitar Petar, who arranged this prank at the expense of his eternal foe Nasruddin, was literally tripped up – by Kaggen of the Kalahari bushmen – and broke his nose on a chair back.

Kaggen in turn suffered a broken nose, and worse, when he was sent over to deliver a message and a beer to a biker in one of Sweetwater's rougher drinking establishments and, owing to his poor command of English, failed to realise that he had been set up so that it looked like he was making a sexual proposition.

By day's end our complement of avatars had been whittled down to twenty-six. All anyone could talk about, though, was my three-in-one coup. It was as brassy and audacious a move as anyone could recall.

"I was right about you," Bill Gad said to me in the bar that evening. "You really are my main competition this time around. And I know what I'm talking about, being as I've won this contest a fair few times."

"So have I."

"But not lately. Past century or so, you've been off your game, spider. I've not been getting the contender vibe off of you that I'd come to expect. Not 'til now. What it is, is it's a good match of rider and horse. You're in synch, the two of you. Simpatico. When that happens, that's when things start to cook."

On my way to my room, I had an encounter with Solveig. She appeared to be having trouble with the ice dispensing machine in the corridor, although I quickly realised she'd been lying in wait for me.

"Can you help?" she pleaded, holding up one of the small tin buckets that could be found in every room. "I've put a quarter in, but this push chute thing doesn't seem to be working."

"Help yourself," I told her, swanning past.

"It probably needs a man's touch."

"You've got that already, haven't you?"

"Anansi..."

Something about the way she said the name – the sudden croaky tenderness in her voice – halted me in my tracks.

I turned. "Yes?"

Her head was bent to one side. She was toying with a lock of her silver-blonde hair. A small smile twitched at the corners of her mouth. "Aren't we too old to be like this with each other?"

"What do you mean?"

Anansi knew full well what she meant. *Ignore her, Dion. Move on.*

"To pretend there's no connection between us," Solveig said. "To be aloof. That's how children behave in the playground. The boy loves the girl but cannot show it, so he punches her and runs away."

"I haven't punched anyone."

"We've been close before. So close." She moved towards me, as if to illustrate her point. "You've not resisted me in the past."

I knew a little of Anansi's history with Loki and the run-ins they'd had at previous contests. "The past is past," I said. "Mistakes were made."

Too right they were, said Anansi.

"Was it a mistake? That night in San Francisco? 1962, I believe it was. We were drawn to each other. You were so passionate, so intense."

You didn't have a dick then, Anansi said, and I relayed the remark to her.

"Details, details," she replied airily.

"And he was a married man," I said. "Anansi's avatar, I mean. That's how you caught him out. His wife phoned the hotel room in the morning, you picked up, and all you did was say, 'Hello,' and it was game over. This time I don't have a wife, so you're not going to get me that way, and thanks to Reynard your little surprise package isn't a surprise any more. That particular cat is out of the bag."

Solveig was right in front of me now. Her perfume was heady, her allure undeniable.

"Are you so sure?"

"I am."

So am I. But Anansi sounded far less adamant than I did.

All at once her hand was cupping my crotch. My breath caught. I stiffened, in more ways than one.

"Feels good, doesn't it?" she whispered in my ear.

It does. It does. Oh, it does.

"I swear I won't embarrass you, Anansi. Or Dion, if I may call you that. No one would ever have to know. It would be our secret. Your room. Now. I'll do anything you desire. Anything."

Anything...?

"For old times' sake. We'll keep the lights low. I'm very skilled. You won't notice any difference."

Oh, Dion, we could, couldn't we? Look at her. She's so lovely. All we have to do is half-close our eyes and it would be like being with a normal woman, just about. Come on, what harm can it do?

Fortunately, when it comes to one's baser urges, I am made of sterner stuff than that.

"I was wrong, Loki," I said, yanking her hand away by the wrist. "I am married. Or at least, Anansi is."

"To silly old Aso, who'd be none the wiser."

"Aso would find out. She always finds out. Anansi's infidelities always end up biting him on the backside."

"I could do that to you if you like," Solveig purred.

"No. You've tried your best, son of Odin, half-brother of Thor," I said, "but your best isn't good enough."

I strode off to my room, very pleased with myself, although Anansi was less than satisfied and kept grumbling discontentedly.

I was even more pleased with myself after a swift search of the room turned up a tiny infrared camera and wireless transmitter which had been inserted into a corner crevice, up where the cork wall tiles met the Artexed ceiling. The camera's lens was pointed straight at the bed, and I had no doubt who had installed it or why.

"She broke in," I said.

Solveig? How?

"Vintage hotel. No key cards. Old-fashioned door latches like these aren't too hard to force with a credit card or a slim jim." Hark at me, the man who's rubbed shoulders with more than his fair share of cat burglars and carjackers.

Devious bitch, said Anansi.

"And if she'd had her way, we'd have been on YouTube before you know it. Every avatar with a laptop would have been watching us over breakfast.

Dion Yeboah *in flagrante* with a shemale. Chances are she'd also send it as an email attachment to my colleagues in chambers. I'd never live it down. My career would be in tatters."

Not to mention our hopes of victory.

"She'll get what's coming to her," I vowed. "Just you wait."

But still... It might have been memorable. Just as a one-off.

"We don't think that way, Anansi. Not if we're here to win."

I was minded to crush the camera underfoot and present Solveig with the remnants, but decided instead to keep it. I lodged it in a drawer. It might come in handy.

DAY TWO OF the contest was crueller than day one. This was the natural order of things, according to Anansi. As the ranks of competitors thinned and the tension mounted, the trickery took on a nastier, more vindictive edge.

So Hershele Ostropoler, the Ukrainian Yiddish analogue of Mullah Nasruddin and Till Eulenspiegel, had his turkey bacon rashers at breakfast replaced by the real thing when he wasn't looking. He wolfed down several mouthfuls of pig-flesh before the substitution was revealed. Given that his avatar was a Hasidic Jew, it was hardly surprising that he dashed straight out of the restaurant in search of the nearest toilet to throw up in.

Someone, evidently inspired by my casual remark outside Reynard's room, placed a live rattlesnake in the bed of the Korean woman who was acting as vector for Gumiho, the Nine-Tailed Fox. The woman was lucky, in as much as the snake only snuggled up against her leg for warmth and wasn't prompted to bite her. She was too terrified to set foot inside the Friendly Inn again, however, and excused herself from the contest.

A razor blade was embedded in the bar of soap used by San Martin Txiki from the Basque region. His hands were badly lacerated when he washed them.

Păcală, whose name literally translates from the Romanian as 'self-deluder,' woke up from a drunken stupor to find himself cocooned from head to ankle in cling film. So much of the stuff had been wrapped around him – and the bed he was on – that he couldn't move a muscle, although his captor had at least been generous enough to leave his nose uncovered to allow him to breathe. A chambermaid found him and cut him free, but not in time to prevent him voiding a full-to-bursting bladder all over himself and the mattress.

Someone stole the laptop belonging to the Norwegian Askeladden, or "Ash Lad," and downloaded child pornography onto it. The young man had no alternative but to destroy the computer and pray that no one in authority traced the download to his IP address.

The Joke Shop Jamboree attendees became unnerved by the change in atmosphere. Several of them closed down their trade stands, gathered up their belongings, and headed home. They weren't quite sure why they did this, but one man within my earshot said, "Doesn't feel right any more. I've stopped having a good time." Another seemed to think the living-theatre actors – for that was what everyone assumed we were, by now – were taking things too far. "Nothing against performance art," he said, "but, I don't know, these dudes... Feels like they've got a mean streak in 'em."

I bided my time that day, watching as the others busily cat-and-moused. Why sully my hands? I noticed Gad doing much the same, and Set, and Loki. The second-stringers could scratch and scrabble amongst themselves all they liked. We top guns were holding back, keeping our powder dry. Let them do the dirty work for us, after which we could pick off the survivors, if there were any.

As evening fell, attention coalesced around a four-way poker game between Gwydion, Huehuecoyotl, Eshu and Hermes. I had long since stopped bothering to learn the avatars' real names. It was hardly worth the effort, and superfluous to my needs. Hermes I think was called Apostolis, but the rest could have been Larry, Curly and Moe for all I cared. I had no interest in them as people, only as rivals, obstacles to be got out of the way.

Now, poker is all about bluff and nerve, everyone knows that. So really it's the perfect game for tricksters. Throw in the fact that all four participants were cheating madly, and each was aware that his opponents were cheating madly, and the stage was set for some of the most devious, unsporting card play ever.

Moreover, the stakes weren't money, or gambling chips, or even matchsticks. These four were playing for punishments. Whoever lost a hand had to accept a punch from all three others. There was no limit to how hard the blows could be, nor where they could land, and they were to be taken without flinching or shying away, otherwise the recipient was disqualified.

So it was a test of physical endurance as well as a battle of chance and skill. The players sat with increasing numbers of bruises, blood dripping from facial injuries, eyes swelling shut, lips puffing up, loosened teeth, through round after gruelling round. Fresh decks of cards had to be cracked open to replace ones that were too blood-smeared to be usable. The baize on the table became more and more liberally dotted with dark brown stains.

The rest of us looked on from the sidelines. It was a grim, but fascinating spectacle. We were in a private room, well away from the main body of the hotel, so the sound of fists smacking flesh, the cries of pain, even the occasional involuntary massed gasp from the audience wouldn't draw any unwelcome attention.

After an hour, Gwydion and Eshu were fighting to stay conscious. Gwydion's co-ordination was off, so an attempt to introduce a queen of diamonds from up his sleeve into his hand was clumsy and he was spotted doing it. "Saw that!" exclaimed

Huehuecoyotl, and because he had been caught in the act, Gwydion's hand was forfeit, with the consequence that it was again his turn to get hit.

Eshu and Hermes both delivered solid punches to his midriff, but it was a devastating roundhouse from the Peruvian that finally put paid to the Welshman's involvement in the contest. Gwydion crumpled to the floor, and no amount of face-patting or limb-shaking could revive him. He was out cold and out of contention.

The remaining three resumed play. The level of card-sharping and sleight of hand in the game was phenomenal. Nothing else could account for the extraordinary number of flushes, full houses and four-of-a-kinds that cropped up, well above the statistical average. Sometimes it appeared there must be six kings in any given deck and even more aces. In any reputable gaming joint, this lot would have been turfed out on their ears long ago.

Eshu was next to go. One moment he was sitting there, cards fanned, head bobbing a little but otherwise essentially steady. Next moment, he was slumped face first on the table, burbling incoherently into the baize. Set and the Monkey King carried him off to a corner.

Which left only Hermes and Huehuecoyotl. Greek and Peruvian glared at each other, steely-eyed. The knuckles of their punching hands were red raw. Hermes's nose appeared to be broken. A gash in Huehuecoyotl's brow bled profusely.

Hermes lost, then Huehuecoyotl, then Hermes again.

The room had the metallic, meaty reek of a butcher's shop.

Trembling, Hermes laid down his next hand. A flush, all clubs, but not high. He knew it was no good.

Silently, triumphantly, Huehuecoyotl trumped it with four tens.

Nobody thought Hermes would be able to carry on after the swingeing chop to the neck that Huehuecoyotl gave him. But the young Greek struggled to his feet, wheezingly retook his seat, and began shuffling the cards once more. He dealt, and with the swaying slowness of punchdrunk boxers, the two of them examined their hands, discarded a couple of cards, and drew substitutes from the pool. Each then gazed across the table to see what move his opponent would make.

"Call it," said Hermes.

"You call it," Huehuecoyotl replied.

If I'd been a betting man I would have laid a wager on the Peruvian to win outright. He seemed sturdier than the Greek, in body and in temperament. He looked like he could withstand hardship far longer and with greater equanimity than the slightly built youngster facing him.

But I was wrong. Hermes laid out a royal flush, to which Huehuecoyotl was able to respond with a mere full house, aces over nines.

Hermes rose and crossed over to dish out the penalty.

Huehuecoyotl, however, held up his palms in surrender. "Enough. No more." His face was half masked in his own blood. "I give in. You have won."

...changes will not be permitted (i) after 14 ...out receipt or (ii) for product not carried by ...ble or Barnes & Noble.com.

...receipt may appear in two sections.

Return Policy

With a sales receipt or Barnes & Noble.com packing slip, a full refund in the original form of payment will be issued from any Barnes & Noble Booksellers store for returns of undamaged NOOKs, new and unread books, and unopened and undamaged music CDs, DVDs, and audio books made within 14 days of purchase from a Barnes & Noble Booksellers store or Barnes & Noble.com with the below exceptions:

A store credit for the purchase price will be issued (i) for purchases made by check less than 7 days prior to the date of return, (ii) when a gift receipt is presented within 60 days of purchase, (iii) for textbooks, or (iv) for products purchased at Barnes & Noble College bookstores that are listed for sale in the Barnes & Noble Booksellers inventory management system.

He stood up and managed three tottering steps towards the door before his legs collapsed under him.

Hermes was rewarded with a round of applause from the avatar onlookers.

"So this is us now," said Gad, looking round the room. "All that's left. We're down to the final eight."

Besides him, Hermes and myself, we had Loki/Solveig, Susanoo-no-Mikoto, Sun Wukong the Monkey King, Crow and Set.

Somehow it felt inevitable. We were the eight best-known names, the ones who were the most celebrated, the ones whose stories were still most often told. Who else was likely to have made it this far?

We all shared a moment in which we basked in our own durability and popularity. Anansi, for once, was quiet within me, almost as if he wasn't there, and yet conversely I had never felt closer to him, never felt more as though he and I were made for each other. He was a part of me and I was a part of him. Anansi and Dion Yeboah, intimately joined, inseparable, like Siamese twins.

Which raised a question in my mind.

LATER, IN MY room, I voiced it.

"What happens when this is over?"

What do you mean what happens?

"When the contest's done, what do you gods do? Do you just... go?"

Yes, we go.

"You leave us?"

Why stay? What would be the point? We have places to be, people to see, tales to be a part of.

"No, I understand that. It's just... After all this, all we've done, it seems a pity."

I thought you'd be pleased to see the back of me. Your life can be yours again. You didn't really want to be in this contest, did you?

"Not at first."

So what's the problem? When it's over, we're over. You go your way, I go mine.

I couldn't find a way of telling him, although I had a strong suspicion he knew anyway, that thanks to him I was evolving into something that I could never have imagined I could be. Anansi had brought an element of anarchy to my world, a sense that rules truly were made to be broken, not just bent. I feared that without him my horizons would shrink back. I would always be good at what I do, but I would never again have the feeling that I had the potential to be great.

I could tell you it'll be like a boy-and-his-pet Hollywood movie, Dion, said Anansi. *You know, that schmaltzy "I'll always be in your heart" bullshit. But I won't always be in your heart. Better get used to the idea.*

I STEPPED OUTSIDE onto the swimming pool area for some air. The night was oppressively hot and muggy, but I could feel a breeze stirring. The weather was changing. Clouds had amassed to the west, blotting out the stars. Lightning flickered in their bellies.

Storm coming, said Anansi, as if I couldn't already tell.

"Storm coming," said a voice nearby. It was Susanoo-no-Mikoto. He edged up to me, and for a time we stood side by side near the rim of the empty pool, a careful, respectful distance apart. We watched the silent jags of lightning over the peaks of the Sierra Nevada and listened to the chirrup of the cicadas, whose song sounded more reticent than normal, fitful and subdued.

"Cigarette?" The Japanese man held out a pack of Lucky Strikes.

I shook my head.

He lit up. "Storms are good," he said, exhaling smoke.

"You would say that."

"Because Susanoo-no-Mikoto is a storm god? Yes. So many of the tricksters are. Storms bring chaos. Chaos is desirable."

"They also bring disaster."

"Disaster. Calamity. Opportunity. Renewal." He shrugged. "All the same thing. The other gods threw Susanoo out of heaven. *That* you could call a disaster."

"He squabbled with his sister over which of them was more powerful. He stole her fertility beads and fashioned new gods out of them, to prove his point. Then he threw a flayed pony through the roof of her house. Getting thrown out of heaven wasn't some kind of misfortune, it was no more than he deserved."

Susanoo-no-Mikoto's avatar bowed, as though he himself had been personally responsible for the god's actions. "It was not a desirable outcome. Yet – and this is my argument – Susanoo turned a bad situation around. On earth, he met an elderly couple who begged him to slay an eight-headed, eight-tailed monster that had eaten seven of their eight daughters. He did, and one of its tails became the famous sword Grass Mower, which he gave to Amaterasu, his sister, as a peace offering. He also gained a wife into the bargain, the eighth, uneaten daughter, who fell in love with him for his bravery. So you see, out of downfall and misery, benefits may still come."

"Point made." I glanced towards the clouds. They were anvil-shaped thunderheads, slowly prowling towards Sweetwater, like a fleet of gigantic battleships closing in. "If nothing else, we should be in for a noisy night, and who knows what will go on under cover of that."

I looked back at the Japanese man, but he was gone. He had slipped away indoors, leaving just a puff of cigarette smoke hanging in the air.

AN HOUR LATER, the storm was on top of us. The lightning now had thunder to accompany it, some of the loudest, most jolting bursts of sound I've ever heard. Each one was like a stick of dynamite going off directly overhead. Ear-splitting. You couldn't help but duck and recoil.

Then came rain, sheeting torrents of it. The rain pummelled the hotel with such force, it seemed a wonder the building could withstand it. And that was only the beginning. The downpour grew more and more intense, until I had serious doubts as to whether there would actually be a Friendly Inn in the morning. Walls, floor, ceiling, everything was vibrating and shaking. This was Mother Nature as we never see her in our temperate British Isles, primordial and unfettered.

At around 10PM the electricity went out, perhaps not surprisingly. It wasn't just the hotel that was affected. A glance out of the window showed me that all of Sweetwater had gone dark. Along the main street, not a single lightbulb shone. The only illumination came from the intermittent lightning flashes, which revealed glimpses of buildings and parked cars through shimmering cataracts of rain.

This could not have been better for Anansi and me. In readiness, I had already synched up Solveig's infrared camera to my iPhone. I panned the camera round my room, and the phone's screen registered a pin-sharp green image, everything as clear as day. I had an edge over my competition. I could see in the dark.

SUN WUKONG WAS my target. Earlier in the day I had ascertained which room he was in by asking Gladys at reception for a quick glance at the register. She had been reluctant to comply at first, but a crisp fifty-dollar bill soon persuaded her to set professional discretion aside. She was only human.

"I'll tell you what," she said. "I'm going to turn my back for a second, just to check for something in these here key cubbyholes behind me. So if you should happen to lean over the desk and take a gander at the computer screen while I'm doing that, well, tain't my fault, is it now?"

There was only one Chinese name among those listed on the rather ancient black-and-white monitor: Xhu Jiang. Room 134.

One other piece of preparation I'd made was buying a couple of dozen peaches from Sweetwater's principal – and indeed only – grocery store.

If there's one thing anyone knows about the Monkey King, it's that he loves peaches. He even went so far as to steal some from heaven, although those particular fruits happened to be the peaches of immortality that grew in the garden of Xi Wang Mu, the Queen Mother of the West. For this act of effrontery, Sun Wukong earned the contempt of the other gods, much as Susanoo-no-Mikoto did for his crimes against his sister, and was exiled to earth for a time.

It isn't always easy being the trickster, the black sheep of the family, the rogue, as Anansi himself would be the first to admit. People don't appreciate being robbed or conned, and summary and arbitrary justice often awaits the perpetrator.

But who can fight one's own true nature?

*   *   *

I LAID THE peaches in a trail starting outside Xhu Jiang's room and leading down the corridor. Then I rapped on the door and ran away as fast as I could, using the infrared camera image to guide me unerringly through the pitch blackness. The pounding of the rain muffled my footfalls.

Lurking at the far end of the corridor, I saw the simian-faced Xhu emerge from his room. He peered quizzically in either direction.

The peaches, the peaches, Anansi urged. *Smell the peaches*.

The peaches were superbly ripe. Their perfume-like aroma had filled my room all afternoon. Now I was hoping that Xhu, even though he was to all intents and purposes blind in the lightless, windowless corridor, would pay attention to his sense of smell. Sun Wukong would take over from the hapless Xhu Jiang and send him straight into my clutches.

On my iPhone screen, the green figure in the doorway raised his head. He was sniffing. Scenting.

Good, said Anansi. *Good monkey. That's it. Take the bait*.

Then he crouched down and started groping on the floor in front of him. His hand found a peach. He snatched it up, took a bite of its flesh and let out a soft hoot of delight.

He sniffed again. More peaches, his nose was telling him.

He tucked the first into a pocket in his pyjama bottoms and ventured along the corridor, not quite on all fours but almost. He soon located the next peach, and the next. He was excited, his head questing this way and that. He'd thrown caution to the wind. The only thought that occupied his brain was all the delectable fruit that someone appeared to have carelessly left lying around. After his pockets were full, he folded up the front of his pyjama top to make a pouch and stowed further peaches in there.

As he advanced towards the junction with the next corridor, I retreated down that same corridor, depositing more peaches as I went. Another peach was placed on the threshold of a janitor's closet whose door I had managed to pry open beforehand. A final peach was positioned inside the closet, far enough in that Xhu would have no choice but to enter if he wanted to get it.

Xhu rounded the corner, picking his way through the dark with painstaking slowness. I thought he was going to miss the next peach. His hand kept feeling around on the floor but not quite touching it. If he believed the trail had run out, he would no doubt return to his room quite satisfied with the haul of fruit he already had, and my plan would have failed.

Eventually, however, his fingers made contact with the peach. He added it to the ones in the pouch and went forwards. He was walking on his haunches, balancing himself on the knuckles of his free hand, more monkey than man at this moment. Soon he was at the janitor's closet, facing its wide-open doorway, although he himself could not know that. I was standing mere feet away, keeping as still as I could, breathing as shallowly as I could. My iPhone showed

Xhu in close-up, squatting there with one arm across his chest to support his makeshift pouch and its bulge of sweet-tasting cargo. Did he sense my proximity? Had it at last dawned on him that he might be heading into a trap? He was hesitating. I could see greed and suspicion vying with each other in his face.

He knows there's one more peach, said Anansi. *It's right in front of him.*

Could Xhu resist the temptation? More to the point, could Sun Wukong?

The answer was no. Xhu loped across the threshold, and that was my cue to move.

Quickly! yelled Anansi. *You've got to hit him fast and hard – harder than you might think. Now! While he's still bent over.*

I darted in behind him and booted him in the backside with all the force I could muster. Xhu went barrelling headlong into the closet, colliding with the shelves at the rear. An avalanche of cleaning products – cloths, sponges, cans of spray polish, bottles of bleach – tumbled down on top of him. Peaches fell from his pyjama top and rolled everywhere.

Without pausing, I yanked the door shut, then wedged a mop handle up inside the door handle, effectively locking Xhu in. I waited for Xhu to start hammering on the door and shouting, begging to be let out. But nothing happened.

Was he all right? He had hit the shelves pretty hard. Perhaps he'd been knocked unconscious.

So what if he has? said Anansi. *He can stay in there 'til he comes round, nice and safe. You were going to leave him there anyway, so it doesn't make much difference, except this way will be a whole lot quieter for everybody else.*

Which was true. But whereas shutting Xhu in the closet was a minor misdemeanour, shoving him so hard into the shelves that he was knocked cold was battery, maybe even GBH. A solid infringement of the law. A felony.

Don't worry about it.

But Dion Yeboah was an upholder of the law, not a breaker of it.

Oh, yes? And framing Veles with that cigarette lighter, lying to a law enforcement officer? What was that? And abandoning those three avatars in the desert? Reckless endangerment, at least. And what about attending the poker game this evening? That at least makes you a party to assault, if not an accessory. Face it, Dion, you crossed the line a while back. You've passed the point of no return. Better get used to it.

"No," I said aloud, covering my face.

Yes. But it's not a bad thing. How much freer do you feel now than you used to? How much more daring and untouchable? Admit it, you were a slave to conventionality. You were a big old stuffed shirt. Now look at you. You've broken out of all that. And you love it. I know you do. I can tell. You've never felt so powerful, so alive.

With his words came a giddy rush of exhilaration. He was right. He was so right. The panic I'd just experienced was the last dying whimper of my old self, the man I had once been and no longer was. I had cast that Dion Yeboah off as a spider sheds its carapace as it grows. I was bigger and bolder and braver than he ever was, and I would never go back to being him, even after Anansi was gone.

See? Anansi said. *I may not live on in an avatar's heart forever, but I always leave my mark.*

I LEFT XHU, a.k.a. Sun Wukong, in that closet. Whatever state he was in – even if he was lying there in a pool of his own blood – it was his problem, not mine. I had other fish to fry.

The storm raged on. I stalked the benighted corridors of the Friendly Inn, steering by infrared like some nocturnal predator, attuned to wavelengths that were invisible to its prey. Ordinary people would be cowering in their rooms, waiting for the power to come back on and normality to return. Not me. And I didn't think I'd be alone, either. My fellow avatars would be roaming the place too, superior beings engaged in an internecine war of wits.

Sure enough, I soon encountered the Greek man, Apostolis, Hermes's avatar. He didn't spot me. He was making his way through the hotel using his phone's screen as a torch. I followed him at a safe distance, intrigued and on the lookout for any opportunity to pull the rug out from under him. He walked with some stiffness, still in pain from the blows inflicted on him during the poker game. Soon he halted outside a room, which presumably was not his own because he knelt at the door and started working on the lock.

Not for him the crudeness of forcing the latch. Producing a set of lockpicks, he selected two, which he inserted into the keyhole and manipulated gently and with obvious skill until the door came open. He kept his phone gripped sideways between his teeth all the while, training its glow on the lock.

Hermes is a thief, Anansi pointed out. *The Greek gods would send him to fetch whatever it was they wanted stolen or recovered – the maiden Io from the giant Argos, Zeus's own sinews from the monster Typhoeus, Helen of Troy from Paris's arms. Stands to reason that his avatar is a thief too.*

Into the room Apostolis went, leaving the door slightly ajar. I moved to a position whereby I could peer in by aiming the camera round the jamb. The bed was empty and appeared not to have been slept in, although there were signs of occupancy. A cloth bag sat on the dressing table, and there was what appeared to be a blanket of some kind slung over the back of a chair. But it wasn't a blanket, I realised. I recognised the zigzag pattern on it. It was a poncho.

The room, then, belonged to the man from Peru, Huehuecoyotl's representative on earth. Not content with beating the Peruvian at punishment poker, he was now taking advantage of the fact that the man was presently at a hospital down the road in Barstow receiving treatment for his injuries. He was raiding his room in his absence.

Very opportunistic. Very sneaky. Taking time out

from the contest to line his own pockets. Anansi sounded anything but disapproving.

First Apostolis tried the cloth bag, rifling through it on the hunt for valuables. He found none. Next he tried all the drawers, and finally, as I'd suspected he might, the wardrobe. Every room in the hotel had a small safe hidden there, the old-fashioned sort with a rotary dial rather than a digital code lock.

He hunkered down and, still with phone between teeth, set to work fiddling with the dial. Sensitive fingers felt for the combination, the moments when tumblers clicked into place and the dial briefly, infinitesimally loosened.

Meanwhile I configured my iPhone to record the image from the camera. This was it. I had Apostolis bang to rights. Footage of him opening the Peruvian's safe would, when made public, surely guarantee his exit from the contest. The simple threat of uploading it onto the web ought to suffice. Hermes was about to join the ranks of the eliminated.

Apostolis opened the safe door and delved in. What would it be? A passport? Credit cards? Cash?

He let out a startled, involuntary yelp and snatched his hand back. There was something on it – *several* somethings – a host of small crawling black shapes. He yelped again and started frantically shaking his hand in the air, trying to dislodge whatever these things were. The shapes clung on.

Spiders?

Close, said Anansi. *Scorpions*.

Apostolis began beating at the afflicted hand with

his other hand. In his frenzy he dropped his phone and the light went out. He slapped desperately at the scorpions, but they hung on tight with their pincers while their tails stabbed again and again into his flesh. The stinging must have been agony. Apostolis's face was contorted in disgust and distress.

In the end he resorted to thumping the hand on the floor, crushing the little arachnids to a pulp. It took the best part of a minute before they were all dead, and then Apostolis collapsed against the wardrobe door, mewling and sobbing. He held up his hand as though it was no longer a part of him. He couldn't see, as I could, that it was already swollen and looking horribly distended. He could surely feel it, though.

Huehuecoyotl had had the last laugh. He must have suspected Hermes might go for his safe and had booby-trapped it. Exquisite revenge on the god who'd knocked him out of the contest.

THERE WAS NOTHING I could do for Apostolis. Correction: there was nothing I was prepared to do. He had his phone, assuming he could find where he'd dropped it. He could call for an ambulance.

It was every man for himself now. And every god.

Through the drumming of the rain and the peals of thunder I heard a faint voice crying, "Help. Help me." It was coming from outdoors – from the swimming pool area, if I didn't miss my guess.

You're not going to fall for that, *are you?* sneered Anansi.

Of course I wasn't. Someone yelling for help? It couldn't have been a more obvious ploy.

But I felt compelled to investigate nevertheless, to see for myself what was going on.

I went to the main conference hall, where the Joke Shop Jamboree stands stood, the ones still remaining after this afternoon's partial exodus. The windows overlooked the pool. I peeked out.

The pool was no longer empty. The rain was filling it, and there were already several inches of water in its deepest part. And, standing on tiptoes, I could just make out a body lying in the water, face to the sky. An arm reached up, flailing, imploring.

"Someone. Please. Help."

The accent was Middle Eastern, the voice the Egyptian's. Set's avatar was in the pool.

"I am fallen in. I am hurt. My back. I cannot move."

I felt a twinge of concern.

Really? said Anansi. *We're still that trusting? Even now?*

"I can't help it," I murmured. "He's a fellow human being."

Have I taught you nothing?

I bowed to his superior judgement, albeit with some reluctance.

Someone else was not as circumspect as I. A figure emerged from the shadowy shelter of the loggia in the corner of the pool area. It was the Australian Aborigine, the man housing the spirit of Crow. He moved tentatively towards the rim of the pool, shoulders hunched against the onslaught of the rain.

"Hey, mate!" he called out to Set. "What's up?"

"Someone heard. Oh, thank heaven!"

"You all right?"

"No. No, it's not good. I have accident. Slip. Fall in. Now my back, it is bad. I try to move, but no good. The water, it keeps rising higher. If I do not get out, I drown. You must help."

Crow looked distinctly unconvinced. "Nah, mate. Not sure I can do that for you."

"Please. You must. Otherwise I die."

"Yeah, I see that, but you've got to look at it from my point of view. What if you're lying?"

"I am not lying. This is truth."

"I go down there, into that water, and there's something nasty waiting for me. Like, I dunno, mantraps, for instance. Right next to you, under the surface where I can't see 'em. One wrong step and *snap!* I'm bitten like a croc's got my ankle."

Same as when Crow hid those echidna quills in a kangaroo rat's nest, said Anansi, *and got Swamp Hawk to fly down and land on them, and the quills got stuck in Swamp Hawk's feet.*

"No! I swear," said Set. "I am in trouble. I need rescue."

Crow was weighing it up. His posture said that he wanted to leave Set where he was, but his conscience wouldn't allow it. If this wasn't a trick, then his inaction could lead to a man's death.

I watched intently, wondering what I would do if I'd let myself become embroiled in the dilemma as Crow had, and feeling rather smug that I hadn't.

Finally the Aborigine gave a huge sigh.

"Fair go," he said. "I'll get you out. But I'm not climbing into that pool, I can tell you that for free. The diving board. You're right under it. I'll shin along and reach down and grab hold. You stretch up, I reckon our hands can just about meet. Okay?"

"Yes. Okay. Thank you," Set said weakly. "But please, hurry. The water, it is almost up to my mouth."

Crow went round to the diving board and placed first one knee on it then the other. It seemed firm. He shuffled along until he was fully out over the pool. Then he lay himself flat and extended one arm down.

The pool was perhaps seven feet deep at its deepest point. Set raised his hand. There was still a gap of five or six inches between his fingertips and Crow's.

"Try harder," Crow said.

"Come closer," Set replied.

Crow may or may not have been aware that manhandling the body of someone with a back injury was not advisable. If Set was suffering from a broken spine, it might leave him permanently paraplegic. As far as Crow was concerned, there was only one way to get the Egyptian to safety – only one way he was willing to do it – and that was hauling him out. Set didn't seem bothered about the potential consequences, so why should he be?

He wriggled further along the board so that he could lean over the tip of it. He lowered his hand again, his head and shoulders hanging down. Set clutched for the hand. Their fingers met and locked.

"There we go," said Crow. "Up you come now. She'll be right."

But just as he uttered this optimistic phrase and took the strain, ready to heave, Set gave an almighty tug. Something creaked screechingly, and all at once the diving board toppled into the pool, taking Crow with it. His cry of shock was cut short by a heavy splash and a meaty thud.

Set, who had rolled sideways to avoid being landed on, stood up. He had, of course, been shamming.

"I win, you lose," he crowed over Crow, dancing a little jig in the water. "I loosen bolts on the diving board. Ha ha! Next time you better check first, eh?"

Crow's only response was a pain-wracked groan. I couldn't be certain, but judging by the way he had fallen and the angle at which one arm lay twisted beneath him, his shoulder had been broken, and perhaps his collarbone too. I felt sorry for him, but at the same time – one less opponent to think about.

Set at least had the decency to move him out of the rising tide of rainwater. He dragged him by the ankles to the shallow end of the pool, then propped him up in a sitting position against the side wall. Crow's head lolled. I think he had passed out, the pain too much for him.

As Set clambered up the nearest stepladder to get out of the pool, I spotted movement on top of the hotel wing opposite. Someone was up there, a man, staggering across the flat concrete roof in a very erratic fashion. The rain-sodden figure came right to the very edge, where he teetered, gazing down, arms outstretched. He was naked, his pale and almost entirely hairless body exposed to the elements.

Anansi identified him. *Susanoo-no-Mikoto. But what's he doing? He looks drunk.*

"Set!" the Japanese man called out. "Se-e-et! I see you. I see you, son of earth and sky, lord of the desert. One god of storms addresses another. Do you hear me?"

"I hear you," the Egyptian answered. "How do you feel, Masayuki? Do you feel well?"

"Well? I feel great! But my name is not Masayuki. It is Susanoo-no-Mikoto, brother of the sun and moon, born from the nose of Izanagi as he washed his face in the river to purge himself of his sins."

Set chuckled. "Are you sure about that?"

"As sure as I am that you killed your brother out of spite. You cut Osiris into pieces and scattered them across the world, because he was loved so much and you were not."

"I did?"

"Set did, and you are Set."

"Maybe it's Susanoo who is saying this," said Set. "Or maybe, I wonder, is it the LSD which I have put in your cigarettes?"

The Japanese man, Masayuki, seemed not to understand. Bafflement replaced the imperious expression on his face, albeit briefly.

"You speak nonsense," he said. "Susanoo-no-Mikoto does not listen to your foolishness."

"Three drops of pure liquid acid," said Set

gleefully. "In all your cigarettes. Smoking is so bad for the health."

"Silence, horn-headed one!" Masayuki declared. He brandished a fist like some manga superhero. "Do not mock me. Do you not feel my power? It rages through the heavens. You should fear me. My anger could destroy us all."

As if to punctuate the remark, a fork of lightning rippled incandescently overhead. Thunder erupted a split-second later.

"It is also Set's storm," the Egyptian replied. "It does not scare me. It will not harm one who has Set within him."

"If I wish, I could summon the lightning down. Then we shall see whose storm it is."

"I dare you to."

"Do not provoke me."

"You are no god. You are just a man. Susanoo talks inside you, but he does not walk in your skin. And also, you have lost. Thanks to me, you stand there naked, ridiculous. You babble like madman. You are not in this contest any more."

"That's it! Enough!" Masayuki bellowed. Both arms shot up, and he began uttering a stream of words in his own language. Oaths, prayers, imprecations, who knows what they were, but he yelled them until he was hoarse, his body shivering from the cold and his hair plastered lankly against his scalp.

Set just let him rave on, clearly relishing the Japanese man's hallucinogenic lunacy. The crazier Masayuki behaved, the more it cemented Set's victory.

And then...

I have to assume that Masayuki's body acted as a lightning rod. A single raised point on top of an otherwise low, flat structure was simply asking to conduct the current from sky to earth. That's the only way I can account for the immense flash that came, a blinding white brightness. It was accompanied by a percussion, a *bang* that seemed to blow my eardrums inward. I reeled back from the window, dazzled and stunned. For a time, perhaps as much as a minute, I couldn't seem to get my bearings. My head rang. Fireworks were exploding in my vision.

Finally I pulled myself together and returned to the window. Through the rain-spattered panes I saw the Egyptian sprawled by the poolside, supine, and Masayuki on top of him, prostrate, having been propelled off the roof. Masayuki's hair was singed and smouldering and there were various scorch marks on his skin. Both men appeared stone dead, but as I watched, they stirred. The Egyptian tried to push Masayuki off him and get to his feet. Masayuki attempted to rise as well, but his efforts were as in vain as the other man's. Their muscles seemed numbed and not working properly. They couldn't disentangle themselves from each other, and in the end they sagged like exhausted lovers and let the rain pound down on their bodies.

Storm gods' avatars, struck down by a bolt of lightning, said Anansi. *If that isn't poetic justice, I don't know what is.*

"Or just irony," I observed. "A cosmic joke."

Either way, they're out. Which, if I'm right, leaves only us, Coyote and Loki.

"Hopefully, Coyote's eliminated Loki by now, or vice versa."

"You could say that's happened," said a voice behind me, in a rough, worn-out croak. "Kind of."

I whirled round.

It was Bill Gad. A glimmer of lightning showed me his weatherbeaten face, his double-plaited hair, his coyote-head tie clasp.

Showed me something else as well.

A knife in his hand.

Blade glistening wetly.

Dripping thick dark droplets onto the floor.

FOR A MOMENT I was dumbstruck. A hundred thoughts rushed through my brain, a hundred different scenarios.

Blood.

He had killed.

He was about to kill.

It was a trick. Fake blood.

It was not a trick. Real blood.

Gad's eyes shone in the next crackle of lightning. They were sombre, grave even. They were also, I realised, frightened.

I knew that look. I'd seen eyes like those a dozen times before. They were the eyes of someone guilty, someone who has done something they wish with all their heart can be revoked, but can't.

"Gad," I said. "What is this? What's going on?"

"I didn't mean to."

"Didn't mean to what?"

"You gotta help me, Dion. It went too far. I overreacted."

"Gad, what the fuck have you done?" I am not normally one who swears, but these were not normal circumstances.

"She... He... I have to show you. It's the only way."

"Give me the knife first."

"Knife?" He sounded genuinely confused, as if he had forgotten about it.

"The one you're holding. I'm not going anywhere with you unless you give it to me right now." I have no idea where the commanding tone in my voice sprang from. I had never been so scared in my life. I just knew somehow that in order to lessen the danger to myself I should be authoritative, take charge.

"Oh. Yeah." His dim silhouette moved. The knife came up, point towards me. Gingerly I took it by the handle, plucking it from his limp grip. It was an inch-wide hunting knife, a heavy thing, the wooden handle inlaid with some kind of precious stone, turquoise I thought. The blood on its steel blade gleamed blackly.

"This way," said Gad, and I followed him to his room.

ANANSI HAD NOTHING to say as I surveyed the scene in Gad's room, and the spider god's muteness was eloquence itself.

My eyes adapted to the gloom slowly, so that it took me a while to assess every feature of what I was looking at – a horribly long while.

There on the floor was the Navajo rug which was the Friendly Inn's idea of a decorative finishing touch – a bit of threadbare local colour – and there on the rug was the body of Solveig, Loki's avatar. It may seem heartless to say so, but she looked thoroughly disgruntled to have found herself in such a situation. Her eyes were half-closed and turned to the side, as if she were rolling them, and her mouth hung slack in a position indistinguishable from a pout.

She was irrefutably, irrevocably deceased. It would have been obvious even if there hadn't been the *prima facie* evidence of a deep ragged gash in her chest and all the blood that had flowed out of it to soak her blouse. The absence of life is the absence of all motion. Nothing lies as still as a dead thing. I know this after having walked into Nanabaa Oboshie's bedroom one morning, aged nine, and discovered her not breathing. I had understood instantly that my grandmother was gone. I hadn't needed it explained to me, and even as my father tried desperately to revive her, and then prayed out loud to God to give her back to him, I'd realised his efforts were futile. Whatever had animated Nanabaa Oboshie and made her *her*, it was no longer around. It had flown during the night, and the thing left in her bed was nothing more than a hollow framework, like the husk of a fly after the spider has drained it of all its nutrients.

So with Solveig. She was a corpse, utterly immobile and lifeless, weirdly beautiful still, but ghastly too, in death.

The knife in my hand, Gad's knife, was a murder weapon.

"Why?" was all I could ask, once I finally regained the power of speech.

"An accident," he replied. "Honest. I was just... just trying to scare her off. She was coming on so strong, like she wouldn't take no for an answer."

"She was trying to seduce you?"

"Hell, yeah. That way of hers, you know, saying all those nice things in that sweet, husky voice. Suggestive. Flicking her tongue round her lips. I kept telling her to go away, no sale, not interested, find some other patsy. She... she was so goddamn *insistent*. You know? But I knew she was no lady, and I wasn't going there, no way." He sobbed the last couple of sentences, his voice breaking up.

"Had you been drinking?" I said.

"No."

"Don't lie. I can smell whisky on your breath."

"Okay. Yes. A little bit." He sniffed wetly. "Guess that might've had something to do with it. Made me clumsy. When I pulled my knife I only meant to wave it at her, threaten her, to make a point. But then she just kinda lunged at me and I just kinda stumbled... Christ, this is awful. This is a nightmare. What'm I gonna do, Dion? I go down for murder, they'll give me the needle for sure."

"Do they have the death penalty in California?"

"Damn straight they have. This ain't such a liberal state as you'd think. Don't forget we elected that Nazi-loving actor as governor for a while."

"Okay, but it isn't necessarily as bad as all that. From what you've just told me, there were extenuating circumstances. Any halfway decent lawyer could argue legitimate self-defence, along with diminished responsibility through alcohol. Manslaughter, not murder. You'd serve time, but I doubt you'd be sentenced to lethal injection."

"Shows how little you understand about America," he retorted. "An injun killing a white person? They don't call it lynching any more, but that's what it'd be."

"Look, calm down," I said. "Panicking's going to get you nowhere. What's done is done. Solveig's dead."

"Was that her name? Solveig? Pretty name."

"It was the name she chose to go by. What we have to do – and by 'we,' I mean you – is summon the police here straight away."

"The cops? No way. Nuh-uh."

"Listen to me, Gad." I grabbed him by the shoulders and shook him. "Yes, the police. It's the only way. You have to be straight-up right from the start. Play it by the book. Let the system do its thing. There's no alternative. Anything else will just get you deeper into trouble and make it worse for you further down the line. Man up. Plead guilty. Show the authorities what you're showing me, remorse and contrition. It'll all go a long way to helping your case."

He swayed his head from side to side. "No. Can't.

Even if they don't kill me, I can't go to jail. I'm not a young man. I don't wanna spend the rest of my days behind bars, having to dodge musclebound Aryan Nation meatheads with a hard-on for me. I won't." His eyes met mine, and they were imploring. "There is another way. I can get rid of her. *We* can get rid of her. No one'd ever have to know. Some white girl from Scandinavia – white man, whatever – disappears on a trip to the US. Some tourist goes astray. These things happen."

"I can't hear this. I'm not listening to you."

"I know of a way of disposing of that." He gestured at the body. "I got it all figured out. Clean gone, so nobody'd ever find it. It's one tiny corpse, and the Mojave's a huge damn desert. Sometimes light aircraft go down here, and even with satellites and GPS tracking and who knows what all else, the crash site's never located. Desert just swallows 'em up. I know what to do."

Lightning glimmered. Thunder rolled.

"And with your help, Dion," he said, "I can do it."

"MY HELP?" I said. "No. Absolutely not."

"Aw, come on. It's a two-man job. I need you."

"How can I make this any clearer? I am a lawyer back home. I can't be – won't be – made an accessory to murder. I will not even consider it."

"You're only an accessory if you're caught. Otherwise you're just a guy who helped out another guy when he needed it."

"I have principles."

Ahem? said Anansi. *You do?*

"Shut up," I murmured. "Stay out of this."

"What's that?" said Gad, raising an eyebrow. "Spider in your head got an opinion on the subject?"

"None that I'm willing to share," I said.

"'Cause I assure you, the coyote in mine is saying this thing has to be buried and done away with, no question. And he's convinced my plan for doing it can work."

"Well, good for him."

"And you wanna know what else? He's saying he's ready to make a certain concession if you'll agree to lend a hand."

"Concession?" I said. "I don't get."

Oh, yes you do, said Anansi.

"Look at us," said Gad. "We're the final two, just like I predicted. The contest's ours to win or lose. What Coyote's offering is to step down. Victory's yours – if you'll just do this one thing."

"Victory by default," I said.

...is still victory, Anansi chipped in.

"Victory by default," I repeated. "I won't have won. I'm just getting a bye in the final. I'm a lucky runner-up."

"No, no," said Gad. "You'll be the winner fair and square, and you know why? Because I'm in your power. You have me at a disadvantage. A material disadvantage. I'm throwing myself on your mercy, Dion. All it takes is for you to dial nine-one-one now, and I'm sunk. You even have my knife, the main piece of evidence. Now that I've involved you in this, there's nothing I can do without your say-so. You may not have outwitted me in the conventional sense, but I have committed a very dumb, a very stupid act, which makes me less smart than you. Therefore you are, in that respect, the cleverer one out of the two of us. Listen to your god. Listen to Anansi. He knows I'm right."

He's right, said Anansi. *Profiting from the blunders of others – no trickster worth their salt is going to turn their nose up at that. It's valid. It's part of what we do.*

"You have my solemn word," Gad said. "Save my neck, and you'll be declared outright winner."

And didn't you say, Dion, that if we enter the contest, we enter to win? That was how you put it, as I recall. No half measures, you said. You don't take on a challenge unless you fully intend to come out on top. I'm quoting you verbatim.

"But..." I could feel myself weakening, my resolve crumbling. The prize was so near, so tantalisingly near, just within reach. Surely I hadn't come all this way, done what I'd done, only to falter at the very last hurdle. Gad was offering me the laurels, in return for abetting him in the commission of a felony. That would make me a criminal too, like him, but at least I wouldn't be in the same category as him, a killer. And no one need ever know. I was thousands of miles from home, in another country, a faraway land.

It was as if Gad read my mind. "Hey, what happens in Vegas stays in Vegas, right?"

My rather feeble response to that was: "We're not in Vegas."

"No, but near enough. Ball's in your end zone, Dion. What you gonna do, my friend? Play or pass?"

WHAT ELSE COULD I do? It was like taking a deep breath and diving in. I could hear Anansi applauding me – in truth, I could hear little else – as I nodded and told Gad I'd go along with whatever he had in mind. Nothing could dissuade me from the idea that what I was doing was totally wrong. Equally, in the most basic way, it was completely right. It was inevitable. It was *necessary*.

We rolled the body up in the rug, lugged it between us through the hotel, and took it to Gad's pickup truck, which was parked just outside. We loaded it onto the flatbed and Gad secured a tarpaulin over the top, fastening it tightly to the side rails and tailgate with a length of bungee cord. We clambered into the cab, dripping wet from the rain, and Gad fired up the engine.

Our first port of call was Gad's home, a static Airstream trailer parked at the mouth of a canyon some way out into the desert. The track that led to it was one of the bumpiest roads I have ever been along, and matters weren't helped by the storm, which turned earth to mud and reduced tyre traction to nearly zero. We slithered as much as drove, and were half-blind, too, the headlights and windscreen wipers scarcely able to keep up with the incessant pelting rain. It was, in hindsight, a miracle that we got there in one piece. Throughout the journey I was acutely aware that I was with a driver who was not entirely sober nor in his right mind. But Gad was the one familiar with the route and the terrain. I could not have taken the wheel. If I had, it's fairly certain we wouldn't have made it at all. After what had happened, Gad's fate may have been in my hands, but for the duration of that drive, mine was in his.

We took refuge in the battered old trailer, which had clearly seen better decades, and waited for the storm to abate. For a couple more hours, the thunder shook the ground and the rain battered the trailer's sides. It was like sitting inside a giant aluminium dustbin that was being beaten by a million mad club-wielding monkeys. Gad and I didn't have much to say to each other, but if we had, we would have had to yell to say it.

Finally, around 4AM, the racket began to die down, and soon the thunder was faint, distant, and then hush descended. Gad went outdoors and busied himself hitching a small boat to the back of his pickup. The boat was a Zodiac inflatable, harking back to earlier times when he had earned a living as a fishing guide, chartered by tourists to go out onto Sweetwater Lake and help them land chub and cutthroat trout. He kept the outboard in good working order and still took the boat for a spin occasionally on what was left of the lake, just for the fun of it. Nowadays his main source of income was part-time employment as a front-of-house meet-

and-greeter at a casino owned by a cousin of his on a nearby reservation; the job remit was, in his words, "Reeling in the high rollers and rousting out the drunks. Ain't pretty, but it pays the bills."

We set off just as the sun was coming up, revealing a tormented, haggard landscape. Flash floods had torn gouges through the desert. Cacti and Joshua trees lay toppled, ripped up by the roots. Rockslides that had fallen across the roads tested the pickup's suspension and four-wheel drive almost to destruction. The steam rising thickly off the ground was like smoke after a great fire.

"Mother of all storms, that one was," Gad remarked. "The Great Spirit sure was pissed." He made it sound personal.

"He and you have never got on, have you? That is, he and Coyote."

"No love lost between those two. The Great Spirit had it in for Coyote from the start. When all the animals were choosing their names, right back at the time of creation, the Great Spirit made Coyote fall into a deep sleep so's he'd wake up late and get last pick. Coyote coveted a cool name like Grizzly Bear or Eagle, but those were already taken when his turn came, so he got stuck with Coyote. The Great Spirit told him, 'You're the lowest of the low. You slink around and boast too much and do too little work. That's why I punished you by forcing you to have the name no one else wanted.' Since then, Coyote's always been sly, quick to take offence, looking out for nobody but himself. Know why coyotes have those slanted eyes they do? It's 'cause they take after their namesake, and Coyote's eyes are slanted 'cause he props them open with sticks every night so he'll never be caught out like that by the Great Spirit again."

"Anansi and Nyame, the Sky God, have a similar relationship," I said. "Combative. Anansi tried stealing wisdom from Nyame once. It didn't work. He dropped the pot he was keeping the wisdom in, and it broke and wisdom ended up scattered in pieces across the world, a little bit of it in everyone. Nyame wasn't best pleased about that."

"Coyote stole fire from the Great Spirit and gave it to mankind. Same outcome: the Great Spirit wasn't happy. Your god and mine, they're a lot alike, ain't they? Out of all the tricksters, they got the most in common. I guess that's why I felt I could trust you with all of this." He jerked a thumb over his shoulder, and I realised, with a twinge of surprise, that I had all but forgotten there was a dead body in the rear of the pickup. Blame exhaustion – it had been a long, fraught night – and also my own conflictedness. My conscience was doing its best not to dwell on the moral bind I was in, the compromises to my integrity that I was making. It seemed to find it easier to just blank out the corpse that we were even now ferrying to its final, secret resting place.

I HAD NO choice but to focus my attention on the corpse once more as we pulled up at the edge of a shallow ravine and Gad jumped out and began

heads. Mine more so than Gad's; he had put on a John Deere cap. The lake surface was laced with flotsam: scraps of wood, strands of vegetation, every now and then the bloated remains of some rodent or other, a jackrabbit or prairie dog, drowned in its own burrow.

Gad steered us far out onto the shining water to a place he knew, somewhere where, submerged right now but not for long, there was a sinkhole that plunged underground. How far down it went, no one could quite say, but it was deep.

I could tell we were getting close to it when the current picked up and the water became turbid. Soon there was an appreciable swirl on the surface, a slow-moving whirlpool some ten or fifteen yards in diameter. Gad set the Zodiac against the whirlpool's rotation and throttled back on the outboard until we were effectively at a standstill.

"You do the honours," he said to me, and I bent and put my shoulder to the grim task of heaving Solveig, in her rug cocoon, overboard.

She was a slight thing but heavier than she looked. I struggled to roll her up onto the Zodiac's gunwale. I asked Gad for assistance, but he said he had to keep his hand on the tiller to hold the boat steady. So, beginning to sweat, I resumed grappling with the corpse and eventually managed to lay it across the rubber float. After that, it was easy enough to tip it off into the lake.

The rug soaked up water but the body stayed afloat, drifting lazily round in the spiralling current and spinning in smaller circles of its own. Gad and I watched it keenly as it was drawn inexorably towards the centre of the whirlpool. I noted the whirlpool gathering speed but didn't immediately apprehend the significance of this fact. All I wanted was for the corpse to be gone, to disappear from sight so that we could be done with this grisly business and leave.

To my horror, and Gad's as well, the rug began to unpeel itself. Solveig's pallid, bored-looking face was revealed, and then one of her arms flopped free, almost as though she were alive and attempting to swim. The arm wafted in the water in a slow parody of volition, while Solveig's hair fanned out around her head, rippling like the fronds of a sea anemone.

It was awful, and yet I couldn't tear my gaze away. Then, to my immense relief, the whirlpool abruptly pulled her under. She was there one moment, bobbing on her back, like a blonde version of Rossetti's Ophelia; gone the next, sucked down into the sinkhole in a single gulp, leaving no trace, not even a few bubbles to mark her passing.

Gad inhaled sharply, as though for the past minute or so he had neglected to breathe.

"Well," he said softly, "that's that over with. She ain't ever coming back. Loki? If you're listening? Sorry, guy. Them's the breaks. For what it's worth, she was a good choice. Or he. This transgender stuff confuses me."

"She," I said.

He nodded. "She did you proud, Loki. Shame it had to end this way for her."

It wasn't much as eulogies go, but it was all poor Solveig was ever going to get.

EN ROUTE BACK to the ravine, I noticed something curious.

"I can see the bottom," I said, peering over the boat's bows. "The bottom of the lake. I'm sure I couldn't when we were coming the other way."

"Yeah, is that so?" said Gad nonchalantly.

"Yes. The water's getting shallower. Definitely." Which would account for the quickening of the whirlpool. I thought of the water around a plughole, turning faster as the bath drains out.

"Guess I'd better pour on the speed, then."

The boat did accelerate but not by much. Our speed climbed, but I wouldn't say Gad exactly *poured* it on. Maybe this was as fast as the Zodiac could go.

I studied the lake with increasing concern. Boulders were appearing above the surface, and other rocky outcrops, all of which I was sure hadn't been there before. In places, the lake was only a couple of feet deep, whereas earlier it had seemed unfathomable. The landscape was emerging from beneath it, like some mythical continent arising, a desert Atlantis.

I turned to Gad. "We really need to hurry. We're not going to make it."

"Doing the best I can, Dion. Lake's drying up faster'n I thought it would. Sun's evaporating it, ground's absorbing it. But we got time, I think."

"You *think*?"

"Ain't an exact science, but I reckon we'll get back to –"

There was a hideous scraping sound, the Zodiac's soft hull rubbing across the top of some hidden stone reef. Gad grimaced but piloted us doggedly on. Shading my eyes, I searched for the entrance to the ravine, but couldn't see it yet. I realised it would be touch-and-go whether we reached it. The flat-bottomed boat had minimal draught, but the waters were receding fast. Lake Sweetwater's brief burst of renewed life was coming to an end. Its mayfly renaissance was over, and the dry times were returning.

Now little low islands were visible, raised patches of glistening mud. Gad circumnavigated them, and although he continued to radiate an air of imperturbability, I caught what I fancied was a flicker of concern in his eyes. He didn't relish the prospect of becoming stranded out here any more than I did. He, like me, was keen to make it back to the pickup and, ultimately, back to the Friendly Inn, where we could tie up any dangling threads and go our separate ways, never to meet again. At that moment I wasn't even thinking about the contest. I was experiencing the low-level nausea of the crook who simply wants to be able to get away with his crime scot-free, even as fate does its very best to thwart him.

Seeing life from the other side of the fence now, eh, Dion?

Snide comments from Anansi did not help.

The Zodiac juddered across something rugged, and Gad swore some Native American curse and veered sharply sideways. For several seconds the boat skimmed freely through the water. Then it hit some other obstruction. Gad and I were jolted out of our seats. We landed back more or less upright, and Gad gunned the motor and the Zodiac charged forward, but not for long. All at once it was ploughing a furrow through mud, and the propeller became clogged, and we lost momentum, and just like that the motor cut out and we were at a halt, beached, going nowhere.

"Well, shit," Gad sighed. "If that don't suck a fat one... Could've sworn the lake'd stick around longer than that."

The boat lay at a slight angle, amid a sea of mud.

"What do we do now?" I said, trying to keep an edge of anxiety out of my voice.

"We could stay put."

"But the way you said that, you don't think it's wise."

"It ain't got much to recommend it. Mojave's not what you'd call a hospitable spot, 'specially to two fellas without a drop of drinking water on 'em. Our best bet's abandoning the boat and going on on foot. Won't be easy, but it's preferable to just sitting here and letting the sun slowly bake our brainpans."

"Then what are we waiting for?" I surveyed our surroundings, the lakebed that was almost entirely land again. "Let's get cracking."

"After you," said Gad.

* * *

WE STEPPED OUT of the Zodiac, onto the mud. Straight away I sank in up to my ankles; Gad likewise.

"Trick is to keep moving," he said. "Stop, and you'll just carry on sinking."

So we hurried, or tried to. We trudged. We slopped. We slurped. We forged through the mud. It accumulated around our calves in clumps, layer upon thickening layer. The further we travelled, the more of it stuck to us, and the more that stuck, the harder we had to struggle just to walk. In some places the mud was so shallow we could virtually skate over it. In others, it swallowed our legs up to the knees and we were wading along, arms swinging, like astronauts in cumbersome spacesuits.

There was the mud, and the heat of the morning, and I could feel them both taking their toll, but I dug deep and carried on. Gad, at least twenty years my senior, was finding the going tough too, but he had a lean, wiry build and I sensed his stamina was well above the average for someone his age He might even be as fit as me. We could do this, I thought. We could make it through to the ravine and the pickup.

But soon my strength was ebbing. The mud was relentless and treacherous. More than once I lost my footing and went floundering into it face first. I managed to pick myself up and lumber on, but each time it was more difficult to recover than before. I lost my shoes, and my socks, and had no recollection of them being wrenched off my feet and vanishing, and didn't care. I began to despair. The ordeal seemed endless. The mud went on forever.

I didn't realised I had stopped in my tracks until Gad said, "Don't just stand there, Dion. Up and at 'em."

I forced my legs to move, hauling them one after the other out of the mud and back into more mud, on and on. Increasingly I found myself bent over, scrabbling along on all fours. I was covered in muck. Dank gluey brownness was all over me, inside my clothes, smeared on my face.

At some point Gad fell behind. When I looked round, he was perhaps a hundred feet back. I'd been aware that he was flagging, but not that he had completely run out of steam. I yelled at him to keep up. All I got in return was a bleak, weary shake of the head and a beckoning gesture.

"Need you," he gasped. "Think I'm in trouble here."

Ignore him. Go on.

But I couldn't. I couldn't just leave him. So I ignored Anansi instead and turned myself round and toiled back through the path I had churned in the mud until I was by Gad's side.

He was in up to his crotch.

"Real soft patch," he said. "Stuff's like quicksand here. I can't lift either of my legs."

"Try."

"Can't. You gotta pull me."

I could feel the mud dragging on my legs, urging me down. It was a sickening sensation.

"Come on." I held out an arm to him. "Grab on. I'll do what I can."

He grabbed. We strained and heaved as one, but it was no use.

"Only one thing for it," I said. "I'll go on. Get to the truck. Fetch help."

Gad nodded.

I tried to turn round again.

I couldn't.

The mud held me fast.

I writhed. I squirmed. I fought to free myself.

I couldn't.

It was above my knees, clawing my thighs. It gripped like a vice. And I was utterly worn out.

I allowed myself to rest for a moment. I would gather my strength, get ready and then exert myself again.

Next thing I knew, Gad was telling me to wake up. "This ain't the time for napping, Dion. We gotta figure out a way out of this."

I opened my eyes and started battling with the mud once more. Somehow, though, I ended up embedded even further in it.

"This is stupid," I said. "Absurd. It can't be happening."

But it undoubtedly was.

Gad and I had managed to trap ourselves in the middle of a mud plain. No one knew we were there. Our chances of getting rescued were negligible, possibly even nil.

* * *

THE SUN CONTINUED its inexorable, blazing ascent to its zenith, and as the air grew hotter, so the mud hardened and set. Talk about adding insult to injury. Gad and I weren't just stuck, we were being cemented in place. Soon the ground around us had become concrete-solid, and it was then that Gad began to laugh.

"Shut up," I told him. "How the hell can you laugh at a time like this?"

"'Cause it's funny."

"We are going to die out here!" I exclaimed. "In what conceivable way is that amusing to you?"

"'Cause it's my fault."

"No argument about that. We wouldn't even be here if you hadn't stabbed Solveig."

"Yeah, but that's not what I meant. Don't you see? Look at us. Anything about our situation at all familiar to you?"

"No."

Yes, said Anansi.

"Anything about it strike a chord?"

"No."

Yes. Oh, you cunning bastard, Coyote. And how dare you. That's my *story. Mine!*

"The tar baby," said Gad.

The sticky gum doll, said Anansi. *The one I caught Mmoatia the Dwarf with.*

"The tar baby that a farmer set up to catch a rabbit with. The more the rabbit struggled to get free of the tar baby, the more stuck he became."

My story! I carved a mannequin out of wood and covered it with tree sap...

"Then Coyote came along, and the rabbit, who was a sly one, explained that the farmer was punishing him for refusing to eat his melons, but he'd promised him a nice fresh chicken if he just stayed there a while."

And I put a yam in a bowl in front of it...

"So Coyote offered to swap places with the rabbit, and he pulled the rabbit free and stuck himself to the tar baby instead."

And Mmoatia saw the yam and ate it, and thanked the doll, who didn't reply, so Mmoatia got cross and hit it...

"And when the farmer came back, he didn't have a chicken, of course, but he did have a big stick."

Her fists became stuck in the gum...

"He beat Coyote within an inch of his life."

And I'd caught her and was able to take her to Nyame, the last of the four gifts which bought me ownership of all the world's stories.

"Tricksters get tricked," said Gad. "Happens all the time. Goes with the territory."

"This," I said, incredulous, "this was all designed to trap me?"

"Bingo."

"Everything? Solveig included?"

"Hell of a plan, right? Suckered you right in from the start." Gad wasn't gloating. If anything he was rueful, which, given our shared predicament, was understandable. "Gained your confidence, strung you along... It just went wrong here, at the very end. The *coup de grâce* – me playing the 'tar baby' – it was always gonna be the hard bit to pull off. Guess I shoulda known it might backfire. Didn't exactly work out so well for Coyote, did it?"

"And letting me think I'd won the contest?"

Gad gave a half-hearted shrug. "A lie."

"But I *have* won!" I declared.

"You honestly think so? Take a look at us. At yourself. This look like winning to you?"

My own trick, used against me, Anansi fumed. *The stories are similar, but even so. I did it first. Coyote stole it from me.*

"Enough!" I yelled at him, clutching my head. "Enough! Get out of my thoughts. Get out of me. Go. I've had enough of you."

"Spider giving you grief?"

"Look at what you've done to me, you bastard. Look how I've ended up. All in the name of your stupid, pointless contest. Go!"

"You tell him, Dion. Go for it."

"Leave me the hell alone!"

I didn't even know who I was shouting at any more. Anansi? Gad? Myself? What I did know was that my voice sounded hopelessly small and faint in that heat-ridden wilderness, a whisper lost in an ocean of sky.

"Anansi?"

There was silence, inside me and outside.

Not a sound except the faint scuttling of tiny legs, dancing off into the distance.

* * *

LATER, SOME TIME later, I have no idea how much time later, Gad said, "You ever wonder, Dion, if there's actually been a trickster god inside you at all?"

"Huh?"

"Coyote's voice. I don't hear it no more. And now he's not talking to me, I'm asking myself, did he ever?"

EVEN LATER, WHEN our lips were parched and blistered and the sun was searing and we were still planted in the ground like half-buried statues...

"Maybe," Gad said, "we're men who thought they were gods. We wouldn't be the first."

"Stop talking. Please stop talking."

"Or men who know too many stories. You think that's possible? To know too many stories?"

"I can't listen. My head hurts."

"Maybe the tricksters' biggest trick of all is that there is no contest. Right now they're laughing their asses off, all of them, over the huge hoax they've pulled. It'll be a heck of a tale to tell all the other gods, how they fooled a bunch of humans into hurting, even killing one another, for nothing, no good reason whatsoever."

"For Christ's sake, Gad..."

"Never trust a trickster. Never trust a motherfucking trickster. That's the moral of the story."

WE WILL BE here forever. They will find our bones, bleached, picked clean by vultures and, yes, by coyotes.

We will be rescued. Someone will miss us and send out a search party. A helicopter full of paramedics will descend from the blue like a roaring angel and bring us salvation.

We will die.

We will live.

Oh, Nanabaa Oboshie, you taught me how to begin a story and also how to end one. Let me end this one with the words that end all tales.

"That was my story which I have related. If it be sweet, or if it be not sweet, take some elsewhere, and let some come back to me."

This is my Anansesem, my Anansi story.

I am Dion Yeboah, and I wish with all my heart that it did not end this way.

AGE OF SATAN

JAMES LOVEGROVE

'The kind of complex, action-oriented SF Dan Brown would write if Dan Brown could write.'
– Eric Brown, *The Guardian* on *The Age of Zeus*

1968

THE SCRUM COLLAPSED. Guy, in the front row, went down with what seemed like the full weight of a dozen boys on his back. He couldn't rise, couldn't move. He was trapped.

Then a rugby boot stamped on his outstretched hand. Steel cleats ground his knuckles.

Guy screamed. He tried to pull his hand out from under the boot, but the boot's wearer only bore down harder, crushing the hand deeper into the grass. He felt the sweaty, suffocating press of bodies on top of him. Guy's nose was squashed into the turf, and the pain from his hand was excruciating. It felt as though small bones were fracturing.

Mr Stevenson the games master gave up frantically and uselessly blowing his whistle and prised apart the tangled human knot with brute strength. Guy was one of the last on either team to see daylight. He rose to his feet holding his hand out limply in front of him, like something which no longer belonged. It was reddened, raw, beginning to puff up. Mr Stevenson despatched him to the sanatorium to have it looked at.

As Guy stumbled off the pitch, a boy on the opposing team hissed, "That hurt, Lucas? It was meant to. Fucking choccie poof."

TWO DAYS LATER, in the dining hall, Guy was carrying his lunch on a tray, searching for somewhere to sit. His hand was thickly bandaged. Matron had given him a chit absolving him from rugby for a week. Instead, he had to go on a five-mile run with Mr Jacks's upper-sixth cross country squad every afternoon. The running was exhausting and made his hand ache, but at least there was little chance of it getting injured afresh.

Guy did not see the foot lash out from under a nearby table, catching his ankle. All he knew was that he was suddenly sprawled flat out and his tray had disgorged its contents across the parquet floor. Pork chop, scoop of mash, diced vegetables, ginger pudding and custard – all of it went flying, mingled with shards of smashed plate and bowl.

There was silence after the crash.

Then the entire dining hall erupted into jeering laughter. The sound ricocheted off the linenfold oak panelling, scurried up past the stern-faced portraits of former headmasters, and lost itself amid the high, solid roof beams.

Everyone was guffawing. The entire school, all three hundred boys. Even the teaching staff up on the top table couldn't hide their sniggers.

Guy painstakingly gathered up the spilled food and broken crockery onto the tray, then hurried out of the room.

THAT NIGHT, AFTER lights out, they came for him in the dormitory. There were three of them. They dragged Guy from his bed and frogmarched him to the bathroom, both arms twisted up between his shoulderblades almost to the nape of his neck. The boys in the other beds were quiet, those awake feigning sleep. They didn't want to know.

A stall had been made ready for him. A freshly laid turd bobbed in the toilet bowl. His three tormentors forced his face into the water. Guy struggled, fought like a cat, but it was no use.

Someone pulled the chain. Water gurgled and churned around his head. Guy strained to keep his lips above the surface so that he could breathe. Lumps of faecal matter buffeted his cheeks and ears.

As the tumult of the flush died down, Guy's tormentors let him up. He sagged against the stall partition, spluttering and gagging. He retched into the clean bowl.

"You were shit brown before, you choccie cunt. You're even more shit brown now."

* * *

GUY CLEANED HIMSELF up, dried himself off, and crawled miserably back into bed.

He had been a boarder at Scarsworth Hall for a little over a fortnight, and already he loathed the place with a passion. It wasn't just the bullying. It was also the food, the hard mattresses, the ever-present stink of linoleum polish, the sarcastic, hectoring teachers, the relentless bells and countless rules. The weather, too. Until now, Guy had known only the tropical climes of south-east Asia, where everything was a perpetual swelter relieved by the occasional warm torrential downpour or air-clearing thunderstorm. His father had been stationed all across the region – Thailand, Burma, Vietnam, Laos – serving as consul at various British diplomatic missions. For the first fifteen years of his life Guy had gone about in shorts and sandals, often shirtless, baking his skin to the colour of mahogany in the sun. If asked, he would have told you he was English, but he had never actually been to England, not until his first term at Scarsworth Hall. He had never before experienced chilly grey skies, drizzle, breezes that nipped and pinched, a sun so pallid you could almost look directly at it even at noon.

His mother was a hundred miles away, in London.

His father was even further away, forever beyond reach.

It was hell.

Guy drew the covers over his head and sobbed.

Springs creaked. Someone had sat down on the bed beside his legs. Guy snapped the covers back and emerged snarling.

"Fuck off!" he cried. "Whoever you are, just fuck the fuck off!"

"Hey," said a low, calm voice. "One: whisper. Don't want a prefect to come in, do you? That'd be extra fagging duties for sure. Two: I'm not here to give you any grief. I just want to make sure you're okay."

"I'm not okay," said Guy, whispering. "Of course I'm not bloody okay."

"I heard them grab you. Who was it?"

"I don't know all their names. One of them's called Mayflower, I think. The others are Bartlett and – is it Thomas? They're all in the lower sixth."

"Thompson. Those three. Thought so. Utter wankers, the lot of them."

"Who are you?" said Guy. The figure at the end of the bed was a dim grey silhouette. He could make out curly hair, narrow shoulders, striped pyjamas, that was all. "Is that you, Milward?"

"Yes, choccie."

"Don't call me that. I'm not black."

"You look black."

"I've a dark complexion and a tan, although it's starting to fade."

"But you're foreign."

"No."

"You live abroad, that's what I heard."

"Used to. Not any more."

"Why not?"

"Don't want to talk about it."

"Okay. Only asking. Why have Mayflower and chums got it in for you?"

"How should I know? I haven't done anything to piss them off, not that I know of. I'm new, I suppose. And brown."

"Doesn't take much, does it? For a bully to hate you."

"Apparently not."

From the far end of the dormitory someone hissed, "Keep it down, you pair of homos. Some of us are trying to sleep."

Milward lowered his voice further, leaning conspiratorially close to Guy. "Listen, Lucas. Those three bastards had it in for me too. Made my life a misery all last year. In a way, I'm glad they're picking on you now. Takes the pressure off me. But I still haven't forgiven them, or forgotten. How do you fancy getting your own back? Giving them a taste of their own medicine?"

Pain pulsed up from Guy's bad hand. He caught a vague excremental whiff from his hair.

"I don't know," he said. "Maybe. What do you suggest? Report them to the Head?"

"Christ, no. At best, old Haemorrhoid Hemingway will give them a stern talking-to, maybe a detention, and then they'll come after you in revenge and you'll be even deeper in the shit. I'm talking about something cool. Something we'll never get caught for and they'll never see coming. You in?"

Guy hesitated. He didn't really know this Milward fellow at all. They were in the same year, but different academic streams, so they shared no classes together. Could he trust him? Was this some kind of trick?

Then again, what did he have to lose? Milward appeared to be offering him the hand of friendship. Rude to refuse. More than anything, Guy needed a friend.

"Yeah, all right. I'm in."

"Tomorrow," said Milward. "Meet me at the clock tower during short break." And he stole back to his bed like a wraith.

AFTER A PAINFULLY protracted double maths lesson, Guy made their rendezvous. Milward said nothing, just beckoned him to follow. He led Guy across the playing fields to the cricket pavilion. The door was kept locked and only the groundsman had the key, but Milward levered up the shutter covering the opening the scorekeepers looked out from. The gap was just large enough for a slender boy to slither through.

Inside, there was gloom and the smells of dust, leather and linseed oil. Stumps and bats lay about in untidy piles, awaiting summer, along with the stacks of rectangular plates with numbers on for tallying runs and overs on the scoreboard.

Milward bent and rummaged under a heap of leg pads, uncovering a small tin box hidden there. From the box he produced candles, a book of matches, some chalk and a carton of Saxo salt.

"What is all this?" Guy asked. "What are we doing here?"

"Over the holidays I did some reading," said

Milward. "Research, you could call it. Tell me, Lucas, do you believe in God?"

"I suppose." Guy's mother kept saying that his father was *with God now,* and *in the arms of the Lord,* so he didn't want to not believe in the Almighty. It would imply that his father's soul did not live on; that there was no such place as Heaven. He couldn't be so disloyal – either to his mother or to the memory of his father. "There must be a God, mustn't there? Millions of Christians can't be wrong."

"Ever pray to Him?"

"Not really."

"Me either, not any more. It doesn't work. Last year I asked Him time and time again to get Mayflower and Co. off my back. Almost every day I'd go down on my knees and say, 'Please, God, do something about them.' He just bloody ignored me. So I decided to ask the other fellow instead."

"The other...? Who do you mean?"

Milward rolled his eyes. "What sort of education did they give you in bongo-bongo land, Lucas?"

"I went to some pretty decent international schools," said Guy defensively. "And I had tutors."

"I don't care. I was just being rude."

"Oh."

"You must know who I'm referring to. The other fellow. God's opposite number. The chap down below."

"The Devil?"

"Light dawns. Yes, the Devil. A.k.a. Satan, Beelzebub, Lucifer, Mephistopheles, Prince of Lies, Lord of the Flies, and a lot of other names besides.

I begged him to deliver me from my oppressors, and guess what? He did. He sent me you. You turned up at the start of this term, and all of a sudden Mayflower and his cronies had a new target. I was free."

"Well, great. That's nice. Glad to be of service."

"And now I want to do the same for you. I know how it feels having those bastards gunning for you all the time. You're always on your guard, never knowing what they're going to do next. And I warn you, it's only going to get worse. Last year, Mayflower cornered me in the showers. It was only me and him there. I swear, I thought he was going to try to bugger me. He had this look about him, like he wanted to, and he was talking about how he was going to duff me up and he was getting a stiffy as he did so. I just barged past him, all covered in soap and shampoo. Didn't rinse off or anything, just grabbed my towel and scarpered. Do you want that to happen to you? Do you want Mayflower sticking his cock up your arse?"

"Of course not."

"So we have to stop him." Milward lit one of the candles, dripped melted wax onto the floor, and planted the candle in the spatter of wax so that it stood upright. "And this is how we'll do it."

"You're – you're going to perform some kind of ritual?"

"Durrh, what does it look like? Yes, I'm going to perform some kind of ritual. It's called a black mass. Now, you light the rest of these. I'm going to draw the pentagram."

Guy stood with the candles and matchbook in his hands, numb, uncertain. He couldn't help but feel that this was profoundly wrong. He didn't know much about Devil worship but he knew that it was something you ought not get involved with. It was tampering with sinister, dangerous forces. It was going against God. It was blasphemy.

"Umm, I've got a history lesson to go to." He realised, even as he said it, how banal it sounded, how pathetic. He carried on anyway. "With Poxy Cox. You know how cross Poxy gets if you walk in late. He made me copy out a whole page of the *Encyclopedia Britannica* the last time."

"You won't be late if you stop dithering," said Milward. "We can have this finished in five minutes. Light the fucking candles, would you?"

Guy wasn't sure why he stayed put, why he complied. He wanted to leave. But instead he struck a match and applied it to the wick of a candle. It seemed easier to go along with Milward's demands than continue remonstrating. He told himself that this was just a game. This wasn't a real black mass. This was just two teenagers messing about in a school cricket pavilion, playing at Devil worship. Nothing would come of it, good or bad.

Milward completed the pentagram – a five-pointed star inside a circle. He positioned a lit candle at each of the star's points. Then he poured the salt out in a broader concentric circle, surrounding himself and Guy.

"Do not, whatever you do, step outside the salt

circle," he said. "Not until the ritual is over. It's a protective barrier."

"What happens if I do?"

Milward gave him a look as if to say, *Do you really need me to spell it out?*

Guy felt a chill. All at once he was conscious of how many shadows hung inside the pavilion, how thick those shadows were, how dark it was in here, how silent. Cobwebs lifted and fell, blown by subtle draughts, wafting like phantoms. The daylight he could see through various chinks seemed impossibly dim and distant.

"I really don't like this."

"Tough. Too late to back out now. I repeat: do you want Mayflower sticking his cock up your arse? No? Then show some balls."

Milward grabbed Guy's hand. He was holding a penknife. Guy hadn't seen him draw it. He sliced the blade across Guy's fingertip. Guy yelped in shock and outrage. Milward flipped his hand over and squeezed drops of blood out onto the pentagram. At the same time he said, "Satan, dark one, ruler of Hell, fallen angel, punisher of the wicked, we come to thee in supplication, thy humble servants Frederick Milward and Guy Lucas. We come to thee craving that you will visit just retribution upon Daniel Mayflower, Jeremy Bartlett and Angus Thompson, all of whom are unworthy wretches who – who have abused us cruelly and – and been really shitty towards us."

To Guy's ears these words didn't sound like a formal invocation, more like something Milward was making up as he went along. That comforted him somewhat. It gave the 'black mass' an amateurish feel, suggesting the whole thing might not be valid. Strict protocols were not being observed. Milward was not calling on Satan properly, therefore Guy had nothing to worry about.

He clung to this hope as Milward continued: "Grant us this boon and we shall be forever in thy debt, o great one. We commit ourselves to thee, Satan, Eternal Adversary, bequeathing you all that we have and promising to respect and venerate you for as long as we shall live and beyond. Show us a sign, Satan, that you have heard us and acknowledge our request. Prove that you are listening."

At that moment, a strong gust of wind struck the side of the pavilion. The thin wooden walls rattled and shook. All the candles were snuffed out simultaneously.

Guy's scrotum stayed scrunched up with fear for a good hour afterwards.

DAYS PASSED, AND Guy alternated between dread and despair. What had he done? He had damned himself, surely. Willingly or not, he had struck a bargain with the Devil, sealing it with his own blood, and the Devil collected on pacts like those in one form of currency only – your immortal soul.

At chapel each evening, as the school chaplain led the prayers, Guy desperately tried to recant. While everyone else intoned the Lord's Prayer and the Apostles' Creed, he sent up his own silent imprecation to the heavens, begging to be pardoned, to be redeemed. He had erred and strayed. He had trespassed. Have mercy on him, Lord. It had been a mistake, a terrible lapse of judgement. Please don't let him pay the full, awful penalty for it.

The bullying continued, with Mayflower as prime instigator. A snide word here, a surprise kick up the backside there, the occasional ugly prank like a fish head in Guy's bed or a dog shit in his tuck box. This in itself was perversely, ironically reassuring. As long as Guy continued to suffer, it meant Satan was holding off. The bargain was not being fulfilled.

But it was only a matter of time, he feared. Only a matter of time before something dire happened to Mayflower, Bartlett and Thompson, and he would then have to face the consequences.

He avoided Milward as much as possible. Milward had suckered him into participating in the ritual, against his will. Milward had abused his trust. Milward could go fuck himself.

HALF-TERM EXEAT ARRIVED, and a London-bound hire coach ferried Guy and a couple of dozen other boys down to the capital. Home for Guy was a mews house in Chelsea, just off the King's Road at World's End. It was quite a comedown from the consular residences he had been used to, those colonial clapboard mansions with verandahs and louvre blinds, ceiling fans and servants. The mews house had a small bricked-in back yard, rather than an expansive garden filled with ferns and lotus bushes where exotic birds hooted and snakes roamed. The hot water tank groaned like a sleeper trapped in a nightmare, and the other taller buildings crowding all around meant the windows let in precious little direct daylight.

It was lunchtime when Guy walked in through the front door, and his mother was already drunk. She sat in an armchair with the morning's *Daily Telegraph* on her lap and an empty tumbler in her hand. She was overjoyed to see him. She tried unsteadily to get up, and he gently pushed her back down into her seat. She wouldn't have made it.

He knelt and let her kiss his forehead. She smelled of gin and Guerlain. Her contour-cut hairstyle was looking a little ragged today. He brushed a stray ringlet away from her eye.

"My boy," she slurred. "My little Guy. You look so pale. How's school?"

He couldn't bring himself to tell her the truth. Her heart, so harshly broken by her husband's death, could only handle so much.

"It's fine," he said. "I'm settling in."

"Bad business in Vietnam." She gestured vaguely in the direction of the newspaper. "President Johnson's sending yet more troops in, as if that's going to solve anything."

"Mum, you shouldn't read those bits in the paper. You know they upset you."

"And that's not all," she continued. "I heard the other day from Margery Crisp. You know, married to the assistant attaché at the Bangkok embassy. Remember her? With the huge wart on her upper lip? She said in a letter that there's been some awfulness up in a place called My Lai. An entire village wiped out by US soldiers for supposedly harbouring Viet Cong fighters. Hundreds dead, including women and children. Happened last spring and the Yanks are denying it, but the rumour mill is grinding."

"It's not our concern. We don't live there any more."

"Your father was right. Maurice, bless him, he was absolutely right. The whole of Indochina is going to go up in flames, I can just see it. American boots on the ground. How long 'til the Russians are there too? A flashpoint waiting to happen. It could start there, like it nearly did in Cuba. The war to end all wars. The war to end everything."

"Let's not think about that, eh?"

"I can't help thinking about it, my darling. Your father tried so hard – so hard – to keep things from escalating. I know he wasn't supposed to. The Foreign and Commonwealth Office never approved. But he insisted on trying to reason with the enemy. He feared the spread of communism as much as anyone, but his approach was always to engage in diplomacy rather than aggression. Like Churchill said, 'jaw-jaw not war-war.'"

"Please, Mum, don't get in a state," said Guy. "Fretting about it isn't going to help. How about I fix us something to eat? I don't know about you, but I'm famished."

"He shouldn't have gone. Maurice should never have gone. Into North Vietnam. He had such a sense of duty, though. Such a strong moral compass."

Guy's father had been killed on his way to a meeting with a high-ranking Viet Cong warlord. He had been travelling overland from Laos via the Mu Gia Pass when his car was ambushed by armed guerrillas from another VC faction. He, his driver and his translator were dragged from the vehicle and lined up by the roadside. They were defenceless. It was a firing squad, an execution.

Publicly, the Wilson government's line was that it disapproved of the White House's strategy in Vietnam. That played well with the Labour Party rank and file and the wider electorate. Privately, however, Wilson had pledged support for Johnson and his military operations in the region. Maurice Lucas's death therefore put the government in a quandary. He had been doing the right thing, but not the officially sanctioned thing. His superiors in the FCO chose to paint him as a rogue and a maverick, describing his venture into hostile territory as well-intentioned but wrongheaded. The incident was swept under the carpet. He became just another regrettable casualty of war, a minor British martyr.

Nonetheless a whiff of disgrace hung about the whole affair, and still clung to his wife. She always used to drink, but never as much as she did nowadays.

"A good man and a fool," she said to her son. "Why are the two so hard to separate?"

Guy couldn't answer the question and didn't think he was meant to. He went to the small galley kitchen and made two cheese and tomato sandwiches using slices of a slightly stale Sunblest loaf. When he returned to the living room, his mother was sound asleep. He rescued the tumbler from her hand before it could slip from her fingers onto the floor. He sniffed the clear dregs inside the glass, then gulped them down. Bitter. Usually she added more tonic.

He ate both sandwiches, thinking.

The idea, when it came, seemed fantastically obvious, as a good idea should.

In next to no time Guy was on the King's Road, heading for World's End Wines, the local off-licence. He was still dressed in his school uniform – tweed sports jacket and tie – so that when a hippie couple passed him coming the other way, the man turned to the woman and said, "That's way too young to be so square." She, in return, chided him, saying, "Give the kid time. He'll turn on and get hip when he's good and ready." Guy ignored them both. They were walking clichés: tinted round spectacles, fur-trimmed suede coats, Afghan hound trotting beside them. Guy had no idea what the future held in store for him, but he had no ambitions to grow up to become a shambling longhair freak. Life was far too serious for that.

The proprietor of World's End Wines, Mr Norrington, greeted Guy with a smile.

"What is it today, young man? The usual? Beefeater Extra Dry is a shilling off at the moment, if I can tempt your mother away from Gordon's for a change."

"No, I'll stick with Gordon's. Three pint bottles, please."

"Three?" An eyebrow curved.

"We're entertaining this evening."

"Fair enough." Mr Norrington bagged the gin in a paper sack printed with his shop's name. "On the account?"

"Of course."

"I should mention, Mrs Lucas hasn't actually settled last month's bill yet. A lady like her, I'm always willing to extend the repayment period, but if you wouldn't mind having a word with her about it...?"

"I'm sure it just slipped her mind."

"I'm sure it did. Just like I'm sure you're eighteen years old. If you catch my drift."

"I'll remind her. Thank you, Mr Norrington."

"Pleasure, young man."

As Guy walked back up the road with his purchases, he passed the hippies again. They were standing outside a record shop admiring the cover of the new Beatles album displayed in the window. Their elegant, silky-furred dog sat at their feet, thoughtfully licking its privates.

"That's, like, so nothing," the man said of the blank white record sleeve. "So nothing it's everything. Genius."

"Hey," said the woman, noticing Guy and the bag he was carrying. "Look. Kid's just bought some booze."

Her partner chuckled. "Wow. I had him pegged wrong. Not so square after all, huh?" He gave Guy the peace sign. "Be cool, brother."

I will be, Guy thought. *I will be very fucking cool.*

HE SMUGGLED THE gin back to school inside his going-away suitcase. He doubted his mother would ever notice that three extra bottles of Gordon's had been charged to her account, and even if she did, he could surely convince her that she had asked him to buy them for her. Anyway, it didn't matter. Sorting out Mayflower, Bartlett and Thompson was all that mattered.

Stashing one bottle in each boy's bedside chest of drawers was easy enough. So was quietly tipping off Mr Hemingway the headmaster. "I'm sorry, sir, this may just be a rumour, but I'm pretty sure I overheard someone saying that some of the boys have brought alcohol to school." Dormitories were searched, the gin was discovered, and Mayflower, Bartlett and Thompson were summoned to Mr Hemingway's study. They came out half an hour later, limping, their backsides having been soundly thrashed. Mr Hemingway then phoned each boy's parents, inviting them to come and collect their son at the first available opportunity and to consider enrolling him in some other educational establishment. Expulsion was not specifically mentioned, but that was to all intents and purposes what this was.

Before they left, the three bullies had just enough time to find Guy and give him the beating of his life.

They knew he had framed them. It couldn't have been anyone else. And even if they were wrong and he was innocent, it wouldn't do any harm to give the choccie one last bashing. They stripped him to his underpants and kicked and punched him until he was sore all over and bleeding freely from mouth and nose.

For Guy it was worth it, every moment of it. The pain and humiliation were victory.

THE NEXT TIME he saw Milward, he told him what he had done.

"Don't mean to swank," he said, "but really, Satan didn't come through for us, did he? So I took matters into my own hands."

Milward was torn between admiration and indignation. "You've interfered with his plans, Lucas. That's unwise."

"What plans?" Guy shot back testily. "Assuming there even were any, we could have died of old age waiting for him to put them into action."

"Honestly, there'll be repercussions. Serious ones. You'll see."

"Well, perhaps. But in the meantime, Mayflower and his cronies are someone else's problem now. That'll do for me."

THE TWO OF them never spoke again. The very next afternoon there was a fire in one of the school attics. It was a place where boys regularly went to smoke.

The floorboards were littered with cigarette butts, spent matches and discarded empty Pall Mall and Capstan cartons.

One of the first-years spotted flames pouring from the roof. The alarm was raised and the fire brigade came. Within an hour the blaze was brought under control. Mr Hemingway conducted a roll call of the entire school in the clock tower quad. There was only one absentee: Clive Milward. Mr Hemingway called out the name three times. No reply.

The firemen found the body later that day. Milward was scorched almost beyond recognition, but just enough of his face remained, to enable identification.

It was assumed, not unreasonably, that the fire had been caused by a stray cigarette ash falling onto the insulation lagging and setting it alight. Mr Hemingway called an assembly and delivered a long lecture on the perils and pitfalls of smoking. "Filthy habit and, as we're now all too well aware, deadly dangerous too." He expressed relief that the fire had been contained and the disaster had not been significantly worse. Then the chaplain led everyone in a prayer in memory of Clive Milward, taken before his time. "We commend his soul unto God. Amen."

Guy wondered if it was God who had taken receipt of Milward's soul, or some other supernatural being. Either way, Milward had had a brief taste of the fires of Hell while still on earth.

Would Satan visit a similar fate on Milward's partner-in-crime, the boy who had collaborated with him in the black mass in the cricket pavilion? Would he destroy Guy too?

Guy guessed he would have to wait and find out. But he wasn't holding his breath.

1971-1972

Her name was Molly and she was a free spirit. She was naturally busty and unnaturally blonde. She came from America – Wisconsin, originally, but more recently Washington, DC – and she was into Woody Allen movies, horoscopes, strong coffee, and the music of Carole King and Van Morrison. Her favourite books were *The Catcher In The Rye* and *Slaughterhouse-Five*, and she said she would find it hard to love anyone who didn't love both of those. She looked great in hip-hugging bell-bottoms and a tight paisley shirt, braless. She smelled of lilies and clean laundry.

Guy was besotted.

They first met during Freshers' Week, at the bar in Oxford's tiniest, most tucked-away pub, the Turf Tavern. Molly broached the conversation: something about liking Guy's sideburns. Guy liked

Guy's sideburns, so as ice-breaking lines went, it was a winner.

His reply was fumbling, a gauche statement of the obvious: "So you're American."

"No shit, Sherlock," Molly drawled. "How'd you guess?"

He redeemed himself somewhat with his comeback. "Wild stab in the dark. It was either that or Hungarian."

She smiled. She laughed. Her nose wrinkled, making the freckles on it bunch together. "You're funny. And kooky. I like funny and kooky."

Guy could have sworn he was onto a sure thing with her. They chatted for a good ten minutes, both seeming to have forgotten why they had come to the bar in the first place. Molly's father worked at the US Embassy. "You know, the place that looks like a prison on Grosvenor Square in London." He was a minister-counsellor, which meant –

But Guy knew what it meant. Assistant to the ambassador, an administrative role.

Wide-eyed, Molly exclaimed, "How in heck did you know that? You're the first person I've met here who does. Everyone assumes he's a priest or something."

"I'm the child of a diplomat too."

"It's kismet, then," Molly said. "You and I were destined to meet."

But it went no further that night. Molly was with friends, a table full of them, all men. She said Guy could go over with her and join them. He'd be welcome. "They're all guys from my college. They're cool."

They were rough and hearty, though. Rowing types, to judge by the broadness of their shoulders. Gales of raucous laughter burst from their table, chasing after coarse jokes. Testosterone city. Guy didn't feel like dealing with them. It would be too much effort. He didn't want to compete with them for Molly's attention. He wanted her all to himself, or nothing.

So he chose nothing. He made his excuses. "Actually, sorry, I've got my own bunch of friends. They're outside."

Her disappointment was fleeting but, he believed, sincere. "Oh. Okay. Another time, huh?"

He took beers out to Terry and Phil, both first-year PPE undergrads like him. Terry was from Wales and into prog rock and fantasy novels, especially Tolkien and Moorcock. Phil was from Humberside and wouldn't stop going on about his girlfriend back home, Julie, who worked in a clothing boutique but had ambitions to be a dancer on *Top Of The Pops*. They were pleasant but dull, but their real problem that night was that neither of them was Molly-From-Wisconsin-Then-Washington. Guy, as he chatted with them, could think only of her. He cursed his own pusillanimity. *Leave that lot. Let's go somewhere else, just you and me*. That was what he should have said to her. Coward.

Eventually, having stewed in remorse for long enough, he went back inside the pub, determined.

Molly and her retinue of oarsmen were gone.

* * *

THEIR PATHS DIDN'T cross for the rest of that Michaelmas Term. Guy looked out for her in every pub he visited, every Junior Common Room, on the street, in the quads, in the lecture halls, even down by the river. He didn't know which college she was at, what course she was doing, anything other than her nationality and her first name. It was a fruitless search. There were other girls interested in him – he slept with one or two of them – but he kept biding his time, waiting for a second chance with Molly. If he got it, he wouldn't bungle it this time. He promised himself that.

Hilary Term came, bitter cold, with mist hanging perpetually over the spires and meadows. Guy was strolling back to his college early one morning after a drunken hook-up with a girl from St Hilda's. He was crossing Magdalen Bridge when who should he see coming the opposite way but Molly. She was on a bicycle, pedalling serenely down the High, lost in her thoughts, a million miles away.

Guy hailed her, but she didn't hear. He darted across the road, narrowly avoiding getting run over by a Hillman Imp. The driver's irate horn-tooting caught Molly's attention; she spied Guy and braked.

"You," she said, sounding both mystified and delighted. "Sideburns boy. Hi."

"Hi yourself," said Guy.

"I haven't seen you since, well, ever. Where have you been hiding?"

"I could ask you the same thing."

"Want to get breakfast? There's this café up Cowley Road serves great bacon and eggs and the thickest toast you've ever seen. Plus real coffee, not instant. I was just going myself."

"Kismet," said Guy.

THEY BECAME AN item. That was the word Molly used for them, so Guy used it too. Item. Not inseparable. Molly needed her space. She didn't want to hang out with him all the time. She was a liberated female. She valued her independence. But two or three nights a week he would stay over at her digs, the tiny terraced house she shared with two other girls in Jericho, down near the canal. She was a second-year, living out of college, so there weren't any restrictions about overnight guests for her as there were for him. On her narrow mattress on the floor, by the soft glow of a batik-draped lamp, with *Moondance* or *Tapestry* on the turntable, Guy had never been happier.

It was Molly who suggested, late one evening, that the two of them hold a séance using a Ouija board. She'd done it with school friends back in Wisconsin. It had been spooky and a bit freaky but still fun. She wasn't sure they had made actual contact with the Other Side, but some of the messages the board spelled out had been scarily close to the truth, stuff she and her friends hadn't known they'd known, things about the other townsfolk, secrets and such.

"C'mon," she said, fetching the Ouija board out of her cupboard, "it'll be a gas."

They sat opposite each other, cross-legged on the floor, the board between them. A candle wedged into the neck of a Mateus Rosé bottle was their only illumination. They had shared a joint earlier and Guy was still a little lightheaded from that, and from the couple of glasses of cheap plonk he had downed. Dimly he recalled his escapade in the cricket pavilion at Scarsworth Hall with Clive Milward, the so-called black mass. He felt less trepidation now than he had then. He and Milward had not managed to raise Satan, had they? It was all bollocks. Childish nonsense. Demons and spirits and séances... But he would indulge Molly. He could deny her nothing. Sometimes her unpredictability vexed him; sometimes her mood swings caught him on the hop. Nonetheless, he was truly this woman's lapdog.

Molly placed the planchette in the centre of the board, rested her fingers on it and instructed Guy to do likewise.

"You have to clear your mind," she said. "Empty your thoughts. There's no room for doubt or cynicism here. You must be open to what lies beyond. We both must. We must let the spirits enter us and speak through us."

Guy nodded. It was cold in Molly's room. A single-bar electric fire was doing little to dispel the damp February chill.

"Wait for it," Molly said. "Wait..."

Guy waited, wondering idly whether his tutor would grant him an extension on his essay on Keynesian Macroeconomics and the Relationship Between Aggregate Demand and Aggregate Supply. It was due in the day after tomorrow and he hadn't done nearly enough of the background reading, let alone begun to plan his argument. He also thought of his mother. How was she doing? It had been a drab Christmas, just the two of them again, her still drinking too much. He kept encouraging her to find a new man, have some fun in her life, but she maintained that nobody could replace his father, and he had to admit she might be right.

"Yes," said Molly, almost a gasp. "Yes, they're here. The spirits are here. Can you feel it?"

To be honest, Guy could not. The air had grown a little colder – a draught sneaking in around the ill-fitting window sash – but nothing else seemed to have changed. If entities from beyond the veil were in the room, they weren't making their presence perceptible to him.

"Ask them something," Molly said. "Go on. Something you've been burning to know."

"All right. Is Molly Rosenkrantz going to give me a blowjob tonight?"

"Asshole!" She was surprisingly cross. "Don't mess about. This is serious shit."

"I am serious. And the answer is..."

He shoved the planchette over to the YES on the board.

"Bingo," he said. "The spirits never lie."

Molly thumped him in the chest. Pretty hard, too. "Guy Lucas, you do that again and you can get the fuck out of here right now and never come back. I mean it. This isn't the time for goofing around."

"Okay, okay. I apologise. I'm British. We find it

difficult to do anything solemn with a straight face. You always say I should learn to hang loose. Well, okay. This is me, hanging loose." He rolled his shoulders, cricked his neck. "I'm ready now. Let's try again. I swear I'll do it properly."

They laid their fingertips back on the planchette.

"Spirits, can you hear me?" Molly intoned. "Return to us. Share with us your wisdom and knowledge. Are you there?"

Nothing happened.

Then, to his surprise, Guy felt the planchette begin to move. He wasn't pushing it. Was Molly?

The heart-shaped piece of wood slid across the board on its three stubby legs. It came to rest with its tip pointing firmly at YES.

"Wow," said Molly. "Groovy."

"Yeah, groovy," Guy echoed uncertainly.

"Go on, ask them a question," she urged. "A real one, this time."

"Okay. Ummm... Will I graduate with a first?"

"*That's* your question?"

"It's important to me."

"Kind of materialistic, though. Thinking about your own worldly progress."

"Well, I don't know. How about this? Spirits, do Molly and I have a future together?"

"You can't expect —"

The planchette interrupted her by moving. It scuttled over from YES to NO.

"Oh," said Molly, and "Oh," said Guy too. She was embarrassed. He was crestfallen.

"Why?" Guy blurted out, before he could stop himself.

The planchette headed for the letters of the alphabet, arranged in two rows across the middle of the board. Gliding from one to another, it spelled out a word.

M-A-D-N-E-S-S.

"'Madness'?" said Molly. "I don't get."

"This is daft. Let's stop."

"No. What is it saying? I'm not mad. Okay, so I can get a little flaky from time to time, but..."

The planchette was on the move again. The whole thing was just too eerie. Guy knew he had nothing to do with its activity, and was almost entirely convinced that Molly wasn't responsible either. She looked genuinely baffled, verging on distressed. Some other force was guiding the planchette, something from elsewhere. Their hands were mere passengers.

P-O-S-S-E-S-S-I-O-N, the planchette said.

Neither Molly nor Guy spoke.

Finally Molly stammered, "W–what's that supposed to – ?"

The planchette raced back and forth, visiting five letters in swift succession.

D-E-V-I-L.

"Oh, God," she breathed.

The planchette darted to the same five letters again.

D-E-V-I-L.

And again.

And again.

Until at last Guy, with a cry of "That's enough!" snatched his fingers away.

The planchette shot across the room, as though fired from a catapult. It rebounded off the wall and skidded under Molly's desk. It was as though energy had been building up in the thing, and the moment Guy let go, the energy had been violently released.

Guy sat trembling, his gaze fixed on the planchette where it lay poking out beside the desk leg. He was aware that his breath was coming in short bursts, as though he had been sprinting. He no longer felt lightheaded. He was as sober as he had ever been, his entire body seeming electrified, every sense and synapse on high alert.

He turned to look at Molly.

Molly's eyes were rolled back inside their sockets. Only the whites showed. Her head was canted slightly backwards. Her chest heaved.

Then came the voice.

It was not Molly's voice.

It was barely even a human voice.

"Guyyy," it grated. "Guyyyy Luuuucassss."

Guy nearly pissed himself then and there.

The voice continued, growl-hissing from Molly's throat like an escape of steam from a broken pipe. It sounded like the voice of someone who had not spoken in a thousand years, whose tongue was dust and whose lips were sand.

"You're mine, Guyyy. We belong together, we two. We have a bond that none can break. Your fate is fused with mine."

"Stop this. Molly, stop this. It isn't funny."

"Molly isn't here. You know who I am."

"No, I don't. Molly, stop taking the piss. You're totally weirding me out." He said this, not because he believed she was playing a trick on him, but because he *wanted* to believe it. So much.

"We're never going to be apart," the voice that wasn't Molly's said. "How else can it be? You made a commitment to me. Did you think that that wouldn't matter? Did you think I'd *forget*?"

Guy slapped her face. It was all he could think of to do. He needed to snap Molly out of this trance she was in, or whatever it was. But there was repugnance behind the blow, too. He had to make the horror of what was happening go away. Somehow. Anyhow.

Molly reeled. Her eyelids fluttered like those of a sleeper coming round. Her hand went to her cheek.

"Ow," she said, and then, louder, "Owww. What the – ? Guy, why the hell did you just hit me?"

"Why the hell did you just talk to me in that creepy voice?"

"What creepy voice? What do you mean?"

"You know damn well what I mean. Like a *Scooby-Doo* monster."

"I have no fucking idea what you're going on about."

"Oh, yeah?"

"Oh, yeah. But I can tell you this, buster. Nobody hits me. Especially no man. Get out. Get out of here, this instant, or I call the cops."

Guy stood. He grabbed his velvet jacket and his army-surplus overcoat. "I'm going, all right. That

was a really nasty little stunt you just pulled, Molly.
Hope you're pleased with yourself. Know what? The
Ouija board was right. Madness. There's something
profoundly wrong with you, you crazy bitch." He
tapped his temple. "Up here. You are one seriously
fucked-up human being."

He stormed out of the room. Molly's housemates
were downstairs, watching *Callan* on a tiny black-
and-white portable. They peered out through the
living-room doorway as he raged past.

"'Bye," Guy said to them, meaningfully, and
slammed the front door behind him.

THERE WAS A note in his pigeonhole in the porters'
lodge the next morning. All it said was:

> We need to talk. The Bodleian. Catte
> Street entrance. 4pm.
>
> M

He made sure not to turn up. He spent the whole
of the next fortnight scrupulously steering clear of
Molly's known haunts and spent as little time as
he could in his room at college in case she sought
him out there. He buried himself in his studies.
His Keynes essay was one of his best, earning him
a rare "A," and he also turned in a pretty good
dissection of the *Critique Of Pure Reason* and
Kant's counterargument to Hume's assertions about
empiricism.

A second note came from Molly. This one he didn't read at all, just tore up and chucked in the bin.

The rational part of him kept insisting that it had all been a sham. Molly had put on a fake voice and groaned out that stuff about them belonging together, their fates being fused, all the rest. What for? Maybe to contradict the Ouija board's initial verdict about their relationship. Maybe to provoke a row, for her own perverse satisfaction. Maybe to get back at him for that blowjob wisecrack. Maybe simply to mess with his head. Who knew? Some barmy reason, at any rate.

But a deeper, less rational part of him couldn't help but ask: what if it had been no pretence? What if the séance had opened a portal to the netherworld and allowed *something* to enter Molly and take up residence inside her? What if she had become a mouthpiece, a puppet, for some malign creature with designs on him?

Guy's nerves were jangled. He felt as anxious as he had in the days immediately following the half-baked 'black mass' in the pavilion. All at once he was a fretful schoolboy again, terrified at having transgressed against God's will. He even attended a Sunday service at the college chapel. Religious observance had been compulsory at Scarsworth Hall; here at university it was optional, more or less an irrelevance. To sit in a pew and sing hymns and pray meant something. But he felt no better afterwards. His inner self didn't feel lighter or unburdened or spring-cleaned, as he had hoped.

So he went home for the weekend. To be away from Oxford. To get some distance from the place, some perspective. He took the train down to London.

There he learned that his mother had followed his advice and found herself a boyfriend.

THE MAN'S NAME was Alastor Wylie and he held a position high up in the civil service, although Guy's mother was unclear exactly what. They had met via a mutual friend, someone in the FCO who had worked with Maurice Lucas a long time back and still kept in touch with his widow. The mutual friend had introduced them at a cocktail party last month. Since then they had been to the opera twice and also attended a preview of the Tutankhamun exhibition at the British Museum.

She told Guy all this with a sly, shy air. "I felt you ought to know. As luck would have it, he's popping round for sherry tonight, then taking me to Claridge's. You two should meet."

Guy's first impressions of Alastor Wylie were not entirely unfavourable. He was silver-haired and handsome, with an effortless suavity about him. He spoke in a languid purr, and his tailored suit, with its wide lapels and shoe-swamping flares, hung comfortably off his trim-but-ever-so-slightly-going-to-seed frame. He smiled a little too hard and a little too often, but all in all Guy was inclined to like him. He seemed genuinely smitten with Guy's mother and treated her with courtesy and respect. Guy wondered if they had slept together yet, then did his best not to think about it. None of his business. His mother was a grown woman, still reasonably young, still good-looking. What she did with her body was up to her.

"So, Politics, Philosophy and Economics, eh?" Wylie said over a glass of Harveys Bristol Cream. "A balanced portfolio of disciplines and, I might add, the degree choice of the ambitious. What do you plan on doing with it, Guy?"

"No idea. It's still early days. I've got two and a half years left to decide in."

"Considering following in your father's footsteps? Something in politics or the *corps diplomatique*?"

"I've not really thought about it."

"You should," said Wylie. "I can see you in Whitehall, striding the corridors of power. You have that air about you. An intelligent young man, well-spoken, reasonably well-groomed – at least, nothing that a shave and haircut couldn't fix. Someone like you could go places, Guy."

"Um, thanks. Really, I just don't know. I want to enjoy life. I'm not sure about settling down into a job as soon as I graduate. Maybe I should get out there and see the world first."

Wylie nodded sympathetically. "Very laudable, but it's vital in politics to get a foothold while you're still young. I know the prevailing trend among your age group these days is to fool around and have fun. We've bred a generation of dilettantes. But for those who wish to get ahead in life, the sooner they knuckle down to it, the better."

"Well, I'll certainly bear that in mind," Guy said.

"You do that, my boy. I'm just an old bore, giving my advice. Pay me no heed. I happen to see something in you, though, something I like. I could help you. I know people. I could give you a leg-up."

"That's kind of you, Alastor," said Guy's mother. "Isn't it, Guy? Very kind of him."

"And now, my dear Beatrice..." Wylie consulted his watch, a handsome gold-and-steel Rolex Oyster Perpetual. "Our table's booked for eight, and my driver is waiting."

As Wylie draped Guy's mother's mink stole around her shoulders, he said to Guy, "Pleasure to make your acquaintance, young man. Don't forget what I've said. I could be a useful ally, if you so choose. A friend in high places. Better the devil you know and all that, eh?"

WYLIE'S PARTING WORDS would not have lodged so firmly in Guy's brain if he hadn't already been obsessing over Molly, the Ouija board, and her apparent possession by some otherworldly being. *Better the devil you know.*

He realised that by running away from his problems, he was only making them worse. He needed to confront them instead, head-on.

He returned to Oxford the next morning and went straight from the railway station to Molly's digs. She wasn't home, and neither of her housemates, Sophie and Tamsin, knew where she was.

"How is she?" Guy asked.

"No idea. Haven't seen her in a couple of days, actually," said Sophie.

"But that row you had with her really screwed her up," Tamsin added.

"We did not have a row," Guy protested.

"Well, whatever it was. She's been frantic ever since. She's not as confident as she acts, you know. She comes across all brash and self-assured, but she's delicate underneath."

"As you'd realise," Sophie chipped in, "if you weren't an insensitive bastard like all men are."

"Thanks, ladies," Guy said, taking his leave. "I appreciate the lecture. Now go back to licking Germaine Greer's fanny and fuck off."

"Chauvinist pig," Tamsin called after him as he set off down the street.

"Tosser," added Sophie.

Guy V-signed them over his shoulder.

HE ARRIVED AT college to find a familiar bicycle leaning against the wall beside the entrance to his staircase: Molly's. Its frame was festooned with stickers – the Stars and Stripes, the CND logo, Road Runner, a yellow Smiley. One of the college porters had taped a photocopied memo to the handlebars, asking the bike's owner to move it as soon as possible, otherwise it would confiscated and sold. The memo had yesterday's date scrawled across the top.

Guy skipped up the two flights of spiral stone steps

to his rooms. He was anxious but hopeful, anticipating a happy reconciliation with Molly. Why else would she have come here if not to bury the hatchet? They could put this whole stupid business behind them and move on. What had happened in her bedroom that night had happened, it was in the past, they were both adults, time to behave like it. In truth, he missed her. She brought a welcome element of anarchy to his life. She was bewitchingly lovely. She was, no question, a damn good lay. What they would do was, they would make up, make love, then perhaps head down to the Isis for a nice riverside walk. It was a bright, brisk day, the first of its kind this year, more like spring than winter. If they got as far as the Trout Inn at Godstow, a lunchtime pint might be in order.

He opened the oak door.

The smell hit him straight away, and he didn't know what it was, but he knew that it wasn't good. It was sweet and sewery, a bloated smell. It touched something deep and dark in his brain, something that made him instinctively want to turn and flee.

He forced himself to stay put. His study was empty, no one there but him. He called out Molly's name, tongue tripping over the word. No answer.

The bedroom door stood ajar.

He pushed it all the way open, stomach knotted with dread.

Somehow he knew what he was going to find.

He didn't want to see it.

He had to see it.

So much blood.

The bedcovers were sodden red. The body on the bedcovers was sodden red too. An arm hung down from the mattress, hand almost touching the floor. It had been slashed open longitudinally, from the wrist halfway to the elbow, on the underside. A razor blade lay below the fingertips on the carpet, an inch from their reach. The gash in the arm reminded him – oh, God – of a vagina. A ragged wet pussy, gaping, revealing a fleshy purple-pink interior.

She stared accusingly at him across the room. Her eyes were open but dulled, the irises pale, almost opaque. Her lips were slightly parted, as though she had something to tell him.

Guy sank to his knees.

He retched. Vomited.

Molly.

A POLICEMAN FOUND the suicide note. Guy, once he had managed to stumble outside and raise the alarm, hadn't dared go back in. The constable who arrived first on the scene handed the envelope to him, saying, "I think this is for you." It had Guy's name on the front. It bore traces of Molly's scent – lilies and clean laundry. Specks of her blood, also.

The note inside read:

Guy,

I know you won't believe me, but I had nothing to do with the thing you thought I did. I've been going half crazy thinking about it and worrying about it. I don't even know what I'm supposed to have said to you. I guess I must have blacked out or something. It wasn't me. I wasn't there when I said it. You have to believe me on that.

You've been avoiding me. I get it. But I've never needed you more than I have these past few days. I've never needed anyone as badly. But you don't care. Fine.

So I'll show you. I'll show you what you mean to me and what I should mean to you.

Here's the girl you turned your back on, Guy.

Guess you won't ever forget me now, huh?

love,
Molly xxx

P.S. Hope you don't mind me borrowing one of your razor blades!

* * *

Days blurred. Weeks passed.

There was a nice large manor house with sweeping, well-kept lawns. Guy lived there. Doctors and nurses looked after him. They gave him pills and injections. They made him talk about himself. They were always pleasant and gentle, trying to get him to open up, to coax him out of his shell. But it was a nice shell. A solid shell. Cottony soft inside, like a cocoon. He wasn't sure he ever wanted to leave.

Sometimes at night he had dreams. Dreams about Molly. She came to him in his sleep. Her arms dripped blood. She held them out to him, beseechingly, and the blood poured from them in crimson cataracts.

Usually she was not alone. There was someone behind her. Someone dark. Guy could never make out this person's face – it was all shadows – but he had a sense of a looming, powerful presence. A strong vigorous force. The figure clung to Molly, as if claiming her for itself, but its focus was always on Guy. It meant him well. It had plans for him. Such plans. Great plans.

He did not confide in the doctors about his dreams. They were too personal. He did not understand them himself; the doctors would never understand. But he knew they were significant.

One day the doctors told him he was better. He had improved immeasurably. They were no longer concerned about him. He assumed they were right. He undoubtedly felt more a part of the world, less shut-in and lost. They told him he was well enough to go home.

A car came to collect him, a Bentley, with a chauffeur up front and his mother and Alastor Wylie in the back.

Wylie had paid for Guy's treatment, apparently. The sanatorium he had been staying in was highly exclusive and terrifically expensive.

"But, for Beatrice's son," Wylie said, "for you, my boy, money's no object. I think you'll be worth it. Look on it as an investment in your future." And he patted Guy's hand, and Guy gazed out of the window of the Bentley as the car cruised down the long sinuous driveway to the main gate, and it was summer, and he never went back to university.

could equally have been *Diamond Dogs* or *Pretzel Logic*. He was wise. He was brilliant.

Come the dawn, he had a splitting headache and felt at best only ordinary. He trudged along the beach to Mr Khun's café shack, where he ordered fresh orange juice and scrambled eggs done Thai-style, seasoned with chilli and coriander. The sand was littered with casualties from the night before, sleeping off hangovers or skinning up a little wake-and-bake. Mr Khun brought over his breakfast, smiling a broad, sunny smile. Guy ate and drank at a plastic table in the swaying shade of the palms while red-clawed crabs scuttled past his feet, making for the water.

Everyone had advised him against visiting this region of the world, from his mother to the travel agent through whom he'd booked the flight. Thailand was too close to Vietnam, where chaos reigned. If he must go abroad, why not Australia? Africa? India? Wouldn't any of those be adventure enough?

But Guy was adamant. Thailand was not under threat. The Vietnam War was in its death throes, less likely than ever to spill outwards and infect the rest of South-East Asia. North Vietnamese troops were closing in on Saigon, the ultimate prize. The endgame was being played out, ugly but self-contained. He would be safe. Besides, Europe was hardly the most peaceful spot at present. A febrile, fissured continent. NATO fighter jets on a state of constant high alert ever since Warsaw Pact tanks rolled into Czechoslovakia back in '68. The Iron Curtain trembling. Terrorist revolutionaries – the

Baader-Meinhof Gang, the Red Brigade – setting off bombs left, right and centre, though mostly left. Olympic athletes murdered in Munich. England itself wasn't immune either, with IRA cells active, carrying out assassinations and bombings, testing the nerve of Special Branch on a daily basis.

Life could be gone in an instant. If nothing else, Molly Rosenkrantz had taught him that. He should see places, have experiences, be his own man, while he still could.

It was a sort of homecoming. Six years on, he was back in the heat and humidity, under the same constellations he had known as a boy. Here was Bangkok with its rush of tuk-tuks and bicycles, the air brown with the fumes from two-stroke engines, the stench of rotting garbage catching you unawares on street corners, the Chao Phraya river greasing its way through the middle of the city. He backpacked north, via the ancient Thai capital Ayutthaya, up to Chiang Mai and Chiang Rai and the jungles on the border with Burma. There he smoked opium and met a former mercenary, a local, who had lost a foot in a Cambodian minefield and was proud of the prosthesis he had carved for himself out of teak. He stayed with a hill tribe for three months, earning his board and lodging by teaching the village children the rudiments of English. The kids, though their parents never found out, became proficient swearers and regularly greeted one another with cheery cries of "Hello, wanker!" and "Good morning, you old hairy bastard!" He loved them. They were never reluctant to learn. They seldom squabbled. They owned nothing but the T-shirts and flipflops they stood up in, yet they were unfailingly happy. The only time he ever saw them sad was when he left. They ran after the pickup truck that carried him away, sobbing their eyes out. Guy's heart ached. But he had to move on.

The beaches of the south beckoned. He caught the overnight train down through the Isthmus of Kra. He slept folded like human origami in a couchette bunk that was far too short and narrow for a lanky Westerner. A puttering ferry took him from the seaport of Surat Thani out to the islands in the Gulf of Thailand. One of the smallest, Koh Maan, became the terminus of his journey. It lay at the far end of the hippie trail, a kind of Ultima Thule for those who had tired of Marrakesh and Goa and wanted to go that one step further. All sorts of oddballs and outcasts fetched up on its shores, from slumming-it rich kids to brain-fried dopeheads, and every night, somewhere, there would be a beach barbecue, a bonfire, beer, music. Somebody would strum a guitar, playing Dylan or Simon and Garfunkel. Girls would dance, often naked, then select a man they liked and settle in his lap. The surf would crash, opium-laced joints would be passed round, and it felt, in every sense, like the end of the world. The furthermost tip of civilisation. The last days of planet Earth. A party to drown out the ticking of the doomsday clock. An orgy in Atlantis.

* * *

WHEN THE AMERICAN approached, Guy resolved to ignore him. The man had a shambling gait and twitchy eyes, and Guy was certain he would try to bum a cigarette or beg for a few spare baht. He kept his head down and concentrated on his eggs.

"Hey, my man."

Here it came. Guy pretended not to have heard. Hopefully the man would give up and go away if he blanked him long enough.

"Those eggs look good."

Buy some of your own was the obvious response to that, but Guy opted for continued silence.

"Want seconds? My treat."

Before Guy could stop him, before he could really work out what was going on, the American had ordered two more rounds off Mr Khun and sat himself down at the table.

"Yeah, nothing like a good breakfast, right?" He extended a hand. "Nick Scranton. And...?" He raised eyebrows expectantly.

"Guy. Guy Lucas."

Scranton's grip was surprisingly strong. "Cool. That's cool. I've seen you around, Guy Lucas. I make it my business to know who's who on Koh Maan. You've been here awhiles, and we've kind of not connected yet, so I thought introductions were in order."

Guy studied Scranton, whom he now vaguely recognised – a face at one of the many Bacchanalian revels he had attended, a jovial presence, invariably squiring at least two women at once. The American, perhaps in his early thirties, had long, grey-flecked dark hair, tied back in a ponytail. A red bandanna encircled his head. He wore jeans and a denim waistcoat, which hung open to reveal a scrawny but still muscular torso. Beads dangled around his neck, and a pair of military dogtags.

"Ah, you noticed those, huh?" Scranton said, tapping the dogtags. "Yep. US Army. Hundred-And-First Airborne, a.k.a. the Screaming Eagles. Did three tours up north, chasing Charlie through swamp and jungle. Now officially demobilised. Well, I say 'officially,' but..." The sentence lapsed into a shrug.

"But Uncle Sam might not see it that way," said Guy.

"Ha ha! Well put, Guy Lucas."

"Absent without leave, isn't that what they call it?"

"When they're being polite. Deserter, when they're not. I prefer to think of it as done with hellholes and terror and bullets and choosing to *live* instead. I figure, I didn't volunteer, right? I got drafted in. So I gave as much as I was willing to, and now I've drafted myself out again."

"Why are you telling me this?" Guy asked. "You don't know me from Adam. I could report you, couldn't I? Make a call to the right people..."

"...and bring the MPs down on my head. Yeah, sure. You could. But you won't. You aren't like that. I'm a good judge of character, Guy. I've got you pegged as the sympathetic type. That's what I said to myself first time I saw you: 'the sympathetic type.' Anyways, what does the army care about one washed-up old grunt? America's falling apart. I tell you, my country hasn't got long left. It may not even live to see its bicentennial. Everything's gone to hell since The Man started killing presidents and black preachers and college kids. By the end of this decade, there won't even be a USA any more. There'll be a giant glowing hole, with wolves and coyotes roaming the edges, eating the corpses. You can bet on that. It's all over for the Land of the Free. And I'm going to sit here, at a safe distance, and watch the whole goddamn country burn. But that's enough about me. You."

"What about me?"

The eggs arrived. Scranton tucked in with gusto, holding his fork like a magic wand and scooping. Guy dug in too.

"You," Scranton said through a bulging yellow mouthful, "have the look of somebody who's seen his unfair share of shit. Kid your age, but you got an old man's eyes. Don't mean to pry. I can just tell."

He leaned closer; lowered his voice.

"You've touched the Devil," he rasped. "Or the Devil's touched you. It's much the same thing."

Guy did not reply, but all at once the old chill was back, the familiar needling in the gut. Two years since Oxford and his spell in the sanatorium. He had put his past mistakes behind him. He had run. There were six thousand miles between him and all that. Wasn't he allowed to escape it? Would it be chasing him forever?

"I know how that is, my friend," Scranton went on. "I know 'cause I've met the Devil myself. No word of a lie. He was out there in that steaming Asian jungle, walking in plain sight, bold as brass. He was out there watching the slaughter and rubbing his hands like it was all part of the plan. Every GI who got cut down by sniper fire or died of sepsis from a punji stick wound, every VC who got napalmed or shot like a rat in one of their tunnels – that was the Devil leaving his mark. He saw me and staked a claim on me too. He's at large in the world and he's after us, and he won't stop until he gets us. All of us."

"No," said Guy. "I don't believe that."

"Don't or won't?"

"Both. There is no Devil." This had been his mantra since Oxford. This was the fragile creed he clung to, most ardently at night, a crumb of comfort in the dark of the small hours. *There is no Devil.*

"You say that, but he has plans for you, and if the Devil has plans for you it doesn't matter what you think or feel or desire, you just have to accept it. Embrace it. And I can show you how. You've less to be scared of than you think, Guy. Open up to the Devil, and you'll soon realise it's not as bad as the alternative, which is to keep shying away from him, when it's inevitable he's going to catch up to you sooner or later. That's just lunacy – denying reality. I can open your eyes, my friend. I can make the fear disappear."

Guy had been all set to leave the table – perhaps abandon Koh Maan altogether. Anything to get away from this crazy person, this Vietnam veteran who'd clearly left several of his marbles behind somewhere north of the 17th Parallel.

But now, almost to his horror, he heard himself saying, "How?"

"Easy. With this."

From a pocket, Scranton produced a small polythene baggie, inside which were squares of blotting paper, each no bigger than a postage stamp. He took one out and proffered it to Guy on the tip of his index finger. On it was ink-stamped a cartoon face: a leering demon with horns and a protruding tongue.

"A gateway," he said. "A portal to truth."

FOR THREE DAYS Guy refused to touch the tab of acid. But neither did he throw it away. It sat sandwiched between two pages of his tattered paperback copy of *Steppenwolf*. It called to him from the book.

A portal to truth.

Most nights on the island, he had been skying on a cocktail of dope, opium and alcohol, getting a decent buzz on and often feeling as though he was close to some sort of breakthrough. He kept receiving glimpses of something vast and intricate and magnificent, an underlying scheme, the solution to everything. It was there, so near, but remained tantalisingly out of reach. It was as though one day he saw a leaf, the next day a branch, the day after that a root, but never the entire tree.

He had travelled, as so many did, in order to find himself. So far, however, all he had found was hedonism, old memories, and an infestation of pubic lice. Guy Lucas's purpose in life was still a mystery to him.

Finally, on a bright, muggy afternoon, he bit the bullet – took the tab.

The blotting paper gradually disintegrated on his tongue. For long minutes he sat outside the beach hut, feeling no different. Maybe it was a dud batch of acid. Maybe Scranton was a bullshitter, or a prankster – went round distributing squares of blotting paper that were nothing more than that, for his own obscure amusement. And maybe that coconut on that palm tree over there was about to fall. Maybe it was already falling. Maybe its fall had happened long ago, and was happening now, and would happen in the future, and was always happening. Guy saw the coconut stay put, and descend, and lie on the ground having descended, all at once. The potential for falling was inherent in it. Latent. Nascent. It was born to fall.

Fascinated by the coconut, he stared at it for hours. Days. Weeks. The beauty of it dazzled him.

Was everything so beautiful?

It was. You only had to look – really *look*. The coconut. The hummingbird flirting with the hibiscus bush. The blades of coarse grass between here and the beach. The beach itself, where the foamy waves curled and the sea unpeeled itself beneath the sky.

Knee-deep in the surf, Guy could feel the rhythm of the tide, the pulse of the universe. The water was as warm as blood. Further out, he floated on his back, until the rollers gently returned him to shore like caring hands.

The answer, he thought as he lay on the burning hot sand, was that there was no answer. There was no underlying scheme. It was only an illusion.

He waved his arms up and down and scissored his legs open and shut, making a sand angel.

You could chase that illusion all your life, and only on your deathbed would you realise it meant nothing. It was just some will-o'-the-wisp. A flickering lie.

The heavens darkened. The sun hid its face. From somewhere came an immense deep groan, and the rain plummeted.

Guy did not move. Droplets pelted him like countless ball bearings. Lightning stalked across the horizon like the legs of a giant. The storm was terrifying, but he submitted to it, giving it the awe and respect it deserved.

As the tempest intensified, he heard footfalls. Someone was coming along the beach.

A faint, acrid smell reached his nostrils. Sulphur.

He looked round.

Scranton had been right.

The Devil was at large.

GUY AWOKE IN his beach hut. He was sprawled in the hammock, soaked to the skin. The rain rumbled on the corrugated tin roof. Thunderclaps rolled against the planks of the walls.

Nick Scranton was sitting in the one and only chair, idly thumbing through *Steppenwolf*. His denim waistcoat was damp from the shoulders to the breast pockets, his jeans from the knees down. His ponytail dripped water on the floor.

"Welcome back, my friend."

Guy tried to get up, but his head swam every time he raised it. He voiced a question, a single guttural monosyllable. It could have been "Where?" or "How?" or "When?"

"Dragged you indoors," Scranton said. "You were lying there in the shallows, out cold, with the waves breaking over you. I thought if the tide didn't get you, a lightning bolt might. Drown or fry – either way, not good. So you tripped, huh?"

Even nodding made Guy dizzy.

"Good? Bad? Indifferent?"

Guy cast his mind back.

Before passing out, he had seen the Devil walking. He was convinced of it. The Devil in human guise.

"Well, anyway," Scranton said, rising to leave. "Guess you're going to be okay. Get dry if you can. Don't want you catching a chill."

"Wait," Guy croaked.

Scranton halted by the door.

"You saw the Devil. You told me."

"I did."

"What – what did he look like?"

Scranton pondered. "Like a man. Like you or me. Like anyone. You've seen him for sure, huh? How'd he look to you?"

"Like someone. Someone I know."

The American's smile was grim and wry. "That'd be about right. Who else would he look like? You wouldn't recognise the Devil if he was a stranger."

* * *

CONFUSED DAYS FOLLOWED, Guy veering from certainty to doubt and back again. The LSD seemed to take a while to work itself out of his system. He could be doing something quite ordinary – brushing his teeth, say – and suddenly there would be a sense of dislocation, of things not quite meeting up, reality blurring. The toothpaste tube would throb as though it had a heartbeat. The toothbrush would twist and writhe like a worm in his hand.

The episodes became fewer and further between. His world stabilised. But still Guy could not decide whether what he had seen on the beach during the thunderstorm had been genuine or just an acid-induced hallucination. He had heard those footfalls, smelled that sulphurous smell. The Devil had stood there, a solid living being, a thing of flesh and blood and bone, looking down at him through eyes Guy had seen many times, familiar eyes. Looking with a calm, acquisitive glint, a gloat of ownership.

And yet the mind could play tricks, he knew. It could even break down completely, as he'd discovered only too well just a couple of years ago. The mind was not to be trusted. It was not you – it was something that pretended to be your friend, but might easily betray you. It was the Judas inside.

WHEN HE NEXT bumped into Scranton at Mr Khun's, he had two things to tell him. The first was that he was leaving for England.

"Oh, hey, man, sorry to hear that. Gonna miss

you. This little community of ours, all these heads and freaks and strays, we're kind of a loose-knit family, right? Always a shame to see one of us go."

"Yes, well, it's time."

"No, that's cool. I understand."

"And listen," Guy said. "I don't know what your motives were, but when you gave me that acid, it helped. It really did."

"You're welcome. I like to share."

"It's clarified things."

"That's what acid's for. Scrubs clean the windows of the brain."

"When I get home, there's stuff to do. Lots of stuff. But what I need to know is..." He dropped his voice. "When you met him in Vietnam, what did he want from you?" There were other people present so he didn't say who "him" was. He didn't need to.

"My friend, I never asked," said Scranton. "Because, you know what? I reckon I'd already been his servant, without realising it. Killing gooks by the dozen – if that isn't his work, I don't know what is. I'd damned myself plenty just by being in 'Nam and obeying orders. You think I'm here on Koh Maan hiding from the Military Police? I'm not. I'm hiding from *him*. He'll come collect his due eventually, but maybe, just maybe, I can stay out of his sights a while longer yet."

"You said it's lunacy trying to run away from him."

"What can I tell you? I'm a desperate man. Could be I've a few bugs in the brainpan as well. At any rate, I'm hoping that, since this is the obvious place to come looking, it's the last place he'll think of."

"The obvious place?"

"Koh Maan, man," said Scranton. "It's in the name. Don't you know any Thai-ish? Means Island of the Devil."

"Holy shit," said Guy.

"Yeah," said Scranton with a raucous cackle. "Holy shit, exactly."

IN BANGKOK, VIA a long-distance payphone call, Guy told his mother he was returning. She was pleased and relieved.

"I've some news for you," she said.

"What is it?"

She tried to tell him, but the connection expired in a fizz of static and he had no money left to make a second call. Her last words were a faint "...it'll have to wait... nice surprise for..."

When he landed at Heathrow, she greeted him off the plane. Alastor Wylie was there in the arrivals lounge with her.

"Look at you," she trilled, clasping Guy's cheeks in both hands. "So thin. But you're brown again, just like when you were a child. Oh, it's lovely to see you. It's been so long."

"Welcome back, my boy," said Wylie.

"Er, yeah," said Guy. "Thanks."

Wylie's Bentley whisked them away from the airport.

"So what's this news of yours?" Guy asked his mother.

By way of answer, she held out her left hand. A large diamond sparkled on her ring finger. It took him a moment to realise that it wasn't the engagement ring her father had given her.

"You're –"

"Getting married!"

"To –"

His mother took hold of Wylie's hand. "Alastor went down on one knee. I said yes. We've been going out together nearly three years. It's about time he made an honest woman of me."

"All this time I've thought of myself as a confirmed bachelor," said Wylie. "Seems I was just waiting for the right girl to come along. Of course, we'd like your blessing, Guy," he added, "if at all possible. I'd be pleased if you were happy about the arrangement. After all, I am going to be your stepfather."

"Uh, yeah. Fine. What do you think I think? It's great. Super. Really."

Guy didn't know what else to say. He could hardly tell them that he had met the Devil on a beach in Thailand, and the Devil was a dead ringer for Alastor Wylie.

1976

THE JOB AT Shamballa (...And Other Dreams) did not pay well, but it had two main benefits. One was that it kept Guy's mother off his back. She had been nagging him repeatedly to get off his behind and find work. Now he had a little money coming in, and although manning the till at a cult bookshop wasn't her idea of a career with prospects, or indeed anyone's, at least he was no longer moping around all day doing nothing and going nowhere. He had a reason to get up in the mornings and a level of professional responsibility, however meagre.

The other benefit was that he could read. Shamballa (...And Other Dreams) was seldom busy, except on Saturdays. For most of the week, only a handful of customers came through its doors, among them regulars like Hattie Jake the enormous transvestite, Angelcat the kaftan-swathed astrologer, and nervous little Mervyn Tingley with his mackintosh and myopic squint who always looked as though he had wandered in expecting to find a sex shop but made purchases nonetheless. The proprietor, Mr Ingram, was often absent for long stretches or else asleep in an armchair in the basement stockroom. This left Guy plenty of time to leaf through whatever from the shelves took his fancy. He could sit at the counter, wombed in the sweet smell of decaying wood pulp, and peruse at leisure, largely undisturbed.

He enjoyed the scary-movie magazines Mr Ingram imported from the States – especially *Famous Monsters Of Filmland* – and the horror-comic anthologies such as *Creepy*, *Eerie*, *Vampire Tales* and the like. He polished off countless trashy sci-fi paperbacks and the whole of Colin Wilson's *Outsider* cycle.

Mostly, however, he concentrated on the shop's extensive occult section, in particular books pertaining to Satanism and demonology.

Know your enemy.

It was from one of these books that he learned that the name Alastor belonged to a malevolent demon, but also could be used simply to denote an evil spirit. From another, he learned that the Devil would walk the earth only if the End Times prophesied in the Book of Revelation were nigh. St John the Divine dubbed Satan 'the deceiver' and 'the dragon' and foresaw him precipitating a war that would bring about the destruction of the world.

The deeper he investigated the subject, the more Guy was persuaded that his experience on the beach had been a genuine manifestation, not a hallucination. Alastor Wylie had been there, a palpable presence. Why would he have imagined seeing him, of all people, if it wasn't of some significance? And then there was that look in the apparition's eyes, that expression that stated quite explicitly "You're mine." Evidently Wylie had been sending him a message on the psychic plane. He wanted Guy to know that there was nowhere he could run to, no way he could break free. By marrying Guy's mother, Wylie had insinuated himself inextricably into his life, and there was nothing Guy could do about it.

That, however, would not stop Guy from trying.

ONE EVENING IN autumn, Guy finally plucked up the nerve to take action. What he wanted above all else was confirmation that Wylie was what he suspected him to be: literally the Devil incarnate. Once he had proved this to his own satisfaction, then he could plan his next move – assuming he could think of a next move that wouldn't imperil his own safety or his mother's.

He closed up the shop early. Mr Ingram had already gone home, complaining of a migraine. Guy's boss lived in a more or less constant state of depression, which was ironic, given the number of self-help titles available in his own inventory. Thomas Anthony Harris's *I'm OK, You're OK* might have done him some good, or Paul A. Hauck's *How To Be Your Own Best Friend*, or even *Jonathan Livingston Seagull*, which was the closest thing Shamballa (...

And Other Dreams) had to a guaranteed seller, its banal platitudes popular with stoners and earth mothers and troubled teens and just about everyone.

Locking the door, Guy headed along the side-alley where the bookshop stood, out into the bustle of Charing Cross Road. It had rained earlier and the glowering charcoal skies suggested another downpour was due soon. Given the long, parched summer that had just passed, however, no one minded. For many, the unpleasant memory of drawing their daily water from standpipes in the street was fresh and acute.

He took the Piccadilly Line from Leicester Square to Gloucester Road. There had been rumblings about a Tube drivers' strike. All the other trade unions seemed to be taking industrial action, why not them too? But so far, the underground trains were still running, if a little more recalcitrantly and less reliably than usual.

A ten-minute walk south from the Tube station brought him to the mews house, which he now had all to himself. His mother had moved into Wylie's Belgravia residence, and who could blame her? It was a palatial five-storey townhouse backing onto the exclusive green oasis of Cadogan Gardens, a short stroll from Knightsbridge. "Harrods is my corner shop!" she was fond of boasting.

Guy would be heading over to Belgravia himself in a couple of hours' time, for dinner *chez* the Wylies. His mother had been pestering him for months to come by for a meal. He had eventually given in, but only because it suited his own agenda.

Before then, he had some preparations to make.

Holy water, as in water consecrated by an ordained priest, was hard to come by. They didn't just hand it out free at church to whoever asked. But he had found out how to make his own. To begin with you blessed some salt, using a benediction from the Renaissance grimoire *The Key Of Solomon The King*: "The Blessing of the Father Almighty be upon this Creature of Salt, and let all malignity and hindrance be cast forth hence from, and let all good enter here in..." Then you sprinkled the salt into some distilled water, uttering an incantation beginning, "I exorcise thee, O Creature of Water, by Him Who hath created thee and gathered thee together in one place so that the dry land appeared..." Hey presto: sanctified water. Effective against all manifestations of evil, apparently. Anathema to hellspawn.

He decanted the holy water into a strawberry Cresta bottle which he had rinsed out thoroughly beforehand. With the stubby little screwtop bottle in his jacket pocket and a marbled kipper tie knotted around his neck, he made his way across town to beard the Devil in his lair.

THE FORMER BEATRICE Lucas, now Wylie, was resplendent in a bead-embroidered peach chiffon evening gown with big floaty ruffled sleeves. "It's Hardy Amies," she told Guy, doing a little twirl for him like Anthea Redfern in *The Generation Game*. "Do you like it? I daren't tell Alastor how much it cost. He'd pitch a fit!"

The fact that she was dolled up to the nines was a strong hint that this was not going to be some small intimate get-together, and sure enough, as Guy entered the drawing room, he found a dozen guests already present. He recognised a couple of famous faces – a Cabinet minister and a prominent member of Her Majesty's Opposition – and the rest all had the sleek, creamy air of the rich and powerful. Wylie introduced him to them as "my somewhat errant stepson," which made Guy's skin crawl, but he smiled bravely and behaved impeccably, the dutiful young man paying court to his elders and betters.

"I do hope you don't mind, darling," Guy's mother whispered in his ear as everyone filed through to the dining room to eat. "I know we've rather sprung this on you, but actually it was Alastor's idea. He's mad keen for you to meet some of his chums. I think he wants to show you off. You're the closest thing he has to an heir, and he still sees potential in you, even if," she added with some asperity, "you insist on frittering it away in that useless bookshop. This could be a huge opportunity, Guy. A chance to show some very important people what you're made of. Try not to waste it, eh?"

To Guy's way of thinking, it *was* a huge opportunity. At first he had been taken aback, but he realised that having this assemblage of high-and-mighty guests in attendance was a good thing after all. They could be witnesses.

They were going to see not what Guy Lucas was made of, but what Alastor Wylie was made of.

*   *   *

DURING THE STARTER and main course, the meal proceeded much as Guy had anticipated. The conversation was stultifyingly boring, focusing mainly on money, the things money could buy, and the exploits of colleagues and mutual acquaintances, none of whom he had heard of. He had been placed next to the wife of one of the politicians, a garishly over-made-up creature with terrible halitosis who gripped his forearm almost every time she spoke to him, as though forbidding him to turn away, restraining him so that he had no choice but to endure the full force of her breath. To get through the ordeal and keep his nerves steeled, he drank perhaps more wine than was wise. It was, at least, damn good wine.

As Wylie's servants cleared away the main course dishes and laid out the cheese and biscuits that preceded dessert, someone raised the subject of the strikes. This prompted Wylie to launch into a long speech denouncing the Callaghan government. The Cabinet minister bore the tirade with good grace, since it was couched in such a genial, ironic tone that only the thinnest-skinned could have taken offence. Besides, Guy could see that both politicians were somewhat in awe of their host, even intimidated by him. Guy knew how Wylie funded his lavish lifestyle. His mother had mentioned overseas investments and a vast inherited wealth. What he was still unclear on was what the man actually *did* in the civil service, what his job title was. On present evidence,

Wylie appeared to outrank almost everyone in the House of Commons and, from the dismissive way he was talking about Callaghan, possibly even the incumbent of Number 10 as well.

"What this country needs," Wylie said, "is a strong leader. Someone with guts, balls and vision. James Callaghan is not that man, and even if he was, he wouldn't have the mandate to achieve anything. A prime minister with a minority government, who only has power because he's done deals with the Liberals, the Ulster Unionists, Uncle Tom Cobley and all, is hamstrung when it comes to policy making. Callaghan can scarcely break wind without clearing it by committee first. Britain is facing immense difficulties. The unions are crippling us with their wage demands and work-to-rules. Unemployment's on the rise. Inflation is through the roof. It's one of our darkest hours, and Sunny Jim, despite his nickname, is never going to be able to bring any light."

Guy spied his chance. He leapt in with, "You mean we need a light-bringer, Alastor? Is that what you're saying?"

He could have hugged himself with glee at his own cleverness. In Vulgate Latin, the word *Lucifer* translated as 'light-bringer.'

"Metaphorically speaking, yes," said Wylie, with a tiny quizzical twitch of his eyebrows. "Someone to lead us out of the chaos and impose some order again. A Churchill for our times."

"And who would that be?" Guy asked. "Anyone in mind?"

"I've my eye on a couple of likely candidates. I wouldn't underestimate the leader of the Opposition, for one."

"Oh, Margaret has no ambitions to be PM," said the Conservative MP, a prim and pompous man with extraordinary bouffant hair. "She herself is on record as saying there'll never be a female prime minister in her lifetime."

"If you think she means it, my dear fellow, then you are well and truly blind to that woman's personal drive," said Wylie. "What did that Soviet rag dub her earlier this year? 'The Iron Lady.' And they're not wrong."

"You don't see yourself taking that role, then?" Guy said. "I can picture you ensconced in Downing Street, holding the national reins."

Wylie was not unflattered. "Indeed?"

"Yes. You'd make a devil of a good job of it, too." Again, Guy's boldness and wit were breathtaking. He took a fresh swig of wine.

"Guy, why would I stoop so low as to become prime minister?" Wylie said, and the others chortled knowingly. "I can achieve so much more as an *eminence grise*. The power behind the throne fares better and lasts longer than whoever's actually *on* it. And I couldn't face all those endless meetings with foreign dignitaries, the gladhanding and backslapping, the cosying up to oil sheikhs and tinpot dictators and all the other loathsome Third World types with damp palms and poor personal hygiene. I'm very happy where I am, thank you. The smoky back rooms. The Pall Mall club lounges. The places where the real business of ruling gets done."

A murmur of approval went round the table. Even the democratically elected politicians seemed to agree that what Wylie had just said was sagacious and true.

Guy tried another tack. "Alastor – it's an unusual name, isn't it? What is it, a variant spelling of Alistair? Like with Aleister Crowley?"

"The notorious Great Beast?" he said. "The so-called 'wickedest man in the world'?"

"Yes."

"Are you insinuating that he and I have anything in common?"

"Do you?"

Wylie gave one of his too-broad, too-frequent smiles. "Not as far as I'm aware. If you must know, Alastor means 'avenger.' It's one of the epithets of Zeus. My mother was an amateur Greek scholar and a lover of the ancient myths. Alastor is also the name of a son of Neleus, king of Pylos, who in turn was a son of Poseidon. He was killed by Heracles, along with Neleus's other sons, over some personal slight or other. Yet another Alastor was killed by Odysseus during the Trojan War. There's an early poem by Shelley called 'Alastor,' where the name is given to a spirit of artistic inspiration. I could go on. Does that answer your question?"

"I think it's a fine, distinguished name," Guy's mother interjected, loyally.

Guy was momentarily becalmed, the wind taken from his sails. His eye fell on a photograph sitting in a silver frame on a rosewood side table. The picture had been taken at his mother and Wylie's wedding. The newlyweds were both beaming at the camera, while in the background skulked Guy, looking considerably less pleased, unable even to fake a smile. He had been the proverbial spectre at the feast that day, a sullen gloomy presence, and remained rather proud of that.

The picture reinvigorated him, reminding him what he was here to do. "Wouldn't you agree, though," he said, "that things are starting to look a bit, well, apocalyptic these days? And nobody in power is doing very much to prevent it. The opposite, in fact."

"Really, Guy!" his mother exclaimed. "What has got into you? Why are you coming out with all these absurd remarks?"

"No, no, Beatrice," said Wylie with a placatory wave of the hand. "Let the boy speak. It's the prerogative of youth to be able to say what's on your mind, without filtering or fine-tuning it in any way."

"But his tone... Your tone, Guy. It's morbid and – and disrespectful."

"I'd call it 'challenging,' myself," said Wylie. "But again that's a prerogative of youth – the willingness to confront authority and question orthodoxy. In what way apocalyptic, Guy?"

"Just generally," Guy said. "In the sense of civilisation gradually breaking down. America and Russia at loggerheads, ready to destroy us all at the touch of a button. Terrorists on the loose. Pollution. The ecology. That Son of Sam killer in New York."

"The Stonehouse affair," someone chipped in, and there was a ripple of laughter as people recalled the corrupt former postmaster general, currently standing trial for fraud and embezzlement, who had clumsily faked his death a couple of years ago.

"Big Ben on the blink," said someone else. "When will it bong again?"

"Jeremy Thorpe ousted," said a third person. "What a pain in the arse he was – in more ways than one."

Lots of laughter over that one.

"It's not funny," Guy protested. "Any of it. You lot can sit here all smug and self-satisfied, but then you're okay; you're old. You've had your fun. People my age, my generation, what sort of future have we got? None. Nothing but death and disaster to look forward to."

"Guy, Guy, Guy," chided Wylie. "It's not as bad as all that. Granted, we're going through a period of turmoil right now. But if you look at it in the long term, *sub specie aeternitatis* as the saying goes, 'from the perspective of the eternal,' this is just a blip. It could be argued that human history is one long litany of turmoil – countless struggles, one apparent apocalypse after another – yet we survive, we live on to fight another day. What seems like upheaval at present is in fact merely the latest in a series of upheavals. They come in waves, with lulls of peace in between. When you're older, a little more seasoned, a little worldlier, then perhaps you'll perceive that we're nowhere nearer the end of civilisation than we've ever been."

"Oh yeah?" Guy said hotly. Adrenaline and alcohol were conspiring to make him angrier and more reckless. "'From the perspective of the eternal'? Who is this 'eternal'? You?"

"I have no idea what you mean."

"Guy, please," said his mother, exasperated. "You're making a fool of yourself." To her neighbour, she confided, "He works at this strange bookshop. 'Esoteric,' I think is the word for it. The sort of clientele they get there! Heaven knows what effect it's been having on him."

"I mean," said Guy to Wylie, "you can afford to take the long view, having been around since the year dot."

"I may be no spring chicken, if that's what you're getting at, but nevertheless –"

"And it's all part of your plan, isn't it?" Guy said, interrupting him. "Your grand infernal scheme. It's what you've been working towards all your life – creating Hell on earth. Whispering in the ears of kings and queens and the great and good. Influencing policy. Nudging mankind slowly and steadily closer to the brink. It's all coming to a head, isn't it? No wonder you can sit here in your mansion, with your paintings and your silver cutlery and your staff, and gloat. Everything's just the way you want it."

"I think," said Wylie, "that you are in danger of crossing a line, young Guy. A line you would be unwise to cross." The amused twinkle was gone from his eyes. In its place was something sterner and flintier.

Guy steamrollered on, heedless, oblivious. "And somehow you want me to be part of it. You want to sucker me in. What happens if I drop my guard and give you the chance? You'll take me up to 'an exceeding high mountain' and show me all the kingdoms of the world? You'll try and tempt me with riches and power? And all you'll ask in return is that I bow down and worship you? Is that it?"

"Guy!" snapped his mother.

"Guy," Wylie growled, "you seem to have me confused with someone else. I am no angel, as I'd be the first to admit, but neither am I the opposite."

Enough was enough, as far as Guy was concerned. He had had an elaborate stratagem mapped out. He had been intending to go out to the kitchen, tip the holy water into one of the water carafes, offer to top up everyone's glass, make sure Wylie had some to drink, then wait to see what ensued. With the domestic staff catering to the guests' every need, it would have been a difficult feat to pull off, but far from impossible.

Now, though, it was too late for such subterfuge. Only a blunt, full-frontal approach would work.

So he pulled the Cresta bottle from his pocket, uncapped it, and flung the contents across the table, straight into Wylie's face.

To describe what followed as stunned silence would be a gross understatement. Everyone forgot to breathe for several seconds, too shocked even to think.

Alastor Wylie sat with water running down his face. His fringe was plastered to his forehead. His collar and shirtfront were soaked.

An appalled sob escaped Guy's mother's throat.

Guy, for his part, waited for the holy water to take effect. For Wylie's skin to start to blister and bubble, as though splashed with sulphuric acid. For his human disguise to peel away, layer by melting layer. For the monster beneath – his true self – to emerge. For the Deceiver to appear at the head of the table, in all his Satanic majesty, so that everyone might see him and know him for what he was, as Guy saw him and knew him.

Slowly, with great care and deliberateness, Wylie began dabbing himself dry with a linen napkin.

Then, in a voice like low, distant thunder, he said to Guy, "You should leave now."

Guy was dumbstruck. The transformation hadn't happened. Was there something wrong with the holy water? Had he not prepared it correctly? Or could he have been mistaken all along about – ?

"I said," Wylie rumbled, "you should leave."

Quietly, falteringly, Guy got to his feet.

As he walked past his mother, she reached out a trembling hand to him.

He brushed it aside and continued out of the room.

HUMILIATION. FAILURE. PERPLEXITY. Resentment.

That was all he felt for months afterward. The emotions dogged him, one after another in a continual cycle.

How could he have been so wrong?

Was he wrong?

1977

HE NEVER EVEN saw them coming.

They pounced one night as he was shambling drunkenly home from the pub. They swept him up from behind, shoved a hessian sack over his head, bound his wrists behind his back, and bundled him into the boot of a car. One moment he was tootling along through the streets of Chelsea, minding his own business. The next, he was a captive, in a confined space, being driven who knew where.

The car bumped and juddered along for what felt like hours. What with the sack and the exhaust fumes, Guy was half-suffocated, not to mention completely terrified. The jolting seemed neverending. Where were they taking him? Who were they?

A horrendous thought struck him. They were Irish Republican terrorists. Of course.

Lately there had been a spate of high-profile

kidnappings by IRA units: Lord and Lady Donoughmere, the Dutch businessman Tiede Herrema, and the German industrialist Thomas Niedermayer, to name but four. All those abductions had taken place in Ireland, but there was no reason why the kidnappers shouldn't have expanded their sphere of operations to mainland Britain. The IRA were all over the country at present.

Guy racked his brains to think why they might have chosen him. The only answer he could come up with was Alastor Wylie. He was Wylie's stepson, and could be used for leverage on Wylie. Technically, at least. Someone evidently did not know how the relationship between him and Wylie stood. There was no love lost there.

Then again, Guy was still his mother's son. The pressure could be put on her husband through her. She would not want to see Guy hurt or killed, even if Wylie couldn't care less about him. Wylie would have to take her wishes into account when considering any ransom demands, which would probably be for political prisoners to be freed from jail. For her sake, he would be obliged to negotiate for Guy's life.

To the best of Guy's knowledge, the IRA had so far released all their kidnap victims unharmed. Wait. No, not all. Nothing had been heard of Neidermayer since he was taken outside his house in Belfast back in '73. Nobody knew where he was, and it was widely assumed that after all this time he must be dead.

A renewed surge of fear made Guy's stomach churn. He fought not to throw up. If he did, he would be stuck with his head in a bag full of his own puke for the foreseeable future.

He mastered his nausea, and was quite proud of himself for doing so.

Then the sound of the car's tyres changed, going from the thrum of tarmac to the crunch of loose stones. A gravel driveway? Or an unmade road leading to a remote farmhouse or perhaps to a disused quarry?

A few more twists and turns, then the car braked to a halt. The engine died. The boot lid opened. Chilly night air rushed in. Guy was manhandled roughly out. He discerned people moving around him, three, maybe four of them.

"Listen," he said. "Please listen. I don't know who you are, but if you are who I think you are, you've got the wrong man. I mean, the right man, but for the wrong reasons. If you're trying to get to Wylie, believe me, I'm not the one you want."

Someone laughed, coarsely.

"I mean it," Guy went on. "Wylie and me, we're not related, not as such, and we don't get on. I hate the man. Honestly, he's everything I detest. I'm more on your side than I'd ever be on his. I know him. I know what he is. I don't want anything to do with him."

"Come on, sunshine." Hands seized his upper arms, and he was steered along. "This way. Got somewhere nice and cosy waiting for you."

The accent wasn't Irish. It sounded Londoner, if anything. That was some small comfort. This was no IRA plot, at least.

"Steps ahead," said the man. "Mind yourself."

Guy shuffled up a short slight of stone stairs. He passed through an entranceway. The acoustics of their footfalls altered, taking on an indoor echo.

More walking. He heard a door being unlocked.

"Another set of stairs. Steep. Try not to trip."

It was a descent this time. Smells of mould and mildew permeated through the sack. A cellar, most likely.

At the bottom, the hands let go. Guy deciding to give ingratiation one last try.

"Just tell me who you are," he said. "Maybe we've got more in common than you think. Never mind who my stepfather is. I'm just an ordinary bloke. Power to the people, yeah?"

"That might have worked for Patty Hearst, mate," said the kidnapper, "but you're barking up the wrong tree here." His colleagues sniggered. "Now, make yourself comfortable. It's going to be a while before we come back for you. Don't even think about taking that bag off your head. And if you need to piss... Well, I'd try and hold it, if I were you."

With that, they left him.

The door slammed.

A key turned.

Guy was alone.

IT WAS A long night. Some of it Guy spent whimpering in misery. Some of it he spent in futile prayer. Mostly he just sat in a corner of the cellar, his mind running through all the ways this situation might play out. The majority of the scenarios ended with Wylie handing over a small fortune in ransom money or else persuading someone in government to grant the kidnappers whatever boon they asked for. A few of the scenarios, however, reached a less pleasant conclusion: Wylie refusing to help in any way, Guy's cold body being found in a field or, worse still, never found at all. Perhaps parts of him would be sent through the post – a finger, an ear – like in the gangster films. God, please not. Not that.

It must have been morning when his kidnappers finally returned. By now, Guy urgently needed to urinate. Last night's pints had worked their way through his system and his bladder was groaning.

He communicated his need, and grudgingly a bucket was fetched. His wrists were untied. He knelt and relieved himself with gratitude.

He was given food. A roll and butter, a cup of milky tea. He was told he could lift the sack just far enough to expose his mouth. He ate and drank.

"Thank you," he said, making it as heartfelt as he could.

"Got to keep body and soul together," said the kidnapper, seemingly the one only of them designated to speak to him. "For now, at any rate."

"What does that mean?"

"You'll find out. Tonight."

* * *

THEY HAD LEFT his hands unbound, so he began tentatively exploring his surroundings. Remembering the admonition against removing the sack, he groped his way around with arms outstretched like a child playing blind man's bluff.

Yes, a cellar. A pretty big one. Brick walls. A number of large, empty wine racks. Several items of – ow, his shins! – discarded furniture and bric-a-brac.

His fingers accrued a fur of dust and cobweb.

Vaguely he had hoped to find a window, a trapdoor, some kind of aperture to the outside world, something he could force his way out through. No such luck.

He sat again. He wondered if his mother and Wylie had been informed he was missing yet. Probably the ransom note had already been delivered, the individual letters clipped from newspaper headlines and glued to a sheet of foolscap, as was traditional. Or it could just have been an anonymous phone call – telephone box, handkerchief over the receiver to disguise the speaker's voice. "We have your stepson, Mr Wylie. Now listen very carefully..."

Wylie would play ball. Guy's mother would see to that. She would never forgive her husband if he let her son die.

Then again, what did her opinion matter to Alastor Wylie? Guy still could not shake the conviction that Wylie was truly the Devil. His mother, by that token, was just a puppet in Wylie's overall scheme, a mere pawn. Wylie didn't love her, he was simply using her in order to get to her son. In which case, it would hardly matter to him if, grief-stricken and angered, she turned on him and rejected him. Indeed, if Guy was dead, Beatrice Wylie would no longer serve a purpose, as far as her husband was concerned. He would no doubt devise some way of getting rid of her – divorce or, worse, an arranged fatality of some sort, a car crash, a skiing accident, a mishap in the shower.

And yet, if Wylie wanted Guy so badly, if, as Satan, he was so keen to sink his hooks into him, surely he would never allow the kidnappers to get away with murdering him. No, he would use his infernal powers to rescue him, perhaps sending in lesser demons disguised as SAS soldiers or antiterrorist police to retrieve him. That, yes, would work in Wylie's favour. A grateful Guy, glad to be alive, would be indebted to him. Enough – or so Wylie might hope – to pledge him his undying loyalty.

In fact, what if Wylie had orchestrated this entire operation? What if he was the mastermind behind it? What if it was the next phase in his long-drawn-out siege on Guy Lucas's soul?

That cast everything in a whole new light. All at once, Guy was the hero of the piece rather than the hapless victim.

He felt a flush of bravery. It was all about him now – his fortitude, his resolve, his obstinacy. Wylie would not get what he desired. No way. Guy would rather die.

HOURS LATER, MANY hours, he had no idea how many, the cellar door reopened.

"Right, my lad. Up you get. It's time."

"Time?" said Guy. "Time for what?"

"You'll see. You're a lucky fellow, you know."

"Yeah, I really feel it."

"Privileged, even," the kidnapper said. "Not a lot of people have been granted the honour of taking part in what you're about to take part in."

"Which is what?"

"Patience, mate. Just for a few minutes more."

Guy was led up out of the cellar. He was taken back through the hall, or whatever it was, the spacious echoing place. Back outdoors and down the stone steps – the front steps to a sizeable house, he reckoned, a mansion.

There was gravel underfoot, then lawn. No light was coming through the coarse weave of the sack. It must be night-time once more. He grass hissed softly when trodden on, as though wet with dew.

The ground sloped upwards and became tussocky and uneven. He stumbled once or twice, but his captors supported him, keeping him upright. An owl hooted. A fox howled.

And then Guy heard something else. Faint. Distant. A rising and falling sound, somewhat like the drone of bees.

It grew closer, clearer, and he realised it was voices.

Voices chanting.

In English?

No, another tongue. Latin, if he didn't miss his guess. It wasn't so much the individual words as the shapes of them, familiar to him from his Classics lessons at Scarsworth Hall. All the *–um* and *–us* endings. The internal rhythms.

Men and women, intoning in a dead language.

Guy was suddenly very afraid. Far more afraid than at any other time during his ordeal so far. The fear went deep, beyond the terror of pain and suffering, down to a more visceral level, a spiritual level even.

Someone whisked the sack off his head.

For all that it was dark, he was dazzled. The moon was full, bright and high, and to his unadapted eyes it blazed like the sun. Squinting, he caught glimpses of the scene it illuminated, silvery impressions.

The skeletal remains of a chapel. Roofless. Broken rafters reaching to the sky. Tumbledown walls. The hollow arches where windows had once stood.

Within the chapel, people. Perhaps twenty of them. All clad in identical, ankle-length robes. Faces hidden inside hoods.

Candles by the dozen, black ones, flickering. A brazier throwing up flames and spirals of ember.

An altar. The chapel's original altar. Covered in a black cloth.

On the cloth, arcane symbols. Principally, a pentagram inside a circle.

Behind the altar, a huge crucifix, inverted.

In front of the crucifix, a man. Robed and hooded like the others. In his hand, a dagger.

Guy looked to his left and right. The men holding him were robed and hooded too. Moonlight etched a feature here and there – the tip of a nose, a grimly smiling mouth.

He tried to wrench his arms out of their grasp, intending to run, but they gripped him all the more tightly. They forced him onward across the grass, covering the final hundred yards to the chapel. Guy writhed. Guy yelled. To no avail.

His protests drew the attention of the people inside the ruined chapel. They broke off from their chanting and fell expectantly silent.

Guy was dragged through the entrance where stout oak doors would once have hung. He was beside himself with terror. He could hear himself trying to plead with the men holding him. He could hear how his own sentences made no sense. They were more or less gibberish.

The celebrants bowed as Guy passed. Their hands were folded inside their sleeves, monk-fashion. They were eerily reverent.

He was weak-kneed by the time he reached the altar. His heart was thundering.

He knew what this was.

Oh, God. He knew only too well, from his researches, his reading.

It was what Clive Milward had attempted so cackhandedly at school. But here, it was being performed by people who were clearly experienced and well versed in the lore.

A black mass.

GUY WAS MADE to kneel before the altar, although in truth he all but collapsed when the men escorting him pushed him down. They ripped his shirt open, baring his chest to the midnight air.

On the other side of the altar, the high priest, officiator, whatever he was, raised the dagger in both hands.

An athame. The word surfaced amid the panicked welter of Guy's thoughts. *A ceremonial knife for a Satanic ritual is called an athame.*

The high priest began to recite Latin phrases, which the other celebrants duly echoed.

"*In nomine Dei nostril Satanas Luciferi Excelsis... Introibo ad altare Domine Inferi...*"

He continued with this profane desecration of the Catholic mass in a nasal, singsong voice, not unlike a vicar leading the catechism. He concluded with a cry of "*Ave Satanas! Rege Satanas!*"

The rest picked up the imprecation, repeating it at increasing volume, lauding Satan all the way up to the dark heavens.

"*Ave Satanas! Rege Satanas! Ave Satanas! Rege Satanas!*"

They proclaimed their blasphemy joyously until Guy was almost deafened.

"*Ave Satanas! Rege Satanas!*"

Then, at a gesture from the priest, silence reigned again.

"Please," Guy murmured. "Please don't do this. It's not right. I don't want to be here. I've tried to be good all my life. This isn't me. This isn't fair."

To his left, a nickering sound. Another celebrant appeared from what had once been the north transept, dragging a billy goat on a rope. The goat peered around, perturbed, but far from alarmed. It bleated again as it was brought up to the altar.

The priest handed over the athame to the celebrant with the goat.

Guy could only watch, mesmerised, numb.

"To you, Satan," the priest said, "we offer this sacrifice of one who bears your likeness. With its death, we pledge ourselves once more to you and ask you to welcome to your bosom a new member of our unholy congregation, this young man, Guy. We offer him unto you as a future loyal servant, sealing the profane compact between you and him with the blood of the beast you have claimed as your own."

The priest gave a nod, and the celebrant with the knife bent and put the blade to the goat's throat. Gripping its horns with his other hand, he drew the athame swiftly from left to right. The goat bucked and writhed. Skin parted. Blood came out, first a trickle, then a tumbling, spattering flood. The goat shuddered, its legs buckling, its bowels loosening. Its eyes, with their curious rectangular pupils, seemed to go blank, and its tongue lolled from the side of its mouth.

Then it was just a dumb, limp carcass. The celebrant lowered the goat's body to the flagstone floor and passed the dripping athame back to the priest.

The priest came round the altar, holding the knife carefully as though it and the blood on it were immeasurably precious. He approached Guy, who strained away from him in a paroxysm of horror.

"No," Guy gasped. "No, I won't. You hear me? I won't. I am not Satan's servant. I don't belong to him. You can't make me."

"Whether you like it or not, Satan wants you," said the priest. "There's nothing to be gained by resisting. Accept your destiny. You are meant to be his thrall. *Ave Satanas. Rege Satanas.*"

"No."

"Say the words. Say them!"

"No!"

The tip of the athame hovered at Guy's exposed chest. A drop of the goat's blood splashed onto his breastbone and dribbled down his sternum. It was still warm. Guy let out an involuntary shriek of revulsion.

The priest sprinkled more of the blood onto his skin. Then, with a fingertip, he drew an inverted pentagram onto Guy's chest, using the blood as paint.

"*Ave Satanas. Rege Satanas,*" he said. "Acknowledge the Dark One as your true lord and master for evermore. Step onto the left-hand path. Allow him into your life, give him your heart and soul, and you shall be rewarded with all the many blessings and bounties that are his to bestow."

"No... I don't want..."

"Don't fight it, Guy. Just repeat after me: *Ave Satanas. Rege Satanas.* That's all. Then it'll be over."

Guy's resolve was weakening. He could feel the blood congealing on his chest, tightening his skin as it dried. Maybe it would be best to do as the priest said. Admit defeat. Bow to the inevitable. Satan had been pursuing him for nearly a decade, flirting with him, trying to ensnare him. Or perhaps it was the other way round. Unwittingly, Guy had been chasing Satan. Milward's black mass. The Ouija session with Molly. Koh Maan. All along, Guy had been looking for the Devil as much as the Devil had been looking for him. He just hadn't realised it at the time. Why would Satan have singled him out, of all people, if it wasn't what Guy secretly desired? Satan must know what was going on deep in his heart. They were drawn to each other; they kept meeting; they were even related now, after a fashion, by marriage. Now, at last, was the moment of consummation. Why not, like a lover, submit?

"Where is he, then?" Guy said feebly. "Tell him to show himself. He must be here. If I'm going to pledge myself to him, I want to look him in the eye."

The priest reared back slightly, visibly flummoxed.

"We know each other," Guy went on. "Might as well do this in the open, face to face."

The priest darted a look across the chapel. Guy had his first clear sight of the man's face. It was oddly familiar. Those arched eyebrows. That neatly trimmed goatee. He was certain he knew this person, had seen him somewhere, and not that long ago either. A younger version. On television?

Something was wrong. All at once, things weren't adding up. The priest's hesitation. His vaguely recognisable features.

"Hang on a second," Guy said, bemused. "You're... him. From a film I saw."

The priest bowed his head, trying to hide himself in

the shadows of his hood, but it was too late. A guilty flicker in his eyes said he knew the game was up.

"A Hammer film. An old one. You were the baddie. BBC2 showed it the other day. You were... you were doing something like this."

Guy couldn't put a name to the face, but the man was a character actor, not terribly famous but remembered for a couple of suave-villain roles in the 'sixties. In the Hammer film, he had played a dissolute Edwardian aristocrat who used dark forces to seduce young virgins and steal their life essence in order to keep himself youthful and virile. He was eventually defeated by Peter Cushing or Christopher Lee, one or other of them, or possibly both, and his body withered and rotted away to dust while his soul went howling down to the deepest pit of damnation.

"Does this mean you're... really...?"

No. That didn't make sense. The actor wasn't a genuine Satanist. The more plausible explanation was that he was just an actor and this was a part.

Therefore...

Applause sounded from a corner of the chapel: a pair of hands clapping.

"Enough, ladies and gentlemen," said a voice – one which Guy had no difficulty whatsoever identifying. "We have been, as they say, rumbled. Our excellent, if rather elaborate, imposture is at an end."

One of the celebrants had stepped forward from the ranks. He lowered his hood, revealing the handsome, sleek and oh-so-self-satisfied head of Alastor Wylie.

Wylie smiled at Guy with all the lofty delight he could muster, which was a lot.

"I'm surprised you didn't twig sooner, to be honest," he said. "Didn't this all seem remarkably stagey to you? Contrived? No? I would have thought an astute, savvy young fellow like yourself would have seen through it in no time. This sort of thing never happens in real life, does it? Only in fictions. Or perhaps you believe it does, and that is why you were so readily taken in."

Guy could only gape. A part of him was wishing he could come up with some snappy riposte. Most of him, though, was too stunned to do anything cogent or clever.

"You've all performed admirably, my friends," Wylie said to the other celebrants, who were adopting relaxed, casual postures, their work done. "I appreciate your efforts. We've had some fun tonight, have we not?"

There were murmurs of assent and a ripple of self-congratulatory laughter.

"And you," Wylie said, addressing the ersatz priest. "A fine piece of thespianism. You still have what it takes, whatever anyone else might say. I will, as agreed, put in a word for you with a certain TV director-general of my acquaintance. Your career is far from at an end. And you." This to the celebrant who had slit the goat's neck. "I very much appreciate you bringing your agricultural expertise to the proceedings, and surrendering an item of your own livestock as well."

"Pleasure," said the man, posh-sounding but with a touch of a Gloucestershire burr. "You must try and get to the shoots more often, Alastor. We hardly see you these days."

"So busy, my dear chap." Wylie turned to the men who had made Guy their detainee. "And you, gentlemen of the Met. I hope this wasn't too arduous an exercise."

"Not at all, Mr Wylie," said their spokesman. "Prisoner couldn't have been any easier to handle. Trust me, we've dealt with far worse."

"I've no doubt you have." Wylie's gaze finally alighted on Guy again. "Well, dear boy. I hope you've learned your lesson. You'd do well to remember this, next time you contemplate humiliating me in front of my friends. I am not a man to be crossed lightly. Nor am I a man who forgives readily. You have got off relatively unscathed today. Were you not my beloved Beatrice's son, I might not have been quite as lenient. Test me again, and I definitely will not be."

He leaned closer, his voice dropping to a hiss.

"You seem to have got it into your head that I am some sort of Prince of Darkness," he said. "I am not. But what I am may be far worse. I am real, I have influence, and my reach is long and powerful. Better men than you have opposed me. Better men than you have lived to regret it."

He straightened again.

"Now go, Guy. Get out of my sight. And do not dare breathe a word of this to your mother. She wouldn't believe you anyway, and it would only make her think you are more of a fool than she presently does. Go.

"I said go!"

Guy scrambled to his feet and ran. He ran out of the ruined chapel, out into the grounds of the stately home which the chapel belonged to, out across greensward and estate, out into the open countryside, fields and woods, racing along with hot tears scoring his cheeks and shame and rage boiling in his chest, beneath stars whose twinkle openly mocked him, beneath the moon's lambent, scornful laugh.

1978

IT COULD HAVE been any south coast seaside town, and it could have been any fish and chip shop, and he could have been any youngish man working behind the counter, serving up battered cod and saveloys, dressed in white apron, checked trousers and embarrassing paper hat. It was an absolutely anonymous job in an absolutely anonymous place, and Guy was more than happy with that.

The routine was dull and unchanging, reassuringly so. Clock in every morning at eleven. Clean out the fryers. Set the cooking oil to heat up. Scrub the floor and the melamine tabletops. Dig a fresh catering-size bag of chips out of the freezer. Wait for the first customers to amble in. Work until late. Close up. Go home to bed. Repeat ad infinitum.

His boss was Mr Fernandinho, a Portuguese man who had come over to the UK after the war on a tourist visa and stayed. He was a squat, frog-faced man, bad-tempered but fair. Possibly he had imagined himself doing more with his life than doling out fried food for thirty years in a dilapidated English resort town that only came to life – and then just barely – during the summer months. But, if he felt he was a failure, he was philosophical about it, and when he was sharp with Guy he usually apologised soon after. Guy was a hard worker, conscientious and reliable, and there were far too few of his type around, so Mr Fernandinho couldn't afford to alienate him.

For Guy, it was all about the safe monotony of the job and the pleasure of never having to think. He lived in a first-floor bedsit a few streets inland from the promenade, and he had bought himself a portable colour telly and a kettle, and there was a second-hand bookshop close by, and this meant he had all that he needed. No one bothered him. No one much cared who he had been or where he had come from. To his neighbours, he was just a drifter who had breezed in last autumn, found himself lodging and employment, and wanted to be left alone.

He had lived in the town for over a year, and it was beginning to seem that he might remain permanently – a victim of inertia like Mr Fernandinho, an accidental fixture, someone who had, in every sense, settled.

Then Petra the Punk walked into his life.

STRICTLY SPEAKING, SHE walked into his workplace.

It was an October evening, midweek, blustery

out, a very slow night clientele-wise. The only other customers on the premises were an elderly couple – Mr and Mrs Arbuthnot, or Armstrong, something like that – who dined out at the chip shop once a week and always ordered the same, him haddock with mushy peas, her scampi and about a pint of vinegar on her chips. Both of them winced in disapproval when a girl with glue-spiked hair, Siouxsie Sioux eyeliner, bondage trousers and cherry-red Doc Martens clumped in through the door. News of the punk movement had reached even this bygone backwater, but an actual fully-fledged fan of the music was a rarity. It was a quiet town that didn't go in much for that sort of thing. The locals would probably have been less shocked by the sight of a Zulu tribesman in full war paint and battle regalia marching down the high street, brandishing his shield and assegai.

The punk girl sidled up to the counter and plonked her elbows on it. Her hands were sheathed in fingerless lace gloves. Metal studs rimmed one ear. The obligatory safety pin speared her nose. She wasn't tall, but she held herself as though she was, rising on her heels, her head and neck posturally correct. Guy was expecting her to affect an angry nasal drawl, just like Johnny Rotten, and was surprised when the voice that came out of her sounded polite and, well, normal.

"Large chips, please."

Instantly – and he couldn't for the life of himself tell why – he was smitten. With those three very mundane words, the punk girl somehow endeared herself to him and stirred the dormant ashes in his heart, kindling a glow.

"Er, yeah. Sure. Coming up." He poured a scoopful of chips onto a Styrofoam tray, and added a second scoopful. It was a bigger helping than Mr Fernandinho formally prescribed as "large," but as he wasn't present at that moment, it didn't matter. Guy bunged in a wooden chip fork and a sachet of tomato ketchup, then asked her about salt and vinegar.

"Nah," she said. "I like them *au naturel*."

"A chip purist," he said, parcelling the portion up in newspaper.

"You what?"

"I said... Never mind."

She frowned at him. Her eyes, amid all that kohl, were hazel with a hint of gold, and dazzlingly huge. Her skin was pale and, to Guy's reckoning, flawless.

"Are you taking the mick?" she said. "'Chip purist'?"

"Nope. Not at all. It was just an observation. Comment. Thing to say. Meant nothing by it."

"Should hope so, too."

"That'll be seventy-eight pee."

She handed over a one-pound note and he gave her change.

"So, erm..." he said as she turned to go.

"Yeah?"

"You new in town?"

"What's that supposed to mean? Why are you asking?"

"No reason. Just... asking. I haven't seen you before, that's all. Here, I mean." He waved his hands, indicating the shop.

"In your mighty domain," she said.

"Yes."

"Well, that's because I'm normally into gourmet dining. If it hasn't got a Michelin star, I'm not interested. I just thought this evening I'd see how the other half eat."

"Oh."

"You don't really believe that, do you?" she said with a derisive giggle. "You dolt."

"So you are new in town."

"So what if I am?" Her head tipped to one side, almost – almost – coquettishly.

"Then hello. Welcome. It's funny, nobody's ever called me a dolt before. Plenty of other things, but never a dolt."

"I was going to say something worse, but then, you know..." She clicked her mouth towards Mr and Mrs Arkwright, or whatever their surname was. "Didn't want to offend the pensioners."

"A punk who's scared of offending."

"That such a surprise? We're not all like the stereotyped idiots you see on TV, effing and blinding and gobbing."

"And pogoing," Guy added.

"Oh no, I pogo. If the guitars are thrashing and some skinny bloke is jumping up and down onstage snarling into a mike, I can't help myself. It's a thrill, when the music's loud and the crowd are going mental. But that doesn't make us all evil drooling monsters. It's like Sid says, 'We're really quite nice and friendly, but everyone has a beastly side to them, don't they?'"

"Ah, yes. Mr Vicious, the great sage of our times."

"He damn well is and all. He's wiser than you'll ever be. You ever listened to any of the Pistols' lyrics? Properly? No, you're too middle-of-the-road and boring, aren't you? Bet you like the Eagles and that Dire Straits. Maybe a bit of ABBA..."

"Hey!"

"Sorry. That was a low blow."

Before Guy could reply, Mr Fernandinho emerged from the back room.

"Why are you standing there gassing with the customers, Guy?" he snapped. "There's work to be done."

There patently wasn't. The restaurant was near empty. But Guy knew better than to argue with his boss. He grabbed a J-cloth and a can of Ajax powder. "I suppose the bins out back could do with a scrub."

"That's more like it."

The punk girl smiled and popped a chip into her mouth. "I'll let you get on with it, Guy." Calling him Guy seemed to amuse her, or maybe it was just that she now knew his name, while he still had no idea what hers was, and this gave her some obscure advantage over him.

As she left, Mrs Allbright (or whatever) loudly and openly tutted.

"Oh, *what*?" the girl said to her.

"Such a shame," the elderly woman said. "To see a pretty thing like you go to such lengths to make herself look so ugly."

"Better that than looking like a shrivelled-up old testicle like you."

The response was a sharp intake of breath and an aghast glare.

Guy hid a smile.

The girl turned on her heel and sashayed out of the shop.

She disappeared along the pavement. Then she backtracked to throw a glance in through the window. Catching Guy's gaze, she stuck her tongue all the way out like a kabuki performer, flicked him a cheery 'V,' then was gone again.

"We can do without her type," Mr Fernandinho muttered.

Guy felt quite the opposite.

ON HIS ONE day off a week, Guy liked to go for a stroll along the seafront, if the weather wasn't too foul. Today, it was only drizzling, and with the collar of his bomber jacket turned up, the chill was bearable.

He was passing one of the shelters that dotted the promenade at intervals when someone called out to him.

"Oi. Chip shop."

The punk girl was huddled on the bench inside the shelter, smoking.

"You," Guy said.

"Yeah, me. Fancy a fag?" She offered him a cigarette from a pack of Silk Cut.

"No, thanks. Bad for your health." Guy made to move on.

The girl rolled her eyes. "I'm asking you to come and sit next to me. It's called a cue. You can either pretend you do smoke, or you can say no, but come back with some kind of line like 'But I'll watch you finish yours.' Either way, you can at least be polite and give me five minutes of your time."

Guy thought for a moment. "But I'll watch you finish yours."

"That's my boy. It's Petra, by the way. In case you were wondering."

"What's Petra?" Guy said, lowering himself onto the bench's unforgiving wooden slats.

"My name, you twat."

"Petra as in the *Blue Peter* dog?"

"No, as in the ancient city in Jordan. Petra 'the rose-red city half as old as time.' Which is from a poem."

"I know. By John William Burgon. It's about the only thing he's famous for."

"Not just a pretty face," Petra said, and then kicked his shin with her steel-toecapped Doc Marten.

"Ouch! What did you do that for?"

"Petra the fucking *Blue Peter* dog," she snorted. "Arsehole."

Together, side by side, they watched the waves hurling themselves onto the shingle beach and shattering against the groynes. Seagulls stomped by, hunched and aggravated, the wind ruffling their feathers. The pain in Guy's shin slowly subsided.

"If you're such a smartypants," Petra said, puffing out a plume of smoke, "how come you're stuck here in the arse end of nowhere, working in a chippie? How come you're not making a mint as a merchant banker or a stockbroker or writing the world's greatest novel or something?"

"Long story."

"I look like I've got somewhere else to be?"

"Is that another cue?"

"He's learning."

"Well, you could say this is the right place for me," Guy told her. "Or you could say I'm here because it's about as far away from all the bullshit as I can get."

"What bullshit?"

"The bullshit of my life so far."

"You're running away from something. Hiding from something."

"Sort of."

"What?"

In reply, Guy said, "What about you? How come you've made here your home and you're not up in London, going to the 100 Club by night and hanging out at Sex on the King's Road by day?"

"Ooh, hark at you, professor of punk. Who says this is my home? Maybe I'm just passing through. And don't think I haven't noticed you avoiding my question."

"My answer is I'm not prepared to talk about it." He added, "Yet."

"Mr Mystery. Well, *my* answer is I've sort of run away too. From a bloke I was seeing. Right bastard. His idea of fun was getting off his face and kicking the shit out of me."

"A punk too?"

"Yeah, but a drunk and a druggie first and foremost. I loved him so much, which is why I stuck it out as long as I did. But when he nearly broke my arm one night, that was when the penny finally dropped. I knew I had to get out, otherwise next time he might kill me. And don't make that face."

"What face?"

"That sad goo-goo face. That feeling-sorry face. I don't want your pity. He was a cunt, and I was a twat for letting him be such a cunt to me. I betrayed my own principles." She shrugged. "You live and learn. You move on."

"You want to go to the cinema?" Guy said abruptly, surprising himself.

"No, ta."

"Okay."

She grunted in frustration. "Don't give up so easily, Guy. Never take no for a first answer when you ask a girl out. If she refuses three times in a row, then perhaps you should accept that she doesn't fancy you. But otherwise, keep trying."

"All right, so if I ask you a second time, you might say yes?"

"Give it a whirl."

"You want to go to the cinema?"

"No."

He was crestfallen.

Petra laughed. "Just teasing. Your expression! Priceless. Yes, let's go to the cinema. There's fuck all else to do in this dump, is there?"

THE TOWN'S CINEMA was old and musty-smelling, with a leaking roof and seats whose stuffing crunched when you sat down. They went to a matinee showing of *Midnight Express*, which was all that was on, and afterwards Petra said, "Well, this clearly isn't a date, because you just took me to the most gruelling, depressing film ever and now I want to slash my wrists," but with a smile, because it clearly *was* a date. Then they went to the amusement arcade and shovelled ten-pence pieces into the Space Invaders machine. Petra was pretty good at the game, whereas Guy struggled to clear even a single screen.

As the sky darkened, they moved on to a pub, The Anchor, where Petra drew stares and the occasional snarky aside.

"Oy-oy, freak show's in town," someone muttered, while someone else said, "Why don't you get in your spaceship and go back to the planet Zarg?"

"Doesn't it bother you?" Guy asked her as they carried their drinks to a quiet corner table. "People making snide comments all the time?"

"If it did, would I dress like this?" she replied. "It's just the look they object to, not me. And that's because *they're cowardly conformist wankers.*" She raised her voice loud enough so that everyone in the pub would know they were being referred to. Lowering it again, she said, "I hate sheep. People who follow unthinkingly, like this lot, with their jeans and their conservative attitudes and their complete lack of imagination."

"Aren't you a follower yourself? I mean of punk."

"Ah, punk's just a fashion statement. It'll have its day and then something else will come along. Already there's people in London dressing like the opposite of punk: frills and flounces and buccaneer boots. They all gather at the Blitz Club and Billy's and dance to glam rock records. That'll probably be the next wave, with bands writing songs that sound like glam but different, just like punk's like rock-and-roll but different, and then there'll be something else, and something else after that. I choose to be a punk but I won't be one forever. I pick whatever suits my mindset at the time. People who follow trends slavishly, unthinkingly, just because it's cool – they despise themselves. They have no self-worth. They get their identity from something outside themselves. Not me. Whatever I wear, I'm still me inside and that'll never change."

"Petra. From the Greek for 'rock.'"

"Look, we already know you're educated. No need to show off."

"I think it suits you. You're stable. Grounded. Solid. Like a rock, you won't be worn down."

"Are you using flattery to try and get into my knickers?" She peered at him over the rim of her lager glass.

"I don't know," he said cagily. "Is it working?"

"You might be better off telling me I'm pretty, not comparing me to a fucking bit of stone."

"You *are* pretty. And the 'rock' thing really was meant as a compliment. I've known some flaky girls in my time."

"Some rocks can be flaky."

"Not the type you are." Guy was beginning to wonder if anything he ever said to Petra would go unchallenged. Her personality was as spiky as her hair. For all that, he was enjoying the cut-and-thrust of the conversation. He didn't even mind that she always seemed to win. "You're... you're granite."

"I'll jot that one down in my diary. 'Dear diary, today a boy said I was granite. I really want to shag him now.'"

"Do you?"

"Buy me another pint and we'll see."

THEY STAGGERED TO his bedsit. Petra mocked the state of the room, the mess of unlaundered clothes, the narrowness of the single bed. Then they kissed, they fumbled each other to nakedness, they fell onto the bed, they fucked as ardently and urgently as any two people ever had.

Afterwards, while Petra enjoyed a postcoital cigarette, Guy examined her body in detail. He hadn't had a chance to in the throes of passion. She had small pert breasts, a smooth flat belly, wide generous hips, a tidy pubic thatch, and there on the inside of her left thigh...

Guy recoiled as if stung by a scorpion.

"Oh, fuck. Oh, Jesus," he breathed. "What – what the hell is that?"

Petra looked down. "What? Oh, my tattoo, you mean."

"Yes. Your fucking tattoo." He sprang off the bed, backing away from her. He was trembling. His balls had clenched up to the size of broad beans.

"Guy, what's got into you?"

"That!" He pointed agitatedly at her leg. The tattoo was small, no larger than a two-pence piece. From a distance you could have mistaken it for a mole or some other sort of blemish. "That thing. Christ in heaven, what are you doing with that on you?"

Petra peered at him, puzzled by his reaction. "It's not what you think."

"Isn't it? Because what I think..." Guy was aware that he had begun to hyperventilate. He fought to steady his breathing. "What I think is that you've got a fucking inverted pentagram on your skin."

All at once he was back in the ruined chapel. He was being anointed with goat's blood. He was being made the butt of Alastor Wylie's extravagant practical joke. The terror, the humiliation, the indignity, the seething rage – all the emotions that the incident had aroused, and which he had fought to put behind him, came flooding back. He could feel the priest's finger inscribing the warm wet pattern on his chest, feel it as thought it was happening right now, again. He was sweating all over. He could barely bring himself to look at the pentagram on Petra's thigh – barely bring himself to look at *her*.

Petra stubbed out her cigarette. "Calm down," she said. "Come here."

He couldn't move.

"Come here," she insisted.

Reluctantly he walked over.

"Sit. Relax."

He perched on the edge of the bed, still trembling. "How could I have missed it?" he murmured. "You're – you're one of his minions. Must be. You've finally come for me."

"One, I'm nobody's minion," Petra corrected him flatly. "And two, I haven't 'come for you,' whatever that's supposed to mean. Stop babbling and look at me, Guy. Look me in the eye."

He did.

"What's scared you?" She tapped the tattoo. "What does this represent for you?"

"Bad things. Very bad things."

"You've some kind of history with it?"

"Yeah. Stuff that's happened throughout my life."

"Want to tell me about it?"

"No."

"You can, you know."

"No. You tell me."

"Tell you what? Why I have the tattoo?"

"Yes."

"All right," she said. "If it'll help."

"But I warn you. I'm this close to kicking you out."

She was unimpressed by the threat. "I'd like to see you try. I've never left anywhere against my will." She lit a fresh cigarette from the tip of the one still in her mouth. "So, you reckon I'm a Devil worshipper? Is that what the pentagram says to you?"

He nodded.

"Well, you're wrong," Petra said. "Robes, virgin sacrifices, all that Dennis Wheatley guff – that's Satanism, right? But only if you believe that Satan is an actual being. You know, the Fallen Angel, God's shadow, ruler of Hell, the personification of evil, all that malarkey. That kind of Satanism is called theistic, and it is, not to put too fine a point on it, a load of old bollocks. Satan the ultimate bad guy is a fabrication of the Church. He's a propaganda tool, a bogeyman used to frighten people into having faith and going to Sunday services and donating to the collection and being good little robots."

"He's not," said Guy. "I've..."

"You've...?" she prompted. "You've met him? Is that it? Have you? Really?"

He was going to say *yes*, but settled for, "I may have."

Petra eyed him speculatively. "Maybe you think you have. Maybe all you did was come face to face with yourself."

"Eh?"

"The other kind of Satanism, you see, is atheistic Satanism. It says there's no such thing as Satan, no supernatural deity with that name. There are no gods at all. There's just us. To follow God or any other supposedly divine entity is to deny life. It's surrendering your humanity, and everything that makes you interesting and useful as an individual. It's abdicating responsibility for your actions and offloading it onto someone else."

"It's bad, then."

"It's not constructive, put it that way. Atheistic Satanism says bugger to all that. Be yourself. Be here on Earth. Enjoy yourself. Don't cower in fear of divine judgement, either here or in some mythical afterlife which doesn't exist. Listen to your heart, indulge your desires, have fun, *live*. It's a philosophy, not a religion, and you can boil its message down to a single sentence."

"Which is?"

"'Do unto others as they do unto you.' If someone loves you, love them back. If someone despises you, ignore them unless they're actively trying to harm you, in which case neutralise them."

"Well, it's certainly shorter and pithier than the Ten Commandments," said Guy.

"Oh, there are other rules," said Petra. "I'm just giving you the *Readers' Digest* version. Hopefully this is helping you calm down so you can stop having this big girly hissy fit."

"I don't know."

"I just don't want you getting the impression that I'm some boggle-eyed lunatic who bites the heads off bats and has lots of strange leather-bound books at home. I'm not. I'm completely sane, and I dare say better adjusted than ninety-nine per cent of

Christians. I mean, holy wars. What's that all about? Christians seem to spend half their time killing other Christians, or failing that people from different religions, all in the name of a supposedly loving God. It's like Pascal said: 'Men never commit evil so fully and joyfully as when they do it for religious convictions.' Look at the Irish situation – Catholics versus Protestants. It's all so pointless, and it could end tomorrow if everyone stopped blowing each other up because they think God wants them to and started being true to their own natures instead."

"That's a pretty simplistic view of the problem. There's politics, history, territorialism..."

"But when you get down to it," she said, overriding him, "almost every conflict is a clash of ideologies. And if you dispense with all forms of orthodoxy – politics, nationalism, and especially religion – then what you're left with is just people, human beings, and human beings by and large want to coexist in peace. They don't want endless death and mayhem. It's common sense."

"And that's what your pentagram represents?" Guy said. "All of what you've just said?"

"And more, but in essence, yes. It's a reminder, a secret token of commitment. Believe me?"

Guy found it hard to look at the tattoo. This was not helped by the fact that it was in such distractingly close proximity to Petra's pussy. He made a conscious effort to focus on the pentagram and not the erotic, enticing pink-lipped slit just a few inches away.

The tattoo was tiny and innocent, just lines etched in ink. Merely a symbol.

"Can I touch it?" he asked.

Amused, Petra popped the stub of her second cigarette in the empty Skol can she was using as an ashtray. "Go on, then. If it'll make you feel better."

Guy placed a forefinger on her skin. Ludicrously, he anticipated some kind of reaction within himself, revulsion, nausea, something like that, or perhaps a sudden burning sensation in his fingertip, as though the tattoo was magically empowered and liable to scorch those who were intimidated by it. But there was nothing, just the soft warmth of a woman's inner thigh.

"You know what would make *me* feel better?" Petra said.

"No."

"If you slide your finger up a bit. Go on. And a bit further."

"Like that?" said Guy, obliging.

"Yes," she purred. "Just like that. A bit further still. Oh, yes."

LITTLE BY LITTLE over the next few weeks, Petra explained her form of Satanism to Guy. She never lectured or hectored. She simply answered when he asked, laying out the fundamentals and leaving him to digest them.

She told him she had started out as a student of the writings of Anton LaVey, the American occultist who ran his own Church of Satan in California and had published two key books, *The Satanic Bible* and *The Satanic Rituals*, neither of which Guy had heard of. Somehow the eccentric and inconsistent Mr Ingram had not seen fit to stock them at Shamballa (...And Other Dreams). She told Guy about LaVey's notion that Satan was the "Black Flame" that burned inside every person, the embodiment of will, a source of great inner power if you knew how to tap it. She talked about the Nine Satanic Statements, a kind of secular Apostles' Creed, and the Eleven Satanic Rules of the Earth, a repudiation of the Ten Commandments. There was also a list of Nine Satanic Sins, among them Stupidity, Pretentiousness, Self-Deceit, Herd Conformity, Lack of Aesthetics – things to be avoided if you wished to lead a productive, fulfilling life.

Petra had eventually drifted away from LaVey's ideas. There was an undercurrent of selfishness there, a peculiarly American brand of *fuck you* which didn't sit well with her. Plus, given that the whole point of LaVeyan Satanism was to foster self-reliance and individuality, then it was necessary, even obligatory, to turn your back on your teacher and find your own way. LaVey had provided her with a template to work from, at least. The rest was down to her.

She was a rational, pragmatic person, so LaVey's penchant for magical rites also held little appeal. She acknowledged that they served a function as psychodramas, enabling one to work through frustrations and mental blocks and emerge the other side with a clearer head and a healthier outlook. She felt, however, that enlightenment could come simply from approaching a problem carefully and with an open mind, confident in your own ability to resolve it.

"The universe is amoral," she said. "It doesn't care how we behave or what we do. The only truths are inner truths. Answers don't come from outside, from other people or some nebulous supreme being. They come from within."

Guy, for his part, began revealing his past to her, particularly his repeated encounters with what he thought must be the Devil. In each instance Petra was able to offer a plausible rationale, showing him that he hadn't in fact bumped into Beelzebub but had instead misinterpreted the experience and seen demonic influence where there was none. Molly Rosenkrantz, for example, had obviously been unhinged, quite conceivably schizophrenic, or at the very least so obsessive and insecure that she had faked being possessed by an evil spirit in order to tighten her hold over Guy. When that had had the opposite outcome, scaring him off, she had got desperate and resorted to the razor blade. And as for his vision of Alastor Wylie on the beach in Thailand, what drug was it he had taken? LSD? Ahem! That was a great big clue right there. Wylie had been busy elbowing his way into Guy's life. Guy had had no wish for him to usurp the role of his late father. So his subconscious mind, liberated by the acid, had recast Wylie as the Devil. His id had been communicating its feelings to his ego in the way it knew best: through symbolism. There was nothing more to it than that.

"But Clive Milward?" Guy said. "He died in a fire. It was as if..."

"As if Satan was punishing him?"

"Well, yes."

Petra snorted. "No, that was just what it was, a teenager disposing of a fag butt carelessly and setting the place alight by accident. I'll tell you what's instructive about that whole incident at school. You got those three boys expelled. You, Guy Lucas, were the agent of their downfall. Nobody else had anything to do with it, and that includes Satan. You triumphed. You did exactly what had to be done. They got their just deserts. That was the Satan here" – she jabbed Guy's chest – "the Black Flame inside you, doing its job. Your stepdad seems to know a thing or two about that."

"Don't call him that. Stepdad. Ugh."

"Your mother's husband, then. Wylie. That whole sham ritual he put together – he got you back, good and proper. That's how it works. Someone fucks with you, you fuck with them in return, at an appropriate level, to ensure they never do it again. No wonder he's such a big cheese in the government. From what you've said about him, Wylie's got Satanism down pat, even if he'd never call it that himself. He's manipulative and shrewd, and I'm sure he never has a moment of self-doubt. He gets what he goes for. He makes the most of his life. He succeeds."

"You sound like you admire him."

"Subjectively, because of what he did to you, I think he's a big fat turd," Petra said. "But objectively, I have to say there's a lot to like about the way he operates. If only he had more of a conscience, Alastor Wylie is the sort of man who could change the world for the better."

AUTUMN GREYED INTO winter, and Guy fell ever more deeply under Petra's spell. She seemed to be the person he had been waiting for all his adult life, the one who came along and made everything clearer, the one who spoke sense and put the world into perspective. He began to be unable to imagine himself without her. His dead-end job in a dead-end town became immaterial. Life was infinitely rich with Petra around.

As Christmas approached, Guy grew convinced that he had found his soulmate. He started to do something he had long since given up doing: making plans for the future. In all of them, Petra featured centrally.

Then, one gusty Saturday afternoon, the Mods rolled into town.

They came in a swarm of buzzing Vespas and Lambrettas, each scooter adorned with a plethora of rearview mirrors like elaborate chrome antlers. There had been fights all along the south coast that year, in places like Brighton and Hastings, gangs of Mods and Rockers coming down from London to clash on the beaches, a revival of a noble tradition going back to the 'sixties and the antagonism between the original Young Moderns and their mortal enemies the Teddy Boys. This particular group were out for a scuffle, but had apparently got lost on their way to the venue. Either that or they were simply enjoying a weekend jaunt to the seaside, although it seemed unlikely. The way they meandered up and down the seafront road on their scooters in close formation, now and then one of them veering across the white lines into the opposite lane, carried unmistakable menace. They were troublemakers, no doubt about it. Whatever they had in mind would be fun for them, but not for anyone else.

Soon enough they got bored of parading around. Hunger drove them to seek food. Mr Fernandinho's chippie was the place they chose to find sustenance.

They entered, all nine of them, with their crash helmets tucked under their arms, bumping tables 'accidentally' with their hips, kicking chair legs. Mr Fernandinho treated them diplomatically, which was out of character for him. He addressed them as 'gentlemen' and enquired politely how he might help.

"Cod and chips all round," said the tallest, skinniest Mod, whose parka bore Union Jack patches, a large RAF roundel on the back, and The Jam's logo, drawn on the sleeve painstakingly in marker pen. His short centre-parted haircut was an almost exact replica of Paul Weller's.

"Guy, you heard the gentlemen," said Mr Fernandinho. "Look lively."

While Guy fried the fish, there was more laddish rowdiness from the Mods. A sugar dispenser crashed to the floor, shattering to pieces. Mr Fernandinho hurried over with brush and dustpan, saying it was nothing, these things happened, never mind, no harm done. Guy just counted down the seconds until the meals were ready and the Mods were gone. The young men had brought an ugly mood with them into the chip shop – along with the smells of unwashed parka and diesel fumes – and he couldn't wait for them to take it away again.

"What are you looking at, twat?" one of them demanded, scowling.

"Nothing," said Guy. "Food's almost ready. That'll be eleven pounds twenty, all in."

"Eleven quid twenty," the Mod said to his friends. "Who's got cash? Anyone?"

Heads were shaken. There were smirking, insolent looks all round. The Mods had never had any intention of paying.

"Tell you what, gents," said Mr Fernandinho. "First-time customers get a free meal."

"What you saying, you little brown shrimp?" snarled the tall Mod, whom Guy had to assume was the leader of the pack. "You think we can't afford your crappy grub? You think we're a bunch of tramps or something?"

"Not at all," said Mr Fernandinho, retreating back behind the serving counter. "It's my usual offer. Open to everyone."

"Here," said Guy, placing the last of nine newspaper-wrapped parcels on the countertop. "All ready. *Bon appétit.*"

"Ooh-la-la!" said the Mods' leader archly. "'Bon appy-tee.' Very sophisticated they are in this town."

"Why's it such a fucking shithole then?" one of the gang remarked. "Nobody around. Rubbish little beach. Hasn't even got a fucking pier. Whoever heard of a seaside town doesn't have a fucking pier?"

"Come on, let's go," said another of them. "I'm ruddy starving."

The Mods gathered up their meals and, to the great relief of Guy and Mr Fernandinho, made for the door.

By terrible coincidence, that was when Petra arrived.

She often dropped by, usually during Guy's break hour, so the two of them could go and get a bite to eat or else just sit and chat while she had a cigarette. Mr Fernandinho still didn't approve of her, but knew he had to put up with her. He was loath to ban her from the chip shop in case his best and only employee took umbrage and resigned.

Guy spotted Petra through the window, saw how the Mods reacted to the sight of her, and knew instantly how things were going to pan out. It had the crushing inevitability of a traffic accident, a juggernaut on a collision course with a car, nothing anyone could do to prevent it happening.

"Hello, what's this?" said the Mods' leader, looming over Petra. "A fucking human hedgehog."

The others cackled.

Petra ducked her head and skirted round the gang. Guy sent up a small prayer of thanks that for once she had elected to keep her mouth shut.

Then one of the Mods grabbed her arm.

"Here, darling," he said and made smoochy noises. "How about a snog? I don't normally fancy your sort, but for you I'll make an exception."

Guy began to move around the counter, picking up a mop as he went, the first weapon that came to hand. Mr Fernandinho waylaid him. "No. Not wise."

"Sod that," Guy said, brushing his boss aside. "I have to help her."

Petra looked up at the Mod gripping tightly on her forearm. "Let go of me," she said, coming across as remarkably calm.

"Snog first."

"I'd rather kiss a dog's arse, you tosser."

A couple of the Mods chortled. "That's funny," one said. "The last thing Graham kissed *was* a dog's arse."

Graham rounded on his colleague. "Shut it, you nob." He turned back to Petra. "In that case, how about a fuck? I've heard about you punk birds. You're slags. Gagging for it all the time. I'll do you, only it'll have to be from behind so's I don't have to look at all them safety pins and whatnot, 'cause they're right off-putting."

"How are you going to manage that with nuts the size of a football?" Petra asked.

"I'm sorry, you what?"

"I said..."

And she kneed him in the groin.

Graham the Mod let out a wheezing gasp and sank to the ground, clutching himself between the legs.

Petra spun round and headed for the chip shop

doorway. Guy was nearly there, the mop brandished like a quarterstaff.

"Get inside! Quick!" he urged her. As soon as she was across the threshold he would lock and bolt the door, then phone the police.

She almost made it.

The gang leader got in her way and brought her down with a punch to the face. As Petra fell, she made a sound halfway between a shriek and a groan. Guy propelled himself through the doorway, not caring what might happen next, not even thinking about his own safety. He rammed the mop at the Mod like a lance, only to find that in all the excitement he was holding it with the head forwards. The clump of thick cotton strings had almost no effect on the Mod, other than pissing him off.

"Seriously?" he said, glancing down at the mop then back up at Guy. "You arsehole."

He snatched the mop out of Guy's grasp, snapped the handle in two across his thigh, and tossed both halves aside. Then he loosed off a roundhouse that laid Guy flat.

Guy had never been hit so hard before, not even when the three bullies had beaten him up at Scarsworth Hall. He rolled on the pavement, unmanned by the impact and the searing pain. He couldn't get up. He just wanted to curl into a foetal ball and never be hit again.

Sadly, the Mods felt differently. They started raining down kicks and stamps on him. Guy's flailing hands seized hold of a foot and he tried to flip its owner over, but another of the Mods booted his elbow and his arm went numb and he had to let go. He could dimly hear Petra screaming, telling the Mods to stop, leave her boyfriend alone. Through the forest of kicking legs he saw her snatch up a discarded crash helmet and swing it at the gang leader's head. The man was hardly fazed; he evidently had a pretty thick skull. He swivelled round and belted Petra in the belly.

The blow bent her double. As she sank to her knees, heaving for breath, the Mod grabbed a handful of her hair spikes and began dragging her. Petra scrabbled for purchase with her heels as he hauled her round the side of the chip shop, into the narrow alleyway that ran between it and the seaside souvenirs emporium next door. Guy scrambled frantically after her on all fours, but a toecap came up under into his midriff and he was sent flying over onto his side. He sprawled in the gutter, winded, paralysed with agony, while the Mods hurried off laughing to join their leader in the alleyway.

The sounds Guy heard then – the tearing of clothes, Petra's rasping screeches of protest, the Mods' inane chuckling – would haunt him for many days to come. He peered up and down the street. It was deserted. Where was everyone? Why wasn't anyone doing anything? Where were the fucking police? Surely someone must have called them by now.

With a Herculean effort, he raised himself to his knees. He spied one half of the broken mop handle nearby. He reached for it, at the same time pushing himself fully upright. The world teetered. The road seemed to rise and fall beneath him. He walked. Every step was a battle, as though he were aboard a ship pitching up and down in a storm. Yet he staggered on.

In the alleyway, most of the Mods were gathered in a knot, shoulder to shoulder, looking on. Beyond them, the gang leader was crouched over Petra, his jeans down, pumping away at her from the rear. Petra lay prone on the sordid brick floor of the alleyway. Her battered, bloodied face wore a look of numb resignation, her mouth hanging loose with disgust. Her whole body jerked each time the Mod thrust into her.

The other Mods were agog, mesmerised by the act of rape, so much so that they barely registered as Guy elbowed his way through. It was only when he reached the front that they realised he wasn't one of their own kind, and by then it was too late.

Guy raised the mop handle above his head with the splintered end pointing downwards. He drove it, hard as he could, into the gang leader's back, using the roundel on his parka as a target.

Bullseye.

The Mod spasmed as though electrified. He tumbled away from Petra, his erect, shit-stained cock flapping wildly. He tried reaching for the mop handle spearing him from behind, but couldn't pull it out. Eventually he collapsed against a dustbin, choking and mewling.

The *nee-naw*, *nee-naw* of a panda car siren skirled above the rooftops, growing louder. One of the

Mods yelled, "Fuck, it's the fuzz!" and they all fled, haring to their scooters.

Guy didn't give a toss about them any more. He crawled over to Petra. There was blood leaking from between her buttocks. He took off his jacket and draped it over her, and he stayed there, hugging her to him, sobbing, until a police officer found them.

AT THE HOSPITAL, Petra lay unconscious, sedated. She had had to have surgery, five stitches, but the prognosis was good. There was no reason why she shouldn't make a full physical recovery.

Guy's injuries were seen to, too. He sported some atrocious contusions and abrasions but, aside from pain and stiffness, he was fine. Nothing broken or ruptured.

The Mod he had stabbed was also there, in the intensive care ward. The doctors were unsure if the man would walk again. The mop handle had partly severed his spinal nerve. "Frankly, if he's left a cripple," a consultant confided to Guy, "it's no more than the bastard deserves."

When Guy had finished giving his statement to a detective sergeant, he was allowed to go free. He stayed by Petra's bedside through the night until dawn. He didn't sleep a wink.

It would be fair to say that that long, lonely vigil was a pivotal moment in Guy's life. He thought again and again about the Mods' vicious, mindless assault. He thought about tribes and factions, confrontation and hatred. He thought about his father, dead now for over a decade, victim of the worst kind of irony, murdered while on a mission to broker peace. He thought about the bigger picture, the blocs the world was divided into, the ever-present threat of nuclear obliteration, the insanity of the superpowers' doctrine of mutually assured destruction. He thought about individuals, who only wanted peace, and collectives, who seemed hell bent on war, a seemingly intractable paradox.

Come the morning, he had arrived at a turning point. A decisive moment.

He went in search of a pay phone.

He didn't have a great deal of change on him, but that didn't matter. He dialled 100.

"Operator. How may I help?"

"Yes, I'd like to make a reverse charge call please," Guy said.

"What number to?"

"It's an oh-one London number." He reeled off seven digits.

"And who shall I say is calling?"

"Guy Lucas."

The distant burr of a phone ringing. Finally, a click of connection.

"Hello? This is the operator. I have a call for you from a Guy Lucas. Will you accept the charge?"

Silence. Then a grumbled, "Very well."

"Putting you through now, sir," the operator said chirpily to Guy.

"Alastor?" Guy said into the receiver. "It's your stepson. I'd like to talk."

"Guy," said Wylie. "I'm not sure you and I have much to say to one another."

"Please, hear me out."

"Do you know what time it is? I happen to have been up half the night trying to sort out this bloody public sector pay chaos. We're in for a wretched bloody winter if this nonsense carries on much longer."

"It is early, and I apologise for that."

"Hmm. Well, that's something, I suppose," said Wylie, partly mollified. "An apology. Are you after your mother? She's still asleep upstairs."

"No, it's you I want," Guy said.

"Curiouser and curiouser. Well? What is it you'd like to talk about?"

"Me. Us. The future. *My* future."

A pause, then Wylie said, "Interesting. Do go on."

2013

Guy Lucas sat back in the plush leather back seat of the Jaguar XJ Sentinel with a sigh and folded his hands across his belly. Through his silk shirt, he could feel a roll of flab like a lifebelt, quivering with the vibration of the idling engine. He was softer around the middle these days, no question. His wife kept hinting that he should lose some weight, and a couple of his aides and advisers actively nagged him to do so. It wasn't good image control to appear bulky and *contented*. People might get the wrong idea.

But Guy didn't care. Fuck image control. He was pushing sixty, damn it, and could be forgiven for carrying a few extra pounds at that age. Besides, the public liked him just the way he was. They could relate to him precisely because he wasn't movie-star svelte and toned.

So, no, he wouldn't flog himself half to death on

an exercise bike or forgo chocolate biscuits and the nightly glass of red. What was life without the small pleasures? No life at all.

It was over a glass of red – Château Lafite Rothschild Pauillac, to be precise – that he and Alastor Wylie arrived at a rapprochement, back in 1979, at the turn of the new year. Guy went to Wylie in the manner of a supplicant, humble, on bended knee. He asked for forgiveness. He apologised for his previous behaviour. He had had time to think, he said. To reconsider. He was not the callow, opinionated, misguided youth he used to be. He had had some troubled years that had given birth to some, ahem, eccentric ideas. He regretted that. He was saner now. He saw things more clearly.

"The prodigal returns," said Wylie. He smiled sleekly. "I had a feeling this would happen sooner or later. We're all allowed to be young and wayward, but there comes a time when a man must shoulder responsibility and enter adulthood. You've taken longer than most, but you're here now. What can I do for you? What do you want from me?"

Guy smiled sleekly too. "I want you to take me under your wing, Alastor. I want you to be my mentor. Teach me all you know. I'm ready to learn."

The chauffeur engaged gear and the Jaguar pulled away from the kerb. Cameras flashed. Journalists clamoured. "This way, Guy!" "Go on, give us a smile!" Within moments the car had reached the end of Downing Street. The huge black steel security gates which had been erected in 1989 were no longer there. Guy had ordered them to be dismantled in 2006, shortly after he began his third term in office. He had called them, rightly, redundant.

It was in that same year that Guy had decreed that he would no longer travel around in specially modified vehicles. The Jaguar he was currently riding in was an ordinary factory model that had come straight off the production line, with no Kevlar lining or bulletproof polycarbonate glass installed. The man behind the wheel was not a special forces close protection driver, but just an ordinary professional chauffeur. His name was Derek, and he was, by his own admission, one of Guy's biggest admirers.

"What you've done for this country, Mr Lucas," Derek once told him, "well, it fair brings a tear to the eye. Not to be a crawler or anything, but you, sir, have put the *great* back in Great Britain."

Today was a momentous occasion, and the usually chatty Derek maintained a respectful silence. He turned left out of Downing Street, onto Whitehall, and guided the Jaguar slowly and sedately north towards Trafalgar Square.

MARGARET THATCHER CAME to power in 1979, the Tories riding a massive upswing in popularity after the disastrous so-called Winter of Discontent and the collapse of the Labour Party. Those in the know credited Alastor Wylie, at least in part, for her success.

Guy spent most of the 1980s scurrying around Westminster in a variety of menial roles – personal assistant to so-and-so, private secretary to such-and-such. Wherever Wylie sent him, he went. Whatever Wylie instructed him to do, he did.

It was hard work, and not always gratifying, but he made useful contacts and got himself known. He also established a functioning relationship with his stepfather, much to his mother's delight.

It helped that he had a devoted, stable girlfriend he could lean on when he got tired and stressed and life seemed too much like drudgery. Petra – tasteful makeup, big shoulder pads, blonde-streaked Princess Diana hairstyle, showing not a trace of the punk she had once been, apart from a tiny piercing scar in her nose – was endlessly encouraging and supportive during these years of struggle and consolidation. She kept Guy on course during the times when he began to doubt himself and wonder whether it was all worth it. She helped him screw his courage to the sticking place.

The day he got an inverted pentagram tattoo to match hers, Petra held his hand. It was done in secret, on a trip to Paris, in some back-alley parlour where nobody recognised him. It bloody well hurt, but Guy was no stranger to pain.

Petra also held his hand on a more public occasion: the day they got married, 26th June 1985, in a costly, elaborate service which was conducted at St Mark's Church in Regent's Park and paid for, in full, by Alastor Wylie. Countless politicians, tycoons and society bigwigs attended. The event marked Guy out, once and for all, as someone to watch, a face of the future, while his bride looked, of course, radiant.

As the Jaguar cruised up the broad canyon of Whitehall, Guy acknowledged the cheers of the crowds lining the pavements. Over the decades, a couple of dozen of prime ministerial motorcades had plied the same route and barely caused a stir. But Guy Lucas was not just any prime minister, and a fifth successive election win – yet another landslide victory – was hardly going to go unnoticed and uncelebrated. Union Jacks fluttered. His name was chanted. In order that as many people as possible saw his face, he even wound down the window and leaned out.

"*I* didn't win," he called out over the roars of approbation. "We all did."

While Guy was learning the political ropes, he was also covertly seeking out allies, likeminded souls, people he felt could be fellow-travellers on the journey he was planning on taking. It was a long, cautious, sometimes tedious process. Quiet chats in the Pugin Room at the Commons. Quick asides in a corridor. Dinner-party conversations that strayed, ever so artfully, down esoteric byways.

Always he deferred to Petra in matters of character judgement. She, better than he ever could, knew how to distinguish sincerity from fraud. She ruthlessly rooted out the phonies, the yes-men, the ones who seemed sympathetic and compatible but would, in truth, say anything to gain advancement. Plenty of people clung to Guy, because he was a comet, rising fast, spectacularly full of promise, but not all of them were trustworthy or without self-interest. Petra, a bullshit detector *par excellence*, never once steered him wrong. With her aid, Guy secured allegiances that would stand him in good stead later on.

In the meantime she raised their children, Beattie and Alex, and played the dutiful wife at drinks parties, Commons functions, and weekend stays in the country. She flirted outrageously with the older MPs and simpered winsomely with other parliamentary wives, sharing their complaints about the punishing hours their husbands worked, the long absences from home, the tendency towards alcoholism.

Sometimes, just sometimes, Guy might catch a tinge of anger or melancholy on her face and knew she was recalling that awful day in '78 when the Mods came to town. But she was strong. She was a hell of a strong woman. She knew how to adapt and survive.

And their mission was as important to her as it was to him, if not more so. They had made a pact in the hospital, as soon as Petra had recovered from the anaesthetic and her mind was clear. This was what they would do. Whatever it took, whatever it cost them, this was their path together.

*   *   *

TRAFALGAR SQUARE WAS packed, too. People clambered up onto Landseer's lions to get a better view. The Jaguar rolled under Admiralty Arch and into the Mall, where there were yet more crowds. Guy saw placards. Many carried his name – WE ♥ YOU GUY and so on – while others sported the Black Flame Party logo, an upward-pointing black arrow on a bright red background.

Guy recalled the day Petra had sketched it on a notepad in their kitchen.

"ISN'T IT A bit, well, Nazi?" he said.

"It's simple," she replied. "It's striking. Unforgettable."

"And calling ourselves the Black Flame? Won't that give the wrong impression? People will only have to look up what it means, and..."

"We're not going to make any secret what we're about," Petra said. "That's the whole point. Absolute honesty, absolutely all of the time."

It was 1989. The Falklands War was beginning to recede from memory. So was the Enniskillen bombing. The conflict between Iran and Iraq had petered out. The Berlin Wall had come down. The Cold War was thawing out.

Change was in the air. It was time to make their move.

*   *   *

"DEREK, STOP THE car," Guy said.

"Right you are, Mr Lucas."

Guy climbed out of the Jaguar. The crowds went wild. He signed autographs, kissed babies, posed for cameraphone pictures, shook hands until his knuckles ached. Someone offered him a toke on a spliff. "Way of saying thanks, mate. Ten years of decriminalisation. Personal responsibility, yeah? We're all grown-ups."

"Yes," said Guy, and drew deeply on the joint.

Half a mile away, at Buckingham Palace, the Queen was waiting.

She would just have to wait a little while longer.

THATCHER WAS OUSTED in 1990, undermined and betrayed by her own Cabinet. The Conservatives limped on under John Major. Labour was still in disarray, riddled with infighting and indecision.

A new political party emerged seemingly from nowhere. Disaffected MPs on both sides of the House were drawn to it like iron filings to a magnet. Its policies were brutally, brilliantly forthright. Its manifesto, in a nutshell, was: *Do unto others as they do unto you*.

AS GUY RETURNED to the Jaguar, he couldn't help grinning. It wasn't just the dope. He was remembering how Wylie had laid into him one evening in the Strangers' Bar. Wylie was patently drunk, which was unlike him. Hitherto he had always struck Guy as a man who could hold his liquor. Tonight he had imbibed more liquor than he could hold, and Guy could guess the reason.

"What's this?" Wylie slurred. "What the hell's going on? You and your cronies have formed a new party. Isn't two enough? Or three if you count the Liberals, which I don't. Two parties is plenty for a country like ours. We don't need some bunch of upstarts coming along and splitting the vote."

"Rocking the boat, don't you mean, Alastor?" said Guy. "Isn't that the real problem here? The Black Flame is something you can't influence or control. We're independent-minded and antiestablishment. We don't do things the way you like them to be done. For once you're – what's the word? – let's say *impotent*. Or maybe irrelevant."

"Don't you get fresh with me, young man," Wylie barked back. "You're not even a constituency MP. You're a nobody. How can you have pulled off a coup like this?"

"Quite easily, as it turns out. By making the right friends. A trick you taught me."

"But I made you! You're mine!" Wylie's voice had risen loud enough to dampen other conversations in the room. People still talked, but they were also listening in. "Without me you wouldn't be where you are. You'd be nothing."

"I'm more than grateful for all you've done for me," Guy said. "But now's my time to move on, to take the next step. It's also your time to bow out.

One generation has to give way to the next. It's the natural order."

He strode away from Wylie, a deliberate act of provocation.

"Don't you turn your back on me!" Wylie spluttered. "How dare you! Come back here, Guy. Come back this instant! I haven't finished talking to you. I can destroy you, you know. As easily as I built you up, I can tear you down."

But the fact that he had to say this out loud meant he was no longer in a position to make good on the threat. He realised it. Guy realised it. Everybody present realised it. Wylie, all at once, was a spent force. He could do little but bluster. Guy Lucas now had the upper hand.

GUY WAS VOTED in as an MP in 1995. His constituency was Kensington and Chelsea, close to home, close to Westminster. The sitting MP there had had to resign after an extramarital affair with his secretary came to light, forcing a by-election. Guy put himself up as a candidate, with the backing of dozens of his parliamentary allies. The Black Flame Party gained its first seat in the Commons.

A general election followed two years later. Black Flame candidates stood in almost every seat. Their campaign was predicated on a policy of truth and self-reliance. Voters were invited to listen, not to manifesto promises, but to their own consciences. They were offered free will to choose exactly as they pleased. The other two parties responded with scare tactics and smear campaigns. Despite that, Black Flame MPs were swept to victory all across the land. Guy Lucas, their leader, became prime minister.

Wylie, who had had some involvement in orchestrating opposition to the Black Flame, keeled over from a heart attack two days after the election. He died a week later, of complications. Guy delivered a moving eulogy at the funeral. His mother was inordinately proud of him and told anyone who would listen that her son had been Wylie's loyal protégé to the end. She was so glad that two of them had managed to set aside their differences and make up, all those years ago. The thought made her grief as a widow that bit more bearable.

THE JAGUAR HOMED in on Buckingham Palace, skirting round the Victoria Memorial, with its bronze statues depicting Charity, Peace, and the Angels of Truth and Justice.

Guy mused idly that there ought to be a fifth statue, that of a Rebel Angel.

Or, to give him his proper name, Man.

THROUGHOUT THE LATE '90s and early 2000s, there had been calls to arms. Britain was invited to involve itself in this or that conflict, send troops in, help quell civil wars and suchlike. Guy steadfastly refused.

"We haven't been attacked," he would say. "Our

interests are not at risk. Why fight? Why send soldiers to die needlessly?"

At first his attitude earned enmity among the international community. After 9/11, President George W. Bush branded him a coward for not lending his support to America's War on Terror. Prime Minister Lucas responded by saying that not being a bully did not equate to being a coward. Many American citizens echoed the sentiment.

When Bush stood for re-election in 2004, he was defeated by a senator belonging to the Black Flame Party's US offshoot, which was called – no surprises here – Black Flame USA.

At home, Guy was busy. He abolished the Whip's Office. MPs were now entitled to vote on legislation entirely according to their own principles and inclinations, and didn't have to toe the party line. He introduced a mandatory fixed four-year term for governments, as in the States. He then instituted a system of political job-sharing, whereby husbands and wives were jointly regarded as a single Member of Parliament. You voted for one, you got both. That way, an MP could attend debates at the Commons while his or her other half got on with constituency work back home. Close collaboration between the two led to a better service for voters and strengthened the domestic bond, which could often become strained between spouses when one spent so much time away from the other.

Guy was re-elected in 2001, again in 2005, and yet again in 2009. Now, in 2013, he was about to embark on an unprecedented, record-breaking fifth term as British PM.

THE JAGUAR GLIDED through the palace gates, saluted by members of the Queen's Guard. The tradition of the monarch inviting the incoming prime minister to form a new government was a quaint formality, but one that Guy liked. He enjoyed his meetings with Her Majesty. She was a game old bird who teased him relentlessly about his cherished moral code, but seemed to respect it, too, and him. She and Petra also got on like a house on fire. She would be disappointed that Petra wasn't with him today, but there was a diary clash. Alex had a trombone recital at school, and Guy and Petra had agreed that one or other of them, if not both, would always attend important dates in their children's calendars.

"I'm Defender of the Faith," the Queen had said to Guy after his second victory at the polls – or was it his third? "But if you lot carry on the way you are, there may not be much of a faith left to defend."

She hadn't been joking, either.

Organised religion was on the wane, dying fast, not only in the UK but abroad, churches, cathedrals, synagogues and mosques all closing their doors. Its decline was matched by the rise of Black Flame movements across the world, a mass, pan-national consensus not to accept the dictates of ancient cults and belief systems any more, and to heed one's own inner promptings instead, to listen to the god within.

With the breakdown of religion had come a substantial decrease in war. Trouble spots and flashpoints were few and far between these days. The UN had more or less been disbanded.

"Do unto others as they do unto you" was now the global mantra.

If you weren't attacked, don't attack. If you weren't offended, don't offend. If you weren't hated, don't hate.

GUY GOT OUT of the car.

The sun was shining. The sky was blue. Pigeons flocked above the palace rooftop, exulting in the warm spring air.

He took a deep breath, savouring the moment.

It was an age of peace.

An age of reason.

An age of Satan.

And behold, it was good.

AGE OF GAIA

JAMES LOVEGROVE

BIRD STRIKE

As Barnaby Pollard stepped out of the Jag, a dead seagull hit him slap bang in the face.

The bird was a large one, nearly four pounds in weight, and it collided breastbone-first with the bridge of Barnaby's nose. He felt a sickening *click*, a momentary numbness, and then a crashing burst of pain. Clutching his face, he sagged back against the car, a luxury sports saloon XJ model. The seagull corpse flopped to the ground, inches from the gleaming toecaps of Barnaby's handmade John Lobb full brogue Oxfords.

"Take that!" someone yelled from close by. "Bird killer! Planet raper!"

Jakob, Barnaby's chauffeur-cum-bodyguard, moved swiftly. Having ascertained with a glance that his boss was not too badly injured, he swung towards the person who had thrown the dead gull.

The culprit was a young man in ripped jeans and a shabby cagoule. His hair was long and matted, somewhere between terminally unwashed and dreadlocked. His neck was swathed in the kind of Mediterranean cheesecloth scarf beloved of gap-year students and eco-activists. From his left hand an empty Waitrose carrier bag hung limply like an old man's ball sac, the container which until a minute ago had cradled the defunct bird.

Jakob sized up the youth. The youth, in turn, took in the bodyguard's immense bulk, the barrel chest that strained the buttons of his double-breasted Tom Ford suit jacket, the close-cropped hair, the rock-solid jaw – and blenched. All at once it occurred to him that he might have just made a terrible mistake.

Actually, no 'might have' about it.

Jakob Beit was a Jewish Afrikaner by origin. His racial heritage was that of both oppressor and oppressed, his personality a thin-skinned mix of superiority complex and inferiority complex. It made him doubly quick-tempered, twice as likely to take offence and lash out.

The gull flinger turned to run, but Jakob caught up with him in three strides. He grabbed him by the hood of his cagoule and spun him round.

"Please, n-no," the youth stammered, hands raised defensively. "I didn't mean to – It was a political statement – My mum's a lawyer –"

Jakob's implacable expression was the warship's bows over which these waves of argument broke uselessly.

"Boss?" he said to Barnaby over his shoulder. "How's your nose? Is it broken?"

"I think so," Barnaby replied. His sinuses felt on fire. It was as though someone was boring upwards into his skull with an electric drill.

"Is that all? Nothing worse?"

"Yes."

Jakob turned his attention back to the youth. "Just that, then, you *bliksem*. A nose for a nose."

A fist smacked.

Blood spurted.

The youth shrieked.

THE SEXINESS STAKES

THE INCIDENT OCCURRED in broad daylight, during the morning rush hour, on a busy central London street, outside one of the tallest of the capital's new skyscrapers, the GloCo Tower.

Which meant eyewitnesses, plenty of them. In particular, it meant phone cameras.

Nobody had shot footage of the assault with a dead seagull. That had come out of the blue, a complete surprise.

The retaliation was what got filmed. Between the attack on Barnaby Pollard and the punch that decked his assailant, a dozen phones came out, a dozen video apps were deployed, a dozen thumbs pressed *Record*.

How it looked was that the bodyguard had carried out a disproportionate act of aggression on a passerby who happened to have shouted a few derogatory comments at Barnaby. This was the story that spread virally, starting in the paddling pool of social media before graduating to the adult swim of the news networks: big business violently and bloodily curbing the common man's right to freedom of speech.

Barnaby had his PR people disseminate the counter-story, with pictures of the dead seagull and his red, swollen nose as proof that Jakob's retaliation was warranted and appropriate.

But his side of things didn't receive nearly as much airtime. It wasn't as interesting. It didn't fit with the ongoing popular narrative. It wasn't *sexy*.

He was outdone in the sexiness stakes by cagoule-wearing Tarquin Johnson, upper-middle-class dropout, self-styled green warrior.

Tarquin lived in a squat in Kilburn while his parents sat snug in a multimillion-pound mansion on Primrose Hill.

Tarquin smoked roll-ups and rode a bike and loved nature and abhorred what he regarded as the environmental sins being perpetrated by Barnaby's corporation, GloCo.

Tarquin was good TV. He hunched on morning-show sofas and played the part of the wounded, blameless victim well.

"I just couldn't, y'know, let it lie," he said, peering out over a broad strip of bandage, his eyes black like a panda's. "Knowing there's sea birds and, like, all manner of marine life *dying* out there – dying in oil spills created by GloCo tankers and rigs and refineries. Pollard's company's sort of, y'know, toxic. Toxic to the earth. He's killing us all. I had to do something. I found the seagull lying beside the Thames at Shoreditch. Like, dead of natural causes. It was a sign, a gift from the universe. Throwing it at Pollard – it seemed like the right thing to do. Fitting, you know what I mean? Poetic justice. I'm sorry I broke his nose. I didn't mean to. But he didn't have to go and have his Nazi goon break mine."

Tarquin's mother, a highly successful human rights lawyer, sued GloCo for damages. By rights Barnaby could have countersued, claiming unprovoked common assault and actual bodily harm, but his legal team advised against. Whatever the technicalities of the case, a jury's sympathies would not lie with him. So instead he settled out of court. The payout was a seven-figure sum, enough to keep Tarquin in Golden Virginia and cheesecloth scarves for the rest of his life.

In fact, Tarquin moved out of the Kilburn squat immediately and used some of his windfall to buy an organic smallholding in Devon, not far from Totnes. He published a blog for a while: *Diary Of An Extreme Farmer*. Toiling on the land in the constant Dartmoor drizzle proved to be too much like hard work, however, so he sold up and moved to India, opening a beachside bar in Goa – a far more congenial climate and job. He died a year later when a tsunami roared in from the Arabian Sea and devastated a whole swathe of the Subcontinent's western coastline. The oceans didn't seem to care much about the valiant efforts Tarquin had made on their behalf, unless this inundation was their obscure way of rewarding him, clawing him into their deep, damp embrace.

RESET

BARNABY'S NOSE RECOVERED, although the same could not be said for his reputation. But then, his reputation had never been that great to begin with.

A doctor reset the nasal bones and said there was nothing further he could do. Time and ibuprofen were all that were needed.

Barnaby resumed work at GloCo, making money. The corporation was a massive entity with an annual turnover equivalent to the gross national product of a small Asian democracy. Its assets were distributed worldwide, most of them in the field of energy generation and distribution. Oil, gas and coal formed the lion's share of its business portfolio, but GloCo owned and ran a handful of nuclear plants as well.

It almost went without saying that GloCo boasted very few green credentials. Its primary concern was making profit from fossil fuels and enriched uranium.

It did not, as a corporation, consider the long-term consequences of its activities. It could not afford to. Its horizon extended no further than the next set of quarterly accounts, the next share dividend payout, the next round of end-of-year bonuses.

Barnaby perched at the vertex of a pyramid he had built, with thousands of employees below him, spread across the world. He orchestrated their symphony of industry with an unerring hand. The staff of GloCo moved in unison to do their CEO's bidding, reaping the earth's natural resources and transforming them into cold hard cash.

The corporation was popular with its stockholders. It was blue chip, firmly ensconced in the FTSE 100, a steady, reliable source of income and capital growth. Barnaby was a celebrity among the City fraternity. Those in the financial know feted him.

The wider world took a somewhat dimmer view of GloCo. In recent years there had been a groundswell of hostility rising against all the energy corporations. Investment banks still headed the anti-capitalists' shit-list, but energy giants such as GloCo ran them a close second. They were icons of greed and rapaciousness, in the eyes of many. Unprincipled. Unaccountable. Crazed monolithic gods gorging on the meat and muscle of the planet. Giant assemblages of human beings who had collectively lost their humanity and their individuality, becoming no more than cells in a mindless-brute body.

So there had been a constant background hum of carping and criticism, mainly in the left-wing newspapers and academic journals; GloCo was not well thought of by the *bien pensant*. There had been the occasional protest rally outside one or other of its places of business, including the corporate headquarters at GloCo Tower. It was nothing, though, that the company could not shrug off, much as an elephant might shrug off the stinging of flies.

Until Tarquin Johnson threw that dead seagull.

This was a catalysing moment. An inciting incident.

What Tarquin had done was actually quite funny. It was an ironic, apposite act of vengeance against a man whose corporation had indeed, as Tarquin claimed, suffered a number of unfortunate escapes of crude oil which had resulted in large, lethal slicks. These were all accidents, of course. Tankers ran aground in foul weather. Offshore drilling platforms experienced wellhead blowouts. It happened. It couldn't be prevented. But what people remembered most vividly about these events were the pictures of sea birds with oil-sodden feathers, wings flapping ineffectually as they struggled to free themselves from a beach that had become a black, tarry mire. The pathetic plight of a stricken guillemot or tern became indelibly etched in the public's minds. They saw a creature that was natural, noble and free, besmirched and doomed by the clumsy, ruinous hand of man. GloCo was to blame. Tarquin's seagull had been a neat, pithy way of making that point.

THE SEAGULL MOVEMENT

A<small>ND SO THE</small> Seagull Movement took shape.

It began in low-key fashion. Overnight, somebody dumped a couple of dead sea birds on the doorstep outside the ground-floor lobby of the GloCo Tower.

The next night, it was ten birds.

The night after that, dozens.

Barnaby made a call to the Commissioner of the Met, who was a friend of a friend. Out-of-hours police-car patrols in the area were doubled. A number of suspects were arrested, caught acting furtively in the vicinity of GloCo HQ. They were found, most of them, to be carrying dead seagulls in their backpacks.

The subsequent phase saw a group of demonstrators turning up at the Tower during the daytime, dressed as seagulls. They prostrated themselves on the pavement and lay stock still, transformed into a representation of avian slaughter. TV stations had been alerted beforehand and reporters were there to capture the protest on camera. It made the lunchtime and evening news bulletins, and featured prominently in all the following morning's papers.

In no time at all, it was an international phenomenon. Wherever there was a GloCo subsidiary, a GloCo plant, a GloCo holding of any sort, there was a flashmob flock of activists outside it, mostly youngsters, clad in bird costumes, playing dead. They didn't necessarily come as seagulls. Some were canaries or eagles or ostriches or swans. The rules were loose. As long as the outfit was suitably birdlike, it was allowable.

They filmed themselves doing it. They posted clips online. They set up Facebook pages. In the space of a month the Seagull Movement went from daft stunt to worldwide meme, and an albatross around Barnaby's neck.

GloCo became the punchline to jokes by stand-up comedians and chat show hosts. Someone at Barnaby's squash club yelled, "Caw, caw!" across the changing room, and elicited a ripple of chuckles. In parliament, the Leader of Her Majesty's Opposition described the Prime Minister's policies "lying in tatters around him like a heap of dead seagull impersonators in front of a GloCo building," not the wittiest quip ever made, but it still brought the House down.

The net result of this campaign of sustained mockery was a small but significant drop in GloCo's market value. The corporation had become a laughing-stock, but that was no laughing matter for anyone who held stock in it.

Something had to be done to arrest the decline. If GloCo shares continued to dip, there might be a panic, a run on the company, investors scrabbling to extract their money before the slide turned into an unstoppable avalanche.

Barnaby held an emergency meeting with his public relations department. His PR team were all bright young things, wedded to their BlackBerrys and iPad minis, Prada-neat, gym-honed, skilled in the arts of looking good and making others look good. They spoke in a pidgin of buzzwords like some futuristic cargo cult: "next-gen," "turnkey," "mission-critical," "bleeding-edge," "client-centric." They advised Barnaby that GloCo should "repurpose its iconic best-of-breed status" and "develop a groundbreaking, feature-rich solution" to its current "cross-platform synergistic perfect storm" if it wanted to stave off the likelihood of a "never-before top-down paradigm shift without an available exit strategy."

Barnaby translated this as: the company needed to do something urgent and radical *now*, or else it was up shit creek without a paddle.

"Ideas, anyone?" he asked.

The PR people had ideas. Oh, they had ideas.

Restructuring. Repositioning. Rebranding.

"Change?" said Barnaby.

"Yes," said someone.

"Genuine change? Or the appearance of change?"

This was a moot point with the PR department, for whom "genuine" and "appearance" were synonyms.

"Whatever you feel comfortable with, Mr Pollard."

As was so often the case with PR meetings, Barnaby found himself having to devise a strategy in spite of, rather than thanks to, the advice he was being given. He treated his PR people as a kind of Delphic oracle: they delivered vague, gnomic pronouncements which he interpreted as he saw fit, to the best of his own abilities. They helped him by raising a cloudy mirror to his thoughts, whose reflection he could then study and clarify. This was their main use to him, and the sole reason he kept them on the payroll. In every other respect they were just a gaggle of jargon-obsessed, otherwise unemployable morons.

"How about we court the eco lobby?" he said. "Woo them? Show them a different face of GloCo, a caring, friendly one?"

Nods all round. Yes, yes, that was exactly what the PR people had been driving at. Exactly. They couldn't have phrased it better themselves. Well, possibly they could have. But yes. Exactly.

"Make nice with them," Barnaby continued. "Let them see we're not heartless, plundering ogres. Slicks and spills and suffering wildlife matter to us, *really* matter. How about that?"

From the gathered PR people there was something like a massed sigh, a mutual, near-orgiastic gasp of delight. Of course. Of course. GloCo cares. These things matter to GloCo. GloCo is good.

"Get onto it," Barnaby instructed them. "Find

LA CIGARETTE

THAT EVENING, BARNABY consoled himself with dinner and a girlfriend. Not both at once; in series rather than in parallel. He ate by himself at Nobu on Old Park Lane, starting with an appetiser of beef tenderloin tataki followed by lobster tempura with creamy wasabi, washing it all down with a 1999 Chambertin-Clos De Bèze Burgundy. Then he met the girlfriend at a rooftop bar round the corner.

She was called Zurie, Marseille-born, Paris-based, sometimes a catwalk model, mostly a woman who liked to hang out with very rich men. She smoked incessantly in order to keep her weight down. Her dependency on cigarettes seemed to sum up everything she was: slim, pale, bad for your health in large doses.

Hence Barnaby had nicknamed her La Cigarette. He nicknamed all of his girlfriends. Pigeonholing them according to quirks or character traits – The Complainer, Persistent Hair Flicking, Licks Teeth, Coke Hound – made them easier to remember. Easier to tell apart, too. Otherwise they might all meld into one amorphous whole, indistinguishable from one another.

Because Barnaby had a type. Whippet-thin. Blonde. Desperately insecure. Clingy. Neurotic. Eager to please.

Zurie, La Cigarette, was a classic example.

"You have eaten?" she asked as she sipped her cosmopolitan, which the barman had made, at her request, with sugar-free cranberry juice.

It was past 10PM. Barnaby could not realistically deny it.

"Why do you not invite me to join you?" Zurie lit her next cigarette from the stub of the last. They were outdoors on the terrace, under a pergola and a gas-fired space heater. "You are ashamed of me? Do not like to be seen with me?"

Barnaby could have told her the truth. Why *would* he want to dine with her? She was hardly the world's greatest conversationalist, her talk usually revolving around fashion designers and her fellow models, every one of whom, if Zurie was to be believed, was a bitch of one kind or another. Also, she seldom touched her food. She would run her fork through it a few times, perhaps nibble a salad leaf or two, meanwhile tapping her foot agitatedly as she counted down the minutes until she could nip out and light up. It was pointless taking her to a decent restaurant. Barnaby could afford it, but there was the principle of the thing to consider. Why waste money on a perfectly good meal if it wasn't going to be consumed and enjoyed?

That was what he could have said. But since he itched to have sex with this woman, what he actually said was, "It was a business dinner. Very boring."

"With who?"

"What?"

"This business dinner. With who were you having it? What did you discuss?"

"An associate from Australia, Bob Shearwater of Port Kembla Collieries. We talked about exploitation rights in New South Wales." He *had* had dealings recently with said man on said topic, but it had been a ten-thousand-mile videoconference exchange, not an intimate restaurant tête-à-tête.

He had, however, given his answer as quickly and adroitly as he needed to in order to make the lie sound convincing.

"Very well," she said. "But Barnaby, I do not like this 'just drinks.' It makes me feel cheap. I am over in England for work, you call me, you want to hook up, it's fine. But I want to feel special, you know? Not just some *putain* you can have for the price of a cocktail or two."

Her expression was forlorn, her lips crushed and bitter.

Now was the right moment for Barnaby to bring out the gift, a necklace from Garrard, a lustrous confection of black diamond beads and a cabochon emerald drop, suspended on thin white-gold chains.

Zurie's eyes widened and sparkled as she opened the velvet-lined case.

Barnaby's PA, Veronica, had chosen well. But then, with the kind of budget he had set her, how could she not?

"Ohhh," Zurie gasped, and that single syllable confirmed, once and for all, that she *would* be coming back to his house this evening.

She wasn't going to make it plain sailing, though.

"I still do not know why I am even seeing you," she said as she stowed the necklace safely in her Louis Vuitton clutch bag. "I do not know if you deserve me."

"You're one of the most beautiful women in the world, and I deserve the best."

"But it hurts. It hurts me every time."

"I'm sorry. I can't help the way I am."

"I always feel so used afterwards, so insignificant."

"Don't you think, somehow, that that's what you really want? Deep down?"

She said, "No," but her eyes were telling a different story.

"Don't you think," Barnaby went on, "that what we have works precisely because of the way it makes you feel, that extreme of emotion? Put it this way: would you rather we were dull and ordinary? Do you really want to be like those millions out there?" He gestured, indicating the brilliantly lit expanse of London – the polite white Victorian façades, the black office-block obelisks. "They don't have nearly the same pitch of excitement as we do. They will never know the intensity of what you and I share. Night after night they couple in their beds, listless and bored and indifferent, barely even thinking about what they're doing, going through the motions. They are tiny flickering little birthday-cake candles, whereas we... we are *incandescent*. We are fireworks. We burn more brightly than they can ever imagine."

"Flames leave scars."

"Which is why we get together so rarely. We both need time apart to recover afterwards. Our relationship will never become stale and routine like everyone else's does, as long as it is intermittent and spectacular."

An old cigarette surrendered to a fresh one. Zurie inhaled a lungful and let it out in a long, controlled plume. Her hands were trembling slightly. Apprehension? Anticipation? Both, most likely.

She drained her drink. "Buy me another," she said.

A SPREE ACROSS THE WORLD

THE PR DEPARTMENT had had a brainwave. They wouldn't simply gather together some ostensibly hostile journalists for Barnaby to charm and win over. Said journalists would travel with him on a spree across the world, flying in his private jet to various GloCo sites where they would meet the workforce, be shown the environmental safety protocols the company had put in place, and above all have a chance to get to know Barnaby Pollard as a person, to see that he wasn't an unfeeling, inhuman monster, to discover the man behind the mogul.

The five who were chosen were a motley lot. One was the environmental issues correspondent for a national left-leaning broadsheet, a shapeless landslide of a woman who wore a crystal pendant and endless layers of chiffon and favoured the colour purple. Another was the founder-editor of a homespun magazine called *Higher Consciousness*, available mostly at health food shops. He looked grubby and malnourished, as though he subsisted on a diet of whatever he could forage from the nearest patch of woodland. There was a blobby eco-blogger whose mushroom pallor suggested he seldom left his basement lair, and a timid Goth documentarian who had won an IDFA award at the Amsterdam festival last year with her short film on the plight of the narrow-mouthed whorl snail in Britain's imperilled wetlands.

The fifth and final journalist was the smartest-dressed and most attractive of them, though that wasn't saying much, given how low the bar was set. She had striking red hair and eyes of a shimmering greeny-blue. Her name was Lydia Laidlaw and she was a freelance writer who contributed articles to a variety of publications, both mainstream and esoteric, offering an ecological slant on everyday topics. She had, for instance, used miniature GPS transponders to track the journeys of numerous items of domestic rubbish from doorstep dustbin pick-up to final resting place in a landfill. Collating the data, she had established that council waste departments did not always use the directest routes or the nearest, most convenient disposal sites but that they could, with a little organisation rejigging, streamline the whole system significantly and thus reduce carbon emissions from their fleet of garbage trucks by nearly a quarter. No one had yet acted upon her findings, although a handful of councillors had made noises about possibly doing so in the near future. She epitomised the slogan 'Think global, act local.'

As Barnaby's Gulfstream G650 soared away from London City Airport, his heart sank. He was committed to spending a little over a week in the company of these worthies and weirdoes. In no way did it look as though it was going to be fun. Already the purple-clad harpy, Dorothea, was muttering darkly about the vast quantities of aviation fuel a plane like this one consumed and how it had been scientifically proved that the "bleed air" being cycled into the cabin from the jet's engines was laced with organophosphate particulates which were incredibly carcinogenic. Meanwhile the man from *Higher Consciousness* – real name Frank Denham, but he had rechristened himself OwlHenry on the advice of his animal spirit guide – had begun badgering the stewardess about the vegan option on the in-flight menu. Could she absolutely guarantee that the dish contained no animal products? Were the ingredients stored in a separate compartment in the fridge, well away from the meat and dairy sections? Was she sure no cross-contamination could occur?

Barnaby broke out a bottle of 2002 Cristal and helped himself to a generous glassful.

It was going to be a long week.

LYDIA LAIDLAW

THEIR FIRST DESTINATION was Alaska, and for at least half of the fourteen-hour journey none of the journalists approached Barnaby. They sat at one end of the cabin, he at the other, with Jakob Beit stationed close by him. The journalists didn't appear openly hostile, but their skulking, suspicious demeanour left him under no illusion that they regarded him as the enemy.

This didn't prevent them from taking full advantage of his hospitality, however. They devoured the delicious snacks and meals the chef rustled up for them in the galley, and kept ordering more – even emaciated, self-mortifying OwlHenry.

Barnaby, meanwhile, teleworked on his Falcon Northwest Fragbook DRX and drank his champagne, getting slowly, quietly tipsy.

Lydia Laidlaw finally broke the détente. She strode the length of the cabin and slid into the creamy, plush leather-upholstered seat opposite him. Barnaby glanced across the aisle at Jakob. His bodyguard, who had spent the most of the time since takeoff dutifully glowering at the journalists, was now fast asleep.

"Too busy to chat, Mr Pollard?" Lydia asked.

Barnaby shut his boutique laptop and forced a smile. "I was waiting for one of you to make your move."

"Shouldn't you be the one making the move?" she shot back. "We're here for your benefit, aren't we?"

"I thought this was a mutual thing. You get unfettered access to me, and I get..."

"Favourable coverage?"

"Something like that. If I win your approval."

"A big 'if,'" Lydia said. "Still, I feel that you should be wooing us, not treating us like lepers."

"Wooing?"

"Wooing. The effort has to come from you. We're your guests. You could be a better host."

Barnaby regarded her. One thing he was sure about – Lydia Laidlaw was not his type. She was a plump, rounded creature, heavily breasted, generously hipped, with cherubic cheeks and a dimpled chin. Her face radiated sweetness, but also a steely inner strength, evident in the straight, forthright nose and permanently arched eyebrows.

At a PR-department briefing yesterday, he had learned that Lydia was not afraid of confrontation. She had once investigated a criminal gang who were charging to dispose of construction industry waste in line with regulations but were in fact fly-tipping it and pocketing the commercial waste rate fees. A man had ambushed her outside her home, beating her with a baseball bat badly enough to land her in hospital. She had published her exposé nonetheless, which had led to prosecutions, fines and jail sentences. On another occasion she had faced harassment and intimidation from the boss of a dye factory which was flushing used toluene into a nearby river instead of sending the solvent off to be properly treated. She had secretly recorded him haranguing her on the phone, saying he knew where she lived and he was going to pay some men to go over there and gang-rape her if she didn't leave him and his company alone. The recording would have been inadmissible as evidence in court since it had been made without his consent, but its mere existence, cached on Dropbox and a number of other data storage sites, gave her sufficient leverage to blackmail the boss into accepting his environmental responsibilities. The upshot was that the factory switched to using closed-loop recycled toluene, the greenest option available.

Lydia Laidlaw, then, was not someone you should fuck with.

Nor was she, as far as Barnaby was concerned, someone you should fuck.

Just not his type.

The very antithesis of his type.

And yet, as she sat in front of him in the smoothly gliding jet, for someone reason he couldn't stop staring at her.

It was her eyes that fascinated him the most. They weren't simply greeny-blue, he realised. They seemed to shift between the two colours. One moment there was more blue than green in them, the next more green than blue. It had to be a trick of the light. Whenever the Gulfstream banked or made a minor course correction, its position relative to the sun changed. The sunlight then struck Lydia's irises from a different angle, exposing some subtlety of pigmentation, emphasising the striations of one hue at the expense of the other. Perhaps that was the explanation. Yes, it must be.

"Mr Pollard?"

"I'm sorry, what?"

"I was saying," said Lydia, "before you somewhat rudely drifted off into your own thoughts, that being standoffish doesn't lend you an air of mystique. If that's what you're hoping for, then I hate to burst your bubble, but it's not working."

"No. I wasn't hoping that at all. That's not the intention. I'm... shy."

She let rip with a snort of pure scorn. "You? Shy? Hah! Yeah, right. The megabucks jetsetting energy tycoon, shy? Pull the other one."

"Reticent, then. Reserved."

"Does that line work with all the supermodels you pull? 'I'm reticent. Please don't be fooled by my aloof exterior. I'm a sensitive soul underneath.'"

Barnaby felt his cheeks growing warm. "I don't only go out with supermodels."

"Actresses, ingénues, fashionistas, professional arm-candy, whatever you want to call them – it's all the same thing. *They're* all the same thing. I've seen the pap-shots in the papers: you at some society event or other – Henley, Ascot – squiring your latest bit of leg-over. Those scrawny size-zeroes, just about identical to one another. Highlights, ribcages, big greedy eyes... You change them as often as most people change their underpants."

"I know what I like when it comes to women."

"And you like what you know."

"Is any of this relevant to the piece you'll be writing about me, Miss Laidlaw?" Barnaby snapped.

"Lydia," she said. "Not Miss Laidlaw." She held out a hand. She grinned.

Barnaby was jolted off-track. The woman was being friendly? Hadn't she just been attacking him a moment ago? Berating him over his taste in women?

Numbly, dumbly, he shook the outstretched hand. Lydia had quite a grip.

"And may I call you Barnaby?"

Barnaby nodded.

"There," said Lydia, getting up. "Ice broken." And, humming a little tune to herself, she returned to the rear of the plane and her fellow journalists.

Barnaby, dazed, topped up his glass of Cristal and struggled to fathom what the hell had just happened.

A FREE LUNCH

THE SHE-WOLF EMERGED tentatively from the forest of pine, spruce and cedar, sniffing the air. Her breath huffed around her in gauzy clouds. She had dark grey fur and a white muzzle and was beautiful, with a haughty set to her shoulders, imperiously pricked ears.

She seemed to sense that there were people not far away, people observing. Her gaze kept drifting towards the hide where Barnaby, the journalists, Jakob and their Inuit guide were bunkered down. The hide was downwind of her and well camouflaged, looking like a low white hummock, part of the landscape, but still she was aware that something was amiss. She took a few hesitant paces out from the shadow of the trees, into the snowfield, placing each paw with precision. She was gauging the threat level, wrestling with her instinct to turn and flee.

Nobody in the hide dared breathe. They stared through their binoculars, waiting, hopeful.

Gradually the she-wolf relaxed, judging that the threat, if one existed, was not imminent. She let out a soft, gruff bark.

Almost immediately, a half-dozen cubs tumbled out from the treeline. They yipped at one another and gambolled in the snow, rolling, fighting, cuffing.

Meanwhile their mother ventured further out into the open, towards the thing that had lured her from her den: a caribou carcass. The guide, John Kunayak, had shot the reindeer the day before and laid it out as bait that morning. The scent of blood and meat must have been unbearably intoxicating for the she-wolf. It was a wonder she hadn't appeared earlier. But then one of the animal kingdom's life lessons was that you should be wary of food that came too easily. There was no such thing as a free lunch.

She approached the carcass by a circuitous route, eyes constantly scanning the horizon. All at once she lunged for the caribou, seized a hindleg between her jaws and dragged the dead beast backwards. Within moments she had rejoined her brood, bringing them a banquet. The cubs set to work with relish, delving into the deer's underside, tearing through the skin and gorging on the soft innards, while their mother gnawed on a haunch. Soon every wolf, big and small, was smeared in blood, its pelt pinkened. The caribou's body twitched as it was devoured, as though somehow brought back to life.

Eventually all had eaten their fill, and the she-wolf

hauled what was left of the carcass off into the forest. Her cubs, bellies distended, waddled after her.

The group of visitors had seen what they had been brought here to see. John Kunayak led them back to the Sno-Cat, a three-mile trek through knee-deep snow. Isaac, the eco-blogger, wheezed and struggled the entire way, demanding a rest stop every few hundred yards. He was not built for physical exertion, and the extreme cold was exacerbating his asthma. OwlHenry soon lost patience with him, calling him a fat, lazy mummy's boy. Isaac retorted that at least he wasn't a fucking tofu-eating scarecrow. The name-calling might have degenerated into a fistfight if Jakob hadn't stepped in and separated the antagonists.

"Here are your options," he told them. "You can stop squabbling like a pair of babies, or I can *klap* you both round the ruddy head 'til I've knocked some sense into you, *ja*? Which is it to be?"

Isaac and OwlHenry fell silent, like scolded schoolchildren.

"That's better," said Jakob.

It was two hours by Sno-Cat back to the oilfield, a noisy, jolting journey over rough terrain, but at least the vehicle's cab was heated, blissfully so after the wind-chilled subzero temperatures of the Alaskan wilderness. Barnaby just so happened to be sitting next to Lydia. The seating was ungenerous, everyone squashed together all hugger-mugger. He felt her flesh pressing against his, her warmth permeating through the duck-down insulation of their Canada

Goose pants and parkas. He concentrated on the landscape outside, making a show of ignoring her. On the rare occasions when he sneaked a sidelong glance at her, she was also ignoring him – yet she was smiling, too. Always smiling.

SCAPEGOATING AND VICTIMISATION

THE GLOCO DRILLING station covered twenty acres of permafrosted nowhere. Rigs and derricks hunched over one-storey cinderblock buildings, all surrounded by a chainlink fence four metres high and topped with razor wire to deter curious fauna, principally polar bears and grizzlies.

The party of visitors ate dinner that night in the mess, surrounded by grizzled, boisterous roustabouts. Country music blared from the loudspeakers, and in the adjoining bar-cum-recreation-area football fans cheered a game on the TV and personal grudges were settled noisily over the pool table.

The food was basic, hearty and none too wholesome. Every main course was meat-based and served with biscuits and gravy. OwlHenry had a hell of a time finding anything he could accept as edible, in the end resorting to a selection of the soggy, overcooked vegetable side dishes.

"So we saw some wolves today," said Isaac in his customary world-weary drawl. "Big whoop. What's that meant to prove?"

"The Alaskan grey wolf is an endangered species," said Aletheia, the Goth documentarian, nibbling at her food like some eyelinered dormouse. "Humans have encroached on its habitat. We're driving it to the brink of extinction."

"But not here," said John Kunayak, who was a game warden with the US Fish and Wildlife Service and also employed by GloCo as the drilling station's designated environmental-impact assessor. "Where we were this afternoon, that was grey wolf breeding territory. The forest is where several packs are known to mate and rear their young. Have done for countless generations. It also lies directly between this site and Valdez on the Kenai Peninsula, where the refineries and tanker port are. As in, if you drew a straight line between here and Valdez, it'd go smack dab through the middle of the forest."

"So?" said Isaac.

"So, oil pipelines tend to be laid in straight lines. Shortest, most economical route possible. They cut across country, only diverting around geographical features they can't go over, like mountains or lakes. Most companies would have ploughed a pipeline right through those trees and not thought twice about it. The wolves would have been disturbed and would have quit the area. They'd have lost their ancestral lair. But GloCo didn't do that. On my recommendation, they agreed to give the place a wide berth. The pipeline to Valdez runs a total of twenty-five miles out of its way, going round the forest in a big arc. It can't even be seen by the wolves. That cost GloCo – how much was it, Mr Pollard?"

"Not sure," said Barnaby. "Couple of extra million at least."

"Couple of extra million it needn't have spent – wasn't obligated by law to spend. All for the sake of a bunch of wolves," Kunayak concluded with an ironic grimace.

"We're supposed to be impressed?" said Isaac.

"You have to admit it shows consideration," Kunayak said.

"But you're still sucking oil out of Mother Earth and pumping it across hundreds of miles," said Dorothea to Barnaby, "all in order to feed our insatiable appetite for petrochemical products. Saving a few wolves doesn't mitigate the damage you're doing to the world, filling the tanks of gas-guzzling cars, heating up the atmosphere with CO_2 emissions..."

"I'm not forcing people to drive their cars," said Barnaby. "I'm not making anyone do anything. I'm just meeting market demand. If everyone stopped using oil tomorrow, I'd have no one to sell it to. I'd have to close down that arm of GloCo and try and make do with its other assets. Don't blame me for giving people what they want."

"We have to blame *somebody*," said OwlHenry. "Might as well be you."

"No," said Barnaby, struggling to control his temper and keep stating his case calmly. "That's not a rational argument, that's just scapegoating and victimisation. You want a sea change in culture, a move away from humankind's dependence on fossil fuels, fine. But it doesn't start with me" – he pointed at himself – "it starts with you" – he pointed round the table – "and them" – the other diners, the roustabouts in their plaid shirts and jeans – "and everyone else. We're all equally culpable, all seven billion of us. Singling me out as the problem achieves the opposite of what you're after. It's denying where the true responsibility lies. It's placing the burden of guilt on one man's shoulders when it should be shared universally. Besides –"

Lydia interrupted him. "Don't."

"Huh?"

"I bet I know what you're going to say next, Barnaby, and I'd suggest you don't. It's not likely to win you any friends."

"Oh? And what am I going to say?"

"'If it wasn't me digging up the oil, it would be someone else,' or words to that effect."

Barnaby blustered, but yes, that had been more or less the tack he had been intending to take. There was no denying it.

"It doesn't absolve you," Lydia said. "It's just a little bit childish, in fact. 'I stole those doughnuts, but only because another boy would have if I hadn't got there first.' Rather than having the moral courage not to steal the doughnuts at all."

"It's not *stealing*."

"Did you pay for the oil? Was it yours to start with?"

"I paid for the land rights to drill for it. I'm the one taking the financial risk, fronting up the capital necessary to get the stuff out of the ground. That makes me its owner, doesn't it? As much as anyone ever could be."

"No one owns anything," said OwlHenry. "We just borrow whatever we have, for as long as we're alive."

"Oh, for God's sake, spare us the hippy bollocks!" Barnaby couldn't rein in his irritation any longer. "Get to grips with reality, Olly the Owl or whatever your stupid made-up name is. People own things. That's how the world works. I have what's mine, you have what's yours. You wouldn't want me to grab your shirt off you, that crappy smock thing you're wearing – not that I'd want it. What's it made of anyway? Hemp?" OwlHenry nodded. "Thought so. Hemp dyed the colour of turd. But if I did for some bizarre reason want it for myself, you'd never let me have it. Why would you? You need it so as not to be naked. Owning stuff is what make us human. It defines us. Those wolves we saw, they don't own anything, and that's why we're better than them. That's why we're the dominant species and they're on the endangered list. Because we possess, we have something to live for, a purpose: acquisition. Whereas they just exist."

He shoved back his chair and strode away from the table in high dudgeon. It was only later, when he was in his meagrely furnished room in one of the accommodation blocks, listening to the arctic wind hiss between the buildings and pepper the window with snowflakes, that his anger began to simmer down.

The bloody nerve of these people. Trying to undermine him. *Him*. Barnaby Pollard. One of the wealthiest, most successful men on the planet. Those ignorant, arrogant little troglodytes...

But he mustn't let them get to him. He must be magnanimous. He was a god, and gods must always learn to tolerate lesser beings.

BORN AGAIN VIRGIN RAINFOREST

THE NEXT DAY they exchanged the bitter cold of Alaska for the swelter and humidity of the tropics. Ecuador, to be precise, where the Gulfstream touched down at Lago Agrio Airport in the east of the country.

The following morning, the group travelled upriver by motorised canoe into the western reaches of the Amazonian rainforest.

The journalists were already sullen and tetchy, thanks to a combination of jet lag and the switch from one extreme of climate to another, but now illness started to take its toll as well. OwlHenry had come down with a severe cold, which he was treating with homeopathic remedies, to little avail, while Dorothea was suffering from an upset stomach – caused, she said, by the travel inoculations she had been given prior to leaving the UK, but more likely a result of her insistence on drinking tap water with her dinner at the hotel last night rather than the bottled water everyone else opted for. "If it's good enough for the locals," she had declared, "it's good enough for me." The upshot of this noble sentiment was a case of cramps and acute diarrhoea.

Isaac and Aletheia had managed to avoid contracting any ailments, but were still tired and taciturn. Isaac had withdrawn into himself, emerging from his shell every so often to grumble or snipe. Aletheia was preoccupied with filming everything on her compact Contour+ HD camcorder, mediating the world through a lens.

Of the five of them, only Lydia remained chirpy and upbeat.

The two long canoes navigated various winding tributaries of the Amazon basin, passing Indian villages and the occasional private landing, consisting of a jetty, a deserted-looking colonial-style hacienda, and not much else.

"There was a time when gringos came," the head guide, Rodrigo, explained when asked about these houses. "They tried to carve out land for agriculture and start up rubber plantations, sugarcane farms, that sort of thing. It never lasted. The jungle was too much for them." He chuckled. "The ones that didn't die went mad."

"Mother Nature can be overwhelming," said Lydia. "You think you can tame her, but at best you can only reach a truce with her."

"You said it, pretty lady," said Rodrigo, beaming. "Never a truer word spoken." He had taken an evident shine to Lydia, and had already asked twice if she was single, to which her only answer had been an ambiguous shrug.

Barnaby's feeling was that if Rodrigo wanted Lydia, he could have her. It puzzled him, however, that he should even care about another man's interest in her. Were she His Type, he could understand being proprietorial about her, even jealous. But since she was not His Type, why did it require an effort to overlook someone else making a pass at her? Why couldn't he simply be oblivious?

The canoes put in on a shallow beach at a bend in the river. Everyone waded ashore and tramped inland for a mile or so, Rodrigo and the other guides cutting a path through the undergrowth with machetes.

Eventually they arrived at a low-lying area, a shallow valley dominated by towering hardwood evergreens. The leaf canopy cut out all sunlight but for a few bright, piercing shafts. Birds warbled, a rippling chorus of competing song. Monkeys and macaques, unseen, hooted and shrieked. The air was thick with biting, stinging flies that seemed to find the insect-repellent gel everyone had slathered thickly on their skin alluring rather than offputting.

"Virgin rainforest," said Dorothea, with something like a sigh. "Magnificent. The lungs of the world." Then she retreated behind a mahogany tree and voided her bowels, groaning with discomfort.

"Yes, yes, all very lovely," said Isaac tersely. He wiped sweat from his bulbous forehead. "But all said and done, it's just a patch of rainforest."

"Rainforests are disappearing," Aletheia piped up from behind her camera. "An area the size of Wales every year. Logging and agriculture are eroding them away. Soon they'll all be gone, and then where are we going to get our oxygen from?"

"From phytoplankton in the oceans," said Barnaby. "Fully half the world's oxygen comes from plankton photosynthesis, maybe even more. Also, your Wales statistic isn't quite correct. Yes, rainforests are getting chopped down, but what many people don't take into account is how quickly they can regrow. Take this spot, for instance." Now was the moment to play his ace. "Would you believe me if I said that eight years ago there was a GloCo oil extraction plant situated right here?"

The journalists looked dubious.

"Tell them, Rodrigo."

"It's true. Señor Pollard isn't lying. I used to work here. There were prefab building units, rigs, a two-track mud road all the way down to the river. We pulled tens of million of barrels out of the ground."

"It wasn't the most lucrative field I've ever exploited," said Barnaby. "The infrastructure and transport costs ate into the profits, and then the global oil price took one of its periodic dips and we were starting to lose money, so in the end we shut up shop and pulled out because it wasn't viable any more. We dismantled everything, loaded it onto barges and took it away, and now look." He gestured at the rampant greenery all around. "You'd never know we'd ever been."

"I call bullshit," said Isaac.

"That's your prerogative. Rodrigo? Why don't you show them the wellhead cap?"

Rodrigo and the other guides got busy hacking away at a huge clump of lianas and vines until they had exposed a flat round concrete plug set into the ground, one foot high and six feet in diameter, like some ancient, forgotten altar. A small tarnished plaque in the centre bore the GloCo logo: the world held between two hands, superimposed over the initials GC.

"That's all that's left," Barnaby said. "The only sign that this was once a GloCo site. A few more years, and even that will be gone from sight, buried beneath leaf mould and soil."

"All this grew up in just eight years?" said OwlHenry, his consonants blunted by his blocked nose.

"The jungle comes back fast," said Rodrigo. "Left to its own devices, it soon reclaims what was taken from it. You could say it's a quick healer."

"What about indigenous tribes?" said Dorothea. "I bet they weren't happy about oil prospectors coming along and churning up their ancestral home."

"On the contrary," said Barnaby. "Most of the manual labourers we employed were locals. Rodrigo himself is half Indian."

"My mother belongs to the Oriente Quichua. And my people were glad of the income. Me especially. I saved what I earned, and it paid for me to study at San Francisco de Quito University. I now have a degree and am a professional geologist."

"So am I still the bad guy?" said Barnaby.

There was a pause, then Lydia said, "Jury's out."

HARMONIOUS COEXISTENCE

BACK AT THEIR hotel that evening, Lydia joined Barnaby on the verandah. Built into hillside, the place boasted views over a part of the rainforest that was preserved as a national park. Wisps of evening steam clung to the treetops. The rumpus of the daytime fauna was quietening down, but the nocturnal animals were tuning up and finding their voices.

"My colleagues are all tucked up in bed," Lydia said. "Need their rest and recuperation, poor things."

"How come you've stayed in such good health?" he asked.

"Clean living. Sturdy constitution. No neuroses. You?"

"I'm one of the ultra-rich. Haven't you heard? We don't get ill."

She laughed. He was weirdly gratified that he had amused her.

"And," he added, "I'm used to flying around the world, flitting between time zones and waking up in all sorts of odd places. Drink?"

He was working his way through a bottle of Ecuadorian Pinot Noir, astringent but palatable.

"The local rotgut? Don't mind if I do."

He filled a glass for her. "Be warned: it takes a few sips to get used to. They say you can't make decent wine on the equator, because grapevines need cold winters to help produce better, hardier fruit. They're right."

"Well played today, by the way," she said.

"You think so?"

"Brilliant sucker-punch move. Touché." She clinked her glass against his. "Not that it's done you any favours."

"No?"

"Nobody likes to be tricked. Nobody likes to be made to feel a fool."

"It was a salutary lesson." He frowned. "Wasn't it?"

"Not exactly. Remember, you're wooing, not browbeating. Haven't you ever had to woo anyone?"

"I don't think anyone's had to woo anyone since about 1930."

"Seduce, then. How do you go about enticing your succession of blonde coat-hangers into bed? Don't you have a technique? Some neat chat-up lines you use?"

"The only line I need is my line of credit," he quipped.

"Gosh, that wasn't at all glib and smarmy, much."

"I thought it was funny."

"Well, you go on thinking that, Barnaby, if it makes you happy. All I'm saying is, if you want to impress us, don't treat us like we're ignorant heathens who have to be shown the light. We're entitled to our opinions, even if they differ from yours. Be nice. Show us some respect, not condescension." Lydia tried her wine. Her nose wrinkled. "Ooh, good Lord. I take your point. That's... novel." She tried again. "But it grows on you."

"I'm not winning?" he asked. "That's the consensus so far?"

"Why does it have to be about winning? In your world, is it so important to always have the upper hand?"

He thought about it. "How else does one measure success?"

"By harmonious coexistence, I'd say," was her reply. "Getting along with other people, not getting one over on them. No doubt you'd call that 'hippy bollocks.'"

"If OwlHenry had said it, yes. But from you..."

She glanced at him. "From me... what?"

He turned away. "Nothing. Never mind."

The sun was going down, burnishing the foothills of the Andes. Barnaby and Lydia stood side by side at the balustrade, drinking their wine and watching the day die.

Barnaby was starting to resent her. She invariably had an effective counterargument, a riposte that kicked the legs out from under him, a question that questioned his question. He hated that. He hated anyone who talked back and, worse, who could wrongfoot him.

He imagined ways he could control her, make her do his bidding, bring her to her knees. He could think of nothing more satisfying than seeing Lydia Laidlaw acquiesce to his wishes and become his thrall.

That was when he realised that he desired her.

It had stolen up on him, caught him totally unawares.

But yes, oh, God, he was actually attracted to this large, buxom woman, with her strange bicoloured eyes and aggravating smart comebacks. He actually fancied her and wanted her.

He had never, ever had a woman like her before.

But that just made it all the more of a challenge, all the more exciting.

A DAMN GOOD MERGERING

Somewhere in an air corridor over southern China, Jakob slipped across the cabin aisle and lowered his bulk into the seat next to Barnaby's. He said nothing. Eventually Barnaby looked up from his Fragbook.

"We're going to have a chat, aren't we?" he said.

"'Fraid so, boss."

"One of your heart-to-hearts. Remind me, do I pay you to do this?"

"You pay me to take care of you."

"My physical safety, yes."

"I see it as extending further than that."

"All right," Barnaby sighed. "What's on the agenda today?"

Jakob swivelled round. The journalists were asleep, sprawled in different postures, seats reclined. Dorothea's snores vied with the Gulfstream's twin Rolls-Royce BR725 engines for loudness. Only

Lydia was awake, but she was listening to music on her iPod Nano, earbuds firmly wedged in place.

"Her." He jerked a thumb. "The redhead." He raised his voice. "Lydia Laidlaw, who can't hear us talking about her." Lydia didn't stir, didn't even glance up. He nodded in satisfaction. "Her... and you."

"There is no 'her and me.' I don't know what you're getting at."

"Come on, boss. Don't take me for some dumb Boer hick. I've seen you making goo-goo eyes at her. I've been working for you for nearly a decade. I know the signs. You get this look about you when you see a *stukkie* you fancy. Same look you get when you've set your sights on some company that's not doing well and you want to buy it out. Next thing, it's hostile takeover and asset-strip. A damn good mergering."

"Are you talking about women there, or business?"

"Both."

"Well, in this instance I can categorically state –"

"Boss," Jakob said, softly but firmly, "I just want to warn you. I don't think this one's for you. I don't think she's the right sort of girl."

"Oh, and you're such an expert on the opposite sex?" said Barnaby. "Correct me if I'm wrong, but don't your preferences run the other way?"

Jakob's expression soured. "Cheap shot, Mr Pollard. Besides, my sexual orientation isn't relevant. Relationships are relationships. The dynamics are more or less the same, whatever the gender."

"Okay, so what's the problem with her?" Barnaby

shot a glance rearward. Lydia was nodding along to a song, gaze unfocused.

Jakob leaned confidentially closer. He wore a bold, spicy aftershave, Jean Paul Gaultier Le Male. Barnaby himself preferred a subtler scent, Paco Rabanne 1 Million. "Look, I was a nightclub doorman in Jo'burg, *ja*? And before that I was South African Special Forces. A 'recce,' *ja*? I've learned how to spot a troublemaker at a hundred paces, and boss, this Lydia, she's trouble. There's something going on there, deep down. Something you don't want to stir up, not if you know what's good for you."

"I've handled a few bunny boilers in my time. I'm battle-hardened on that front. Your concern is touching, but –"

"No, listen," Jakob insisted. "You have your tastes. Your very specific tastes. They work for you, and that's fine. Who am I to judge? Give me an all-male sauna and a glory hole any day. But there's a level of give-and-take with what you do with your ladies. They accept how you treat them because secretly it's what they want. They don't have a lot of self-esteem, and you confirm that for them, and they're grateful. That's not going to fly with Miss Hourglass Figure back there. She's made of sterner stuff. She's not going to be plain sailing. She's shark-infested waters."

"Don't go there, you're saying?"

"Definitely don't. It won't end well for you."

Barnaby deliberated a moment. "You realise that when somebody tells me not to do something, I usually go ahead and do it, just to spite them?"

Jakob sighed, his meaty hands dropping into his lap. "*Ja*, I know. But I at least had to try."

"It's appreciated." Barnaby patted his bodyguard's shoulder, which felt as solid as a side of beef. "Let me just deal with Lydia in my own way and see how things develop. Who knows? Maybe nothing will come of it."

"Whatever happens, boss," said Jakob, rising, "I've got your back. And, aside from everything, she has got a cracking pair of *tiets*. I'll give her that."

"Are you sure you're not a closet straight, Jakob?"

He laughed. "No. But I'm still Afrikaans. We're expected to be vulgar, eh?"

ARROWS OF PRAGMATISM, ARMOUR OF IDEALISM

ON A BEACH a few miles south of Baku, crowds of Azerbaijanis sunned themselves, picnicked, and cavorted in the waves. It was Republic Day, a national holiday, the sky was cloudless, and there was barely a square inch of sand unoccupied.

Less than two miles offshore lay a cluster of interlocking triangular drilling platforms, connected to the mainland by a chain of pontoon bridges. They were jack-up rigs, mobile barges with three legs that could be lowered to the seabed, anchoring them in place. The excess lengths of leg rose above their superstructures like skeletal towers. Each rig bore a GloCo logo and each had a flare-stack flame at the top, flickering like a lambent orange banner.

The holidaymakers seemed unperturbed to be in such close proximity to petroleum industry activity. The breeze carried a faint whiff of burning, but the seawater was blue and pellucid, innocent of the rainbow sheen that would have indicated oil pollution.

"Why are we here, you're no doubt asking yourselves?" said Barnaby.

"Not to admire *those*, that's for sure," said OwlHenry with a contemptuous sneer at the jack-up rigs. "Ugly monstrosities."

"Did you bribe some government official to get permission to stick them there?" said Isaac. "Scratch the question; how *much* did you bribe the guy?"

"Everything about the negotiations and the deal was fully above board, I can assure you," Barnaby said. "Not a single backhander involved. What you're overlooking" – *probably deliberately*, he didn't add – "is that Azerbaijan itself gets a decent cut of the profits we make. This drilling is good for its economy. Azerbaijan, in fact, is now one of the highest-GDP countries in the Caucasus, largely thanks to its energy sector. The standard of living here exceeds that of any of its post-Soviet rivals. Beneath the Caspian Sea, within Azerbaijani territorial waters, lies one of the last great commercially developable hydrocarbon deposits, a vast resource we're only just starting to tap. I'm proud that GloCo is leading the way in exploring and extracting that latent wealth."

Lydia raised a hand. "But..."

"Yes, Lydia?"

"Wasn't it right here that GloCo had its most recent spill?"

Barnaby didn't miss a beat. He had anticipated this query. "I'm glad you mentioned that. Last year, as I'm sure you all remember, there was a mishap. It occurred on this very coastline, a few kilometres east. One of our rigs became dislodged during unusually heavy weather. The seal on the wellhead sheared and split. A blowout preventer valve failed. Oil began to leak. That was the bad news. The good news was that we had divers down at the site within the hour. They removed the drilling riser and installed a new one, stemming the flow. The entire operation took the best part of twenty-four hours, but full credit to my employees, they worked nonstop, round the clock, until the job was done. Nearly a million gallons of crude was lost, but it could have been so much worse."

"And then beluga sturgeon started washing up dead on the shore," said Lydia. "Not to mention seagulls."

Barnaby winced.

"I'm sorry, that was insensitive of me." Lydia's smile was less apologetic than her words. "Sore point, clearly. How is the nose, by the way? Better now?"

"It only hurts when I sneeze. The dead-fish situation was undesirable, I admit. Caviar has long been one of the staples of the Azerbaijani economy, and when the beluga sturgeon population took a hit, so did the caviar industry. I regret that."

"Of course," said Isaac. "Poor you. Had to find something else to put on your toast at breakfast for a while."

"Actually, I don't eat the stuff myself. What GloCo did, however, was compensate the local sturgeon fishermen handsomely for their loss of revenue. We also instituted a comprehensive development programme all along the coast here. You see those hotels and holiday apartment complexes?"

Blocky white buildings hunkered a short way inland, like an assortment of sugar cubes.

"Built using start-up funds donated by GloCo. This region is already turning into something of a hot tourist destination. You've got Russians flocking here, Iranians, Turks, Eastern Europeans... I'm not denying that what happened was a great pity, but GloCo has done its best to make amends and offer reparation. If anything, Azerbaijan is better off now than before."

"As I recall," said Aletheia, "wasn't the government planning to sue you for millions of dollars?"

"The President did make noises about punitive damages and restitution. But rather than put everyone through the whole rigmarole of trials and legal wrangling that could have dragged on for years, GloCo held up its hands, said '*mea culpa*,' and ponied up."

"Would you have, if you hadn't been threatened with prosecution?"

"I'd say yes. Look, nobody's perfect. No energy company has a flawless safety track record. For want of a better phrase, shit happens. You can't prevent accidents. It's how you deal with them that matters. If you own up to them and do your utmost to mitigate their effects, isn't that acceptable? Isn't it the most anyone can hope for?"

He stared at the journalists. They stared back. He could feel every arrow of pragmatism he shot at them rebounding off their armour of idealism, unable to find a chink. It was hopeless. The week of the charm offensive was nearly at an end, and he had little to show for it. He had wasted a great deal of money and, more importantly, time. All for nothing.

If he was going to salvage anything from the whole futile exercise, it would have to be her. Lydia. She alone could make it worthwhile. So it was all the more imperative that he didn't let her slip through his fingers.

DEPARTURES AT ARRIVALS

TOUCHDOWN AT LONDON City Airport, in the drizzly greyness of a British spring dawn. The Gulfstream coasted up to a private gate, and its seven passengers disembarked, all of them bleary-eyed, some more than others. Even Barnaby was feeling a bit stupefied after their whistle-stop globe-girdling expedition. Around the world in eight days.

The farewells in the arrivals lounge were stilted. Dorothea hurried off, saying she needed to start typing up the notes she had recorded on her Digital Dictaphone and then prepare her feature on the trip. OwlHenry wasn't convinced his experiences were worth turning into an article – they wouldn't teach readers of *Higher Consciousness* anything they didn't already know – but he might go ahead and write one anyway. Isaac had been updating his blog en route via his BlackBerry and murmured something to the effect that the subscriber feedback so far had not been broadly sympathetic towards Barnaby. Aletheia had raw footage to assemble and edit and expected to have a mini-doc ready for upload onto YouTube within a fortnight. She hoped it would be impartial and allow viewers to make up their own minds.

"You 'hope'?" said Barnaby. "You mean to say it's out of your control?"

"The footage decides," Aletheia replied. "It is its own message. I'm simply the conduit."

That left only Lydia to say goodbye to. Jakob hung back at a discreet distance, though not so far off that Barnaby could ignore his presence.

"So," Barnaby said.

"So." Lydia smiled. "Well, it's been interesting."

"Is that all?"

"Isn't it enough?"

"The others don't sound as though they're going away with a better opinion of me."

"I don't think you've made many converts, it's true."

"Not even one?" He raised his eyebrows hopefully.

"I reckon the best that can come of this," Lydia said, sidestepping the question, "is media coverage showing you as fallibly human. Someone who means well, who tries, but doesn't always get what he wants."

"Could be worse, I suppose."

"It'll take some of the gloss off you, but that's not necessarily a bad thing."

"Didn't having a seagull chucked at me already do that?"

"Not to the extent that a clumsy, half-baked propaganda tour will."

Barnaby's shoulders slumped. "Damned if I do, damned if I don't."

"Cheer up." She patted his cheek. "You're still a squillionaire. Money is the best form of insulation. It's like living inside an impregnable bubble. Even if you fall, you bounce."

"Listen, Lydia..."

Jakob coughed into his hand. "Boss. We have somewhere to be."

"Do we?"

"That thing. You know. That meeting."

There was no meeting scheduled. Barnaby glared at Jakob, then turned back to Lydia.

"I'm just going to come right out and say it. I'd like to take you out to dinner."

She snorted a laugh. "You're kidding."

"Not the reaction I was expecting."

Lydia spread out her arms. "Have you seen me? Do I look anything like the sort of woman Barnaby Pollard has dinner with?"

"You will do if you say yes."

"Is this a wind-up? Has one of your rich friends dared you? Did Richard Branson ring and say he'd give you a million Virgin shares if you ask a chubster out on a date?"

"Don't be so self-deprecating."

"I'm not. It's preposterous, that's all. I'm not even blonde."

"I like you."

"That's odd, because when we talk you act as though I'm driving you nuts."

"Maybe that's why I like you. You never say or do the predictable thing."

"Well..." She made a pretence of studying him. "You're not that bad-looking. You obviously keep yourself in shape. You don't mind a drink. You don't come across as a creep. I'm going to say... I'll think about it."

"That's it? 'Think about it'?"

She grabbed the handle of her wheel-along suitcase and turned to go. Five paces on, she halted. She looked round.

"I've thought about it."

"And?"

Her blue-green eyes flashed. "Go on, then. I'm free tomorrow night. Do your worst."

THE LONG GAME

HE WENT LOW-KEY, nothing flashy: the Wolseley. He sensed that a grand gesture, a really expensive restaurant, might not be welcome at this early stage in the proceedings. Might even scare her off.

They had a good evening. Lydia wore a turquoise lambswool dress, designer unidentified, but the colour showed off her blue-green eyes.

"Is it just me," she said, halfway through the main course, "or is everybody staring at us?"

"It's just you. By which I mean, with someone as gorgeous as you at this table, nobody's paying *me* any attention."

"I reckon they're scratching their heads, wondering who that fat lass is with Barnaby Pollard. They probably assume I'm your sister."

"For God's sake, will you stop calling yourself fat? You're not fat."

"Compared with your usual bulimic beanpoles, I am."

"Then perhaps you should stop measuring yourself against them."

She took a mouthful of her lemon sole Saint-Germain, then said, "Wait a mo. Did you just call me gorgeous?"

"I believe I did."

"Flatterer. Anyone would think you were trying to get into my knickers."

"I'd be lying if I said it hadn't crossed my mind."

"Well, buster, for the record, I don't drop them for just anybody."

"Good thing I'm not just anybody, then. I'm Barnaby Pollard."

"Oh, you smug git," Lydia said, but she was chuckling.

The date ended with a peck on the cheek and Lydia disappearing into the night in a taxi. Barnaby hadn't expected it would go much further than that, although he wouldn't have minded if it had. He understood that this was going to be a long game, that victory would come after a protracted campaign rather than a single, decisive battle. He also knew that there was no way he was going to lose. It was asymmetrical warfare. He had all the firepower. He outgunned her financially and socially, in all the ways that mattered. There could only ever be one outcome: her eventual and total capitulation.

BOMBARDED

HE ARRANGED FOR flowers to be sent to her home the following morning and every morning thereafter – a dozen Burgundy velvet roses, fresh from the Netherlands.

He flew her to Rome to see a new production of *Tosca* at La Scala.

He obtained VIP tickets for the Rolling Stones at the O2 Arena.

He whisked her down to Epsom race course for Derby Day, where she won big with the £500 stakes he subsidised.

He arranged a private, after-hours shopping spree for her at the Hermès boutique on New Bond Street.

He took her to the premiere of the new George Clooney movie, even though she warned him there was a very strong likelihood she would throw herself at the star and gush over him like some breathless teenage fangirl, which, at the post-screening party, was exactly what she did.

"I could get used to this lifestyle," she said as Jakob drove them away from the party venue in the Jag. She added quickly, "But I'm not sure I should."

"Crisis of conscience?" said Barnaby.

"Tell me straight, Mr Pollard..."

"You sound awfully serious all of a sudden, Miss Laidlaw."

"None of what's happening – the attention, the glamorous nights out, the flowers – none of it has anything to do with me being an environmentally-conscious journo?"

"I don't see the connection."

"You're not trying to *defuse* me in any way? Nobble me?"

"How would that work? You're going to have to explain yourself a bit more clearly."

"I'm feeling overwhelmed, that's all. Bombarded. And a part of me's asking whether there isn't some ulterior motive behind it. Whether Barnaby Pollard isn't simply trying to secure some favourable publicity. You struck out with the other four. I'm the one you think you can win round somehow, if you throw enough cash and trinkets at me. You can razzle-dazzle me into coming onside."

"Do you honestly think I'm that sort of man?"

"I have no idea. This is all so outside my realm of experience. I feel like Julia Roberts in *Pretty Woman*. Only without the whole, you know, prostitute thing. Or the teeth." She held his gaze steadily. "I'm just saying, if you're messing with me, if this is all some elaborate business wheeze, some cunning strategy, you need to come clean right now. Because, if it is, I won't take it well, but if I only find out much, much later, I *really* won't take it well. And I am not the sort of woman you want pissed off at you. Trust me on that."

"I don't doubt it," Barnaby said. "And no, this has nothing to do with your job. It isn't anything underhand or sinister. I'm as sincere about this – about us – as a man can be. I don't know how else I can prove that to you, other than by saying so."

"You could kiss me," she said. "Properly. That might do the trick."

So he did.

The Jaguar purred through London, zigzagging around the late-night traffic on its way towards Kensington, where Barnaby lived.

Barnaby and Lydia continued to kiss.

Tongues flickered, touched, entwined.

She tasted of showbiz wine and arousal.

He knew that she would be coming home with him tonight.

He caught a look from Jakob in the rearview mirror, a disapproving scowl.

He closed his eyes and carried on kissing.

ACROSS THE LINE

SHE STEPPED OUT from the en suite bathroom. She had changed into a white satin negligee, which she had brought with her, secreted in her handbag. It hugged the contours of her body. Its lacy hem came down to the tops of her thighs, just hiding her crotch. She had been planning this, he realised. She had decided in advance that tonight would be the night. All she had needed from him was that last little bit of reassurance to get her across the line.

He was naked under the covers. She approached the bed with slow, stately grace.

"How do I look?"

She gave him a twirl.

"Magnificent," he said, and he meant it. There was so much of her. Her breasts were immense, mountainous, possibly larger than the breasts of all the other women he had slept with combined. They gave a delicious ripple as she moved. Her buttocks, across which the base of the negligee was stretched taut, had the ripe roundness of watermelons. Her legs were thick and powerful, and already he was imagining them scissored around his pelvis, squeezing, applying intense pressure.

He was hard as she clambered onto the bed. His groin had become a tight, pulsing knot.

He grabbed her and pulled her to him. The negligee stayed on for perhaps another five seconds.

There was such ampleness to her that he almost didn't know where to begin. He seized and pawed and kneaded, amazed at how soft she was, how her skin seemed to sink and glide under his touch.

Lips crushed lips. His hand slithered over the mound of her belly, venturing into the dimpled fold between her legs. His palm brushed the coarse tuft of her pubic hair. His fingers found her pillowy pudenda. Her cleft was wet. A forefinger slid in. The heat and moistness of her. The gaping, eager void.

All at once his cock was inside her, and she gasped, and so did he. He thrust, and quickened, and *blazed*. She cried out, raking his back with her nails, while he was beyond words, beyond sounds, his mouth wide but nothing emerging except a breath, an exhalation of pure ecstasy.

Later, as they spooned together, woozy and half asleep, he marvelled at how snug her body felt next to his. He was accustomed to women who were all bones and high-strung rigidity. This... this was comfortable and pliant and welcoming. Cotton wool instead of barbed wire.

Yes, it had been perfect.

As far as it went.

A few more straight fucks like that – no problem. Plenty of pleasure to be had there.

But then would come the time when he wanted something else from her. Something more.

Once he had lulled her, once he had gained her trust sexually...

There would be other games to play.

Other avenues to explore.

Other doors to open.

THE *PHWOAR!* FACTOR

THE MEDIA WEREN'T slow in noticing that the founder and CEO of GloCo had a new woman – and a woman who broke the mould as far as he was concerned.

"From seagull to G-cup gal," wrote one gossip columnist. "Maybe that bonk on the bonce from a bird's beak has done something to bachelor Barney's brain. Pictured here is the latest lass he's been lording it with around town, and she's not one of the usual Pollard Lollipops. This larger-than-life lovely is Lydia Laidlaw, 35, freelance journalist, and she's busted our preconceptions about Big Bad Barnaby in more ways than one. As the saying goes, you don't get many like her to the pound. Luckily, oil oligarch Barney's got plenty of pounds!"

The paparazzi took to Lydia. She was photogenic and had the *phwoar!* factor. Hers was the name they shouted loudest at red-carpet events, hers the cleavage that captivated their zoom lenses.

Soon, opinion pieces were appearing in the middlebrow tabloids with headlines such as "Singing The Praises Of The Fuller-Figured Woman" and "Is Our Obsession With Skinny Finally Over?" The articles, all penned by female hacks, couldn't decide whether it was a good thing or not that Barnaby had dumped the waifs and plumped for someone statuesque and Rubenesque instead. On the one hand, it gave hope to larger girls everywhere. They, too, might be able to bag a handsome billionaire. On the other hand, there was a distinct undertone of resentment and chagrin. It seemed that all this time women had been exercising and dieting like mad, thinking that thinness was what men found attractive, only to discover that they might as well have ditched the Zumba classes and splurged on the Chardonnay and chocolate biscuits all along.

When a bestselling chick-lit author went on Twitter and referred to Lydia as "that jammy heifer," she was deluged with indignant comments and trollish accusations of jealousy and gender-betrayal. The truth was, though, that many of her sistren secretly agreed with her. How dare Lydia Laidlaw be so voluptuous, so comfortable with her curves, not to mention so damn *lucky*?

One byproduct of this minor media frenzy was that it drowned out the carping commentary on Barnaby's round-the-world PR tour. Dorothea, OwlHenry, Isaac and Aletheia could barely get their

Brava! Magazine, August Issue
Interview Excerpt

Brava!: Lydia, you've made a career out of crusading environmental journalism. Now you're going out with GloCo oil magnate Barnaby Pollard. How do you reconcile the two things?

Lydia Laidlaw: They're not incompatible. I don't see the problem. Just because Barnaby does what he does, it doesn't mean I have to stop doing what I do. We're both grown-ups. I'm an independent woman. I'm not going to change my worldview just to please my boyfriend.

B!: But don't you think some people might find it a bit hypocritical, you enjoying the rewards of his industry, an industry that's about as environmentally-unsound as it's possible to be?

LL: The money's there. Barnaby's made it. If he wants to spend some of it on me, that's his choice. It's not as if I could stop him.

B!: How did the two of you meet, anyway?

LL: GloCo needed to raise its profile in the eco-media-sphere after a string of industrial accidents, and that whole unfortunate, but still quite amusing, seagull affair. I was one of the journos they targeted. Barnaby and I just clicked.

B!: I'd have thought, to someone like you, he'd be the Devil himself.

LL: But you can't help who you're attracted to, can you? And he is, let's face it, a very attractive man. I'll be honest, I didn't want to like him at first. I tried not to. I gave him a pretty hard time, as a matter of fact. But Marlee, haven't you ever fallen for a wrong 'un? Someone you know you shouldn't fancy but you just can't help yourself? I doubt there's any woman who hasn't, at some time or other.

B!: Are you hoping to tame him? Is he a challenge? A project?

LL: A handful, maybe, but tame him? Why would I want to do that?

B!: Change him, then.

LL: Again, why? He's not broken. He doesn't need fixing. He is what he is.

B!: But someone like you, in a position to influence his decision-making...

LL: I'm his girlfriend, not his wife.

B!: You could do so much good for the planet. You could be the Melinda Gates to his Bill, the Jane Fonda to his Ted Turner.

LL: I can do good with my writing. I don't know if you've noticed, Marlee, but women these days can exert power directly. They don't have to work their wiles on their menfolk in order to have influence, not any more. Like the song says, sisters are doing it for themselves. Barnaby's a king of the world, for sure, but I'm a woman, and that means I'm in a whole different league.

B!: No argument here.

LL: Let me tell you something. There's a lot of talk about women having an "inner goddess." About how we're all of us connected in some way or another to the source of things. We give birth – create life. Our menstrual cycles echo the lunar cycle. We're natural, elemental beings. Now, some would dismiss that as mystical poppycock. Sentimental nonsense. But there's still some truth in it. You can't deny that, in the ways that count, in the areas of life that really matter, women are and always have been far superior to men.

B!: Again, I'm not going to dispute that for a moment.

LL: Here's what I think. We may not individually be goddesses, but collectively, as a gender, you might describe us as a goddess, as aspects of a divinity, multiple parts of a much greater whole. Compared to a man like Barnaby Pollard, I might appear to be nothing very much, not in material terms or the effect I can have on society. But I'm linked to something larger than me, something he's excluded from by virtue of his

Y-chromosome, something no amount of money can ever buy him, and that gives me strength. Infinite strength.

B!: Mother Nature? Is that what you mean?

LL: A bit simplistic, but yes. "Mother Nature" always sounds so kindly and caring, doesn't it? I think it's stronger and stranger than that. Fiercer. Nature is not necessarily a cosy, cuddly thing. So there's my counterpoint to Barnaby's status, how I'm his equal.

B!: Much as I hate to round things off on a "cosy" note, *Brava!* readers I'm sure will want to know if you and Barnaby have any plans. What does the future hold for you two?

LL: Who knows? It's still early days. Are we going to get married, you mean?

B!: He is eminently eligible, he seems serious about you, he's in his mid-forties so he really ought to be settling down – and there's no question you'd make a terrific wife...

LL: It depends. I haven't got to know him properly yet. There are layers to him. Many layers. I feel I've only just scratched the surface so far.

PREJUDICE AND FREEFALL

SHE RODE ON top, her pendulous breasts swinging just inches from his face. She was gripping his cock tightly inside her, her vaginal muscles slowly clenching and unclenching. It was exquisite procrastination. She was holding both of them on the brink of climax, drawing the moment out as long as she could. He thrust upwards with his pelvis, urging her to go quicker, to finish things. She resisted. She pinned his shoulders to the bed with her hands, reinforcing her control. Her mouth was a full-lipped O of anticipation, her eyes squeezed shut.

He almost couldn't bear the delay. He could feel the orgasm swelling up inside him, begging for release, ready to explode, but she kept the tension going, moving only enough to bring satisfaction that tantalisingly tiny bit closer. His cock seemed so engorged, it was a wonder she could fit it in. There was nothing separating them. He filled her.

He seized a breast in each hand. His groping fingers found the nipples, which were erect and proud, big as his own thumb tip. He pinched them experimentally, and when she gasped with approval, he pinched harder.

It had the desired effect. She started to rock faster on him. She tossed her head back. He felt tremors begin to shudder through her. Her hands clawed his shoulders. Her whole body became one massed effort of pleasure, with no function now but to take them both over the edge of the precipice and into the freefall of ecstasy.

They came as one, like a single organism, bucking and bending, bellowing.

PARADISE LOST

"BLIMEY," SHE SAID afterwards. "I think the whole of bloody Kensington heard that."

"Soundproofed glass in every window," Barnaby said. "Keeps the traffic noise out."

"And the shagging noise in."

"Pure coincidence, I'm sure. A happy byproduct."

She lay on her back, gazing up at the moulded ceiling. On first seeing Barnaby's bedroom she had remarked that it was larger than her entire flat. Yet it occupied only a quarter of the second storey of the house. In a crowded city like London, Barnaby's wealth bought him the one thing that was at a real premium: space.

"Did you read my *Brava!* interview?" she asked. "I sent you a link to the online version."

"Hmm. Yes."

"What did you think?"

"I liked it. You came over well. Smart, composed..."

"But?"

"Why does there have to be a 'but'?"

"Because of your tone of voice."

"Okay." He grimaced comically, like someone about to undergo a body cavity search. "The goddess stuff. That Mother Nature bit. Really?"

"What's wrong with it?"

"I just would never have expected it from you. I thought you were more grounded than that."

"Obviously you don't know me as well as you think you do."

"Unless you were simply giving them what you thought they wanted. *Brava!*'s pretty right-on and feminist, isn't it? 'The Magazine For The Woman Who's Special.'"

She rolled over, leaning up on one elbow. Her breasts pooled weightily against each other. "What is it about that sort of thing that bothers you so much anyway?"

"Feminism?"

"No. Spiritual matters."

"Nothing. It doesn't bother me."

"You seem dead set against anything that isn't empirical, straightforward, factual, practical."

"Are we having a row?"

"A genial postcoital discussion."

Barnaby reached for the wine glass on the nightstand. They had been drinking Domaine Ramonet Montrachet Grand Cru immediately prior to tumbling into bed together.

"Right," he said, taking a swig. "Since you broached the topic... I don't believe in nature as this sort of *entity*, this sentient, holistic super-being. I don't subscribe to that point of view. Never have. When I look at a bunch of trees or a mountain or a valley, I don't sense some sort of spooky magical presence there, the way a lot of people do. I just can't understand that at all. Trees, every kind of plant – they're just organic machines. Animals and insects too. There's nothing to them other than their basic imperatives, which are to consume and survive and procreate. And to see the hand of God – or whatever – in a landscape or a pastoral scene, that's just absurd. It's rocks and grass and earth. It can be pretty, yes. Dramatic, even. It can have aesthetic appeal. But to come over all misty-eyed and reverent and talk of 'majesty' and detect a living intelligence buried within... Well, I find that airy-fairy and foolish."

"So the natural world is just *stuff* to you. No more significant than – I don't know – this mattress we're lying on." She thumped the bed.

"Yes. Yes, it is. Let me tell you a story."

"Oh, do."

"A story from my childhood."

Lydia sat up, wrapping the duvet around her. "You never talk about your childhood."

"It wasn't that interesting, frankly. It was just a pointless interlude, a period of waiting until I was finally old enough to get on with my life."

"Jesus, you poor sod." She rolled her eyes. "You were born an adult, weren't you?"

"Pretty much. I used to roam a lot when I was little. Those were the days when a kid could. There weren't so many cars. There weren't paedophiles lurking round every corner, ready to pounce. There weren't videogames and twenty-four-hour TV to keep you indoors the whole time. I had my own front door key, and would go out on my bike for hours on end. It was good to be away from home, where all my mother did was drink all day and bitch about my father when he wasn't there and squabble with him when he was."

"Only child?"

"Yes."

"Explains a lot."

"May I continue?"

"Please do."

"Where I lived was a small town, countryside all around. I had this place I liked, not far out, a mile or so. Fields, a copse, a stream. My own secret spot. I'd park my Raleigh Grifter and sit and maybe smoke a fag I'd bought off one of the older boys at school. Someone once dumped a load of porn mags in a hedgerow nearby. Probably had just got himself a girlfriend, maybe a wife, and he was having a clear-out. I found them and salvaged them. Kept them safe and dry inside the trunk of a half-rotted oak."

"Like a squirrel hoarding nuts."

"If you like. *Penthouse, Club International, Fiesta, Men Only...* I'd thumb happily through those, undisturbed, in absolute peace and quiet."

"Heaven."

"Damn right it was. And then one day they went and built a bypass right through the middle of it."

He mused on the memory, drinking more wine.

"First sign that something was up," he said, "was when I spotted some blokes in council-worker donkey jackets fiddling around with measuring rods and theodolites. I didn't know what a theodolite was; I thought it was a camera, and they were taking pictures. They did it for about a week. I couldn't for the life of me figure out why, what it was all for, what they were up to. Then I overheard my dad talking to one his friends about a bypass. The friend was a shopkeeper, ran a chemist's on the high street. He was worried about losing passing trade. He said a bypass would be the death of the town.

"Everything went quiet for a while. No more men in donkey jackets trampling all over my secret spot. Then, a couple of months later, the mechanical diggers arrived. And so did the protestors. There were standoffs. Plenty of chanting and placard-waving. 'Save Our Town,' et cetera. But the diggers got their way in the end. The workmen started churning up the earth with their JCBs very early one morning, before the protestors turned out. After that it was a *fait accompli*. The ground had been breached. No going back. No point trying to resist any more.

"I watched it over the months that followed: the farmland disappearing, the foundations of the road being raised, this whole massive undertaking, this *change*. They uprooted my tree, the one containing my porn stash, along with most of the others. They

engines, often many of them, in multi-part harmony. The Doppler shift as each vehicle sailed by. I loved it."

"You're a nutter."

"No, but I did," he insisted. "That bypass, you see, represented achievement. Success. Man taking his environment by the scruff of the neck and doing exactly what he wanted with it."

"But didn't the road kill the town, like your father's friend said it would?"

"Not so's you'd notice. His chemist's didn't go out of business. I don't think any shops did. Passing trade – it's overrated. If somebody wants to go to the chemist's, or the greengrocer's, or the newsagent's, or the florist's, they'll go. Just wandering by the shopfront isn't suddenly going to make you stop and turn and walk in. The town still got visitors from outside. What it didn't have, now, was endless queues of traffic clogging up the high street and forming a jam around the war memorial. I'd say that was a win."

"But at the expense of countryside."

"A couple of square miles of it at most. Plenty more where that came from."

"Some animals' natural habitats."

"If they had any sense, they'd have moved on. If they stayed and found they didn't have a nest or a burrow any more, then it was their own damn fault."

"You're only saying that to wind me up."

"Or I could mean it," said Barnaby. "Either way, hand on heart, the construction of that bypass was a formative event in my life. A pivotal one, even. I realised then that I wanted to impose my will on the world too, the way those road builders did. I wanted to accomplish what they had – helping people to travel, making life more convenient for others, accelerating the pace of civilisation. In a nutshell, progress."

"Progress," said Lydia with a curl of her lip. "Such an old-fashioned, Victorian concept. Antiquated. In the circles I move in, it's a dirty word. It always has connotations of a backwards step, not a forwards one. Something lost rather than gained – a site of natural beauty, a way of life, someone's home, a tradition. Something we should have kept hold of, needlessly sacrificed on the altar of modernity."

"As far as I'm concerned it means only improvement. And I knew it was my... Well, my calling. My vocation. I left school at sixteen. Didn't want to waste any time faffing around with university. Wanted to get on with things. Joined a small London firm doing business with Burma, as it was then, for oil – Rangoon Overseas Petroleum Ventures Ltd. A rump company, all that remained of a much larger firm that had been going since colonial times. I was the office boy, making the tea and trying to get the primitive computer system to work. Within three years I was running the company, and the majority shareholder. Another three years and Rangoon Overseas Petroleum Ventures had swallowed up a dozen similar-sized companies and had been renamed GloCo, with me as sole owner. A decade on, while I was only just in my early thirties, GloCo was a FTSE One Hundred corporation and I was climbing fast up the *Forbes* rich list."

"Am I supposed to be getting moist again? Are you telling me all this because you think it'll turn me on?"

"No," said Barnaby. "I'm telling you all this because... because I want you to know. This is me. This is who I am. I believe it's called sharing. Women are supposed to want it from their men. But if you're going to be like *that*..."

"Please don't get all huffy. I'm sorry. I shouldn't have sneered. My mistake." The apology was sincere.

· He almost said it then: *I have something to show you*. The words were on his lips. He had given her something of himself, a token. It was often how he proceeded to the next step with a girlfriend. Soften her up with a revelation about his past. Bait the hook with an honest confession, a glimpse into the real Barnaby Pollard, an insight into his soul. And then – *bam*. While she was off-guard. While he looked vulnerable.

But he held back. He sensed Lydia wasn't ready.

Not yet.

Soon, though.

He couldn't wait much longer.

ON A ROLL

DURING THIS PERIOD, as Barnaby and Lydia became cemented in the public's perception as a couple, GloCo went from strength to strength. The share-price wobble brought about by the Seagull Movement protests stabilised. There were no more ructions or fluctuations, just a steady incremental rise in profits and dividends. Barnaby swooped on a number of his rivals, making bids for them using loans leveraged against his existing corporate holdings. In well over half of these attempted buyouts he was successful. He expanded further into the American and Asian markets, while leaving the Middle East more or less alone. It was an impenetrable cartel down there in the deserts, and the region as a whole was just too volatile. Much the same was true of Russia, which held the world's largest natural gas reserves, second largest coal reserves and ninth largest crude oil reserves. It was too much of a closed shop; the discovery and extraction costs were high on account of the vastness of the country, its harsh climate and its lack of decent infrastructure; but above all, Russian businessmen were, as a breed, mad, and almost impossible to deal with in a civilised manner. Contract negotiations invariably involved drinking Herculean quantities of vodka, more than even Barnaby's hardened liver could handle, and quite often letting off assault weapons in the wilderness as well. The hassle and hangovers weren't worth it. As both Napoleon and Hitler had learned to their cost, Russia should be left well alone.

GloCo flourished, and so did Barnaby's relationship with Lydia, much to Jakob's disgust.

"You're always bloody together," he complained in the Jaguar one morning on the drive in to work. "Every spare minute you have, you spend with her."

Barnaby looked up from his *Financial Times*. "Seriously, Jakob, is it your place to cast aspersions on my girlfriend? Let me answer that for you. It is not. You bodyguard, me employer. There are boundaries. Clear?"

"I'm not casting aspersions on her," Jakob said. "Just on how close you and her are getting. It's not like you to be so... smitten. It's not normal for Barnaby Pollard."

"I think Barnaby Pollard is the best judge on what's normal for Barnaby Pollard."

"It used to be one inconsequential *loskind* after another." *Loskind* was Afrikaans for 'woman of easy virtue,' only not so polite. "And now you're all serious about this one chick who seems to be taking over your life. It's not good for you."

"In what way not good, Jakob? Everything's pretty rosy from where I'm standing. Have you seen GloCo's share price lately? And look at this."

He turned the newspaper round, pointing to a column. Jakob glanced at it in the rearview mirror.

"Print's too small, boss. Read it out to me."

"*FT*'s tipping the valuation to go even higher. Comment here says, 'GloCo's on a roll and shows no sign of stopping. CEO Barnaby Pollard combines acumen with aggression in a high-risk, high-reward industry. He's an old hand, a seasoned campaigner. He knows the ropes and he's got the track record and the assets to underwrite his adventurousness. With the per-barrel price of crude unlikely to drop in the foreseeable future, and demand for gas on the increase in the developing nations, there aren't many safer or more lucrative places to stash your spare cash than GloCo.'"

"All well and good," said Jakob, "but – *jislaaik*!" He braked hard as a black cab swerved out from the kerb right in front of the Jag. Both cars screeched to a halt. Jakob followed a volley of blares on the horn with a volley of insults out of the window: "*Maafoedi*! *Stront vir breins*! Call that driving? You drive like a wrinkled old *krimpie*, you dickhead!"

The cabbie responded no less colourfully, cursing Jakob and flipping him the bird.

"*Ja*, I'll break that *fokken* finger off and shove it

where the sun doesn't *fokken* shine, pal. You know whose car this is you just cut up? Fellow who earns more in an hour than you do in a year."

Barnaby didn't catch the cabbie's reply, but it was strongly worded enough to make Jakob unbuckle his seatbelt and open the door.

"No," said Barnaby. "Let's not. Remember Tarquin Johnson? Best avoid a rerun of all that, eh?"

Jakob grumbled, but stayed put, and the black cab pulled away. The Jag continued on its journey, joining the Westway eastbound.

"It's occurred to me, Jakob," Barnaby said, "that you may be a wee bit jealous."

"Of Lydia Laidlaw?"

"And her relationship with me."

Jakob gave a gruff, staccato laugh that managed to convey both amusement and scorn. "Not a chance, boss. No offence, but you're really not the sort of man I go for. You're about twenty years too old, for one thing. No tattoos, for another."

"Just felt I should ask. You wouldn't be the first employee, male or female, to fall for me."

"Don't flatter yourself, Mr Pollard. I like you as a person, but that's all. I regard you as a friend. And I respect you also, which is why I don't like to see you getting yourself into hot water."

"But I'm not."

"Have you shown her the basement yet?"

The question hung in the air between them. The Jaguar swept down from the flyover onto Marylebone Road.

"No," said Barnaby. "Not yet."

"Didn't think so. But you're planning to?"

"When the moment's right."

"That's when everything's going to change. You mark my words. And I don't know that she's going to be able to make the transition. It's a big gamble with someone like her. It might all go horribly wrong. You could be setting yourself up for a fall."

"But I can't not do it. I can't keep that side of me hidden from her forever."

"Even if it spells the end for the two of you?"

"If it does, then so be it," Barnaby said peremptorily, and he flapped the newspaper in a way that indicated the subject was closed.

Jakob took the hint and drove the rest of the way in silence.

A VERY GOOD TIME TO
BE BARNABY POLLARD

GLOCO'S RUN OF good fortune continued. It was awarded a government permit to release shale gas reservoirs in Lancashire using hydraulic fracturing. The county council was cock-a-hoop, as this would bring employment to a depressed area. Local environmentalists were not so happy, predicting that the fracking process would cause earthquakes, groundwater contamination from flowback from the pumping, and air pollution from the benzene in the shale gas.

Meanwhile, a GloCo exploratory platform up in the Arctic Circle, on the rim of the East Greenland Rift Basin, made a spectacular find: an undersea oil reserve estimated to contain half a billion barrels or more. Barnaby ordered three spar rigs to be towed to the site, and soon they were moored in position with their six-hundred-foot caissons probing down into the gelid water towards the ocean floor, ready to insert drills and suck up oil like mosquitoes siphoning blood.

A GloCo open-cast coal mine in Botswana, which was believed to be virtually exhausted, had an unexpected fresh spurt of life. A new seam appeared, almost magically, running down at a steep angle through the rock strata. The surface mining operation was converted to deep mining, a longwall shearer boring into the ground with its cutting drums and a scraper chain conveyor hauling the raw carbon booty up to be crushed into manageable chunks and carted off in trucks.

At the GloCo Tower, Barnaby sat in his penthouse office, overseeing the company's international business via telecommunication.

Before him, the GloCo logo was inlaid into the Carrara marble floor in brass. It extended from the foot of his desk all the way to the expanse of plate-glass picture windows. The world cupped in two hands.

The earth was yielding up its riches, making him even richer than he already was.

He had a woman who seemed suited to him in nearly every way.

It was, without doubt, a very good time to be Barnaby Pollard.

EMERGENCE AND RE-SHEATHING

SHE WAS ON her knees, hands braced against the headboard of the bed. He was thrusting into her from the rear.

Each time he rammed himself into her, her entire body shook, her fleshiness quivering with the force of his entry. He could see the shockwaves running through her. Her breasts, hanging like udders, undulated. The clap of his groin against her buttocks was like insistent, rhythmic applause.

Her moans invited him to pound into her that much harder. He withdrew almost to the tip of his glans, then lunged hilt-deep, and withdrew again and lunged, over and over. It was slick and slippery and rapid, a continual emergence and re-sheathing.

He looked down. The creamy expanse of her behind was too alluring. He couldn't help himself. He had to slap it. He raised his right hand and did.

She let out a yelp of pain. It was indignant, surprised, perplexed.

He saw his own handprint, a pink flush on the whiteness of her skin.

He slapped again, still thrusting enthusiastically.

Again she cried out.

"Does it sting?" he said through clenched teeth, panting.

"Yes."

"Should I stop?"

He slammed himself into her once, twice, three times, before she answered.

Her voice was low and small, a little bit husky.

"No."

He began delivering firm smacks to her buttocks, timing the impacts to his thrusts. A noise arose in the back of her throat, part groan, part scream. It crescendoed to a shuddering climax, as did she. He followed suit in swift succession, feeling himself erupt inside her as though unleashing a stream of molten silver, a torrent of pure exultant joy.

THE DOOR

"Lydia?"

"Yes?"

Her voice was doughy. She was in a drowse, already half asleep.

"There's something I have to do."

"Didn't we just do it? I've got a sore bum cheek as proof."

"Something I have to show you."

"Can't it wait 'til morning? I'm tired."

"No. It has to be now. Now or never."

She rolled over, frowning at him quizzically. "What's up?"

Instead of replying, he hopped out of bed and fetched bathrobes for both of them. "Put this on. We're going downstairs."

Downstairs they went, padding barefoot through the airy silence of the house. Past the dining room and Barnaby's study lay a door, panelled and painted white like all the others, innocuous-looking. It was situated between a bookcase filled with leather-bound first editions and a pedestal on which perched a gaudy Murano glass vase, its shape reminiscent of an orchid.

"Have you ever been curious about this door?" he asked her.

"Not particularly. Seen it a couple of times. I assume it leads down to the cellar, right?"

"To the basement. It's..." He groped for the right phrasing. He was suddenly, weirdly inarticulate. "It's a special door."

"Could have fooled me."

"What I'm saying is, it's a door that, once opened, can't be closed."

"Bloody stupid door, then. What, does it get stuck or something? A carpenter could fix that."

Her obtuseness, he realised, was her way of coping with the unexpected turn of events. She was aware something out of the ordinary was happening, something odd and unprecedented. His behaviour was disturbing her. She was stalling for time while she tried to process it.

Patiently he said, "I want you to know that you are an amazing woman."

"Thank you."

"We've been together for four months now."

"More like five."

"I am completely yours. I never thought I could be like this with anyone. I always thought I could keep my women at a distance, compartmentalise them so that they wouldn't intrude on other aspects of my life. You've overturned that for me. You've made me break all my own rules."

"Barnaby, you're actually starting to freak me out a bit here," Lydia said. "What's going on?" She glanced at the door. "What's behind that? What's down there?"

He faltered. "Maybe this was a mistake. Maybe it's still too soon, even now."

"No, it's not too soon," she said firmly. "You can't start down a road like this and not see it through to the end. Now I really bloody have to know what's down there." She tried the handle. The door was locked. "Open it," she demanded.

Barnaby knew he had manoeuvred himself into an inescapable position, perhaps unwittingly, perhaps not. The die was cast. There was no alternative now but to carry on, come what may.

He pulled a copy of *The 120 Days Of Sodom* out from the bookcase. Inside, embedded into a custom-shaped section cut out from the pages, was a key.

He inserted the key into the lock.

He turned it.

He opened the door.

Taking Lydia's hand, he said, "Come on."

She baulked. "If there's the mummified corpses of your previous conquests down there, I swear..."

"No. Nothing like that." He tugged her hand. "Come and see."

THE BASEMENT

BARNABY FLICKED A light switch. Together, him leading, they descended a carpeted staircase. To his consternation, Barnaby found that he was trembling. Normally when he took a girlfriend down to the basement for the first time, he was perhaps a little apprehensive, but confident nonetheless that he was doing the right thing and that there would be only a positive outcome. But with Lydia, he was anxious. No, downright scared. He feared her reaction. He feared her rejection.

They reached the foot of the staircase, where a second door stood. This one was padded and silk-lined. The same key unlocked it.

He ushered Lydia in before him, at the same time reaching for another light switch.

This was it. No turning back now.

Lights came on in recessed wall sconces. Their

glow of their low-wattage bulbs was soft and tinged crimson by cranberry-glass Art Deco shades.

Lydia stared around.

The basement had the dimensions of a triple garage. Indeed, 'triple garage' was how it had been described in the architect's blueprint when it had been excavated out under the house, and with the addition of a set of external roller doors and a ramp leading up to the front driveway it could easily be converted into one.

At present, though, it contained no cars. Nothing but a set of very specialised equipment.

Lydia continued to stare around. Her blue-green eyes were wide, her expression unreadable.

Barnaby waited with bated breath. When was she going to speak? Was she going to say anything at all?

"What," she said at last, "the hell," she went on, "is this?"

"What does it look like?"

"I'll tell you what it looks like. It looks like a medieval torture chamber crossed with a brothel boudoir."

Which was more or less correct.

The basement was a sex dungeon, kitted out with an array of bondage and domination furniture, all of it handcrafted and designed to Barnaby's own specifications. Everything was made from the very finest materials: Brazilian rosewood, Sheffield steel, top-grain calfskin leather. The walls and ceiling were flock-papered, underneath which was a layer of sound-absorbent tiles, while the floor was tight-packed parquet, smoothly varnished and easy to wipe clean.

Barnaby was inordinately proud of it. He had worked hard to get the place exactly right, and he maintained it himself, doing all the cleaning, giving it a thorough once-over with duster, vacuum and mop every month. No housekeeper had ever come down here. None of his private staff had a clue the dungeon even existed, save for Jakob.

There was a pillory with padded holes for neck and wrists. There was a spanking bench with cuffs and restraints. There was a Berkley Horse, a six-foot-tall A-frame contraption for upright flogging. There was a bondage table with a pair of shackles at either end. There was a St Andrew's Cross frame, for spread-eagling.

There were various thick hooks screwed into the ceiling, for the purposes of suspension and strappado. There were ringbolts fitted to the walls to accommodate chains of assorted diameters.

Shelves and cubbyholes were filled with fetish paraphernalia: harnesses, gags, fetters, hoods, blindfolds, clamps, muzzles and spreader bars. These were arranged methodically according to type and size. Display cabinets contained whips, riding crops, bamboo canes, knouts and paddles. Drawers held cotton ropes of every conceivable thickness and length, plus lubricants, disposable latex gloves, and an astonishingly broad selection of dildos and vibrators.

"So?" Barnaby said.

Lydia slowly rotated her head to look at him.

"It's..." she said. "It's incredible."

He felt his spirits leap. "You think? I put my heart and soul into it. I sourced the best BDSM furniture makers. Germans, mostly. They have the real expertise in this field, by general acknowledgement. I chose every item personally. I had it all tailor-made. You won't find anything here in any shop or on any website. It's bespoke stuff, unique, the best that money can –"

"No." She held up a hand – which, he noted, was shaking. "No, you misunderstand. It's incredible as in 'I can't fucking believe it.' This. All along, in your house, there's been *this*. Barnaby..."

Her face registered a range of emotions, none of them good. Hurt. Anger. Bafflement. Horror. Disgust. Contempt.

"This is you, isn't it?" she said. "Jesus fucking Christ, this is what you really are. I always sensed there was something off about you, something I was missing, wasn't getting. I put it down to you being so rich. Billionaires are never normal. Now I know what it actually is. Oh, my God. It was so obvious. So bloody obvious."

He reached for her, placing a hand on her arm.

She snatched the arm away.

"Don't touch me," she said tightly. "Just... don't."

"Lydia..."

"You big fucking pervert!"

She wheeled round, away from him, making for the doorway.

"Lydia, please."

"You silly sick sod!"

She scuttled up the stairs, tripping a couple of times. Barnaby followed. He was wracked with dismay.

"Lydia, please don't run away. I'm sorry you're not taking it well."

"Taking it well?" she shrieked. "How am I supposed to take it? My boyfriend's a fucking pervo freak. He's got a bloody sex dungeon in his house that he's neglected to mention to me in all the five months we've been going out together, until one day we have a little bit of mildly rough horseplay and suddenly he thinks I've turned all kinky and I'm going to bend over and beg to be flogged. Jesus!"

She hurtled along the ground-floor hallway. She rushed up the stairs. Barnaby remained in pursuit, still imploring.

"Just hear me out, will you? I have certain predilections, that's all. I'm... I'm into things that quite a few people are but most people aren't. That doesn't make me bad or wrong."

"Predilections!" she echoed, framing the word in a bitter howl of laughter. She was halfway along the upstairs landing now, sailing towards the bedroom. "That's like saying the Borgias were 'a little bit naughty.' I should have guessed when I saw you take that book down. That's when the penny should have dropped. The Marquis de bloody Sade! Shit, shit, shitty shitting shit."

"It's part of my makeup. It's something I just can't help."

"And that makes it better how exactly?" Lydia said, and she slammed the bedroom door behind her.

Barnaby stood outside, frozen in a paroxysm of anguish. "Lydia? Lydia!"

No answer.

Should he go in?

He couldn't decide. He was no longer Barnaby Pollard, the ruthless business magnate who pursued his aims with single-minded tenacity and regarded wavering as weakness. He had been totally unmanned. He had expected anything from Lydia except this outburst of shock and vituperation.

Finally, he made up his mind and determinedly grasped the doorknob.

It turned before he could turn it, and Lydia strode out. She had dressed in a hurry. Her blouse was misbuttoned, her skirt on back to front.

She shoved past him.

He seized her elbow.

"Let go," she said with quiet menace.

"Just hear me out."

"Let go this instant."

"I only want to expl –"

"You're hurting me. I bet you enjoy that. I bet that's what you want; hurting women. What you get off on. I don't. So let go, or I'll call the police. I will."

She held up her smartphone so that he could see the screen. The numbers 999 had already been inputted. Her thumb hovered over the *Call* icon, less than a centimetre away from activating it.

Reluctantly Barnaby relinquished his grip on her.

"Yes," she said. "Didn't think you'd want that. Didn't think you'd care for a big scene with the

authorities *chez* Pollard. I'm leaving now, Barnaby.
I'm going, and you aren't to contact me. You aren't
to try and visit. You're to leave me alone. Got that?"

"But Lydia..."

Her eyes brimmed with tears. Furious tears.
"I loved you, you fucking idiot. We were terrific
together. And now you've gone and... and utterly
buggered it up. Why didn't I see it earlier? Why
didn't I realise all this was too good to be true?"

She spun on her heel and stormed off. Moments
later, Barnaby heard the front door open and then
whump shut. He went to the window and watched
Lydia cross the driveway and exit via the deliveries
gate at the side. Out on the street, she raised a hand.
A taxi drew up. She climbed in.

Barnaby remained at the window for half an hour,
looking out at the desultory to-and-fro of summer
night traffic and pedestrians. A full moon hung high
above London, pale and lonely and desolate.

WHITE AND RED

HE DID AS she asked and refrained from contacting her. That wasn't to say he didn't keep tabs on her. He hired a private investigator to maintain discreet surveillance. At any time, on any given day, he knew where she was and what she was up to. Just by calling the investigator, he could find out what she had had for breakfast, who she had met for lunch, and where she planned on eating dinner. The man even sent him jpegs of long-lens photographs of Lydia. Here she was, glimpsed through her living-room window. Here, trotting down the street to catch the bus. Here, coming home with a bag of groceries.

Technically it was stalking. But Barnaby was able to justify it to himself on the grounds that he had revealed something about himself to Lydia which he would rather the rest of the world not know. He needed to keep a close watch on her, for his own sake and the sake of GloCo, just in case she did something impetuous. He doubted she would, but there was always the risk, and risks should be minimised.

Previous girlfriends had all understood the deal. The fabulously expensive gifts he lavished on them were the price of their silence. Most of them, besides, were into sadomasochism. If that wasn't the case to start with, it soon proved to be, once they had undergone two or three sessions in his dungeon. They responded to the crack of the whip as though it awoke some truth in them they hadn't hitherto been aware of. They learned that they had been born to enjoy pain and submission, and that it gave them an erotic thrill. The tighter he tied the knots that bound them, the harder he thwacked their bare flesh, the more they loved it. Barnaby would listen as their whimpers of discomfort were replaced by moans of delight, and he would be transported. He would push them to greater heights of delirious suffering, sometimes beating them until they passed out. Afterwards, they would be drained and fragile, holding themselves as delicately as though they were broken china, but the look in their eyes – gratitude and gratification – told him everything he needed to know. And they almost without exception came back for more. Whenever he rang one of them up, she would be glad to hear from him. She might take a little cajoling, a little bribing, but soon enough a contract would have been agreed for the night, a safeword established, and she would be letting him fasten her to one of the items of apparatus, quivering as she awaited the snap and smart of the first blow.

Barnaby's own satisfaction was always deferred until he was sure he had wrung every last drop of ecstasy and humiliation he could out of his disciplinee. He would be in a state of iron-hard tumescence through the process of inflicting pain on her, but would never touch himself or allow himself to be touched before she had achieved full arousal and climax, whether through the beating alone or with the aid of a sex toy or, occasionally, intercourse. Only then, as she was coming down from her endorphin high, would he permit himself ejaculation.

It was about control. Control of himself. Control of another.

Often his semen would mingle with blood spatters on the floor, white coiling amid red. Those were the purest colours imaginable, in Barnaby's eyes. The two most precious fluids in the human body, mutually spilled, falling onto the floor in a libation to the gods of lust.

HASN'T IT BEEN A STRANGE SUMMER?

IT WAS THE private investigator who alerted Barnaby to the article in the *Daily Mail*. The investigator had been tipped off by an insider contact, a subeditor, who informed him that Lydia Laidlaw had been commissioned to write an opinion piece for the paper. Lydia's new-found celebrity status meant that she would now command a handsome per-word rate, and that if she pitched for an article it was unlikely to be turned down. The investigator was able to obtain a preview of the text, in return for a sizeable sweetener which the poorly-paid subeditor was only too happy to accept.

He passed the file on to Barnaby via email late one evening, with a note saying, *'Thought you might like to see this. It's going in tomorrow's edition, but unfortunately the presses are already rolling, so we're too late to do anything about it if we wanted to. Doesn't appear defamatory to me, but you may be able to read a subtext I can't.'*

The article was entitled 'Hasn't It Been A Strange Summer?' and appeared in the pages of the paper's *Femail* section.

You've probably noticed we haven't seen much of the sun here in Britain lately.

It rained throughout May, June and July. August was mostly overcast and not particularly warm. As we edge into autumn, the mercury's dropping but there are still no clear skies.

Has anyone on these islands managed a tan this year, without travelling abroad? Or an outdoor picnic?

And what about those poor people whose summer was blighted by flooding? Dozens of rivers burst their banks, flood protection measures could not cope, homes were inundated.

Wimbledon was a washout. The Test was played on a quagmire, not a cricket pitch.

The weather has gone haywire. That's a fact on which we climate-obsessed Brits can all agree. There hasn't been a summer as wet as the one just past, not in living memory, nor indeed since records began. Why?

The quick and easy answer is global warming. Carbon dioxide emissions continue to rise unchecked, reflecting thermal radiation back into our planet's atmosphere. Across the board, the mean global temperature is inexorably on the rise.

In the specific case of Britain, we can look to the influence that global warming is having on the Atlantic Ocean in order to account for the increasingly erratic behaviour of our weather.

In the normal course of events, the Atlantic's "heat transport" effect cycles warmer water up from the tropics to keep northern and western Europe more temperate than other landmasses on the same latitude.

Meltwater from the dwindling polar icecaps is interfering with that process. The waters of the Atlantic are becoming colder and denser and its "heat pump" is weakening, meaning that while the rest of the world hots up, our corner of the continent is getting cooler and the levels of precipitation here are amplified.

The science is complex, but in simple terms, the UK is starting to get the weather it ought to have, and has been protected from for centuries by the prevailing ocean currents.

But there's more going on than just a waterlogged tennis tournament and hundreds of householders stacking sandbags outside their front doors and baling out their living rooms. More danger signs we should be aware of.

There's the steady drop in songbird numbers. The loss of millions of honeybees to disease and pesticide. The decline in wildflowers and butterflies.

We may not notice these things, but they're happening all around us. Small deviations from baseline don't impinge on our everyday perception. Tiny gradual losses go unremarked.

Yet they're part of a pattern, a wave of changes that is gathering pace and momentum.

Avalanches start off small. All it takes is a thin layer of snow to become dislodged. Suddenly, it's an unstoppable, deadly cascade.

So many factors feed into the global-warming doomsday equation.

There's loss of albedo from the shrinking of glaciers and sea ice, meaning less solar radiation is reflected away from the Earth.

There's the melting of tundra permafrost, releasing methane, another greenhouse gas like CO_2.

There's yet more methane being given off by cattle as the demand for meat and dairy products intensifies in order to sate the appetites of a fast-growing world population.

These anthropogenic (human-generated) causes of global warming can be – and hopefully will be – mitigated by international laws and by changes in social behaviour.

But there is reason to believe that the worst of the damage has already been done. That it's too late. A runaway process has begun which cannot be halted or reversed and which is liable to make life incredibly hard, if not intolerable, for future generations. Flooding, famine, disease, death on an unprecedented scale.

Mother Earth has been ravaged and despoiled and is in distress. We feel it instinctively. We know it.

For just over a century, since the advent of the combustion engine and the great industrial boom, the human race has been engaged in a hedonistic fossil-fuel orgy. We have sported around in our cars. We have turned up the thermostats in our houses without a second thought. We have plundered and squandered the planet's resources with all the self-restraint of a gang of children let loose in a sweetshop.

Our world is an organism, an enclosed, self-regulating system. The environmentalist and futurologist James Lovelock came up with that idea. He also gave it a name: the Gaia Hypothesis.

Gaia is our Earth. And Gaia is not happy.

Gaia, of course, was the personification of the Earth in ancient Greek mythology. She was a primordial goddess, mother to Titans, Giants, and all the other gods in the Greek pantheon.

Hesiod, in his poem the *Theogony*, tells how Gaia's husband, the sky god Uranus, began hiding their many monstrous children one after another as they were born. He buried them inside Gaia, causing her pain.

Her revenge was to forge an adamantine sickle, which she gave to their son Cronus, who despised his priapic father for his passions and his relentless lust.

The next time Uranus tried to have his way with Gaia, Cronus stepped in. He castrated Uranus with the sickle. From the blood which gushed out from the wound sprang the Furies and various kinds of nymph, and from Uranus's severed testicles arose Aphrodite, goddess of love.

The lesson we can draw from this is obvious.

You do not mess with Gaia.

It's true of all women. Down through the centuries, men have learned to their cost that no woman is to be trifled with or abused. Love us, and you will be rewarded with all that you could desire. Cross us, and you're in for a sound thrashing.

Perhaps the men who have exploited and abused our planet, this other Gaia, for their own personal gain will take heed at the treatment dished out on Uranus and start treating her with more respect.

Because it is men – not mankind, but males – who have dug up Earth's bounty and used it to line their own pockets.

Men who have been so reckless with our planet's ecosphere.

Men who have sucked every last drop of goodness out of Gaia's heart.

Men who mistakenly believe they can keep on taking from her with impunity.

And maybe it's up to us women to persuade them to change their minds and mend their ways. Maybe we, as fecund, fearsome and feminine as Gaia herself, are the human race's last and only hope.

It could be that the planet is past the tipping point. Any effort to pull us back from the brink is futile. Our civilisation is doomed to extinction.

But that must not prevent us from trying.

LITTLE POISON DARTS

BARNABY COULDN'T HELP but regard the *Daily Mail* article as a thinly veiled personal attack. He suspected that the editor who had commissioned it viewed it in much the same light. Rumours of a split between Barnaby and Lydia had been doing the rounds for days. The pair had not been seen together in public for well over a fortnight, whereas before they had seemed inseparable. The article seemed to harp on the idea of tension between masculine and feminine, a rift between the sexes, echoing Lydia's own situation, which the editor must have been cognisant of. And Barnaby himself could hardly miss the targeted tartness in lines like "men who have exploited and abused our planet, this other Gaia, for their own personal gain" or in the use of sexually-charged phrases such as "hedonistic fossil-fuel orgy" and "relentless lust."

The entire piece was laced with little poison darts aimed straight at him.

He consulted his lawyers first thing the following morning, but their conclusion only confirmed his gut instinct. There was nothing in the article that was actionable, nothing that would warrant taking out an injunction against its being reproduced on the *Mail*'s website or reprinted elsewhere, nor any grounds to sue whatsoever. It was just a bit of surreptitious score-settling that he would have to take on the chin.

He fumed about Lydia all that day. The nerve of her. The ingratitude.

Jakob bore the brunt of his anger. He took it up to a point and then snapped back.

"Look, boss, I hate to say I told you so, but I did," he said. "I warned you exactly what would happen when you showed her the basement, and you, like the big *domkop* you are, ignored me. Lo and behold, she's gone, and you're left with a whole heap of egg on your face. Better than seagull, maybe, but still."

"Jakob..." Barnaby growled.

"No, with all due respect, boss, shut up and listen. You've been lucky. It could have been plenty worse. The red-tops could right now be screaming 'Barnaby Pollard – Bondage Pervert!' in eighty-point type headlines on the front page. She let you off mildly. Consider yourself rapped on the knuckles and move on. Plenty more fish in the sea."

But were there?

Barnaby doubted he would ever meet someone else like Lydia. She was one of a kind.

What he wouldn't give for a second chance with her.

What he wouldn't pay for another glimpse of those extraordinary blue-green eyes.

Even after the article, her act of barbed retaliation, he still wanted her.

He *loved* her, damn it.

Only now, when it was too late to make a difference, could he admit that to himself.

He loved Lydia.

THORNS AND NETTLES

WHEN HE ARRIVED home that evening, he was astonished to find her waiting for him inside, in the living room.

"Still have my door key," she said. "Still know the alarm disable codes."

"Lydia," he breathed.

She was seated on the chaise longue, hands in her lap, back straight, poised, composed.

"It's strange," she said. "On the way over, I had this brilliant speech mapped out. Now I'm here, I'm not sure what to say."

He moved towards her. She stayed him, pointing a finger.

"No, sit down over there."

He did as bidden.

"I'm not even going to ask if you read today's *Mail*," she said. "I'm kind of regretting what I wrote. Parts of it. In hindsight it seems like a cheap shot. You didn't deserve that, me sniping at you in the public domain. I've come to apologise."

"Oh," he said. "Well, I suppose I –"

She interrupted. "Please, just hear me out. This is phenomenally difficult. I look at you and I think of the man I thought I knew and the man I now know you to be, and it seems incredible that the two can be the same person. I'm not a prude, Barnaby. I realise there's a whole subculture of fetishes and kinks, people out there who like to walk on the wild side sex-wise. I've nothing against them or what they do. As long as it's consensual, as long it isn't coerced, as long as it's adults only, then I can't see the harm. Each to their own. I just..."

She looked at her hands, then back at him.

"I just never would have suspected you were one of them. It was a hell of a shock, I'm sure you can appreciate that. You sprang it on me out of the blue. And I... I didn't react in a very mature fashion. It was too sudden, too big for me to make sense of. All the while, we'd been going down this path together, you and me, this sunlit road paved with gold and lined with roses, and suddenly here's you suggesting we take a detour through the woods where it's dark and there are thorns and nettles. I wasn't expecting that at all. I wasn't ready."

She hesitated. Barnaby detected a note of trepidation in her voice, the sound of someone teetering on the verge of a momentous decision. He wanted to speak, to coax her across the threshold, but he kept silent. The wiser course was to allow her to take the final step all by herself.

He was on tenterhooks. A cherished dream was close – *this* close – to coming true.

Lydia took a deep breath, like a swimmer about to dive.

"I may be ready now." She held his gaze, anxious but resolute. "If it's what you'd like. If it'll bring the two of us closer. If it's the only way we can be together again. I'm prepared to make the sacrifice. I'm prepared to try, at least."

Barnaby stood up, hearing his heartbeat loud in his ears, feeling the blood rushing through every vein.

"My God," he said, hoarse. "Really? You have no idea what this means to me, Lydia. This is the best news I've ever had. I love you. Truly, I do."

"And I love you too. Even after everything. I must be crazy, but yes, I still love you."

"So when can we start?"

She shrugged gamely. "Now would seem as good a time as any."

SAFEWORD

HE LAID OUT the basics, the rules. Informed consent had to be established beforehand. That was the grounding for any kind of sexual power exchange. They must be clear which of them was going to be the Top and which the Bottom, who was going to dominate and who was going to be dominated, although that should already be quite evident. He wouldn't take her any further than she wanted to go, especially as it was their first session, and above all else they must agree on a safeword. It couldn't simply be "no" or "don't," since sometimes in a bondage context those meant nothing. The safeword needed to be incongruous and easily remembered and recognised.

"How about 'Gaia'?" Lydia said. "That's been on my mind a lot today."

"Mine as well. Gaia it is." He couldn't see a reason why not.

"And the moment I say it, you stop whatever you're doing?"

"That's the general idea."

"What if you don't? What if you just carry on? What do I do then?"

"You have to trust me. That's the whole point. If you can't trust me when you submit to me, then we have no business doing any of this stuff."

"I see. So I'm placing myself entirely in your hands. I'm at your mercy."

"You are," Barnaby said. "But I'm no ogre, and I promise you I've never once lost control or gone too far. You've nothing to fear."

"I must be mad. I can't believe I'm even considering going through with this." Lydia nodded to the sideboard, where cut-crystal decanters sat on a salver. "Any of those whisky, by any chance?"

"Will Laphroaig thirty-year-old single malt do?"

"Don't care how fancy it is. Just pour me a snifter. A large one."

She took the tumbler and drained the scotch at a gulp.

"Right," she said, exhaling hard. "Shall we?"

KEEPER

DOWN IN THE basement he made her strip off all her clothes. He himself undressed to his underpants.

"Don't you get to be naked too?" she asked.

"I'm in charge. I choose. I want you without a stitch on, so that's how it has to be. And if I want to keep something on, I will."

"Ooh, masterful."

"Now be quiet." Barnaby surveyed the various pieces of apparatus. "Where should we begin? The Berkley Horse, I think."

He led her to the A-frame device. Her feet went into slots in the bottom. He lowered her forward on the angled, padded board, fitting her face into an oval hole. He buckled canvas straps across her legs, waist and arms, fastening her flat. She was immobilised, helpless.

He deliberated over what to beat her with. In the

end he settled on a fibreglass riding crop. The thin leather tongue at the tip, known as the 'keeper,' was designed to lessen the force of the blow and not leave a mark. It was a good selection for a novice.

He positioned himself beside her, his target the enticing plump mounds of her buttocks.

He extended his arm, crop raised.

"Don't tense up," he told her. "Relax. You know you want this."

He flicked the crop.

Keeper met skin with a glorious sharp *snap*.

Lydia shook from head to toe. A small gasp escaped her.

Barnaby drew the crop back and flicked it again, a fraction harder this time.

The keeper struck smartly. Lydia flinched and shuddered.

Barnaby looked down to see the front of his underpants tented outwards. The pressure of restriction down there was painful, terrible – wonderful.

He started to beat her with a regular, consistent rhythm, revelling in the impacts and the intervals between.

He kept expecting the safeword to come, but it didn't.

Lydia took her punishment stoically. Now and then she let out a hiss or a little cry. But whenever he checked her face, Barnaby was pleased to see that she was smiling.

FIVE ON THE MERCALLI INTENSITY SCALE

BARNABY ARRIVED AT the GloCo Tower the next morning in a spry, sprightly mood. His PA, Veronica, couldn't remember when she had seen him cheerier. He positively breezed through the antechamber, past her desk and into his office, like a man who hadn't a care in the world, and she hesitated before going in after him. But she had to. She had bad tidings to deliver.

"Mr Pollard, I'm sorry, but we've just received a flurry of emails from Japan. There's, er, there's been an earthquake. Nothing devastating," she hastened to add. "A minor tremor, that's all. Only, it was on the south coast and the epicentre was on the Atsumi Peninsula, not far from Ise Bay..."

He filled in the rest. "Which is not far from Cape Irago, which is where a GloCo nuclear power plant sits. Shit. How severe's the damage?"

"Unclear. The site manager's running an inspection right now. He seems to think it's just superficial, a few cracked walls here and there. But of course he's shut the reactor down and evacuated all non-essential personnel, as a precautionary measure."

"No radiation leaks?"

"None detected so far."

"Thank fuck for that." Barnaby paused to give himself time to think. "Okay, Veronica, contact Hayashi at GloCo Japan and tell him to get his arse out of Tokyo pronto and head down to Atsumi."

"I believe he's already on his way, sir."

"Good. Then put me through to his mobile, so that I can tell him I want him smiling and shaking hands with every technician at the plant, and I want photographers taking pictures of him doing it, and I want that reactor back online by close of business here in the UK."

"Right away, sir."

Barnaby spent much of the rest of the day on the phone, marshalling resources halfway across the world. It was evening in Japan, but GloCo employees there responded admirably, working into the small hours to establish the plant's integrity and make sure full safety protocols had been adhered to. The plant operated a third-generation advanced pressurised water reactor, generally held to be the most efficient and securest of its kind, equipped with countless passive safety features and a plethora of active failsafe measures to contain meltdown. According to the seismology department at the nearby Aichi

Prefectural University, the quake had been low on the Mercalli intensity scale, registering as a 'Five – Rather Strong,' a category in which the worst that could happen was slight damage to buildings. All that the Cape Irago plant suffered was the odd bit of broken plasterwork and the collapse of the Styrofoam-tile false ceiling in the staff canteen. By mid-afternoon GMT, past midnight Japan Standard Time, the reactor was up and running again, churning out its customary two thousand megawatts of power.

In the wake of the Fukushima disaster, the Japanese were understandably paranoid about a repeat incident, but Hayashi, as GloCo's national head of operations, did a bang-up job reassuring the media that there was nothing to worry about and never had been. Barnaby himself conducted a couple of Skype interviews with BBC World and NHK's *News Watch 9*, calmly allaying any lingering fears.

All in all, a good day's work and a well-executed exercise in crisis management and brow soothing. Barnaby went home pleased, and that night manacled Lydia to the bondage table in a prostrate position, face down, backside aloft, and whacked her with a wooden spanking paddle until her buttocks glowed red.

THE *GLOCO BYZANTIUM*

TWO DAYS LATER, a GloCo TI class supertanker foundered on shoals one hundred miles off the coast of California.

The *GloCo Byzantium* was transporting its cargo of light crude from the La Plata terminal in Argentina up to the Port of San Francisco when extreme weather, coupled with some calamitous navigational decision-making and a glitch in the automated course correction software, saw it deviate out of the shipping lanes and stray onto the Cortes Bank. It struck the Bishop Rock, the highest peak of the undersea basalt ridge, which at low tide lay only a few metres below the surface. The *Byzantium*'s double hull was torn open like tinfoil, and oil began gushing out. Within moments the supertanker was listing horribly and the captain had no alternative but to give the order to abandon ship. The twenty-man crew all made it safely into the life rafts, but had to endure several hours of being tossed about on heavy seas before a coastguard helicopter located them and a US Navy frigate arrived on the scene to rescue them.

Meanwhile the *Byzantium*, battered by hundred-mile-an-hour winds and thirty-foot waves, was dragged further across the Cortes Bank, spewing oil helplessly. Compartment after compartment ruptured into a relentless cascade. Soon the ship was semi-submerged, sinking into a brown sludge of its own making, an emulsified mix of oil and seawater which foamed over its bows and onto its decks. The keel succumbed to the strain and, back broken, the fatally wounded 450-metre-long leviathan plunged under, tumbling to the seabed, still bleeding as it descended.

With a deadweight tonnage in excess of 440,000, the *Byzantium* could hold three million barrels of oil at full capacity. On the trip up from Chile it had been carrying approximately two thirds of that, but two million barrels of oil was still a huge amount. Conditions at sea were too rough for it to be worthwhile sending aircraft out to spray detergent onto the slick, but luckily the prevailing wind and currents carried the oil west into the open Pacific rather than east onto the Californian shoreline. Within three days the slick had dispersed naturally and the nightmare scenario of oil-blackened beaches at Malibu and Baja did not come to pass.

Barnaby, nonetheless, had an uncomfortable time of it. The press and news media did not give GloCo an easy ride, either at home or in the States, where he was vilified by CNN and Fox News and ridiculed on *The Tonight Show* and *The Daily Show*. The *Byzantium* incident was agreed to have been the worst supertanker disaster since the *Exxon Valdez*, and vied with the *Amoco Cadiz* for being the worst ever. Had oil reached US soil, the cost of cleanup and compensation would have been astronomical. As it was, Lloyd's of London fulfilled its duties as maritime accident insurer, but the premiums on the rest of GloCo's shipping fleet immediately went through the roof, so Barnaby was still left significantly out of pocket. GloCo's share price also took a hit.

To add to his woes, the Seagull Movement returned to plague him. People dressed as birds once again littered the concourse in front of the GloCo Tower, sprawled on the paving stones like the aftermath of some mutant avian massacre. Rather than pick his way through or around them each morning and evening, Barnaby was obliged to use the entrance in the tower's below-ground parking garage when he arrived and left each day.

It had always been a source of great satisfaction to him that he could walk through the revolving front door of his very own skyscraper. He enjoyed seeing the building stretching above him: his palace, seat of his empire. He loved the feel of the spacious main lobby, with its marble walls and its soaring atrium that reached all the way to the hemispherical skylight at the top and which had, as its centrepiece, a giant sequoia transplanted from the slopes of the Sierra

Nevada. He preferred to come and go like a king, not skulk about in sublevels where the lift doors were utilitarian steel and the floor was nothing but concrete. But for the time being, the bird-costumed protestors had made it impossible for him.

CANE

"I CAN UNDERSTAND if you don't feel like it," Lydia said, that Friday. "If you're not in the mood."

"No," Barnaby said. "I need this. I need you."

"It's been a bad few days for you. Nobody could blame you for wanting nothing more than to put your feet up and have a quiet night."

"I need the release. I've been thinking about nothing else all week. Let's go."

"If you insist."

"Oh, I most definitely do."

In the basement, Barnaby instantly felt on top of things again. Nothing outside these four walls mattered any more. The real world could not impinge. He could forget the earth tremor and the *GloCo Byzantium*. There was only him and Lydia, and a range of toys to use and games to play.

He spreadeagled her on the St Andrew's Cross

frame. He spent a long time pondering his choice of beating implement, eventually settling on a plain bamboo cane.

He relished the *swissshh* the cane made through the air and the neat red line it left on Lydia's pale skin with each stroke. He swung it at her until his shoulder ached. Several shrill yelps came from her, but never the safeword. Soon she was striped from shoulders to knees in an overlapping crisscross pattern that reminded Barnaby somehow of *kanji* script, as though he had inscribed a secret message on her flesh in a language he couldn't read.

He chose a thick, knurled dildo to insert into her. It slid easily into place. He chose a second, smaller-calibre one and, having applied lubricant copiously, found a berth for that too.

Finally he finished himself off, exploding all over Lydia's hips and spine.

To leave the basement after that was a heavy act, like rousing himself from a rapturous dream. Barnaby couldn't help wondering if the world had any further shocks in store for him and GloCo – and dreaded that it might.

CAVE-IN

At 11.36am, India Standard Time, the cave-in struck.

Seventy-three coal miners at the GloCo colliery just outside the town of Talcher in Odisha province were trapped underground, four miles from the entrance to the pit. A section of ceiling in a newly excavated tunnel that had shown no sign of instability gave way suddenly. Two miners were killed outright in the collapse.

The rescue operation began immediately. Expert volunteers went down to ascertain the precise location of the cave-in and see if it was possible to establish communications with the survivors. They quickly determined that there was no way they could dig through the rubble to free them, or even shout to them. They estimated the cave-in to be at least a hundred feet long, and the tunnel remained in a dangerously unstable condition, so precarious that even reinforcing the ceiling with additional braces or shoring it up with roof bolts might have the reverse effect, bringing more of it crashing down.

Exploratory boreholes were sunk from the surface, seeking the spot where the survivors were likely to be, two thousand feet below. One drill bit eventually returned with a scrap of cloth tied to it, the material torn from a miner's overalls.

The borehole was painstakingly widened until it was large enough for food, water and a two-way shortwave radio to be passed down through it on cables. It also brought the trapped miners much-needed ventilation.

The seventy-three men were stuck in a chamber little bigger than two train carriages. They had been down there for almost a week when the hole was made that promised them salvation. Eleven were badly injured, and most of the rest were afflicted by respiratory ailments as well as eye trouble owing to the acrid clouds of coal dust still swirling in the air after the cave-in. They were beginning to suffer from intense claustrophobia, too, and there were several cases of dysentery arising from the cramped, unsanitary conditions. Their desperate pleas for the rescuers to hurry up were transmitted over the radio and relayed to a watching world by local broadcasters. The miners begged to be reunited with their families, asked for forgiveness from loved ones they had wronged, and prayed to the gods to be delivered from this hellhole they were in.

The only possible way to get them out was to

create a two-foot-diameter escape borehole and extract them one by one in a purpose-built metal capsule, the method famously used in 2010 after the accident at the Copiapó mine in Chile. But time was pressing. It was plain that the miners were in bad shape mentally as well as physically. Some of them were starting to crack up. The escape borehole would take days to drill. The miners might not be able to hold out that long. Their foreman was one of the pair who had been killed by the cave-in. A respected and charismatic figure, he might have been able to keep his men's spirits up, had he still been alive. As it was, a kind of grim anarchy was evolving among the survivors. They were squabbling and fighting down there in the dank, foetid dark, battling over how the food was portioned out, turning on one another like animals over perceived or actual slights.

Barnaby arrived on the scene three days after the initial disaster, and stayed for the next fortnight. Ostensibly he was supervising, but in truth there was nothing practical he could do. The rescuers and the drillers all knew their jobs and didn't need some expensively-suited CEO on hand to give them instructions. Mostly he just hung around the site, giving interviews to journalists and speaking to the miners' families, repeatedly expressing his great concern for the men's wellbeing and his hopes for a successful resolution to a terrible predicament. He dismissed accusations that the colliery was notorious for its lax safety record and higher-than-average level of injuries and deaths. He pointed out that coal mining in India was a vast industry, meeting the energy demands of a billion-strong – and fast-growing – population. Some of the largest reserves of coal in the world were to be found on the subcontinent, and India used more of the stuff per capita than any other nation save for China. Naturally, then, there were likely to be more mining accidents here than elsewhere, thanks to the sheer scale of the business and the numbers of people involved. It was pure statistics.

Then a reporter from an Odisha province newspaper asked Barnaby if he was aware that children as young as fourteen worked at this particular mine. Barnaby pooh-poohed the idea – "Absurd!" – until he was brought face-to-face with proof: a couple of colliery employees who were clearly adolescents and ought to have been in school. He was then informed that one of the seventy-three trapped men was in his teens. It was quite common for minors to be miners here, he was told. Kids were shorter and skinnier than adults, and therefore able to worm into narrow crevices inaccessible to their grown counterparts. India's labour laws prohibited anyone under eighteen from working in a mine, but under-eighteens routinely applied for jobs, lying about their age, and colliery managers routinely ignored the obvious falseness of their claims and hired them.

Barnaby was ill for the next few days. He confined himself to his hotel suite, and for much of the time he genuinely was unwell – the inevitable digestive complaints brought on by the local cuisine – but he was sick at heart, too, sick to the soul. There was a teenager underground, in peril of his life. A *boy*. How had GloCo's own CEO not known what was going on at the colliery? How could one of his companies do such a thing?

He re-emerged from confinement just as the borehole was due to break through to the tunnel. Once that happened, the capsule would be readied and would begin shuttling back and forth within the next twenty-four hours. The miners' ordeal was near its end.

Jakob was with him as the truck-mounted Schramm T130XD air core drilling rig augered down through the last few feet of unconsolidated regolith. Already the ground had ruined three tungsten-bladed drill bits, and the fourth was growing blunt but looked likely to last out the task. Compressed air, blasted down the hollow rods, brought the pulverised cuttings spewing back up and out.

The sense of hope and expectation was immense. A crowd of fellow miners and relatives of the trapped men looked on, beneath a ferocious, beating midday sun and a sky like a magnesium flare.

GloCo was bankrolling the rescue effort, and Barnaby had no idea exactly how much it was costing – it had to be nudging eight figures – but he honestly didn't care. All he wanted was a positive outcome, every single one of the miners hauled to the surface alive and well.

A deep rumble underfoot was the first hint that all was not as it should be. The Schramm T130XD shuddered. The drill accelerated to a tremendous pitch, over-revving shriekingly like a car suddenly thrown out of gear. Then the entire rig jerked downwards, canting the front of the truck into the air. People screamed in alarm. Circuit breakers kicked in, the drill motor cut out, and an unearthly hush fell. Then came further subterranean rumbling, as though some gigantic, terrible gate was being rolled shut. Another hush followed, this one interspersed with frantic sobs and gasps from the crowd. Everyone sensed that something had gone horribly wrong. No one was quite sure what or how.

In fact, it was simple. The drill, on the point of penetrating the roof of the tunnel, had hit the same geological flaw that had been responsible for the original cave-in: a jagged air pocket between two strata. In attempting to save the miners, it had instead finished them off, triggering a second cave-in. Their meagre, sordid refuge had become a tomb.

Radio silence from underground confirmed the awful truth. Several of the rescuers sank to their knees, overwhelmed with shock and dismay. Others took off their safety helmets as a mark of respect, tears rolling down their cheeks.

Barnaby, numb, decided to approach the crowd and offer condolences. Barely had he begun to speak, however, when a woman in a saffron sari shouted, "Murderer!" The rest of the crowd joined in, calling him all the worst words they could think of in English, and countless more in Hindi, Urdu, Bengali and the regional language Oriya. Then rocks and stones were thrown: a few at first, but swiftly becoming dozens.

Jakob hustled Barnaby away, shielding his boss from the rain of projectiles with his own broad back. The crowd gave chase, a mob howling in grief and outrage. A few frontrunners caught up with the fleeing plutocrat and his bodyguard, but Jakob despatched them easily with backhand blows.

The bulk of the crowd gained on them; they were mere metres away as they reached their hired Tata Safari VX. Jakob bundled Barnaby into the passenger seat, then vaulted over the bonnet and dived into the driving seat, locking the doors. As he gunned the engine, people swarmed around the 4x4 and began hammering their fists on the windows and bodywork. Jakob floored the accelerator, powering through the throng. Bodies scattered. Anyone who didn't leap out of the way was knocked aside. The Tata veered away from the mine, fishtailing on the gravelled approach road. The crowd receded behind it, still pursuing, a wall of waving arms and fury-etched faces.

Jakob didn't bother stopping at the hotel in Talcher to pick up their belongings. He headed straight for Biju Patnaik Airport near Bhubaneswar, ninety miles away. Their luggage and other paraphernalia could be sent on later. Jakob's priority was getting Barnaby onto the Gulfstream and in the air. He phoned ahead as he drove, and by the time the Tata pulled up on the tarmac beside the runway, the pilot had the turbofan engines cycling and had obtained clearance for immediate takeoff.

BENDER

THE CROWD AT the colliery couldn't follow Barnaby, but the shame did, all the way back to the UK. Opprobrium was heaped on GloCo from all quarters. Newspaper editorials castigated him. TV pundits berated him. He became a public whipping boy as never before.

It was as though he had somehow deliberately caused the cave-in, as though he were personally responsible.

He started to drink, harder and more intently than he ever had. He holed up in his house and went on a week-long bender. Whenever he felt himself sobering up, he would reach for another bottle. He had plentiful supplies, a whole cellar full of wines and spirits. He could have stayed in the house and drunk for twelve months straight before he ran out of booze.

He woke up on the sofa late one afternoon to find

Lydia standing over him. Her nose was wrinkled. She was looking down at him as she might have at a pig wallowing in its own filth.

"The state of you," she clucked. "Have you no self-respect?"

"Think I pissed it away this morning. Along with half a kidney." He groped for the bottle of Mersault Premier Cru that stood on the coffee table, uncorked and half empty.

Lydia slid it out of his reach. "That isn't the answer."

"It is," he said. "Especially if the question is, 'Did a teenage boy just die down one of your mines? Quite aside from the seventy-two grown men?'"

"Alcohol won't solve your problems."

"No, but it does mean I don't have to think about them. Everyone hates me, Lydia."

"Since when has that bothered you?"

"Since I started hating myself too."

She grabbed him by the shoulders, hauling him upright. "You go and have a shower – a long one – and shave. When you come back, I'll be downstairs. All the way downstairs." She nodded towards the basement.

"You want to...?"

"Don't you?"

He was drunk, but not that drunk. "Yes. God, yes, I do. I just assumed you wouldn't, given... how I am, at the moment."

"If you keep on talking, I might change my mind."

He stood. He swayed. He made for the door. "I'll be as quick as I can."

WORLDS IN HER EYES

SHE WAS NAKED except for a PVC corset that strained around her, as though trying to withhold a flesh explosion. Barnaby hadn't seen her wearing it before. She was, he thought, really getting into this.

"I don't trust you to tie a knot or fasten a shackle properly right now," Lydia said. "I'll just bend over that sawhorse there, okay? I won't move, I promise. I'll stay put. I give you my word. Do you trust me?"

"Yes."

"Then do what you have to."

She draped herself over the sawhorse provocatively, offering him her rump. Barnaby grabbed a whip and began flailing. He wasn't as accurate as normal, but made up for that with enthusiasm. The whip's cracks were deafening in the enclosed space of the basement. Bright scarlet weals appeared across Lydia's buttocks and thighs. She flinched, but didn't

425

cry out. Blood beaded from the wounds. Barnaby kept going. He thrashed and thrashed, breaking into a sweat. No safeword – none that he heard, at any rate. The whip lashed out. He was panting hard. He wasn't aroused at all. That wasn't what this was about. He just wanted to hit and hit, hurt and hurt. He hated the world. The world hated him. Why wouldn't everyone go away? Just fuck off and leave him alone? He hadn't done anything wrong. He was simply making money, same as everyone did. He hadn't forced those miners to go down into that pit. They had gone of their own volition. They got paid. They knew the risks. It wasn't his fault. It wasn't his fault. It wasn't his fault. It wasn't his... It wasn't...

He collapsed to the floor, lungs heaving. The room spun around him. The pattern of the flock wallpaper became swirling mandalas. The cranberry-glass lights pulsed like hearts.

Lydia crouched over him. Her legs were streaked with blood. He looked into her eyes. The blue, the green...

Good God, they were the world. How come he had never realised that before? There were patterns in the irises. The blue, the oceans. The green, the continents.

"Barnaby," she said. "It's time. Time for you to take your turn."

He slurred out some words. "What are you talking about?" Something to that effect.

"Don't you see?" she said. "Isn't it obvious? Hurting me hurts you. And I am everything. What you do to me, I give back to you. It's nature's way."

Was she even speaking? Her lips were moving, but they didn't seem to synchronise with what she was saying. The voice didn't sound quite like hers, either.

"It's no coincidence, Barnaby. You started beating me, accidents started happening to GloCo. There's no act without consequences, especially where a woman like me is concerned. I'm not one of those emaciated nothings you used to use and abuse. Those *girls*. I'm more, so much more. I'm trying to teach you a lesson here. Hoping you'll understand. Hoping you'll learn."

She took his hand, helped him up, led him across the room.

"The Berkley Horse, I think," she said. "As good a place as any to start."

He should have protested, could have resisted. Too drunk still, perhaps. Too exhausted. But also... It felt right. As though it was meant to be.

People could switch. People could change.

"You think you're at your lowest ebb," Lydia said as she fastened the straps around him. "But it could get worse. Equally, it could get better. Depends on what you're prepared to do, the sacrifices you're prepared to make."

"I want it to get better," he murmured.

"Then it will. But it won't be easy. You continue to fuck the planet. Get ready for the planet to fuck you back."

He was pressed tight to the Berkley Horse, his back, buttocks and legs exposed. He couldn't have writhed even if he wanted to. He was held fast.

He had thought that to be immobilised like this would be unpleasant, constraining, inhibiting. But, strangely, it was the opposite. Liberating, almost.

Lydia fetched the riding crop, the same one he had used on her, their first time. He glimpsed her out of the corner of his eye. She ought to be walking stiffly on account of the weals, but she seemed unhampered by them. It was as though she was not fully present, her mind elsewhere, transported out of her body, beyond sensation.

She flexed the crop, testing it.

Barnaby waited for the pain, and when it came it was tortuous, bewildering, dizzying, deserved, and wondrous.

TOP TO BOTTOM

BARNABY ON ALL fours, his ankles parted by spreader bars.

Barnaby, ball-gag in mouth, suspended from manacles.

Barnaby bent double, a rope around his testicles, tightening.

Barnaby with Lydia squatting on his face, smothering.

Barnaby in the pillory, Lydia behind him, thrusting.

Barnaby on his back, feeling a jet of hot urine hit his belly and trickle off the sides.

Barnaby and the cold, searing bite of the nipple clamps.

Barnaby never once saying, "Gaia."

A CHANGED MAN

GLOCO'S FORTUNES BEGAN to pick up.

For a time its prospects had looked dicey. Its CEO was AWOL, nowhere to be seen. Its shares were nosediving. The Talcher mine tragedy had turned it into a toxic brand. There was talk in the City of a shareholders' revolt, hostile takeovers by any number of rivals, even nationalisation by the government, GloCo being one of those British companies that was 'too big to fail.'

GloCo was a captainless ship, sailing on under its own relentless momentum, but who knew where? What reefs or maelstroms lay ahead of it, with no one at the helm to steer it safely past?

Then Barnaby Pollard reappeared.

He was not the same Barnaby Pollard who had vanished into self-imposed isolation a month earlier, after the events in Talcher. Anyone could see that.

He was thinner, gaunt almost, no longer exuding the sleek, glossy confidence of the billionaire businessman. His hair was discernibly greyer. Occasionally he would walk with a very slight limp, as though his hip or lower back was sore.

But he was Barnaby Pollard nonetheless, visible once again, taking his seat at the summit of GloCo Tower, making calls, doling out commands.

GloCo was under control. Stockbrokers, bankers and financiers breathed a collective sigh of relief. All was right with the world again.

He was a changed man, though. Easier to deal with. Less ruthless. The deaths of those miners had done something to him, clearly. Brought humility. Chastened him.

One person who was more acutely aware of the alteration in Barnaby than anyone was Jakob. The boss whom Jakob ferried to and from work and escorted through all public appearances had become a shadow of his former self. They didn't banter in the car any more. Barnaby was subdued in the back seat, seldom engaging in conversation, never rising to the bait when Jakob made some mildly insulting quip.

"Boss," Jakob said to him one evening as they dawdled through unusually stodgy rush-hour traffic, "where are you? What the hell's happened to you? I barely recognise you. It's like I'm bodyguarding a ghost these days."

He got nothing in reply, just a look in the rearview mirror from eyes that were sunken and grey-rimmed, set in a face that was weary and haggard.

"I'm worried," Jakob went on. "Seriously I am. I think you're sickening for something. You should go see a doc. Get a check-up. Have the old prostate looked at. That's a silent killer, you know, prostate cancer. Slowly sucks the life out of a man, then *blam*, he's gone."

Barnaby gave him a bleak smile and shifted in his seat. "I'm fine on that front. Getting plenty of that sort of thing."

"That sort of thing?"

"You know. Examination, kind of."

Jakob's forehead creased into a set of thick, meaty ridges. "I don't get."

Barnaby dismissed the topic with a flap of the hand. "Never mind."

Jakob had to help him up the front steps of the house. His boss was almost hobbling.

"You sure you're all right?" he asked.

"Never better," Barnaby told him. "I'm how I'm supposed to be. It's all great. Stop fussing, you old woman."

Jakob paused, then turned away to go back to the car.

FIGHTING THE TIDE

LYDIA WAS HOME. She had more or less moved in with Barnaby. One of his walk-in wardrobes was now hers. The fridge was filled with the sort of food she liked to eat. One of the bathrooms was a riot of scented candles, essential oils, makeup remover and ethically-sourced, bleach-free tampons.

She was already kitted out in readiness for the evening's shenanigans. Her boots were thigh-high. Her corset was leather, laced under great strain. Her dog collar was festooned with short, sharp spikes.

Barnaby meekly let himself be taken downstairs. He knew this was what he had to do. What must be.

You continue to fuck the planet. Get ready for the planet to fuck you back.

It was a penance, of sorts. A price to be paid. An offering to the goddess.

He loved Lydia. Lydia was his world. He had to

take everything she dished out. That way, balance was restored, happiness ensured.

He submitted to the restraints. He surrendered to the humiliation.

After she had flogged him for a while, tenderising him, she buckled a strap-on dildo into place. Through the muzzle gag that enclosed his head like a horse's bridle, Barnaby groaned, half in eagerness, half in dread.

"Brace yourself," Lydia said, positioning herself behind him. "Don't clench."

Then the basement door opened.

"*Fok* me! I knew it!"

Jakob's near-rectangular bulk filled the doorway.

"I knew something was up," he said. "Boss. What's this bitch been doing to you?"

"Nothing," Barnaby replied. "Go away." But the words were so muffled by the muzzle as to be all but incomprehensible.

"Oh, my *fokken* God, she's got you completely turned around and back to front. This isn't right. This isn't how it's meant to be at all."

"It is," said Lydia. "What's happening here is none of your business, Jakob. Leave."

"I will do no such thing," Jakob said. "Untie him. That's Barnaby Pollard. He's not like that. He's the one who hands it out, not the one who receives. Bloody hell, this explains everything. She's destroying you, boss, inch by inch."

"I said leave!" Lydia barked, with deep menace in her voice.

Jakob advanced into the room. "You," he said, pointing a finger at her, "are not my employer. I do not take orders from you, you *doos*. You may be all got up like a dominatrix, but you're not dominating *me*, got that?"

Lydia took two steps towards him. Her bearing was imperious, for all that she had an eight-inch rubber penis bobbing between her legs. "You have no idea what you're messing with, little man. Lay one finger on me, and you'll regret it."

"You're mad," Jakob scoffed, laughing.

"Try me."

"Jakob, no!" Barnaby yelled through the muzzle. He hoped his tone would carry, even if the words didn't. It wasn't an order he was giving, it was a warning.

The Afrikaner moved closer to Lydia, hands spread. "I've never liked you. You know that? I've always said you're dangerous."

"You have no idea."

"I'll drag you out of the room by your hair. I'll throw you out into the street, where you belong."

"You can't fight me," Lydia said, "any more than you can fight the tide."

Jakob dwarfed her. She gazed up at him wholly without fear.

Barnaby knew there was something inside Lydia Laidlaw that you mustn't resist. It filled her to the brim. She was only outwardly a woman. Within her lay a terrible power. If roused, it could ruin.

But his hands were tied, literally. He couldn't intercede. He could only make noises, imploring

Jakob to back off. But his pleading grunts fell on deaf ears. Jakob was too loyal. He loved his boss too much. He believed what he was doing was right.

He made a grab for Lydia.

She ducked, kneeing him in the groin.

As he slumped to the floor in agony, she snatched a chain from the wall and wrapped it round his neck. She placed her foot in the small of his back and pulled. Jakob struggled, pawing at the improvised garrotte. His face purpled. He tried hitting backwards at Lydia, but she leaned away out of range, hauling on the chain with far greater strength than she ought to have possessed. Her eyes were huge and ferociously, intimidatingly blue-green.

She let Jakob go when he was half strangled. He keeled forwards onto his face, twitching and retching.

She found the hugest, fattest vibrator in the room, and clubbed Jakob on the head with it.

Savagely.

Viciously.

Repeatedly.

Until the thudding impacts turned crunchy and wet.

Barnaby could only look on in abject horror.

When Lydia was done, she sat back, chest heaving. The bloodstained vibrator had been switched on by accident during the bludgeoning. It buzzed like some monstrous mosquito, glutted on the juices of its prey.

Lydia looked across at Barnaby.

"We're in this together now," she said. "All the way. You understand that, don't you, Barnaby?

There's no getting around what we've just done here. No getting away from it. I can dispose of the body. I can find a way. I'm a familiar sight at various landfills around the country. It shouldn't be too difficult. Black plastic bags. A piece here, a piece there. But you're implicated, my love. You're as guilty as I am. This isn't going to end at all well for you if you try to wriggle out of it. Think of the scandal. Think of the disgrace. There wouldn't be a GloCo left, if this got out. The only hope you have is if you go along with me. Do as I say. From now on. In everything."

She rose, dropping the vibrator with a *splat* onto what was left of Jakob's skull.

"We need a new contract, you and me," she said, dressed as a sinner, smiling like a saint. "One that'll apply everywhere, not just within these four walls. A new, very simple agreement. One without a safeword. You do what I tell you, or else."

She stroked Barnaby's hair.

"What do you say to that, my love?" she crooned. "Well, nothing, of course. You can't. But you can nod, can't you? So nod."

With tears spilling from his eyes, Barnaby lowered his head.

"Is that a yes?" said Lydia. "I'll take it as one. Oh, this is going to be so good for us, Barnaby. So good for everyone. Such an opportunity! You'll see."

SWITCH

WHEN GLOCO ANNOUNCED that it was diversifying its portfolio, the general assumption was this meant branching into other consumables, perhaps upping its investment in nuclear power and fracking.

Nobody could have foreseen that the company would commit to a regime of renewable energy production. Wind farms, hydroelectric dams, tidal barrages, massive photovoltaic panel arrays – GloCo sank billions into them all, selling off its existing assets piecemeal in order to fund the purchases.

Most people called it madness. Some called it glorious madness. Many said it was commercial suicide. Everybody predicted that GloCo would be bankrupt and in receivership within the year. 'GloCo Goes Loco,' ran the headline in the *Wall Street Journal*, adding, 'Putting All Its Greenbacks In One Green Basket?'

CEO Barnaby Pollard oversaw the fraught process of restructuring his company with a mixture of regret and resolve. It was not a dismantling, he told himself. It was just change. Radical but doable.

Always Lydia was by his side, administering to him, offering instruction.

His mistress.

His guide.

His Gaia.

JAMES LOVEGROVE'S *PANTHEON* SERIES

THE AGE OF RA

UK ISBN: 978 1 844167 46 3 • US ISBN: 978 1 844167 47 0 • £7.99/$7.99

The Ancient Egyptian gods have defeated all the other pantheons and divided the Earth into warring factions. Lt. David Westwynter, a British soldier, stumbles into Freegypt, the only place to have remained independent of the gods, and encounters the followers of a humanist freedom-fighter known as the Lightbringer. As the world heads towards an apocalyptic battle, there is far more to this leader than it seems...

THE AGE OF ZEUS

UK ISBN: 978 1 906735 68 5 • US ISBN: 978 1 906735 69 2 • £7.99/$7.99

The Olympians appeared a decade ago, living incarnations of the Ancient Greek gods, offering order and stability at the cost of placing humanity under the jackboot of divine oppression. Until former London police officer Sam Akehurst receives an invitation to join the Titans, the small band of battlesuited high-tech guerillas squaring off against the Olympians and their mythological monsters in a war they cannot all survive...

THE AGE OF ODIN

UK ISBN: 978 1 907519 40 6 • US ISBN: 978 1 907519 41 3 • £7.99/$7.99

Gideon Coxall was a good soldier but bad at everything else, until a roadside explosive device leaves him with one deaf ear and a British Army half-pension. The Valhalla Project, recruiting useless soldiers like himself, no questions asked, seems like a dream, but the last thing Gid expects is to find himself fighting alongside ancient Viking gods. It seems *Ragnarök* – the fabled final conflict of the Sagas – is looming.

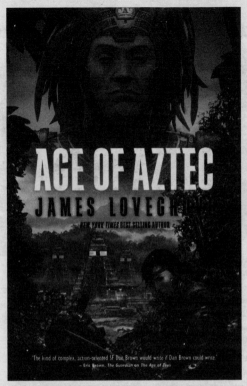

'The kind of complex, action-oriented SF Dan Brown would write if Dan Brown could write'
– Eric Brown, The Guardian on The Age of Zeus

UK ISBN: 978 1 78108 048 1 • US ISBN: 978 1 78108 050 4 • £7.99/$7.99

The date is 4 Jaguar 1 Monkey 1 House; November 25th 2012, by the old reckoning. The Aztec Empire rules the world, in the name of Quetzalcoatl – the Feathered Serpent – and his brother gods.

The Aztec reign is one of cruel and ruthless oppression, fuelled by regular human sacrifice. In the jungle-infested city of London, one man defies them: the masked vigilante known as the Conquistador.

Then the Conquistador is recruited to spearhead an uprising, and discovers the terrible truth about the Aztecs and their gods. The clock is ticking. Apocalypse looms, unless the Conquistador can help assassinate the mysterious, immortal Aztec emperor, the Great Speaker. But his mission is complicated by Mal Vaughn, a police detective who is on his trail, determined to bring him to justice.

 WWW.SOLARISBOOKS.COM

Follow us on Twitter! www.twitter.com/solarisbooks

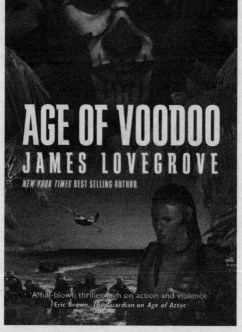

AGE OF VOODOO

JAMES LOVEGROVE

NEW YORK TIMES BEST SELLING AUTHOR

'A full-blown thriller, high on action and violence.'
Eric Brown, *The Guardian* on *Age of Aztec*

UK ISBN: 978-1-907519-40-6 • US ISBN: 978-1-78108-086-3 • £7.99/$8.99

Lex Dove thought he was done with the killing game. A retired British wetwork specialist, he's living the quiet life in the Caribbean, minding his own business. Then a call comes, with one last mission: to lead an American black ops team into a disused Cold War bunker on a remote island near his adopted home. The money's good, which means the risks are high.

Dove doesn't discover just how high until he and his team are a hundred feet below ground, facing the horrific fruits of an experiment blending science and voodoo witchcraft. As if barely human monsters weren't bad enough, a clock is ticking. Deep in the bowels of the earth, a god is waiting. And His anger, if roused, will be fearsome indeed.

'difficult to put
down... a thoroughly
entertaining novel that
I would recommend
to those looking for a
summer blockbuster'
*Sacramento Book Review
on Age of Odin*

New York Times Best Selling Author
JAMES LOVEGROVE

UK ISBN: 978 1 907992 04 9 • US ISBN: 978 1 907992 05 6 • £7.99/$7.99

POLICING THE DAMNED

They live among us, abhorred, marginalised, despised. They are vampires, known politely as the Sunless. The job of policing their community falls to the men and women of SHADE: the Sunless Housing and Disclosure Executive. Captain John Redlaw is London's most feared and respected SHADE officer, a living legend.

But when the vampires start rioting in their ghettos, and angry humans respond with violence of their own, even Redlaw may not be able to keep the peace. Especially when political forces are aligning to introduce a radical answer to the Sunless problem, one that will resolve the situation once and for all...

 WWW.SOLARISBOOKS.COM

Follow us on Twitter! www.twitter.com/solarisbooks

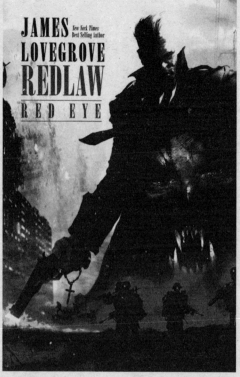

UK ISBN: 978 1 78108 048 1 • US ISBN: 978 1 78108 050 4 • £7.99/$7.99

A BAD DAY IN THE BIG APPLE

The eastern seaboard of the USA is experiencing the worst winter weather in living memory, and John Redlaw is in the cold white thick of it. He's come to America to investigate a series of vicious attacks on vampire immigrants – targeted kills that can't simply be the work of amateur vigilantes.

Dogging his footsteps is Tina 'Tick' Checkley, a wannabe TV journalist with an eye on the big time.

The conspiracy Redlaw uncovers could give Tina the career break she's looking for. It could also spell death for Redlaw.

 WWW.SOLARISBOOKS.COM

Follow us on Twitter! www.twitter.com/solarisbooks